SCARAB IN THE STORM

The Lost Pharaoh Chronicles Book III

LAUREN LEE MEREWETHER

Edited by
SPENCER HAMILTON

LLMBOOKS PUBLISHING

For my mom

EXCLUSIVE READER OFFER

GLOSSARY

CONCEPTS / ITEMS

1. Amphora – large clay jar primarily used for transport and storage of wine
2. Ba-en-pet – iron from the sky; metal of heaven
3. Captain of the Troop – a mid-ranking officer of the military; one rank below Troop Commander
4. Chief royal wife – the premier wife of Pharaoh; Queen
5. Coregent – a ruler second to Pharaoh
6. Cubit – a measure of length equal to about 20 inches
7. Deben – weight of measure equal to about 91 grams
8. Decan – a ten-day period; three decans in a month
9. Dynasties – lines of familial rulers in the Old Kingdom, then Middle Kingdom, then New Kingdom (where this story takes place, specifically the 18th Dynasty)
10. Faience – a popular blue-glazed ceramic

11. "Gone to Re" – a form of the traditional phrase used to speak about someone's death
12. General – highest-ranking position of Pharaoh's Armies
13. Great royal wife – the chief royal wife of the Pharaoh before
14. "Greatest of Fifty" Commander – the second-lowest military rank; a commander of fifty men
15. Hedjet – white crown worn by Egyptian regents of the 18th dynasty
16. Ka – spirit
17. Kap – nursery and school for royal children in the royal harem
18. Khopesh – a sickle-shaped sword
19. Master of Pharaoh's Horses – highest-ranking position of Pharaoh's Chariotry; second-in-command to the General
20. Mistress of the House – the title for the wife of a non-royal estate owner
21. Modius – the crown for a Queen
22. Overseer of the Fortress – one rank below Commander
23. Overseer of the Garrison – second rank below Commander; under the Overseer of the Fortress
24. Pharaoh – the modern title for an ancient Egyptian king
25. Pshent – the great double-crown of Pharaoh
26. Royal harem – a palace for the royal women, usually headed by the chief or great royal wife
27. Royal wife – a wife of Pharaoh
28. Season – three seasons made up the 365-day calendar; each season had 120 days
29. Sed Festival – traditionally, the celebration of the Pharaoh's thirty-year reign, and then every 3–4

years; Akhenaten celebrated several sed festivals, although his reign was not that long
30. Shat – weight of measure; twelve shat equaled one deben
31. Shendyt – a pleated apron / a royal shendyt is lined with gold worn by Pharaoh
32. Sidelock – a long lock of hair above the ear that is kept despite a shaved head, to signify childhood; is usually braided
33. Silphium – a now extinct plant used for contraception and/or to induce menstruation after conception
34. Sistrum – a musical instrument of the percussion family, chiefly associated with ancient Iraq and Egypt
35. Troop Commander – third rank below Commander; under Overseer of the Garrison
36. Vizier – chief royal advisor to Pharaoh

GODS

1. Ammit – goddess and demoness; Devourer of Hearts
2. Amun – premier god of Egypt in the Middle Kingdom
3. Amun-Re – a name given to show the duality of Amun and Re (the hidden god and the sun) to appease both priesthoods during the early part of the New Kingdom
4. Anubis – god of embalming and of the dead
5. Aten – the sun-disc god of Egypt (referred to as "the Aten"); a minor aspect of the sun god Re
6. Bes – god of childbirth

7. Hathor – goddess of many aspects of life, including childbirth
8. Osiris – god and judge of the dead; god of resurrection and life
9. Ptah – god of creation, art, and fertility
10. Re – premier god of Egypt in the Old Kingdom; the sun god
11. Tawaret – goddess of childbirth

PLACES

1. Aketaten – city of modern-day area of El'Amarna
2. Akhe-Aten – necropolis for the city of Aketaten
3. Ipet-isut – modern-day Karnak at Luxor; "The Most Selected of Places"
4. Malkata – palace of Pharaoh Amenhotep III
5. Men-nefer – city of Memphis; south of modern-day Cairo
6. Saqqara – necropolis for the city of Men-nefer
7. Waset – city of modern-day Luxor
8. Washukanni – capital of the Mitanni empire
9. Valley of the Kings – royal necropolis across the Nile from Waset

PEOPLE

1. Amenhotep III – deceased Pharaoh and father of Amenhotep IV and Thutmose III; died in Book I, *Salvation in the Sun*
2. Amenhotep IV / Akhenaten – deceased Pharaoh; second son of Amenhotep IV and Tiye; died in Book II, *Secrets in the Sand*
3. Amenia – wife of Horemheb
4. Amenket – royal guard

5. Ani – royal scribe
6. Ankhesenpaaten / Ankhesenamun – daughter of Amenhotep IV / Akhenaten and Nefertiti; royal wife of Akhenaten; chief royal wife of Tutankhaten / Tutankhamun
7. Ay – father of Nefertiti and Mut; brother of Tiye; vizier to Pharaoh Tutankhamun
8. Bay – servant of the Malkata palace
9. Beketaten – deceased daughter of Pharaoh Amenhotep III; born with the name Nebetah; wife of Pawah; died in Book II, *Secrets in the Sand*
10. Hentmehyt – steward of Ankhesenpaaten / Ankhesenamun
11. Horemheb – military general; future Pharaoh
12. Hori – royal guard
13. Ineni – royal guard
14. Ipwet – cupbearer for Ankhesenamun
15. Jabari – deceased chief royal guard; died in Book II, *Secrets in the Sand*
16. Kha – chief royal architect
17. Kiya – deceased Mitanni Princess sent to seal foreign relations through marriage to Pharaoh; died in Book I *Salvation in the Sun*
18. Maia – nurse to Tut
19. Meketaten – deceased daughter of Pharaoh Amenhotep IV / Akhenaten and Nefertiti; died in Book I, *Salvation in the Sun*
20. Meritaten – deceased daughter of Pharaoh Amenhotep IV / Akhenaten and Nefertiti; chief royal wife of Pharaoh Smenkare; died in Book II, *Secrets in the Sand*
21. Merka – Malkata servant of Pawah
22. Mut ("Mutnedjmet") – half-sister of Nefertiti; daughter of Tey and Ay

23. Nakhtmin – Master of Pharaoh's Horses
24. Neferneferuaten Tasherit – daughter of Pharaoh Amenhotep IV / Akhenaten and Nefertiti; also called Nefe; exited series in Book II, *Secrets in the Sand*
25. Neferneferure – deceased daughter of Pharaoh Amenhotep IV / Akhenaten and Nefertiti; died in Book I, *Salvation in the Sun*
26. Nefertiti / Neferneferuaten – deceased daughter of Ay; chief royal wife and Coregent of Pharaoh Akhenaten and Pharaoh Smenkare; Pharaoh in her own right as Pharaoh Neferneferuaten; died in Book II, *Secrets in the Sand*
27. Paaten ("Paatenemheb") – military general; exited series in Book II, *Secrets in the Sand*
28. Paramesse – military commander
29. Pawah – former Fifth Prophet of Amun; husband of Beketaten; Vizier of the Upper to Pharaoh Tutankhaten
30. Raia – servant of Mut
31. Sennedjem – tutor of Tut; Overseer of the Tutors in the royal harem
32. Setepenre – deceased daughter of Pharaoh Amenhotep IV / Akhenaten and Nefertiti; died in Book I, *Salvation in the Sun*
33. Simut – First Prophet of Amun during Pharaoh Neferneferuaten's reign
34. Sitayet – Captain of the Troop
35. Smenkare ("Smenkhkare") – deceased son of Pharaoh Amenhotep III and Sitamun; half-brother and nephew of Pharaoh Akhenaten; died in Book II, *Secrets in the Sand*
36. Suppululiuma I – King of the Hittites

37. Temehu – deceased mother of Nefertiti; died in Book I, *Salvation in the Sun*
38. Tener – servant of Mut
39. Tey – wet nurse and step-mother of Nefertiti; mother of Mut
40. Thutmose – deceased firstborn son of Pharaoh Amenhotep III and Tiye; died in Book I, *Salvation in the Sun*
41. Tiye – deceased chief royal wife of Pharaoh Amenhotep III; sister of Ay; died in Book I, *Salvation in the Sun*
42. Tut / Tutankhaten / Tutankhamun – Pharaoh; only son of Pharaoh Amenhotep IV / Akhenaten and Henuttaneb
43. Wenamen – High Steward of the Malkata palace
44. Wennefer – First Prophet of Amun during the reign of Pharaohs Tutankhamun, Ay, and Horemheb
45. Yey – soldier messenger

PROLOGUE

THE TIME OF REMEMBERING

"DID YOU LOVE HER MORE THAN ME?" QUEEN MUT FIXED HER gaze upon her husband, Pharaoh Horemheb, as he sat in his throne staring at the five empty seats before him. She pinched the skin between her thumb and forefinger as she rested a hand on her pregnant belly.

The sun had not yet risen and its preceding glory fell through the columns of the council room at Malkata. They waited for the five prophets of Amun to enter before the morning light, as ordered the day before.

Pharaoh Horemheb dropped his chin at the strain in his chief royal wife's voice, but only for a second. He had already answered her the night before, but she'd refused to listen. So, he gave her the answer she wanted, needed, to hear. "No, Mut, I love you more than her."

He glanced up at his wife and saw her chewing her lip. His mouth grew a pensive smile as he stood and drew her to his chest. As he smoothed the strands of her golden-laced wig with one hand and rubbed her back with the other, the memory of his Nefertiti caused a deep ache in his throat as he pressed his lips to Mut's.

At the kiss's end, he placed his hands on his wife's belly. Even though he was twenty years her senior, he did love Mut. He loved her because Nefertiti had asked him to take care of her when she died, but also because he found admiration in Mut's eyes and a warmth in her heart.

"You carry my child. You are the only woman who warms my bed at night. I will take care of you and provide all that you could ever ask or need," he told her as he lifted his fingers from her belly to the side of her cheek.

She smiled briefly, but her eyes averted to her half-sister's gold-and-blue lapis ring on his finger. "You still love Nefertiti, don't you?" Mut asked, her voice soft.

He remembered the previous night—he'd left most of her questions about him and Nefertiti unanswered. He had only asked for silence, saying he needed to be alone to think about the hard days ahead, because she already held a perceived truth in her heart and wouldn't believe anything he said. A mistake to stay silent, perhaps . . . but maybe not? She had at least come to the third day's retelling. Some part of what he had said must have stuck with her; otherwise she would not be asking these questions.

Horemheb rubbed her arms. "Nefertiti is gone." His voice cut through the air between them in contradiction to the softness of his touch. "She will never be remembered after I sign this edict. After we are gone to be with Re, no one will ever speak her name again—" A lump formed in his throat, his words forced back at the realization of her true eternal death among the living. "Do not press me further, Mut, please, my wife."

Mut seemed to shrink as her spine and shoulders slumped. Horemheb opened his mouth to speak and tried to rub her arm, but she pulled away and the door to the room opened, jarring their moment together. Horemheb dropped his hands and took his seat in his throne as his gaze lingered upon his wife. *I'm sorry,* he wished he could say—but not now, not as the five prophets of Amun gathered to their seats for the day.

He pulled his stare from his wife and looked around to the prophets as he stalled, hoping maybe another idea would come to him before he must sign that cursed edict. Future Egyptians would never remember her, Nefertiti, his love, and only those who were now gone would remember his unborn son, perished with his mother. The weight of the past and the weight of the future hung on Horemheb's shoulders. He clamped his jaw shut, knowing the more he spoke the story of those to be erased, the closer their condemnation would ensue.

He looked to the face of Amun for the second time this morning. *You ask for much.* He took a deep breath and closed his eyes to gather his thoughts. Still he clenched his jaw, knowing that to seal Pharaoh's power over the priesthood he must blot out their names:

Pharaoh Akhenaten, who in his own madness worshipped the Aten far longer and with much more zeal than planned, robbing people of their faith and work and draining Egypt of its wealth and foreign powers . . .

Akhenaten's brother, Pharaoh Smenkare, who fell into Akhenaten's trap of false faith and murdered his own people for their faith in Amun, bringing a bloody purification never seen before upon Egypt . . .

Then there was the one he loved, the mother of his unborn son, Pharaoh Neferneferuaten—his Nefertiti—murdered by Pawah, the former Fifth Prophet of Amun, in his struggle for the throne . . .

And, now, Pharaoh Tutankhamun . . . born Tutankhaten . . . Tut.

His eyes remained closed as he remembered each of their faces, lingering the longest on his Nefertiti and his

Tut. A tightness overcame his chest as he took a deep breath.

Forgive me . . .

He opened his eyes and looked again to the face of Amun. *The people cannot remember what Akhenaten and Smenkare did to this empire. They cannot see the weakness Akhenaten and Smenkare brought to the throne, and because of them, their actions, they condemn the entire royal family to eternal erasure. . . . They force my hand. The people cannot remember my Nefertiti and my Tut because there cannot be weakness from Pharaoh in the people's eyes.* He pleaded with his god: *Is there another way? Please give me wisdom to see before I sign this cursed edict!*

Amun only looked straight ahead, mute, in his stone image.

A touch on his shoulder alerted Horemheb to Mut, eyes wide and glistening. She pushed out a whisper, saying, "Be strong, Pharaoh."

His brow furrowed in appreciation of her gesture; he knew those words meant more than their sum. Closing his eyes again, he thanked Amun for granting him an understanding wife—a wife to whom he had been unfair. He took a cleansing breath, opened his eyes, and grasped her hand, bringing her fingers to his lips, never losing eye contact with her.

"My sweet Mut," he whispered, and kissed her hand, this time not caring what the prophets saw. "What would I ever do without you?"

She smiled, but it didn't reach her eyes. However, Horemheb knew the prophets sat waiting for him on this third day of the tale, and he would need to wait to comfort Mut. He patted her hand and she pulled it back to her side, and then he turned to address those prophets who sat with unamused faces.

"Today"—Horemheb felt a sharp tightness in his chest as

he continued, his eyes surveying each of the five men—"we shall recount the boy king, Tutankhamun, firstborn son of Pharaoh Akhenaten." He stopped and closed his eyes one final time; simply speaking the young boy's name drew a painful tug on his soul. His voice wavered; he knew the time neared when he would sign the edict to erase them all from their great country's records.

"Be still and hear his tale . . ."

He opened his eyes to the day ahead.

". . . before we remember no more."

CHAPTER 1
THE TIME OF LEARNING

QUEEN AND CHIEF ROYAL WIFE ANKHESENPAATEN LUNGED AT Sennedjem, her fighting stick raised over her head. She chopped it down, but Sennedjem parried upward, blocking her advance. His stick swung around, trapping hers pointed at the ground. They locked eyes as she considered releasing her weapon or risking another tap from him. She hesitated—and then it was too late. He brought the back end of his stick up to her face and halted his training weapon right before it smacked into her nose. Ending the match, he brought his feet together and straightened his back as he lowered the fighting stick from her face to his side.

He bowed to her, his student, as the Overseer of the Tutors in the royal harem.

Her cheeks flushed; if it had been a real fight, death would have followed. Her heart beat within her chest as the sun poured over the two of them in the training yard. She couldn't quite catch her breath as she remembered her mother's body lying dead in the council room. Tension filled her jaw despite her labored breaths and she wrapped her hands tight around the fighting stick until her knuckles lost their color. Knowing her mother's murderer, Pawah, lurked about the palace fulfilling her duties while Pharaoh was away only intensified her glare fixated on her tutor.

"Again!" Her order rebounded off the distant stone walls surrounding the royal harem's spacious training yard.

With every purposeful stride, Ankhesenpaaten envisioned Sennedjem as Pawah, remembering Pawah's threat and the hot stench of his words upon her cheek—

"Even your own throne room is not yours."

Her teeth shone through her curled lips as she swung her stick at Sennedjem, who blocked it and countered. Ankhesenpaaten parried and attacked again, her eyes narrowed in fury as she heard her mother's scream echo in recent memory.

Sennedjem let out a short, disappointed breath. With ease he became the attacker, putting Ankhesenpaaten on the defensive, until, shortly thereafter, he once again ended the spar with a halted strike to her neck. She fell to a knee, but willed herself to stand upon her wobbly legs, using the fighting stick as leverage.

The only person she could trust—her grandfather, Ay— was in Waset by order of Pharaoh. Loneliness made sleep elusive as she wondered who stayed loyal to the throne, who stayed loyal to *her*, and who followed Pawah. The lack of sleep, in turn, made her tired in her lessons and thus an easy target.

A doomed vicious cycle . . . but this I know: I will not fall victim like my mother.

"Chief royal wife," Sennedjem said, interrupting her thoughts as he looked at her wobbly legs. "My Queen, perhaps we rest for now." He gazed up at the sky, shielding his eyes from the sun's rays; they had been out in the sun for the better part of the day.

"No," Ankhesenpaaten huffed. Her muscles twitched as

would certainly die in the next skirmish, and not necessarily by the enemy's hand." His brown eyes traced the outline of her face as he pulled his hands away from her arms as she regained her balance.

Ankhesenpaaten's jaw drew tight. Her mother's scream echoed in her ears. Pawah would not kill her in the same way. She would be ready for him when he came for her, and she would be ready to take her revenge for her mother's murder. She opened her mouth to speak, but Sennedjem spoke first.

"My Queen, I admire your determination, but even the fiercest of warriors still need rest."

At this, she felt a weight drop from her shoulders. She looked to the ground. He took a step back from her as she noticed how close they were. She looked up at him as he stepped and felt the ground spin as she dug her toes into her sandals to keep her balance. He reached out again to steady her, and she let out a stubborn breath as she gave in—*But only for this one moment,* she promised herself.

"You are a good tutor, Sennedjem. We shall rest now."

Sennedjem nodded and she led them to the shade, using Sennedjem's arm as a counterbalance. Once there, Sennedjem ordered the servant boy to get more to drink.

Secretly, Sennedjem wanted to know if what Ankhesenpaaten told Tutankhaten that day in the training yard was true. He had stood right there when she told the crown prince that Vizier Pawah had killed her mother, Pharaoh Neferneferuaten; but since then, he dared not ask her. To him, it seemed too coincidental that the very day she relayed her eye-witness account, news traveled that Pharaoh Neferneferuaten had died in her sleep.

Now, watching her drink from the goblet, he could only assume it was true. She had been in his training yard every day since her husband, the now-Pharaoh Tutankhaten, had left for war in the North, and it seemed to him that she was possessed with an unquenchable desire to learn to defend herself . . . and, even more so, to attack. Her vigor and sweat made him appreciate her grit; but there lay a sadness in her eyes, just behind the rage. He could only assume why she trained so hard: to protect Pharaoh, should Pawah attempt to kill him too . . . and perhaps to kill Pawah for taking her mother from her.

But that seemed too primitive for a chief royal wife; he rebuked himself for the thought. Regardless, her determination sparked a certain primal admiration in him.

Just then, she caught him staring at her while he thought. Hoping to avoid the questions that were sure to follow, he looked to the yard and bit his tongue.

"Why do you stare at me, Tutor Sennedjem?" Ankhesenpaaten asked him, her voice low.

"Few are granted the privilege of looking the chief royal wife in the face," Sennedjem said, and felt the day's heat seep into his bones in contrast to the cold lump growing in his chest. "I do not disrespect you. I only admire your desire to learn my trade." He kept his eyes on the training yard, examining the training weapons that hung on the walls. *But I want to know why,* he thought.

"No," Ankhesenpaaten said with a curt shake, and tossed her empty goblet to the servant boy.

"What?" Sennedjem asked, snapping his head to her.

"You want to know why I learn a man's skill with so much, as you said, 'desire.' " Ankhesenpaaten stood as he tried to form a response. "I'll tell you," she whispered, making sure the servant boy could not hear them. "You already know why."

Sennedjem dared himself to look into her eyes. "It was true, then, what you said to Pharaoh . . . ?" He studied her face: straight nose, heavy lids covering big brown eyes, high cheeks, full lips.

"Yes. Pawah killed my mother. But we mustn't say that, lest the position of Pharaoh were to fall in the people's eyes." Ankhesenpaaten peered up at him and lowered her eyebrows at the widening of his eyes. "Pawah bribes the people with royal grain in return for blind loyalty."

His jaw fell ajar.

Her eyes darted between his own. "Are you in his favor?"

"No . . . I have never received royal grain other than my payment as a tutor." Sennedjem looked her straight in the eyes and stood tall, his chest growing into a proud stance. "Nor would I ever accept such a bribe. I am loyal to Pharaoh."

"I wish I could believe you," Ankhesenpaaten whispered as she cocked her head to the side and narrowed her eyes at him. "Although I trust you in some regards, I don't fully trust anyone here." She circled him and then stepped backward toward her chair.

Sennedjem watched her cautious actions and thought it funny, albeit sad. If he wanted to kill her, he could have done so already. Could she not see this? He held their stare as he chewed the insides of his cheeks, wondering what he had done to his queen to garner so much distrust.

"Why do you still stare?" she asked him, her voice tense as she crossed her arms.

"Chief royal wife, my Queen Ankhesenpaaten." His words held strong in the air. "I am no traitor."

Ankhesenpaaten ran her eyes up and down his body until she finally accepted his response—for the moment—and commanded him to sit next to her. Swallowing a hesitant lump in his throat, he pulled up a stool beside her, although slightly behind her chair.

"I want to believe you are no traitor, Sennedjem. You taste my drink before me . . . and yet all I wonder is if it is an act to gain my trust." She stared into the training yard as she spoke. She ran her tongue along her dry, cracked lips as her throat longed for more to drink, but she dare not ask after insulting perhaps her only friend left in the palace.

"My Queen, may I speak freely?" Sennedjem asked.

Ankhesenpaaten tapped her front teeth together as she debated his request, but finally nodded.

"The way you speak tells me you are headed for a lonely life if you always second guess who you can trust," he said, and then at the snap of her gaze toward him, he quickly added, "I do not wish that life for anyone, and especially my Queen. I have always been true. You have my loyalty. I will die protecting Pharaoh and his family." He bowed his head and then lifted his eyes to find her stare again.

Ankhesenpaaten shook her head. "I can't—" Her words died before they reached her throat. *I can't what—trust him? He has shown me no reason to not trust. Then again, Chief Royal Guard Jabari had never shown any of us that he could not be trusted, yet he led Mother to her death.* She stiffened as the breeze chilled the sweat on her body. "I can't . . ." Again, the words failed her.

"I would never hurt you, my Queen."

His soft voice cushioned her mind. "How can I be sure?"

Her whisper summed all of her fears in five little words: sure of loyalty, sure of safety, sure of the premier and sole god of Egypt. All her life she had worshiped the Aten disc, but then, at the end of her mother's life, she tells her, *"No! The premier god of Egypt is Amun-Re."* Where did that leave her with life after death? To the Aten? To Re? Was there a god of Egypt at all? Was she to go only to dust at the end? She lifted her chin, so as not to give away her mental debate under Sennedjem's stare.

"I am teaching you to defend yourself and how to attack, but otherwise you have only my oath, for which I will die before I break." Sennedjem's mouth opened again, but no sound came out. With nothing else to offer her, he closed it and laid his arms by his sides.

Ankhesenpaaten's eyes somehow rummaged up a glisten despite the sweltering heat and her own dehydration. "I mean you no insult, Sennedjem. I apologize if I have offended your oath."

"No, my Queen, you do not apologize, even if you are wrong. Pharaoh and his Queen do not apologize." Sennedjem chuckled softly.

Ankhesenpaaten knew the expectation of her position, but, more than that, she felt she needed to talk to someone or her insides would burst forth. He already knew most of what happened; why not tell him more of the truth? She needed someone to help carry her burden. He needed to know why she didn't trust him—and yet, in telling him, she would lend him her trust. But before she could stop her words, they flowed unimpeded, her whisper barely reaching his ears: "I heard her scream, Sennedjem." She pressed a fist to her lips as she shut her eyes. Two tears, each from one eye, raced down her suddenly pallid cheeks to her chin.

Sennedjem leaned forward. His gaze dropped to the ground and he shook his head. His mouth moved, but words never came out until he finally mustered, "I'm sorry."

Ankhesenpaaten drew a deep breath and looked all around, making sure they were indeed alone, the servant boy still on the other side and out of earshot. "My mother trusted Jabari, and he led her to her death." Her hands trembled as she leaned back, away from Sennedjem. "Who to trust?" she whispered. "Who to trust?"

"I will never hurt you," he repeated, and reached for her arm in an attempt to comfort her, but stopped just short of touching her sweat-glazed skin.

Ankhesenpaaten shook her head. "I want to believe you."

Sennedjem was silent for a moment, having decided words would mean nothing to her; but he vowed to try his entire life if that's what it took to prove himself loyal to her and to the throne. He nodded his head. "I understand."

Then he stood and signaled for the servant boy to bring more drink; he tasted hers before handing her the goblet. Together they drank from their goblets, and then he grabbed their fighting sticks. He tossed one to her, which she finally caught after a few months of practice. A light smile crept into the tiny corners of her mouth—but she still had much work to do and much to learn, and so she erased it. Sennedjem tapped the dirt in front of him. "Are you ready to fight, my Queen?"

She stood, let out a captive breath, and wiped the tears from her eyes. A hard scowl plastered on her face, she nodded and lunged for him. His offense had slackened since earlier in the day, as she noticed he could have struck but refrained.

"Lessen your rage. Think through your next steps. Anticipate my advance."

They circled around each other each with their sticks raised, and then he lunged, but she parried. He missed her counterstrike, and, she assumed, let her strike him on the arm. Blood rushed to the spot on his skin where she hit him, but he showed no pain.

"Good, my Queen. If someone betrays you, they will be sorry." He nodded.

"When he comes for me, I will kill him," she murmured as she lunged again, faking a right attack, and smacked Sennedjem in the left leg. That one, she knew, she landed with her own skill.

Sennedjem winced. "Who comes for you?"

"Pawah," she said through her teeth, remembering his ultimatum.

To stay by my side as my wife and Queen, or to die with what is left of your family.

She lunged again, but this time Sennedjem did not allow her to hit him.

He stopped cold in the heat of the day. "Did he tell you he would come for you?"

Ankhesenpaaten narrowed her eyes at Sennedjem. Maybe she could trust him, but her mind toyed with her. What if it was all just a ploy to gain her trust and then kill her? What if Pawah had contracted Sennedjem to kill her in an accidental training incident?

No. She put to bed the possible scenario.

Sennedjem already knows enough. Just tell him. Sennedjem is my only chance at learning to defend myself. He needs to know the source of the threat. He is very concerned and genuinely surprised. Pawah said if I ever told anyone he would kill me; no choice, just death . . . after he had his way with me.

The memory of Pawah's touch sealed in her mind that she needed Sennedjem whether he was truthful or not. She slammed her eyes shut and shook away the fear of dying by Pawah's hand.

"Yes . . . he said he would come for me."

Sennedjem grimaced. "Then you have much more training to do."

She opened her eyes at his blunt response, thinking there would be a smirk or an "Aha, now I can kill you," but instead he gave a serious response to a serious threat.

She half smiled and felt a weight somewhat lift from her chest. Maybe he wasn't lying after all.

Sennedjem lowered his fighting stick. "Why have you never told me this? I didn't know what you were fighting against or why you wanted to learn to fight."

Ankhesenpaaten stood straight. "I didn't trust you."

Sennedjem shook his head. "We should have been

learning how to use a dagger, not fighting sticks. They will be of no use if he attacks you. A dagger would be the better weapon."

Ankhesenpaaten went cold at the word *dagger*.

He grabbed her stick from her limp hand and threw it and his own stick against the wall. He snapped at the servant boy. "Get the training blocks," he yelled as he went to the wall and grabbed the small training blades. He came back and handed one to Ankhesenpaaten. "Here." He thrust it into her hand and then noticed her ashen face as her empty gaze fell upon the weapon. "My Queen?"

As she held the training dagger in her hand, Ankhesenpaaten only heard her mother's screams; she pictured the bloody dagger on the floor next to her mother's dead body. Then, without a moment's notice, she dropped the training dagger and the drink which had for a moment felt good in her belly came back to the surface.

Sennedjem stepped back as she vomited, then offered her a rag to wipe her mouth. "The sun can do that to a person."

She looked at the rag and wondered if poison lay on its surface, and instead wiped her mouth with the back of her hand. "No," she whispered as she grabbed the training dagger from the dirt. "I will not be my mother. I will be ready when he comes for me." She stared the dagger down to conquer the harrowing memory of her mother's death, and then lifted her gaze to Sennedjem. "Prove your loyalty to me."

Sennedjem nodded, then took her hand and adjusted the way she held the weapon. "We train now because your life depends on it."

AT THE END OF THE DAY, ANKHESENPAATEN'S FEET ACHED AND her arms twitched in exhaustion. Sennedjem gave her a real dagger and showed her how to conceal it in her belt. It was a little awkward at first, untying her belt in front of him so he could show her, but he seemed to not think anything of it. Why would he? He was an official, a professional; he was Overseer of the Tutors. After he tied her belt around her waist for her, he resisted putting a hand on her shoulder and let her turn to face him.

"My Queen, I only have domain here in the training yards. Should you be here, know you are safe. However—" He looked up at the royal guards, Hori and Ineni, who had come to escort her back to her bedchambers and stood off at the entrance. "I cannot protect you when you leave. You need to find others who are loyal to you as well. Remember our training today. Come back when you are able—tomorrow, even—and I will teach you more. I promise you, chief royal wife Ankhesenpaaten, you will be able to defend yourself when Pawah comes."

A brief wave of comfort fell over Ankhesenpaaten's expression. She hadn't told him everything, but it felt good to at least have an ally—for now, anyway.

She nodded. "Thank you," she whispered. "I will no longer doubt your loyalty."

But her eyes made the true message clear: *Unless you give me reason.*

Sennedjem smiled, and she noticed his eyes did too as she turned and left with Hori and Ineni.

HORI AND INENI ESCORTED HER TO HER BEDCHAMBERS IN silence. Tut had yet to name a chief royal guard in Jabari's absence, and with Pawah literally sitting on Pharaoh's throne, Ankhesenpaaten's mind drifted to what horrible things either of these men would be ordered to do to please the Vizier of the Upper and be bestowed the honor of Chief Royal Guard. Hori had stood guard at the door to her bedchambers for many years now. She felt he of the two would have more loyalty, but she would not assume anything —that was how her mother had gotten herself killed.

I need a test, she thought. *A test to see where their loyalty lies.*

They had given her no reason to doubt them, but corruption filled the whole palace and city of Aketaten, from servants to high-ranking officials. They were all under Pawah's thumb; it was how he'd escaped accountability for her mother's murder.

She peered over her shoulder as the door closed behind her, and her steward, Hentmehyt, came to her and bowed, her smooth voice cutting into Ankhesenpaaten's thoughts.

"My Queen, we have drawn you a bath after your day at the training yard."

Her body longed for the water, but she remembered the dagger Sennedjem had tied in her belt. Ankhesenpaaten studied her steward's face and chewed her lip, deciding to keep her belt close just in case. Hentmehyt gestured toward the bath chamber and Ankhesenpaaten followed as other servants added blossoms to the water to perfume it. She could smell her own stench, but letting the servants see her with a dagger might bring more doubt than she wanted—or maybe she did want them to know her doubt in their loyalty.

A servant came to her and bowed and began to untie her belt. An impulsive "No!" fled Ankhesenpaaten's lips, which made the servant girl jump back a bit.

Ankhesenpaaten caught her breath as she clenched the gold-lined linen belt between her fingers. She turned to Hentmehyt, who nodded to her Queen and ushered the two servant girls from the room. She grabbed both doors to the bath chamber as she left and turned and bowed again to her Queen.

"We shall leave you to yourself, chief royal wife."

When she was alone, her clenched-white knuckles slowly released the captive fabric, and her heartbeat fell back into a normal pace. She looked around the room; she knew she was alone, but somehow she felt as though she wasn't. She undressed and slid the hidden dagger close to the bath's edge so that she could clutch the wrapped handle as she leaned her head back, yet still she was unable to close her eyes. The water beat against her heat-flushed skin and cooled her aching muscles. Her head dipped as she began to doze, but at the water's touch against her chin she snapped back, looking at the closed doors, and grabbed the handle of the dagger a little harder as she realized her grip had weakened when she lost her focus.

"I am alone," she told herself, and the thought sunk even more. "I am alone." The statement held a deeper meaning. "Who can I trust?" She leaned her head back again, but her eyes stayed on the door. "Sennedjem, for now. Perhaps Hori. Maybe Hentmehyt." She rocked her head side to side, feeling the cool water slosh on her neck. "Trust no one at Aketaten."

A deep breath filled her lungs, and soon she fell asleep, and she dreamt of her mother's cold, lifeless body on the floor of the council room—all because she had misplaced her trust.

Ankhesenpaaten woke to water in her nose and her hands sprang into action trying to defend herself. She coughed and gagged as she splashed around thinking someone was trying to drown her, but soon she realized she had only fallen asleep in the bath. She looked around and shivered as her heart rate and breath fell into a normal rhythm. The water had fallen to room temperature, but she sunk lower in its comfort until the tingling in her fingers and toes resided.

She opened her mouth to call in her servants, but clamped her mouth shut. Were they on Pawah's payroll and so would not hesitate to kill her, making it look like she had slipped and hit her head?

No. She took a deep breath. *Pawah said when Tut came back he would give me a choice. but can I trust what Pawah said?*

"No, I can't," she whispered to herself.

Ankhesenpaaten looked to the dagger, still on the edge of the bathtub, and heard her mother's screams.

"I will not be my mother. I will not die defenseless. I will not die a victim. I will not die because of who I trusted."

She climbed out of the bath and dried and dressed herself, trying her hardest to repeat the folds Sennedjem had made to hide the dagger.

She came out of the bath chamber and saw her servants and steward waiting for her, and the sight of them caused her to jump. They could have killed her at any time she was in the bath, but instead they had waited for her and pulled back her bed.

It didn't matter—they were just biding their time.

Her eyes darted between the three of them. "You are dismissed."

As soon as the doors closed, she ran over and pulled a chair to their back. Her shoulders slumped as she let out her breath, finally thinking she might be safe in her room. She climbed into bed and as the woolly and feathery bed and soft, padded headrest absorbed the ache from her body, she had no choice but to obey her eyes, despite her intense watching of the door, and she fell asleep yet again.

CHAPTER 2
THE TIME OF DISTRUST

THE NEXT MORNING CAME TOO SOON AS SHE AWOKE WITH A start. Half of her body lay off of her bed. Her linen sheet had been ripped from the folds under the mattress and was now wound tightly around her leg hanging off the bed. Her heart beat like the wings of a frightened bird within her cage of a chest as she realized she was still in bed; each *thud-thud* became less of stab wound to the chest and more like a knock on the door. She turned over and looked up at the sunlight bathing the wood ceiling above. It seemed too peaceful for the life she had found herself in. Blinking rapidly, she tried to push the aches out of her joints as she let out her first conscious breath of the morning.

Knocks came at the door. She tried to pull herself fully onto the bed, but it felt like every fiber of her muscle broke as she flexed and collapsed. Her leg was still captured by the linen sheet, and she thought it may be better to go the other way: to the floor. She had never trained as hard as yesterday in all of the last season she had spent with Sennedjem. She groaned. Every muscle in her body yearned for more rest. She pushed herself off the bed and then lost her balance with her tangled foot and fell, hitting her bottom on the stone floor.

"I'll make an easy target today," she muttered, and finally gave up and called for the guard to push open the door.

Hori and Ineni pushed the door open and the chair she had used as a makeshift barricade made a clamor as it slid across the floor. Her shoulders rose to her ears until the screech stopped.

At least, Ankhesenpaaten thought, *if in the night someone tries to open the door, I'll hear it for sure.*

Hori looked to the chair to see what was the clamor, and then looked to Ankhesenpaaten before returning to his station outside the Queen's bedchambers.

Hentmehyt and the two servant girls entered and bowed before her, ready to bathe her and get her dressed for another day in the training yard. Her eyes darted between them, but the way her body ached, she decided it was worth the risk to let them help her free her leg so she could save as much energy as she could for practice with Sennedjem. But she grabbed her belt with the hidden dagger off of the bedside table before they made it to her.

Just in case.

⸻

As Pawah came up behind her he whispered, "Chief royal wife Ankhesenpaaten." Then, to Hori and Ineni, he barked, "Leave us."

They nodded their heads and walked away. Hori peered over his shoulder, careful not to let her out of his sight—although, to follow orders, he walked out of earshot. Every time the vizier came near the guard was reminded of Pawah's story of how Pharaoh Neferneferuaten died. When he and the others had let Pawah go, that morning, after his tale of how Pharaoh Neferneferuaten ended up with a stab wound to her chest, something had not seemed right to Hori.

———

"AH, MY QUEEN," PAWAH SNEERED, AND HE LOOKED HER BODY up and down.

Ankhesenpaaten crossed her arms to avoid his penetrating gaze. To the forefront of her memory came the stench of his breath, the feel of his hard lips pressed against hers. She too well remembered his threat of her life in the Aketaten throne room. The motivation to never feel that again made her mind flee to the training yard. Her fingers slipped unseen under her belt and grasped the handle of the small dagger Sennedjem had given her.

"What do you want?"

The ache in her hand made her realize how hard she gripped the handle. The desire to yank it out and stab Pawah in the chest right here and now, just as he had done to her mother, almost caused her hand to do what it willed, but the paralyzing effect of fear kept it at bay. His height and weight outsized her in every way. Her strength waned from yesterday's practice, and her lack of training with a dagger finally succeeded in stilling her hand—even if she did attack him, he could probably wrangle it away from her and kill her with her own weapon. But she still kept her fingers wrapped around it. All she needed was one good strike if he came too close to her.

A slow smiled crossed his lips, as though reading her mind. "Aketaten belongs to me now," he reminded her. "When your precious husband comes home, I will do away with him, and you will choose me or death."

"And if I choose death, will you kill me in secret like you

did my mother?" Her stomach twisted inward on itself as she spoke, but she forced her voice to stay strong.

I will not be weak.

I will not be a victim.

I will not die defenseless.

"No, silly girl." Pawah ran the tips of his fingers down her cheek; she jerked her face away from his touch and he clenched his jaw from the blow to his ego. "I will have you executed for your crimes against Amun and Egypt's people. The masses will love to see vengeance on the family that set food upon Aketaten's eight hundred offering tables to spoil in the sun for the Aten disc while the people died of starvation. The family that depleted the royal treasury of its grain on extravagance while turning their backs on the people . . . finally gone. A day of celebration."

"If you were so keen on taking the crown, why didn't you just kill Tut when you had the chance after my mother's murder? Why not just kill me now?" Her fingers tightened around the smooth bronze of the dagger handle.

"A mistake I will not soon forget." Pawah's lips enunciated each word and he lowered his gaze to hers. "I thought I needed more supporters. But now all of Egypt stands behind me."

"Not all," Ankhesenpaaten whispered, knowing at least her mother's family in Waset, General Horemheb, and maybe Sennedjem still fought for her and Tut. "My mother allowed the worship of the gods again. The people have no reason to hate us now. You need a reason for them to fight for you. I know that is why you have not killed us. My mother watched out for us. She knew you and your ways."

Pawah curled his lip and shuffled a step backward. Then he widened his stance and leaned forward. "The people will follow me. They believe what I tell them, just as they have done in the past."

"They will see through the lies, and when they know the truth, when they know you took the life of a divinely appointed ruler, they will see you impaled per the law. They will demand it." Ankhesenpaaten's eyes flared as she narrowed her focus on him.

He only chuckled and shook his head. "You will watch what you say, *Queen*. The only reason you are still alive is because I want a warm body in my bed when I am Pharaoh."

Her full lips peeled back in disgust and she let out a gagging breath.

He chuckled again. "If the other does not go the way I need it to, all I have to do is marry you. I offered the same deal to your mother, but she refused me." His voice became innocent and soft, but took a hard turn. "Maybe you will not be as foolish as she."

Ankhesenpaaten felt her heart beat out of her chest as she stood up straight and rooted her feet to the floor. "You will *never* touch me again."

"I will get my satisfaction, one way or another." Then he peered over to Hori, who stared him down, and Ineni, who played with a rock with his toe. "Tell me, Queen . . . do you trust your guards at night?"

Ankhesenpaaten set her jaw. "I trust no one."

Pawah smiled and patted her cheek. "You are already smarter than your mother. It might keep you alive long enough to see my coronation."

"I will tell Pharaoh Tutankhaten what you have done here in his absence, and he will—"

"If you say one word, my Queen, I will *rip* your throat out in front of my supporters and label you an adulteress to the throne." Pawah saw the flinch in her eye and smirked. "Haven't you been with Sennedjem while your husband is away? There are many who saw you with him. You enjoyed his touch and his kiss and his—"

"Those are lies!" Ankhesenpaaten slammed her fisted hands to her side in a rush of fury.

"Oh, my dear little girl . . ." Pawah laughed and waved his hand in dismissal.

Her ears turned to flame. She was nearing sixteen—a woman old enough to bear children and have a family of her own. She was no little girl.

"Anything can be truth when multiple people say the same thing." Pawah pursed his lips. "What do you think your husband would do to you and Sennedjem if he found out about your little transgressions?"

Ankhesenpaaten growled at him. She rolled her shoulders forward, ready to pounce.

"Better yet, if you say anything, I will make you out to be an adulteress and see you executed along with your lovers. I know those still loyal to the throne. Those men will have been with you too. Most all have seen it." Pawah smiled. "And then, when the young King dies from an unfortunate tumble off his balcony, who shall take the throne?"

"You're a monster. He hasn't done anything to you. He is still a boy."

"He was *born*, Ankhesenpaaten, and that is enough. If it weren't for him, I would be marrying you right now and claiming my place on the throne."

"I would never marry you. I'd rather die. And if you kill me, you have no right to the throne."

"Ah, you do hold a point there . . . but you see, I am the closest male relative, and seeing as the people did not want a female Pharaoh, I do not need you in order to become King of Egypt. I just need enough people to want me as their leader to not cause a riot when the throne is left empty."

"You are despicable."

"I know." Pawah smiled. "It is one of my best qualities."

Ankhesenpaaten wondered why he didn't try to take

advantage of her. Perhaps he feared someone still loyal to the throne. Was it Hori or Ineni? Hori was an intimidating man, standing a full head above Ineni, and held an athletic frame.

"So," Pawah said, breaking her from her thoughts. "You will not say one word."

"And sit idly by while you plot a way to kill Pharaoh?"

"I only need him to name me Heredity Prince. When he does, there will be no bloodshed in Egypt because I will then be not only the closest living male relative but also the named successor." Pawah clasped his hands together in front of his chest, as if satisfied that everything would happen as he said it would. "You see, I am not so despicable. I do care if there is bloodshed in Egypt."

"That didn't stop you from spilling the blood of my mother and my husband—"

"And your father, dear."

Ankhesenpaaten knew what her mother had told her, but for some reason it did not phase her until now. Her body grew numb. This man killed her parents. He'd orphaned her. She wet her lips in the desert heat and her eyes focused on his mouth as he spoke:

"Tut will die one way or another, but if you keep silent and help me, you can be my wife and we can save much Egyptian blood. Hasn't there already been enough spilt?"

"You disgust me, Pawah."

"Believe me, you have made that very clear. But no matter. I am a very forgiving man." He winked at her. "I tell you what . . ." A half smile grew on his face as he looked to her breasts and then back to her lips. "Even though our young Pharaoh will always choose me over you, I'm willing to gamble. I'm always up for a game, so let us each take a stake here. If you decide to stay silent, I will not kill Pharaoh for one year. At the end of the year, if he still trusts me over you, I win and you will be my wife once the boy passes in a horrible accident and you will do as I say when I say it until the day you die. If he believes you over me, however, we will call it even. You get to live as Queen to the crippled child the rest of your days."

He let her digest what he said and then continued.

"But if you speak of the horrors"—he raised his fingers to the air as if to mock her pain and began to circle her—"that have gone on here, and he believes *me*, I will make him execute you and your lovers, and then the same nasty fall will kill him . . . and who shall take the throne? Me." Pawah came to face her again and then shrugged. "But if he believes you over me and my many witnesses, then I will leave Aketaten."

"No, you will leave *Egypt*. I am no fool." Her hot breath sizzled in the morning heat. "You would leave Aketaten to only go back to Waset and live in Malkata as King."

"My dear," he said as he reached out to touch her face, but then pulled away at the last second, his eyes flitting to the royal guards standing in sight. "You are no fool."

"You will address me with my title: chief royal wife." Ankhesenpaaten's nostrils flared as she spoke.

"No. I won't." The words tailed the end of a chuckle. "Not while we are alone. Those are my terms. Do you agree to a wager?"

"You will leave Egypt if Pharaoh trusts me over you."

"No, I will leave *Aketaten*." Pawah shook his head with a *tsk-tsk*. "What leverage do you have over me? What would you do to make me change my own terms?"

"I know you killed my mother." Ankhesenpaaten's voice cracked but grew more bold with each passing statement. "And I will let the people know. I will scream it until my throat is—what did you say, ripped out? I will plant the seed of doubt in the people's minds. No one kills Pharaoh."

"Ah, I admire your strategy. Sounds a little like mine."

Ankhesenpaaten swallowed. "I am not like you." She

paused to make sure he knew it, then she lifted her chin and rolled her shoulders back. "You will leave Egypt if Pharaoh trusts me over you," Ankhesenpaaten repeated. Her knees shook as she stared this man down, but her feet stayed firmly planted. She held her breath for fear he might hear her racing heart.

"I have waited sixteen years for this crown," Pawah grumbled. "A woman will be the last thing that keeps me from it."

"What's the matter?" Ankhesenpaaten smirked, satisfied to have finally upset him. "Are you afraid? Do you think there is a small chance I can win?"

Pawah narrowed his eyes. "No. There is no chance, girl."

"Then make the deal. You have nothing to worry about."

She had him. She'd found his ego and squeezed.

After a moment, Pawah nodded. "You're right. If you win, I'll leave Egypt."

"Good." Her senses told her it had been too easy to get him to agree to her terms, but she accepted her small victory nonetheless and felt free to take a relieved breath.

"Good," Pawah repeated in a low hiss as Ankhesenpaaten turned and walked away.

When she reached Hori and Ineni, she peered over her shoulder to Pawah, who still watched her.

"Are you all right, my Queen?" Hori asked her.

"Yes, I am," Ankhesenpaaten said, rolling her shoulders backward and standing straight. "I'm ready to go to the training yard."

Sennedjem will teach me to defend myself. I will teach Tut—no, General Horemheb is teaching him now and telling him the truth about Pawah. I will learn to defend myself. I will kill him if he touches me again. I will kill him. I will kill him.

She would take poison before she ever allowed him to take her by force, she reasoned, and wished her grandfather

Ay were in Aketaten to help keep her safe. She didn't like feeling all alone. But maybe in Waset he would be rallying the people for her and Tut and leading them to disown their precious Pawah.

"Yes, my Queen." Hori bowed his head and took up the tail as they went onward toward the training yard.

PAWAH WATCHED HER LEAVE AS HE MUTTERED TO HIMSELF WITH a nasty sneer, "I have no intention of keeping my end of the bargain if you win, girl . . . but I will delight in seeing your own husband sentence you to death for your betrayal of his bed." He remembered changing the sweet little Nebetah into his conniving late wife, Beketaten, with the same tactics. He remembered plunging Jabari's spear into her heart, and chuckled at the utter confusion on her face as the light in her eyes died. He watched Ankhesenpaaten round the corner. "And in the off-chance he does not, you'll meet the same fate as she when I have no more use of you." He rocked back on his heels and sneered, his eyes hidden in the shadow of his brow. "Bide my time," he whispered. "Bide my time."

CHAPTER 3
THE TIME OF WASET

Ay looked out from his second-story roof deck, over and across the Nile, toward Malkata, and then to the city of Waset on his side of the river. Waset once again bustled, with Pharaoh Neferneferuaten's edict undoing her late husband Pharaoh Akhenaten's ban of all gods except the Aten. The merchants, chanters and chantresses, priests, dancers, and singers were all back to work again for the gods of the kingdom. Ay remembered a season ago when he, in his newly appointed vizier role by Pharaoh Tutankhaten, stepped onto Waset's banks from his two-day journey on the Nile from the capital of Aketaten. His heart was glad Egypt finally was brought back to the old gods, but weighed down at the cost—the life of his precious lotus blossom, his only child of his first wife Temehu.

Nefertiti.

He narrowed his eyes and set focus in his mind. Even in his old age he would find revenge, one way or another. The young Pharaoh Tutankhaten had given into his advice to move away from the city associated with the heresy of Akhenaten and move the capital back to Waset. He was to make preparations for the move. Guards had flanked him as they made their way to Malkata, the palace of Akhenaten's father, Amenhotep III. The doors opened as the few servants who were tasked to upkeep the giant fortress bowed and rushed to their places, trying to remember how to act in the presence of Pharaoh's appointed. Ay had looked around to the old walls and one of the many courtyards beyond the terrace and then taken a deep breath. Nodding, he placed his hands on his hips.

I'm sorry, my daughter. This is where you should have grown old and died.

His thoughts drifted to the present. "My sweet lotus blossom, how I miss you." The breeze comforted his solemn lips as the morning sun rose behind him. "I will make this right for Ankhesenpaaten," he promised Nefertiti's ka, "if she still lives when I return to Aketaten." His fist hit the wall of his roof deck. "If she still lives." He looked up to the sky. "I'm sorry, my Nefertiti. I did not want to leave her." He bowed his head and let out a breath. He flattened his fist and gripped the wall. "He will die for his crimes." Ay nodded, not knowing how he would ensure such a death; but one day he would be able to kill Pawah through the system of justice. Pawah would make a mistake and it would cost him his life. Ay was sure of it.

After a few more moments on the roof in silence, he descended to head back to Malkata to start another day in preparation for Pharaoh to move back to Waset.

A servant coughed as Ay entered with guards all around him. Ay looked at him, realizing the servant wished to say something.

"Speak if you must," Ay told him.

The servant, with a shaky foot, stepped forward. "In peace, Vizier Ay . . . Pharaoh Neferneferuaten was a hero in our eyes. She fell ill too young. We wish her only the best on her journey to the sun." The servant nodded and then added, "I only wanted you to know." Then he stepped back and kept his head bowed.

Ay chewed on his lip. His heart beat faster within its cage as he thought back on the events of his lotus blossom's death.

If only you knew the truth, he thought.

"Yes, I thank you for your sentiments." He looked forward again, but then an idea struck him. He looked back to the servant and motioned for him to draw near. "What is your name?"

"My name is Wenamen, High Steward, son of Surero, Overseer of Amun's Cattle." He dipped his head in respect of Ay's higher rank.

Ay looked him up and down. "High Steward?" Ay considered his loyalty to the throne; he had identified a few others during his time in Waset, but they were all in low positions—maybe useful in turning the common man against Pawah in some circles, but he needed someone with influence. If this Wenamen could be trusted, he might be that someone.

He waved the guards away, as he felt safe now whilst in the palace. When the guards had left, Ay commenced circling Wenamen in a slow pace.

"Well, Wenamen, High Steward," Ay began, and increased his speed. "I do not remember you. I served as Overseer of Pharaoh's Horses in Malkata under Pharaoh Amenhotep III. When did you become High Steward?"

Wenamen tried to keep eye contact, but as Ay began to walk faster, he looked straight ahead. "I became High Steward the last year Pharaoh Akhenaten lived in Malkata. He did not take me to Aketaten."

"Why?"

"I am High Steward. He left me here to take care of his father's palace."

"So where is your loyalty?" Ay tailed Wenamen's response, coming to stand in front of Wenamen and probing his face with his eyes.

"My loyalty?" Wenamen cocked his head to the left then dipped his chin. "Vizier Ay, if I have done something wrong, please tell me."

"Answer me this, Wenamen, High Steward." Ay took a step forward and leaned into Wenamen's personal space. "Have you spoken with an associate of Vizier Pawah?"

Ay waited for Wenamen to blink or show some tell of deceit, but nothing came.

"No," Wenamen answered. "This is the first time I have seen any of the royal officials since Pharaoh Akhenaten's time at Malkata. We, the servants and long-forgotten officials here, toil night and day to take care of such a palace as Malkata. We never have time to leave its walls. Our families live and work here as well."

Ay studied his face for anything and then darted his eyes, taking in the cleanliness and orderliness of the palace. Ay pursed his lips and nodded, finding him truthful—for now.

"Well then, Wenamen, High Steward"—Ay leaned back to stand up straight—"I have a proposition for you. It carries no grain as payment, only honor and the knowledge of protecting Amun's divinely appointed."

"I am an honorable man. I will die fulfilling my oath to protect Pharaoh."

Ay smiled and hoped this Wenamen was not playing him a fool. But he needed allies here and so took the chance to trust him. "Do you accept then?"

Wenamen stood tall and lifted his chin. "Yes."

"It would be an honor to Pharaoh Neferneferuaten and Pharaoh Tutankhaten."

Wenamen nodded and filled his lungs with a proud breath. "I have lived for an honor such as this."

"Good," Ay said, and turned to lead him down the hallway to where only a few trusted men could hear him. "If you speak a word of what I am about to tell you, I will deny it and you will be imprisoned for treachery to the throne. Do you understand?"

Wenamen's face fell solemn. "Yes, Vizier."

"Have you heard of any associates of Vizier Pawah coming to Malkata and rallying support for the former Fifth Prophet of Amun or encouraging rebellion against Pharaoh Akhenaten when he was still with us?" Ay asked, turning to look again for any sign of deceit in Wenamen's face.

"No, I have not heard such things." Wenamen's mouth contorted into a scowl and his head shook at the shame of such actions against the throne.

Pleased with Wenamen's lack of visible deception, Ay continued with his request: "I would like you to find out if any of the servants here have been approached for these propositions, or if they know of anyone outside of Malkata who have been approached. But, Wenamen, when you inquire, do not raise suspicion. Are you able to do such as I have asked?"

"Yes, Vizier. I can do this for you in the name of our Pharaoh."

"Good. Come back to me in a decan's time and let me know what you have uncovered."

"Yes, Vizier."

Wenamen bowed, and Ay nodded his dismissal.

"Pawah, your time is going to be cut short—just like you cut short the time of my daughter," Ay muttered under his breath as he watched Wenamen walk away, observing his hunched shoulders and closed fists. "Perhaps there are many still loyal to the divine authority of the throne."

A deep, hearty laugh bounced on the stone walls and Ay took a sharp look to his left, trying to find the source, his eyes searching for the familiar sound of his Temehu . . . his Nefertiti . . . but when his gaze landed on a young girl playing in the courtyard far off, he chided himself for thinking such a ridiculous thought. His chest sank and his gaze fell to the floor as he interlaced his fingers behind his back.

No, he would never hear her laugh again.

———————

A DECAN CAME AND WENT, AND WENAMEN REPORTED BACK TO Ay under the cover of night in a forgotten corridor of Malkata.

"So?" Ay asked.

Wenamen released a heavy sigh and pressed his lips into a grimace before speaking. "Many of Malkata's servants had not been approached, but some knew of others outside the palace walls who had been bribed with grain to support a movement called the People's Restoration of Egypt during Pharaoh Akhenaten's reign." Wenamen's cheeks flushed, accompanied by a bitter smile. "They then persuaded the people to follow the former Fifth Prophet of Amun, Pawah, the Pharaoh's vizier, in return for grain and a promise for flowing luxuries as we had under Pharaoh Amenhotep III."

"Do you know how much they paid?" Ay asked, prepared to bribe the people back if grain was what they wanted.

"I do not know," Wenamen said, breaking eye contact, and his voice dropped lower. "There was rumor among those loyal to the throne that Pawah used the royal treasury."

Ay snorted, threw his hands on his hips, and shifted the anger out through his shuffling feet. He looked to the ground.

That was why the treasury was drained so fast. Corruption and fraud helped Akhenaten into an early grave.

He closed his eyes, his heart aching to ask the next question.

"Do you know if the people wanted Pharaoh Neferneferuaten to die?" Ay asked with a shaky voice, almost afraid of the answer.

"I do not know. I will find out," Wenamen said; his lips itched to ask why, but he held his tongue.

"Then do so," Ay said. "Is there someone you trust with your life and the lives of your wife and children?"

"Yes," Wenamen answered. "There are three men."

"Are you sure?" Ay asked, peering down at the man.

"Yes." Wenamen stood straight and tall and looked Ay in the eye to show his unwavering loyalty.

"Good. Enlist them to help you if you are sure they are loyal to the Amun's appointed," Ay commanded with a flick of his wrist.

"Yes, Vizier."

"Then go," Ay said. "I will remember what you are doing for your country, Wenamen."

Wenamen nodded and bowed slightly. "Thank you, Vizier Ay, for the honor to serve our true King of Egypt."

Then he left to seek the truth from the people.

Once alone, Ay put his hand on the stone corridor wall and remembered the night he bumped into his newly crowned daughter, wandering the halls after an argument with her new husband. *Trust and truth are united in marriage,* he remembered saying to her, encouraging her to go back to the man who did nothing but cause her pain for the rest of his life. Curling his hand into a fist, he placed his forehead there.

"Oh, my daughter, my Nefertiti, my beautiful one, I'm so sorry. I'm so sorry I did not protect you when you needed me. I failed you." He strained to hear her laugh in his mind, his last memory of her and her mother. Bringing his other hand to the wall, a tear burst from his eye. "I did this to you. I agreed to your marriage to Tiye's sons. I wish you could have been happy with Thutmose, and even if he died, I wished you happiness. I wished you peace. If I knew about you and Horemheb, I would have . . . I would have . . ."

Ay's words got jumbled in his head.

What would I have done? Told the people she died and they could have lived in his house—her gaining a new name, a new identity. She could have been happy. She could have had his son. She could have stayed alive.

He banged his head against his hands as the tears came forth. "She could have been alive," he whispered. "I'm so sorry, my lotus blossom. I promise you, Ankhesenpaaten will not be forced with the same fate. You will live through her. I promise you her happiness. Please forgive me, daughter."

THE NEXT DAY CAME AND WENT AND AY WENT HOME THAT evening under guard. He found Mut in the garden when he entered his estate. She turned to face him.

"Father."

Mut pressed her lips into a half smile as she greeted him. Since Nefertiti's death, they had not spoken much to each other. The truth about her sister's death lived on the edge of her lips. She longed for people to know who killed her, that she did not die of illness. It drove her to stay in her father's estate, so she would not disobey her father and Horemheb's command.

Her father had dimmed from the heroic vision she held of him. He didn't stand for truth and justice. He stood for cowardice and the way of least resistance—at least in her mind. He was still her father, though, and she still loved him. She rationalized to herself that it was the same way her mother looked at Nefertiti when Meritaten was killed. She knew her mother still loved Nefertiti, but there was an eternal disappointment, a sort of blame, that lurked behind her eyes. The same disappointment now lurked behind her own eyes when she looked upon her father.

She went back to studying the lotus blossoms in the garden and enjoying the evening sunset as she sauntered toward the shadows cast by the home's walls. She heard her father's footsteps come closer to her. She stopped and turned to face him again.

He said nothing, but wrapped his arms around her, kissing her forehead, and then pressed her body into his. "I love you, Mut," he whispered, and kissed the top of her head. He squeezed her. "My Mut."

She chewed her lip before responding. "I love you too."

He had only shown her this much affection after her sister had died. She knew he loved her, but there was a special bond between him and Nefertiti, and now that she was gone, it seemed to Mut as if he was trying to fill the void with her.

He pushed back and rubbed her arms before dropping his hands into her palms and bringing them up to his chest. He nodded at her, studying her face. "Mut, as I told all of your sisters, trust and truth are united in marriage. So when you choose your husband, choose wisely, and choose one who believes the same."

The corners of Mut's mouth turned upward into a polite smile as she nodded. She knew he didn't approve of her not being married yet, thirteen years old with no candidate in sight and still at home as her fourteenth birthday drew near in the coming months; all of his other daughters had been married off by twelve or thirteen. Nefertiti had set the precedent. None of them had waited until the age of fourteen, and certainly not later than that.

He ran his hand down the side of her face and rested her chin in his palm. "Choose wisely, my daughter. As long as it takes."

His eyes held a wetness in them and a longing, Mut noticed. Her eyebrows raised in a little surprise and wondered if maybe he didn't care if she stayed in his house for a while longer. Perhaps he truly wanted the best for her. Her lips held no smile as she attempted to learn his hidden motives.

At the lack of response in his daughter, Ay dropped his hand and looked about the garden to the main house. "Now, where is your mother?"

"She is sleeping." Mut's monotone voice cut through her father's sentiments.

"Then I will go to rest as well," Ay said. His shoulders hunched as if waiting for any response from his daughter. When he received none, he only whispered, "Do not stay up too late, Mut."

Mut nodded as he walked off. Her gaze drifted back to the lotus blossoms as they closed for the evening, wishing that even at one time of her life her father had a sweet term of endearment for her like he had for his lotus blossom, his Nefertiti. Then she chided herself for her thoughts. Nefertiti was murdered, and she stood there selfishly pitying herself.

THE NEXT MORNING, MUT WOKE UP AND FOUND HER MOTHER eating at the table.

"Where is Father?"

"He went back to Malkata," Tey said. She sipped her wine and took another small bite of bread.

Mut took a seat next to her mother. Tener, a servant girl,

placed a plate of bread in front of her and poured her some malted beer. Mut cut a hard stare at Tener.

"Beer?" Mut said, unamused, knowing the servant girls all laughed at her behind her back for still being in her father's house at nearly fourteen.

Tener's eyes darted between Mut and the cup made of fired Nile mud.

"I am no child."

Tener's eyes almost rolled, but instead she removed the cup and replaced it with a cup of wine.

Mut stared at her bread, her appetite lost.

Tey peered up at her and then blinked a few times. She opened her mouth to speak, but instead she reached over and squeezed Mut's hand. Drawing her eyebrows together, Tey let out a sigh and asked, "Mut, tell me your thoughts. Why do you not eat?"

Mut knew she already halfway knew the answer. She hadn't talked to her mother as much since Nefertiti died of her sudden illness—or at least that was what Egypt had been told it was. Her mother knew no different.

"I will eat," Mut said, and tore a piece of bread and put it in her mouth. It lay limp on her tongue, as the flavor meant nothing to her. Then she chewed and swallowed it and with half a heart she smiled at her mother.

Tey removed her hand and leaned back. "Do you miss your sister?"

"Miss her? She was never here. Life is as usual. Father, gone. You, tending to his estate. Me, with my studies. Nefertiti, at the palace—only now she is in Akhe-Aten."

All of a sudden, Mut threw her hands up in the air.

"Do I miss her?"

Mut stood up and slammed her chair back under the table.

"No. I don't miss her."

She marched out of there and back to the home's harem, hating herself for being so honest with her mother.

I don't miss her at all, Mut told herself. *She's gone and Father dotes on me now. She's gone and yet I still feel compared to her. Everything she did I can never compare. She was the chosen one. Queen Tiye chose Nefertiti for both her sons. No one chooses me. I hate her!*

"I hate her."

Mut's hot breath tickled the bottom of her chin as she mumbled, walking into her room. She fell into the comfort of her soft wool and straw bed and cried. She didn't have to worry about any of her sisters in there—she was the only one left in her father's house.

"I really don't hate you, sister," she whispered, sobbing between breaths. "I . . ." Mut's hitched breaths overtook her shaking body. "I don't miss you, but I don't hate you. I'm sorry. I'm sorry." Mut wiped the tears from her eyes. "I wish justice for you."

Tey knocked at her door.

"Go away," Mut whispered.

But Tey came in, sat on her bed, and rubbed her back.

"Mut, please talk to me."

"There is nothing to talk about," Mut mumbled as she buried her head in her arms.

Tey chewed on her lip and then shook her head. "Mut, you are acting like a child."

Mut snapped her head to her mother and looked at her with rage in her eyes. "I am no child!" She pushed herself off the bed, ready to march out again.

"Then *talk* to me, woman to woman."

Tey's firm and calm voice settled Mut's march and she heard Tey tap the bed. She turned around, still with a scowl on her face. Mut hated when her mother did this to her. If she did what she wanted, it would prove her mother right.

Every time, she played well into her mother's hand; and so, step by step, she came near to the bed and sat down.

Mut sat silent, so Tey looked around the room. "You know, this room used to belong to Nefertiti. One time, her and Meritaten, Meketaten, Ankhesenpaaten, Nefe, and Neferneferure all stayed in this room. Setepenre, too, since she was in Nefertiti's womb."

Mut looked around. "And now they are all dead except Ankhesenpaaten." Mut shook her head, knowing even Ankhesenpaaten's time may be cut short, since now she was alone with Nefertiti's murderer in Aketaten.

"Mut," Tey said, her eyes wide at the poor taste in her daughter's words.

"What? It is true." Mut crossed her arms. Her mother's silence drew her attention, and Mut saw tears running down her face. "It *is* true," Mut whispered again, feeling her heart shrink within her chest and hating herself for causing her mother to cry.

"Yes, it's true," Tey said as she wiped her cheeks. "They were all taken before their time."

"I did love Nefertiti, Mother," Mut said as she grabbed Tey's hands, hoping to help stem the flow of her mother's tears. "I miss all of them."

Tey shook her head. "We must move on with our lives. They all would want that for us." Tey nodded, as if in agreement with herself. "We mustn't dwell on the past." She smiled with watery eyes at Mut.

Mut let out a deep sigh. "I'm getting older . . ." Her words trailed off.

Marriage weighed heavily on her mind. Maybe she could live on her own or become a concubine, but her singing or dancing skills weren't good enough to fetch a high price. She couldn't even play a musical instrument. She shook her head at the notion. She still dreamed of Horemheb, but after witnessing him gaze at Nefertiti the way she wished him to gaze at her, her dreams had changed from him falling in love with her at first sight to something happening to Nefertiti so that he would fall in love with her instead. A selfish dream that came true in the most horrible of ways. She blinked back her tears as her mother watched her think.

Such a selfish girl, Mut thought to herself. She had never wished death on Nefertiti, but she had wished that for once Nefertiti was out of the way, so she didn't have to live in her shadow. *Never me as Mut,* she thought, *only Nefertiti's half-sister, as if people were trying to force a connection to Nefertiti's greatness.*

"You *are* getting older," Tey repeated. Mut looked to her, knocked from her thoughts. "You are a beautiful woman with a bright future ahead of you."

"Only if I marry someone," Mut muttered.

Tey nodded.

A long-term single woman, while faring well enough to get by, was looked upon as odd by society as they wondered what was wrong with her that she never accepted marriage or found a man to be with.

"Well, did you have someone in mind?" Tey prodded.

Mut bit her lip. She did, but last time she mentioned him, her mother and Nefertiti laughed at her, so instead she shook her head.

"Would you like to go through some of the young men we know?" Tey asked.

"No," Mut said, her cheeks flushed pink.

"Why not?"

"I don't want to marry any of them."

Tey watched her, and then, as if a spark in her memory lit, she lifted her head and ran her gaze over her daughter. "Is it because you want to marry someone of whom I will not approve?"

Mut yanked her hands away and crossed her arms. "Who I marry is my choice. I do not need your approval."

Tey's voice went cold as her eyes widened underneath a furrowed brow. "You still live here. You will get my exact thoughts on who you marry."

Mut pulled her hands back to her side. "Please, Mother, I don't want to talk about it anymore."

"Is it Horemheb?"

Tey's curt tone cut to Mut's heart. She knew it was absurd to still think about him. And although he agreed to keep Nefertiti's murder secret, she remembered the way he rushed to her to shield her from the death in that council room. He had protected her while her own father stayed with *his* Nefertiti. Horemheb had stayed by her side until she left that room. It had sealed her loyalty to him, and this longing, this primal attraction, toward him held her heart.

He has to feel it too, right?

Mut bit her tongue and shook her head.

"Oh my, Mut. I have told you—he is too old for you. And your sister told you that it is not good to be a second wife."

Mut hated the fact that her mother could see through her with ease.

Tey sent her hand sailing through the air as if Mut had thrown her advice to the wind. "He was involved in Pharaoh Akhenaten's demise, and yet you still want him for your husband?"

He did what he had to do with Pharaoh Akhenaten—Father even said that man tormented Nefertiti.

Maybe she admired him for his less than honorable involvement in the Pharaoh's death. Maybe it was her sister's idea—but they never spoke ill of her; she was the victim in the entire plot. Mut shook her head, knowing she'd thought herself into a corner.

"I can't stop thinking of him, Mother." Mut stood up and

began to pace. "It doesn't matter what I do. He . . . he is here." She pointed to her heart.

"Mut . . ." Tey's gaze fell to the floor and then back to her distressed daughter. "He will never think of you in that way. He will never ask you for marriage. You will grow old and alone waiting for something that will never come. He is twenty years older than you. Do you think he will live as long as you? You will be a widow for half your life. You are nearing an age where the young men will raise an eyebrow wondering why you aren't married, and instead of court *you* they will ask the younger women, assuming something might be wrong with you. Do you want that for yourself?"

Mut crossed her arms and looked toward the window as tears welled in her eyes. She knew the rational response, but she also knew that Horemheb permeated her mind and dreams whenever she even thought of being with another man, let alone spoke with another. He smiled at her. He stared at her. He chuckled with her. He protected her. He must feel this attraction too.

"No."

"Then consider Menna, Nehi, or Setka."

"I don't want to consider them." Mut crossed her arms even tighter over her chest, her gaze still to the window—mostly because she did not want to look at her mother.

"Mut, you have a young girl's infatuation. Horemheb has a *wife*. If he wanted you as a wife, he would have asked you by now—he is plenty wealthy and could afford many wives, and the fact he has not asked you for marriage means he will *never* ask you for marriage. Let go and move on with your life. That is what your sister would have wanted."

"No! My sister would have wanted me to be happy!" Mut's arms dropped to her side.

"You will not be happy waiting for Horemheb."

Her pulse raced. "Don't tell me what to do to be happy!"

Tey stood up and smacked Mut in the face. "You will not yell at your elders."

Tey's eyes bore down on Mut, whose blood rushed to her cheeks. Mut bit her tongue as to not enrage her mother more; she reminded her she was still a girl living in her father's house.

"You are thinking with a child's heart. You are a woman now and need to mature past this and learn to live with the life given to you. We never always get what we want. Menna is now a priest for Anubis. He is polite and adores you. He would make a great husband and father. And he holds a noble rank and will be able to provide a luxurious life for you and your children."

Mut stopped listening and crossed her arms again. She didn't want to marry Menna. Yes, her mother's words rang true, but she did not find him attractive in any aspect— although certainly more so than Nehi and Setka. Menna's dull humor and the tang of his overpowering southernwood perfume lingered in her memory of him, and she shook her head.

Tey kept the tears welling in her eyes from falling as she watched her daughter sort out her mental anguish. "Sometimes life is hard." She kept her voice calm as she spoke again. "When you are willing to have a mature discussion about marriage, I will be at the dinner table."

Then she left the room and closed the door behind her.

Mut didn't bother to watch her leave. She simply closed her eyes and let the tears fall once she heard the door close. She whispered to herself, "I look enough like Nefertiti. He will call on me." Then she beat her hands against her head. "What a stupid thought," she mumbled, hating herself for the little bit of relief she had felt when Nefertiti died. "What is wrong with me?" she cried as she crawled back into her bed. "He will come to me because he sees how wonderful I am, even if Nefertiti were still alive. I will wait a little longer. I will wait."

She closed her eyes again and his face came into view as she imagined him holding her in his arms.

"I will wait."

CHAPTER 4
THE TIME OF LOYALTY

Wenamen caught Ay's gaze as he supervised some lower servants cleaning the stone floors. Ay squared his shoulders to him as he continued to talk to the chief royal architect, Kha, about building a monument wall in Ipet-isut for their new Pharaoh and the plans for Tutankhaten's burial in the Valley of the Kings alongside his grandfather's tomb.

"Yes, yes," Ay answered Kha's question, and shooed him away with a wave of his hand.

The chief royal architect bowed to the vizier and went on his way. Ay narrowed his eyes at Wenamen, signaling him to meet. Each man took their own way to their meeting spot in the long-forgotten corridor of Malkata.

"So?" Ay asked, his arms crossed in an attempt to shield himself from any ill news.

"Vizier Ay," Wenamen began with a slight bow. "I do not bring good news."

Ay's stomach tossed from a wave of turbulence and he clenched his jaw, holding back anything that might come up. He regained control of his stomach and spoke. "The people wanted my daughter's death." Ay's gaze found the floor as he assumed the answer.

"No. The people seem genuinely sad Pharaoh Neferneferuaten died. They did not want her death."

Ay snapped his head up to look Wenamen in the face. "Then why would you lie about not bringing good news?"

"I did not lie." Wenamen dipped his chin before he began again. "The People's Restoration of Egypt runs throughout Waset, and it seems Pawah paid good amounts of grain for their loyalty."

"Even now, when the temples are open and people have returned to work? Does the bribe still hold much clout?" Ay cocked his eyebrow, not understanding.

Wenamen's voice dropped. "Yes. They do not forget Pawah, who saved them during their time of need under Pharaoh Akhenaten and Pharaoh Smenkare's reign."

"What of the servants and people of Malkata and Ipet-isut? Surely they stay loyal to the throne?"

"We are loyal to Amun and Amun's divinely appointed."

"Are you sure all in Malkata and Ipet-isut are loyal?" Ay leaned in to study Wenamen's face yet again. His eyes, he noticed, had started to fail him in his old age.

Wenamen did not lean away at the old man's inquisitive stare, but instead stood tall. He had nothing to hide. "Malkata, yes."

Ay rubbed his chin, thinking of how to turn the people from Pawah and remember his bribes no more. Only one thought lingered, and it drew a deep grief within his chest. "You say the people, even those who supported the movement, did not want Pharaoh Neferneferuaten to die?"

"Yes, that is what we have found out. They did not want her as their Pharaoh because she was a woman, but they did not want her to die because she was their Pharaoh. They still saw her as Amun's appointed through her position of Coregent of Pharaoh Smenkare."

"Then I must tell you something . . ."

Ay hesitated, but continued. It was the only way to decrease Pawah's support; but at the same time, he risked the perception of the position of Pharaoh—especially after all these years of trying to regain its power. He shook his head and let out a breath as he made his decision, and selfishly he felt some relief that the truth would finally be made known.

"Pharaoh Neferneferuaten did not die of illness. She was murdered by Pawah and his wife, Beketaten."

Wenamen's nostrils flared and his jaw dropped. His breath quickened by the sharp rise and fall of his chest. "Why was he not impaled outside of the temple for his crime?"

"He would be a martyr for his movement, especially given Pharaoh Neferneferuaten's relation to Pharaohs Akhenaten and Smenkare. It would bring weakness to the throne." Ay squeezed his arms tighter across his chest as he felt his dagger, hidden underneath his shendyt, wishing he could have ended Pawah there as he stood that day. Had they made the wrong choice in letting him go? Would the people have revolted and praised Pawah as a martyr? They just didn't know at the time. "Trust runs thin. I am placing trust in you because you have been shielded from the results of Pharaoh Akhenaten's heresy."

"I am loyal to the King of Egypt and to our premier god, Amun-Re. Your trust is well placed."

"Pawah was the Fifth Prophet of Amun," Ay tested him.

"He was never King of the Upper and the Lower, the Pharaoh, the divinely appointed." Wenamen looked Ay in the eyes. "Pawah has never held my loyalty, and his briber's grain has not crossed the threshold of my house. He himself propagated the lie that Pharaoh Neferneferuaten died of illness."

"Good." Ay nodded at Wenamen's loyalty. "We must weaken Pawah in the eyes of his supporters. If you are correct and the people did not want her to die and you think they will react as you do now, then subtly spread the rumor that Pawah may have had a hand in her untimely demise, gauge the reaction, and report back to me."

"Yes, Vizier."

Ay tilted his head to dismiss Wenamen, but Wenamen stayed.

"I will not rest until I see justice for Pharaoh Neferneferuaten."

"I hope you are not the only one," Ay muttered, and as his thoughts drifted to Horemheb. He hoped he had a chance to undo some of Pawah's hold over the young Pharaoh while they fought at the northern border together.

A FEW DAYS CAME AND WENT UNTIL WENAMEN MET AY AGAIN.

"What have you found out?" Ay asked, crossing his arms over his chest.

"The people here in Waset associate Aketaten with hunger, poverty, and spiritual death. Any Pharaoh who resides there only gains wariness from the people." Wenamen shook his head. "The fact you are here making plans for Pharaoh Tutankhaten to come here is great news to the people. I suggest that he not only come here, but he move here. He abandon and disown what his father has done."

Wenamen took a deep breath and shuffled his feet. Vizier Ay hadn't asked him for his opinion, but Ay only nodded, not noticing Wenamen's shifting.

"You make good suggestions." Ay squinted, trying to plot a plan to do what Wenamen said. "Now . . . how to persuade our new Pharaoh to move here with Pawah in Aketaten."

53

"I have no suggestions. But know this: Aketaten is isolated from the rest of Egypt. All people know about Aketaten is that riches flow in and never out. Food flows in abundance there but is never replenished. The people hate Aketaten."

Ay clenched his teeth, hating Pharaoh Akhenaten even more. He tightened his arms across his chest and found Wenamen's gaze. "Does Pawah still hold clout here in Waset? Or does he not know what the people of Waset think or believe?"

"He may or may not, I do not know. But I do know his influence has been great here. There are many still in his debt. He stole from the royal grain house to feed many families during the reign of Pharaoh Akhenaten and provided safe harbor to those who chose to worship Amun under Pharaoh Smenkare's purification executions. I would still not underestimate him."

Ay nodded, thinking over Wenamen's last statement. "A great enemy from within," he muttered. "And what of the people's reaction to the rumors of the true reason behind my daughter's death?"

"We tried, but none would have it. They don't believe someone who is loyal to Amun, one of Amun's own prophets, would kill Pharaoh, Amun's divinely appointed."

"Then we need to show them Vizier Pawah is not loyal to Amun. I don't even think he believes Amun exists."

"A man who harms Pharaoh would not believe in Amun." Wenamen's pinched lips and furrowed brow mirrored Ay's face.

Ay lifted his chin and his eyes searched the heavens for answers, but found none.

CHAPTER 5
THE TIME OF BATTLE

THE HAZE RISING FROM THE GROUND BLURRED THE ENEMY AS they approached. The sun beat on the now-General Horemheb as he drew in the dusty air through his nostrils and let it out through his teeth. He raised his hand, and his mind cleared as it always did before battle to gain one last moment of peace before life or death rushed upon him. Her dark brown eyes flooded his memory and her deep, hearty laugh rang through his ears as his mouth contorted into a frown. He swallowed with guilt as the pit of his stomach rose to the top of his throat. He looked past his memory of her into the horizon—the enemy gained and were almost within the archers' distance. He made a fist with his raised hand, signaling the archers to draw their arrows. Death would come to all, but in his last moment before he dropped his hand commanding thousands upon thousands of arrows upon the men in the distance, he only regretted one death.

Hers. Nefertiti's. He should have been there. He should have saved her.

The air filled with the hum of arrows as they flew in the

air and gave some small shade to his head. He watched men fall and more replace them.

Looking over to Pharaoh Tutankhaten, in his own chariot helped by his chariot driver, he thought: *Tut replaced Nefertiti. No one gave second thought. Death comes to us all.*

He raised his hand again to command the archers to notch another arrow.

He watched the boy Tut's face bounce between elation and fear. Their trip to the northern border to fight the Libyans who invaded Egypt's lands had seemed a short one despite its lengthy duration—he had tried to teach Tut everything he needed to know, but time was not on their side. He pressed his lips together and narrowed his eyes at the eleven-year-old Pharaoh. Tut had insisted he be on the frontlines to show his military that he was chosen by the god Amun to lead them.

So young, yet he smiles. He doesn't know the perils of war.

He looked to the sand dunes, knowing his Commander Paramesse and his divisions laid in wait for the encroaching enemy. The poor Libyans stood no chance.

He made a fist and dropped his arm.

He looked and saw more men fall from the Egyptians' lethal arrows.

His heart rate quickened, as it always did right before combat.

A small tear came from his eye as he heard Nefertiti's laugh again somewhere in the hum of the arrows.

He told his own chariot driver to grab the reins of his chariot, feeling a sense of unease. Because Pharaoh had not yet named a Master of Pharaoh's Horses, Horemheb took the burden as General to lead the elite charioteers, a feat he felt he was unskilled for.

He was young for General, but he couldn't show any fear or incompetence. He needed his men to respect him.

Nodding to Pharaoh Tut, he remembered his promise to him: he would protect him should he need help. His men would protect their Pharaoh.

Tut smiled as he held himself against the brace in his chariot for his crooked leg, excited for his first battle. Horemheb only half smiled.

He will soon learn.

His and Tut's charioteer cracked the reins, and the horses took off. Horemheb steadied his legs on bent knees, absorbing the shock of the ground as the horses raced toward the Libyans. The rumbling of earth told him he was not alone; his yell was matched by the multitude of men behind him. He glanced over and saw Tut holding on for dear life as he struggled to raise his right arm to lead his army's charge into battle. His spears were still tied to the chariot; it looked like they weren't going to be much use.

The Libyans came into view.

Horemheb drew his sickle-shaped khopesh.

As the horses parted the tide of the enemy, he swung.

His mind drifted, still behind him at the battle line from whence they came, as his body took over from years of experience—until he saw Tut almost fall from the chariot. He hooked his khopesh back on his belt and grabbed the reins from his own chariot driver, steering his chariot toward the boy. If Tut fell, his own men would crush him as they barreled past. Horemheb yelled to Tut's chariot driver to slow down and to let the men pass, but as Tut's driver's attention turned to Horemheb, trying to understand what he was saying, Tut's chariot bumped over a body and his driver lost control of the reins.

Tut screamed as the side of the chariot went into the air; he clutched his brace, hunching over to protect his head. Horemheb pulled up ahead and got close enough to grab him as Tut's chariot toppled over. Horemheb banked hard to the right to avoid the crash—but now his own chariot was at risk of being toppled by oncoming chariots. Throwing Tut to the floor of his carriage, Horemheb grabbed the reins with both hands to gain better control while his chariot driver locked Tut against the carriage with his leg. Again Horemheb banked hard to the left, then straightened out and pulled back on the reins to slow his own horses. He let up enough so that eventually the whole of the chariots passed through and Paramesse and his men were coming up behind them, killing any enemy who still remained alive and cutting off the digits of the dead for an extra reward for the number of enemies slain.

As the horses settled and the three men exited the carriage, Horemheb's chariot driver huffed at him, "If you would have told me what to do, I could have done it as well, instead of you endangering all of our lives."

"You will silence your tongue," Horemheb said, "or I will remove it." He stared down his subordinate as his bronze armor captured the sun's reflection. "Go see if Pharaoh's chariot driver survived."

"Yes, General." As the driver took off toward the wreckage, Horemheb noticed him scrunch his nose and wipe his forearm across his face.

Horemheb extended a hand to Tut, who sat frozen on the floor of the carriage.

The stench of death filled the boy's senses as his gaze extended beyond Horemheb and into the massive slaughter that lay there. He shook his head at Horemheb's hand as his eyes darted from his savior to the dead and to his surroundings until he focused on his own deformity.

"They will see me," he stuttered, holding back his tears as he hit his leg with his fist. "Curse my birth . . . curse my foot."

Horemheb retracted his hand and drew in a breath as he placed his hands on his hips. He sat down next to Tut and exhaled. He knew it was not his place, but he saw a scared young boy in need. He joined Tut in his survey of the bloody field.

"Pharaoh, I was only a few years older than you during my first military encounter. I remember taking a man's life. I will never forget the look in his eyes." Horemheb shook the memory away. "It is something I wish on no one. But to keep Egypt secured, we must go to battle. We, as Egypt's defenders, make that sacrifice. You, Pharaoh, are Egypt's highest defender—"

"I can't defend anything," Tut snapped, and pulled his leg into his chest. He put his head on his knee. "I can't even ride in a chariot without falling off."

Horemheb chuckled. "I fell out of a chariot in every practice."

Tut looked up to him with wide eyes. "You?"

"That was why I refused to be a charioteer or archer. I only wanted to be a foot soldier. I like the feeling of solid ground beneath my feet." He stamped his foot on the ground and smiled at Tut, who tapped his toes on the ground a short moment afterward.

"But you are so good at it." Tut turned his attention back to his leg. "You saved my life while also driving the chariot."

"And yet even *I* think I need improvement," Horemheb said, and leaned both elbows on his knees. At Tut's silence, he rocked back up. "It will come with practice, Pharaoh. Most boys your age are not in battles like these. They still spar with each other in practice."

"I should have listened to you." Tut looked and saw his chariot driver unmoving.

Horemheb followed his gaze and chewed the inside of his cheek while his mind raced to figure out a way to distract Tut's attention. "Pharaoh," he said, and looked to him again, finding his eyes. "Each man must learn how his body moves with the chariot and how to steady himself. You will learn in time."

"I am not a full man," Tut said, looking pointedly at his club foot and gesturing to his child's sidelock.

Horemheb bit his tongue. He had never seen a man with a deformed foot in a chariot, or even in the military. A soldier needed to be able to walk, and if he couldn't keep up he was discharged. But that was the last thing Tut needed to hear.

"You are Pharaoh. It does not matter your age or ability," Horemheb finally said. He winced as he thought of the woman he formerly called Pharaoh. He dropped his chin to his chest for a moment and then looked out to the carnage as Paramesse and his men came into view under the dusty storm the battle produced.

"I am still not a full man," Tut said again, and rubbed his aching leg.

Horemheb leaned over and then glanced at him. "You are still Pharaoh." Then he leaned back when Tut did not return his attention to him. "When I was young, my father did not think I would make it in the army like he did. He said I was too afraid and too weak."

Finally Tut looked at him again. "You?"

Horemheb smiled, knowing he now held Tut's attention. "Yes, me. But my friend told me if you act with courage, then you will have courage." Horemheb returned his elbows to his knees. "Even when I am afraid or I feel weak or lost or hopeless"—his head hung and he pushed Nefertiti from his mind—"if I act like I am not, then people believe I am not, and then I begin to believe it as well. So in a way, it is true. Perhaps for you, the saying goes: act as a full man, and you will be a full man." Horemheb squinted at the boy, who absorbed his words. "Now, what say you, Pharaoh? Are you going to cower in this chariot's carriage? Or will you face your military men who have shed their blood in Egypt's defense?" Horemheb nodded his head out to the carnage.

Tut puffed his chest and lifted his chin, inspired by Horemheb's words. "Pharaoh does not cower."

Horemheb smiled. "That's right, my King."

He let Tut pull himself to standing first before he stood himself. As they walked to meet Paramesse over the bodies, Tut carefully placed his left club foot leaning to the right as much as possible so he could hop and walk using his arms to steady himself. Horemheb spotted a javelin, picked it up, and broke it across his knee, giving it to Tut to use as a cane.

As they neared, Horemheb could hear Tut's repeating whisper.

"Act as a full man, and I will be a full man."

TUT HOBBLED ACROSS THE DEAD MEN TOWARD COMMANDER Paramesse. The stench that arose from the bodies rendered him unable to look down at the carnage at his feet. The sight turned his stomach; those dead eyes looking up sent a shiver down his spine. He tried to hold his breath to keep from breathing in the stench as he locked his eyes on Paramesse before him. His thoughts drifted to Horemheb behind him.

Horemheb didn't seem as bad as Pawah had told him he was. Horemheb didn't seem to want to kill him as Pawah had told him he would do. He had saved him, had he not? And at risk of his own life! He glanced over his shoulder to Horemheb. Indeed, he had helped him to stand, given him courage to step out from the chariot's carriage. Why would he do that if he wanted to kill him? Horemheb smiled at him and nodded as if to encourage him to continue. He turned his sights back toward Paramesse and hobbled forward with his makeshift cane—

But his foot stumbled on a bodiless arm; he fell face-first into a dead man and let out a guttural scream of utter fear upon seeing the bloody, half-decapitated man, his eyes half rolled back into his head and his blood spayed across his face. Tut pushed off of him, only to fall into another dead man's chest where a broken spear had penetrated it, and blood came over his body as he flopped around in the blood-churned dirt. The sea of dead men drowned him as his lungs let out one gut-wrenching scream after another, until he felt the warm grip of Horemheb on one arm and Paramesse on the other.

They both pulled him to standing, and Paramesse handed him another makeshift cane. Tut's eyes were wide and his breathing hitched as he quickly grabbed his cane from Paramesse. The memory of his screams filled his cheeks with the red hue of humiliation. Paramesse stared at him, expressionless and cold. He thought he heard Paramesse's men laughing at him, and looked to Horemheb, who looked in turn to Paramesse. Horemheb's eyebrow slid higher than the other and his lips pressed together.

Heat gave rise to a nasty tingle on Tut's neck as his pulse rang in his ears.

Horemheb is trying not to laugh at me! Why did I ever listen to him?!

A rock sank to the depths of his stomach, and he suddenly felt completely alone amidst his army.

Everyone laughs at me.

His ribs squeezed around his rapidly beating heart as he looked around, hoping no one saw the two grown, well-bodied men holding him to stand up. Despite the heat of the sun glaring down upon them, his sweat turned cold.

"Let go of me," Tut said, now more than ever aware of his unwanted presence. He yanked off their hands, only to fall yet again into the deceased. He froze and tried to swallow another scream. He wanted nothing more than to be home in his room at the royal harem so that his nurse Maia may rub his aching legs.

Why am I here? Why did I come? Why did I let Horemheb bring me here? Why did I ever get out of the carriage? Why did I listen to him?!

He again felt the grips of the two men on his upper arms, hoisting him to standing.

Horemheb wanted me to fall. The realization hit him hard in his stomach as he staggered to get a good footing on the ground. *That's why he gave me the cane and urged me out of the carriage. He wanted me to look the fool so it would be easier to kill me.* He looked to Horemheb, who he thought had a certain light in his eyes. *This is what he wanted. Pawah was right all along. Why did I doubt him? I want Pawah here. He would know what to do. He would protect me. He wouldn't lie to me like Horemheb.*

That was when Horemheb swung him into his arms and began to carry him across the sea of dead men, back toward camp. His stomach twisted as his cheeks boiled. He didn't want to walk, but he certainly didn't want to be carried like a child! Horemheb and Paramesse said nothing, but he caught sight of Paramesse's expressionless stare yet again.

"Put me down!" Tut's voice cracked as he tried to whisper.

"It may be better if you let me carry you back to camp," Horemheb whispered back.

"Why, so you can humiliate me more?" Tut seethed. "What happened to 'Act as a full man'?"

"Pharaoh, I am not trying to humiliate you."

"It seems you are. You knew I would fall. Everyone knew I would fall. *I* knew I would fall. Yet you told me otherwise, and look what happened!" Tut's hands wrenched around his cane, wanting to hit Horemheb. "You did this on purpose. You wanted everyone to see you carrying me as a babe."

Horemheb shook his head, letting out a frustrated breath, but kept silent all the way back to camp.

THE DAY DREW TO AN END AND PHARAOH TUTANKHATEN lay in his cot under his royal tent in the middle of the Egyptian campsite. His cheeks flushed as he remembered Paramesse's stare and his own childish screams and being carried by Horemheb.

He pushed himself over to his side and yanked the linen sheet over his shoulder. His dinner sat untouched by his bedside. "Why did I ever trust the General? 'Act as a full man and you will be a full man'? What nonsense! He just told me that to make me look a fool. Pawah was right. They all want me dead," he whispered to himself. "Why didn't I just listen to Pawah? Now the men laugh at me."

"Pharaoh Tutankhaten," a servant's voice came from the entrance to his tent. "General Horemheb wishes to speak to you."

Tut's mouth contorted to a scowl as he yanked the sheet higher onto his shoulder. "No."

"It is about tomorrow's strategy. He has reason to believe the enemy may attempt an ambush."

"He is General—he can do whatever he wishes," Tut said, not moving from his cot.

"Pharaoh." General Horemheb's deep voice caused Tut's heart to race as he sat up. "I need to speak with you."

"I said *no*," Tut growled, and threw himself back on his bed, looking away from both Horemheb and the servant.

The General clenched his jaw as he glanced to the servant and nodded him off. Once the servant had obeyed and they were alone, Horemheb made his way around to the other side of the bed to face Tut.

"Your men may die unnecessarily if you refuse me," Horemheb whispered as he knelt next to Tut's bedside. He clasped his fingers together over his knee and waited in silence for Tut to acknowledge him. Tut eventually peered up at him. "Do you wish death upon the men who fight for Egypt?"

"No," Tut whispered, scowling at Horemheb.

"Then please speak with me," Horemheb whispered, his eyes urging him from his bed.

"I don't *want* to *speak* with you. Last time you spoke to me, you made me look a fool in front of the Commander. The men don't follow me—they follow *you*. Pawah was right. He was right all along." Tut buried his head in his arm. "Why don't you just kill me now like I know you want to? It would be easy. I can't even defend myself."

At the mention of Pawah's name, Horemheb's knuckles went white and heat overcame his neck and head. "If Pawah—"

"Pawah warned me." Tut looked to Horemheb and, noticing the glare in his General's eyes, shrank a little farther into his bed. "He warned me that anyone in Pharaoh Neferneferuaten's court would conspire to kill me. You just want me to fail first, so the men won't hate you when you do it."

"Pharaoh, if I wanted you dead, if I wanted you to fail, then why would I risk my life to save yours?" Horemheb said through his teeth. "Wouldn't it have been easier to let you die today? We could have all sat around and laughed afterward at the fact that Pharaoh could not even ride a chariot and died in his first battle."

Tut sat up and looked at Horemheb as his mind raced for an answer.

Horemheb, content with Tut's lack of response, stood, grabbed Tut's cane, and handed it to him. "We can talk about this later." Tut took his cane. "Now, Pharaoh, we have matters to discuss. Commander Paramesse waits for us in Pharaoh's outer tent."

Tut stood and began to walk out, but Horemheb stopped him and pointed to his crown on its stand by his bed. Tut let out a sigh and muttered, "I can't do anything right," as he put his crown on his head.

"Remember you are Pharaoh," Horemheb said before he opened the curtain of Tut's inner tent, letting him walk first into his outer tent. "Everything Pharaoh does is right."

Horemheb took his place behind the table alongside Commander Paramesse and nodded to Tut to begin their meeting.

Tut cleared his throat as the two large men dwarfed the table and himself. "What does General and Commander wish to speak about with Pharaoh?" Tut stumbled through his question, trying and failing to sound the part.

Horemheb gestured to the Commander to begin.

"Pharaoh, our scouts say our enemy amasses another large number of men just out of sight." Commander Paramesse jammed a finger into the papyrus map sprawled on the table between them. "We think they plan to attack in the morning. We need to have the men ready for an ambush or a counterattack. I—"

"Then do what you see fit to do," Tut said, not really understanding the gravity of the situation and not realizing Paramesse was not finished speaking.

At the resulting momentary awkward silence, Horemheb asked a leading question: "Pharaoh, would you like to hear our plan?" He gestured to the map.

"Yes." Tut nodded. "Of course." He rolled his shoulders back, trying to save face. "Show me your plan."

Tut tried to stand a little taller under the weight of the eyes in the room. He shuffled his feet. His hands slipped from their growing clamminess. His eyes darted to Horemheb, who gave a little nod, to bolster his confidence. Tut smiled and lifted his chin as he peered over his nose to the map.

Horemheb drew his finger along the map as he explained. "We draw out the Commander's division of the camp, and when the enemy attacks, our men will be awake and waiting for them. Then Commander Paramesse's division will close in around them, cutting them off. Do you agree with this plan?"

"Why not just attack now?" Tut asked.

"Our men are weary from today's battle. They need rest before another encounter. Their men are fresh, not having seen battle yet. I don't think we would be victorious," Paramesse reasoned.

Tut's heart thudded within his chest. He should have known that; now he looked a fool yet again in front of the Commander. "Then why did you need to speak with me?" Tut said, throwing his arm into the air in exasperation, which in turn almost toppled him over on his cane. His cheeks blushed with embarrassment; he prayed to whatever god was the true god to not let him fall again in front of the Commander. Regaining his balance, he continued, "If you already know what you are going to do, then do it. Why do you need me?"

Commander Paramesse let out a blast of air through his nostrils as Horemheb, looking to save the situation, drew in a quick breath. "Pharaoh, the decision is yours. You are Pharaoh. You make the decisions for your army, especially now as you are here on the battlefield. We are your advisors, but the decision is ultimately yours." Horemheb tapped the map. "Now, what shall it be? We need to act quickly one way or the other."

"Do the one you said first." Tut shook his head, scowling.

"You both know this more than me. I don't know what is best for the fighting." His voice cracked and his cheeks regained their pink hue. *These men with their deep voices . . . and here I am with this one.*

"Pharaoh has spoken," Horemheb said, looking to Paramesse. "I shall see you in the morning, Commander. Hopefully under victorious conditions."

Paramesse nodded to his friend. "Sleep well tonight. Tomorrow you will need your strength." Then the Commander left, not bothering to be dismissed by Pharaoh.

Horemheb didn't look at the boy until Tut said, "Are you going to leave, too?" Tut's leg ached, but he didn't want anyone in his camp to know it. He already looked a fool with his club foot and chariot mishap; he didn't want anyone to think any lesser of him than they already did.

"Pharaoh . . . you must *act* like Pharaoh." Horemheb leaned both hands on the table and nodded for the servant to leave them alone in Pharaoh's tent. The servant obeyed. "If you want the respect of the men, you must act like Pharaoh. We all know you are a boy. We all know you have never seen battle. We all do not expect you to know these things, but . . ." Horemheb shook his head. "You must *act* as Pharaoh."

"I don't know what you *mean*," Tut said, and slammed a fist into the table. "Act with courage, act as a full man, act as Pharaoh." Tut leaned on the table; a vein in his neck throbbed as he remembered falling in front of Paramesse. "You fill my head with lies to make me look a fool!"

"Tut, you make *yourself* look a fool," Horemheb whispered. Leaning his head in, he cocked an eyebrow at Tut as if begging Tut to chide him, as would any other Pharaoh, for not using his title, and what was more, calling him by a pet name reserved only for family.

Tut's lower lip, despite his severe overbite, pushed out

into a pout and his eyebrows squeezed together. "You will c-call me *Pharaoh*," he stuttered.

"See?" Horemheb said, and leaned back on the table to match Tut's stance. "Pharaoh would not tolerate someone calling him by his name, just as Pharaoh would not admit that his subordinates know better than he. Pharaoh would have ordered Commander Paramesse to stay until he was dismissed. Pharaoh demands respect and fear. You are Pharaoh. If you fall like you did today," Horemheb said, watching the rage creep into Tut's cheeks again, "you stand up and act as if it never happened. Your men did not laugh at you. If you keep up this"—Horemheb threw his hand in the air—"whatever this is, they might laugh at you if you do it again."

"But I am Pharaoh," Tut said, his chin falling, not wanting to be laughed at.

"Say it again. But this time, *mean it*," Horemheb commanded, and stood up, crossing his arms over his chest.

"I am Pharaoh," Tut said a little louder.

"With more body," Horemheb said, as he himself dropped his voice. "Take a deep breath and then let it out with your words."

Tut drew in a deep breath. "I am Pharaoh." Then he smiled.

Horemheb nodded. "Good." He raised his eyebrows. He spoke truthfully. "Now, Pharaoh, may I suggest you sleep. The morning may be . . . busy."

"I am Pharaoh. No one tells me when to sleep." Tut's voice cracked and a slightly wide-eyed look came over his face, but when he found Horemheb not laughing, he returned to his serious countenance.

Horemheb smiled, nodded, and waited to be dismissed. Tut began to walk away, but Horemheb cleared his throat.

"You can leave, General," Tut said, and waved him off.

"Thus Pharaoh says," Horemheb said, and turned to leave.

EIGHT SENTRIES GUARDED PHARAOH'S TENT AND FOUR guarded his own. He noted the Commander was already moving his men to outside the camp and decided to get some shut-eye before the morning was met with more bloodshed.

He fell into his cot, wondering if his own son, had he had the chance to live, would have been like Tut. What if he'd had a deformity? What if he was strong like he and handsome like his mother?

Nefertiti, my love . . .

Sleep overtook him almost as soon as his head hit the cot. His thoughts twisted to dreams of his homecoming. He walked into his Men-nefer estate as Nefertiti came to him, holding his son and kissing him as he stepped into his house; but once inside, Pawah stabbed him right in his heart and then killed his family in front of him, laughing as he did it.

He awoke a few hours later with cold beads of sweat on his brow and his heart racing within his chest. His linen sheet tossed to the ground in his fitful sleep. Rubbing his temples with the palms of his hands, his mind drifted to Ay's plan: *Get close to the boy and pit him against Pawah.* He gritted his teeth, thinking back to what Tut told him in his tent— that he and the others were conspiring to kill him. That cursed Pawah had poisoned his mind. The boy was not guilty of anything. He was a *victim.* Just like his Nefertiti

Don't let my daughter die in vain, Ay had said.

"A vain death," Horemheb whispered. "Not for my Nefertiti." He rubbed his bald head and then his eyes. "I hate myself," he murmured under his breath. "I should have saved you." His head hung and his hands clenched into fists.

A moment later a soldier muttered, "General."

"Yes," Horemheb answered, snapping his head to attention. He could make out the soldier's silhouette in the dusk's half-light.

"A messenger is here to see you," the soldier said.

"I will be right out."

He stood and splashed water on his face and put on his armor. Walking outside his tent, he surveyed the horizon; a blood-red dawn awaited them.

He found the messenger waiting for him. The messenger dipped his chin out of respect for his status. "General, I bring a message from the northern border in the land of Canaan. The Hittites close in and reinforcements are needed."

"Of course," Horemheb said under his breath. He looked out to the morning sun. "There will be a battle here. If we are not victorious, I will send the Commander Paramesse to their aid. Otherwise both the Commander and I will join them."

The messenger dipped his chin again and took the message with him.

Horemheb looked again to the growing dawn, remembering Nefertiti asking him, *Don't you wish every morning to be like this?*

"I do," he whispered to her memory, and, closing his eyes, he felt the softness of her skin against his, just as a distant war cry filled the morning air. He gathered his moment of peace before the coming bloodshed, and then ordered his men to arms.

CHAPTER 6
THE TIME OF EMPOWERMENT

THE EGYPTIANS PROVED VICTORIOUS AGAINST THE LIBYANS. On the day of victory, the cloudless sky in Goshen gave birth to a line of clouds. The men looked up and pointed at the fair speed of the streak of clouds above them as a sign of a gift from the gods.

Pharaoh Tutankhaten whispered to Horemheb, "What is it?"

"It may be ba-en-pet," Horemheb said under his breath, watching the white clouds dissipate in the east and grow bigger in the north.

"Ba-en-pet?"

"Every now and then, when the gods are pleased and want to gift us, they send ba-en-pet, a strong metal, iron, the same fiber that comprises their bones. It signifies their approval." Horemheb said, still watching the skies.

"Their approval of what?" Tut asked, following Horemheb's gaze.

Horemheb dropped his gaze to the boy. "The approval of Pharaoh."

Tut's head spun around and stared him in the eyes. "The

gods and goddesses approve of me?" Tut pointed to his chest, eyes wide.

"It seems so." Horemheb smiled and pointed in the direction the cloud streaks were headed. "Now hear this. I've never heard it, but I've been told the sound of ba-en-pet is so powerful that it causes men to stumble."

"A *sound* causing men to stumble?" Tut laughed, shaking his head, and pointed to Horemheb. "General Horemheb, I think you need more sle—"

All of a sudden, a loud *boom* rattled their bones and jarred their teeth, causing Tut to wobble on his cane and fall into Horemheb's arms, but Horemheb stood him upright before anyone could see.

"Yes, Pharaoh, a sound apparently *can* cause a man to stumble. Imagine that!" Horemheb laughed. "I shall never forget the gods' sign of ba-en-pet. We are all honored. You, our Pharaoh, should be honored Amun-Re and the others have sent you their gift."

"I am. They approve of me." Tut beamed as he looked to where the clouds sped, beyond their place of camp. Smoke rose in the far distance where the boom had sounded. Then Tut's smile fell as he turned to look to Horemheb. "Does that mean my *father* approves of me . . . ?"

Horemheb pressed his lips together into a sad smile. He took a knee so he was eye-level with the young Pharaoh. "Your father always approved of you, and he wanted you more than you will ever know."

"Then why did he not make me his successor?"

Tut's shoulders shrank away from the answer he assumed he would receive: *He loved you, but you were crippled. He loved you, but you were just not what he thought for Pharaoh.* But instead, Horemheb rubbed his chin and responded with something Tut was not expecting.

"Your father did not make wise choices," Horemheb said,

letting his words sink in; but he knew more questions would come, so he changed the subject, not wanting to discuss more mature topics with the boy. "Now, what are you to do with the gift?"

"The gift?" Tut asked, as if being knocked from a trance.

"Ba-en-pet." Horemheb gestured off to the distant smoke.

"Oh, yes!" Tut nodded then chewed his bottom lip as his words stuttered out, "I . . . sh-shall . . . retrieve it?"

"If I may, Pharaoh, I would send my servants to retrieve it and send it back to Waset with Vizier Ay to oversee its molding into something you can carry on your body. Something powerful for Pharaoh . . . maybe something deadly to show your might. Something for war to show you are a warrior king—"

"I'm not a warrior king." Tut scowled.

"But you have been through five battles and caused the Libyans to retreat! That is a warrior king," Horemheb said, hoping this would pick up the boy's spirits.

"No. You and Commander Paramesse did that. I only hid in the chariot and stayed in my tent because I am not a full man and I cannot fight."

"The *gods* think you capable," Horemheb countered. "You led with strategy and presence. You, our Pharaoh, our warrior king, being here with us—that is reason for our victory."

"You only *say* that, General. I know my worth."

Horemheb drew in a deep breath and pressed his lips together. He debated putting a hand on his shoulder, but when he saw the poor boy's countenance, pity filled his heart. This boy never knew his mother, and his father wanted nothing to do with him. Tut would want someone to touch his shoulder and reassure him he would be a man they were proud of, but Horemheb stayed his hand. He had gotten too close to Nefertiti, and look at the pain he held now that he had failed her. Should Pawah win, it would be easier if he kept his and Pharaoh's relationship as separate as could be.

Nevertheless, there was fire in Horemheb to help the ones who needed help. So he let out a breath and placed a hand on Tut's shoulder to encourage him. "You are Pharaoh. You are worth all to the gods and to Egypt. You are the son of Pharaoh Akhenaten, the grandson of Pharaoh Amenhotep, the most Magnificent King." A soft smile fell on his lips. *And the step-son to Pharaoh Neferneferuaten,* he thought as he continued to speak. "Their blood runs through your veins." Horemheb felt a tug in his soul when Tut looked to him with tears welling behind his eyes. "You will do great things, and you will live eternally on the lips of your people and in the eyes of the world. Your image will live on the great stone walls at Ipet-isut for all eternity to see." He gave a slight but firm shake of Tut's shoulder.

A smile crept on Tut's lips. "Do you really think so, General Horemheb?"

"I know so," Horemheb responded, and patted Tut's shoulder before pulling his hand away and standing up, looking around to make sure no one saw him touch Pharaoh. He looked to the smoke in the distance. "How about a dagger?"

"What?"

"Ba-en-pet, my Pharaoh. Make a dagger from it. It will be your sign from the gods that they have appointed you, and it will signify your divine right to rule Egypt. It is fierce, showing you are a warrior king. It is small, so you can always have it on you, and if needed, you will be able to use it in case someone dares to commit treason against you." Horemheb watched a version of the future play out where Pawah attacked the boy; he hoped Pharaoh would come out victorious.

Tut nodded hesitantly.

Seeing the confusion on Tut's brow, Horemheb chomped his teeth, wondering if he should warn the young boy about the dangers of sitting on the throne—especially now. But he knew of the boy's admiration of Pawah; Tut would never believe him, even if he told him the truth.

Perhaps hold back a little, he told himself. *Distance yourself. When Pawah strikes him, too—no,* Horemheb corrected himself, *if . . . if Pawah strikes him down, too—I will not hurt like I did with Nefertiti. I cannot. I will not. No more. I will be his advisor, but not his mentor like his father should have been. His father. I am not his father. My son is dead. I will never be his father. I will never be a father to any child—not anymore.*

Tut nodded again after the awkward silence and finally said, "All right." Clearly the boy was wary of asking what he meant about treason, lest he seem childish again. "I will order some men to go retrieve the . . . ba-en-pet . . . and make me a dagger."

"That is a very wise choice, my Pharaoh." Horemheb nodded, smiling with his lips but not his eyes, adding, "I would send it to Waset and let Vizier Ay take oversight of its manufacture."

Tut crossed his arms and steadied himself after removing support of his cane. "Why not to Aketaten with Vizier Pawah?"

Horemheb shifted his weight uncomfortably, looking off to the ba-en-pet smoke. After a few moments and a soft sigh, he looked upon Tut again. "Aketaten is home to the Aten cult, which the people have despised for a long time and believe the gods have turned their back on. In light of your ascension to the throne, ba-en-pet is a gift from the gods. Amun lives in Ipet-isut of Waset. It would be unwise to send Amun's and the other gods' and goddesses' gift to the home of the Aten-disc worshippers where they were banned."

Tut's slow nod and pursed lips showed his understanding. "I will do as you say."

"You are wise, Pharaoh. Your father did not understand how great a son he had. Your grandfather would be so proud."

A smile beamed forth from the boy's eyes and a fresh air filled his lungs. "I will be a wise King, General."

"No, you *are* a wise King, my Pharaoh." Horemheb said, and watched as Tut's crossed arms fell to his normal, comfortable stance.

"Thank you, General, for believing in me."

"Always," Horemheb said, gesturing for him to lead the way to the main camp so he could give his decree about the gods' gift. "Shall you address the men?"

Tut smiled further. "I shall," he said, and hobbled along. From a brief change in the wind, Horemheb heard Tut whisper to himself, "Act as a full man, and I will *be* a full man."

Horemheb smiled, and watching the crippled King hobble from behind, a prideful pity filled his heart. He wondered what his and Nefertiti's son could have been. Perhaps he needed the young Pharaoh to fill the emptiness that ate at his soul—and perhaps the young Pharaoh needed a father.

Then he emptied his mind; he would not entertain any more fantasies.

A "GREATEST OF FIFTY" COMMANDER LED HIS GROUP OF FIFTY soldiers to retrieve the ba-en-pet and take it back to Waset per the order of Pharaoh Tutankhaten. The army could only spare fifty men in this endeavor, as reports of the Hittite battles grew more drear with each messenger, and to supplement the Overseer of the Fortress that stayed at the

Libyan border permanently, they had left a Troop Commander and his regiments to detract a second attack on Egyptian borders.

The rest of the divisions marched to the northeast along the Mediterranean coastline toward the Hittite border. Horemheb, at Tut's order, drove the royal chariot as the army followed behind. Most of the morning had been in silence, but Tut kept looking at Horemheb as if he wanted to say something, until finally Horemheb smiled as he looked out across the lush Canaan to their right.

"Pharaoh, is there something you wish to say to me?"

Tut peered up at his General and blew out a large breath. "I just can't . . ." He trailed off, shook his head, and looked out to sea.

"Can't what?"

As the chariot rolled along, Tut finished, "I can't stop thinking about what you said that night in the tent."

Horemheb's mind raced. What had he said in the tent? What night?

"Why can't you?" he finally said, hoping Tut would answer his unasked questions with his response.

"Pawah told me you would conspire to kill me . . . but, then, why did you save me? Surely it would have been easier to let me die in my first battle." Tut's brow furrowed in his contemplation. "You have been like a tutor to me. Why would you do that? Why would you save me when Pawah told me otherwise?"

Horemheb slightly tilted his head back in relief before answering. "I saved you because I am loyal to Pharaoh. I would never take up arms against Pharaoh." His insides warped with that last statement—he *did* have a hand in Pharaoh Akhenaten's untimely death—but he hoped to the gods that Tut would never find out his lie.

Tut looked over to Horemheb as his head bobbed along with the chariot. "Then why would Pawah tell me that?"

Horemheb swallowed the lump in his throat. "The truth, my Pharaoh?" He looked out to the land in front of him. "You may not like it."

Tut looked steadily at him, his gaze firmly set upon Horemheb's face. "I want the truth." Then, after a pause: "Pharaoh demands the truth."

Horemheb let out his breath slowly, calculating his words. "Pawah wants the crown. Pawah is trying to isolate you from those who would protect you."

"That isn't true," Tut scoffed, and grabbed the edge of the chariot for more stability.

"I tell you the truth, Pharaoh, but what you choose to believe is up to you." Horemheb shrugged. "But know this: your wife, Vizier Ay, myself, and Commander Paramesse will never bring harm to you."

Horemheb stayed silent after this, to let the young boy mull it over and come to his own conclusions, like a man would.

Silence fell upon Tut as he battled his thoughts, comparing and contrasting what he was told to what he had known to be true. He doubted his wife would never bring harm to him; she did, after all, participate in her mother's attempt to kill him. At least, that was what Pawah had made him to believe.

THE DAY WANED AS THEY CAME TO MEET PART OF THE Egyptian army that held off the Hittites at the northern border. The time to strategize fled as the battle lay in front of them. Horemheb and Paramesse took it upon themselves to divide the divisions and to descend upon the Hittites, while

Tut nodded in agreement with whatever they said. The archers notched their arrows as their chariot drivers went full speed ahead, straight toward the fortress that only barely stood their ground, to meet the Hittites head-on in battle. Horemheb ordered his driver to not lead the charioteers so that he may stay with Pharaoh. Paramesse and his divisions marched in perfect time behind the charioteers, wielding their khopeshes at those the archers missed in their advance.

"I should be leading the army into battle!" Tut yelled to Horemheb over the clash as they fell farther and farther behind the charioteers.

"I must protect you, Pharaoh. I do not know if I can do such a thing if we are at the frontlines. The Hittites are fiercer than the Libyans!" Horemheb yelled back.

"No! I am their Pharaoh. I should be at the frontlines!" Tut yelled again, and then told his chariot driver to speed up.

The chariot driver looked back to General Horemheb, helpless, and then followed Pharaoh's order.

Horemheb let out a grunt and motioned to his chariot driver to keep pace. Alongside Tut, Horemheb yelled back, "Pharaoh! I think it would be wise to pull back." Horemheb observed Tut's stance against his brace in the chariot and thought, *Well, at least he is keeping steady this time.*

"No! You said you are loyal to me! Keep me safe, certainly, but do it while I go where I need to be."

"Pharaoh!"

But it was too late: they had met with the clash near the frontlines.

Horemheb notched his arrow and, with his exhale, let his arrow fly right into a Hittite who was about to stab Tut with his spear. Horemheb blinked a few times, surprised his aim was so good. The bow was not his weapon of choice, but he continued with it, glad the charioteers had done most of the killing with their superior skill.

The battle sweltered under the sun's intense heat; the wet air coming from the sea only clogged the desert men's lungs as they labored to breathe in the humidity, but the Hittites, accustomed to the climate, fought on with force.

Tut and his driver ventured too far away from the front line, and Tut fell from his chariot after it hit a fallen tree trunk. The chariot driver tried to spin around but ended up getting stabbed in the back as he turned the defensive chariot away from the advancing Hittites.

Tut, seeing he had no protection, curled into a ball on the ground. "Aten, pray my death be quick and not hurt much more than Sennedjem's wooden training sticks." He heard a battle cry and squeezed his eyes shut as the shadows fell over him.

But instead of death descending, warm droplets of blood fell on his back and then a head rolled in front of him. Tut screamed at the bloody sight, and tremors overcame his body. He looked up with a trembling lip and saw Horemheb's chariot heading off the remaining Hittites. Horemheb had pulled out his khopesh and severed limb and head from the bodies of the Hittites who had been unwise enough to descend upon Pharaoh.

Horemheb jumped from the chariot and ordered the chariot driver to get back to Pharaoh. He hacked away at Hittites to defend the driver as his back turned to the enemy. Dodging spear jabs, Horemheb killed each advancing Hittite with his khopesh. He blocked a dagger-throw to his face with his wood-and-leather shield. He moved back slowly, knowing it was only a matter of time before the Hittites overtook him; but he had to give Pharaoh enough time to get up and into the chariot, and so he would hold them off as long as he could.

"General!" Tut's young voice called out once he was safely mounted into the carriage.

Horemheb heard Tut's call over the noise of war. As he hacked off a man's limb and blocked a dagger thrust with a parry, he prayed the gods be good to the boy and that Pawah meet his deserved fate, as he knew he would probably not be there to protect him.

"General!" Tut yelled again.

"Come, Pharaoh, we must get you to safety!" the chariot driver said, and began to steer away.

"No! General!" Tut reached his arm out over the chariot's side toward General Horemheb, his newfound mentor. "General!" At the chariot driver's lack of obedience, Tut threw both hands against the carriage rim. "Get him! I am *Pharaoh*!"

"No," the chariot driver said, taking Tut away from the front line.

But Tut grabbed the reins from the driver's hands and yanked them to steer the chariot back toward the fighting. The chariot careened toward Horemheb.

"Pharaoh, you will die!" the chariot driver yelled, trying to make the boy see sense, and grabbed for the reins; however, the other Egyptian charioteers took notice of their Pharaoh charging head-on into battle and began to charge as well, seemingly empowered by his show of power and might and ferocity.

Horemheb glanced back to see Tut's chariot careening toward him, the many Egyptian charioteers following close behind. A kick sent him to the ground as his eyes left his enemy. He rolled out of the way and onto his feet, avoiding a spear thrust.

"Pharaoh saves the General!" Horemheb heard the charioteers yell as they readied their bows and let their arrows fly.

At that moment a spearhead slid by Horemheb's shield and sliced his outer arm. Horemheb looked back to whence the spear came and saw nothing but dead Hittites, feathered with arrows.

The chariot driver pulled up alongside Horemheb, who jumped into the carriage, holding his arm. "Fall back, driver!" Horemheb ordered.

"Yes, General," the chariot driver said, and turned and went to the back of the front line.

THE DAY ENDED, BUT DESPITE THE LONG STRUGGLE UNDER THE brutal sun, Egypt had pushed back the Hittites into their own land and reclaimed their boundary. They rebuilt their boundary wall during the night, while Pharaoh paced in his tent, screaming.

A guard came to check on him, but Tut threw his water vase at him, yelling, *"Get out!"*

The guard ducked, letting the vase hit the tent and roll to the ground, and left soon after.

He hobbled around his spacious room, hitting and throwing things, muttering to himself, "Act as a full man. I could if I *was* a full man!" Then he hit his chest with his fist. "I hate myself!"

He looked up to the tent roof. "Why did you curse me?!" He held his fist to the sky as his heart pumped blood racing through his veins. "Was it not already humorous to you that my father had nothing to do with me? And now you curse me forever with this?!" He hobbled around so the gods could get a good chuckle at his deformities. "You send your good wishes to mock me!" He wanted to yell at the gods that he hated them, but the sheer fear of their wrath made him hold his tongue in that one regard.

A servant entered a moment after Tut fell silent in his rage, and announced General Horemheb had come to see him. Tut yelled at him to get out, and after many attempts, Tut finally accepted the General into his room.

Tut's back faced Horemheb as Tut sat on his cot, looking at his club foot. His heart still pumped hard in his chest, and his breath came out shaky through his nostrils. A scowl sat on his lips.

"Pharaoh." Horemheb bowed as he entered.

"In peace, General," Tut said, and swung his legs up to the cot and around so he faced Horemheb, his eyes narrowed and his teeth clamped together. "You needed to see me?" He crossed his arms, waiting for the General to gloat over him—gloat at how he had to save the young, disabled Pharaoh yet another time.

Horemheb didn't know what bothered the boy so much. The murmurings outside the tent from Pharaoh's screams and yells didn't yield much more clues when the guard came to get him. He studied Tut's defensive arms and could only guess that he was suffering from embarrassment—again. Perhaps he could help alleviate the situation, as clearly there was nothing for Tut to be embarrassed about.

"I wanted to give thanks to Pharaoh for saving my life today in battle." Horemheb nodded his head and let his shoulders roll forward in gratitude.

Tut's jaw dropped. But as he closed his mouth, he sighed and looked at the crown on its stand by his cot. He slumped and pulled the corner of his mouth into a despondent scowl. "I wouldn't have had to if you did not need to save me first." He shook his head. "Maybe *you* should be Pharaoh."

"Nonsense," Horemheb said, and stared the young boy down. Tut only slumped farther and pressed his arms into his chest.

Horemheb approached and knelt before him. "May I?" He hovered a hand over the boy's knee. Horemheb yelled at himself: *Too close! What are you doing? Stand up. Don't touch him.*

Tut's mouth twitched before he nodded, and Horemheb's hand fell on Tut's knee.

"Pharaoh Tutankhaten," Horemheb began, "the gods are proud of you today."

Tut scoffed. "Why? I almost got us both killed."

"That's not what I remember," Horemheb offered, and after he found Tut's eyes, he lifted his hand and sat next to him. "I remember a warrior King, a Pharaoh, Defender of Egypt, rushing to the front line to lead his army against the enemy."

"But I was witless to think I could fight. Look at me!" Tut yelled, and jerked up his club foot. Tears sat behind his eyes, waiting to drop. He rubbed his leg as he gently put his foot back on the ground.

" 'Witless'?" Horemheb shook his head as he watched Tut rub his leg. His heart hung heavy for him. The days of travel and chariot riding were enough to tire a man with *both* his legs. "No. You were brave. You were a leader today. I only did what I gave my oath to do, and that was to protect you—even if it meant my own life. Today I saw a selfless leader, one who rushed back head-on into the dangers of battle, head-on into death, to save his General. The men respect you for your actions today. And because we both lived, the ba-en-pet only solidifies the gods' approval of you and your reign as Egypt's Pharaoh."

Tut peered up at him and sniffled back the tears that had fallen. "Do you really see that, or are you just telling me lies so I don't know when the men laugh at the turn of my back?"

Horemheb shook his head emphatically. "My Pharaoh, the men never laugh when your back is turned. If you find one or two who do so, you must tell them they no longer have the honor of serving Egypt."

Tut remained silent for a moment, and then he laughed. "I can do that, can't I?"

Horemheb smiled at Tut's childlike innocence. "Yes. Yes, you can."

Finally relaxing, Tut leaned over and put his head on Horemheb's shoulder. "Thank you, General."

Horemheb clenched his jaw at the affection from Tut. His mind raced to his own son with Nefertiti. No—he couldn't let himself feel anything for Tut, not again, not in case Pawah gets his way again. Horemheb cleared his throat and stood up, drawing in a jittery breath. He turned to look at Pharaoh, whose face almost made him wish he had wrapped his arm around him, but rather than bringing him into his embrace, he bowed to break their eye contact.

"No, Pharaoh, thank *you*." His voice broke as he straightened. He took a deep breath to calm his emotions. "Pharaoh . . . if you need anything in the night, your men and I are at your service."

Tut looked to the floor and nodded. "Thank you, General."

Horemheb waited for Tut's dismissal, and Tut finally looked to him and nodded his dismissal.

As Horemheb left, he looked back before letting the tent's curtain fall. He saw Tut curled up on his cot, hiding his tears, and a deep heaviness set upon Horemheb's heart. His thoughts went back to Nefertiti and the last time she asked to marry him.

Will I ever have love?

Horemheb closed his eyes and realized that his own selfish fears should not outweigh the child's needs. The next time Tut showed any affection toward him, he would return it.

CHAPTER 7
THE TIME OF FRIENDSHIP

DUSK HERALDED THE RENEWED MORALE THAT CAME WITH THE arrival of reinforcements. The men drank in their battle's victory.

Horemheb peered at Tut and nodded his head toward the men. "You should say something. To inspire them. Maybe use the ba-en-pet."

Tut looked out toward the men and gulped. His shoulders rose to his ears as the sheer number of men over the horizon compelled him to silence. "I don't think I c-can," he stuttered.

"You are Pharaoh," Horemheb said, sitting up straight. "There is nothing you cannot do."

"Right," Tut whispered to himself, and nodded his head with force to make himself believe he could do it. He cleared his throat and took a deep breath.

He hobbled toward his men to address them. One by one, they looked up to him, and Tut buckled at the knee, almost falling; but to his surprise, the men did not laugh, nor did they even snicker. Tut stood up straight and pulled his shoulders back at their respectful silence.

"I am Pharaoh," he whispered. "There is nothing I cannot

do." He felt his breath come as quick as his heartbeat as he counted all the eyes on him, but they all patiently waited for him to speak.

Horemheb coached quietly behind him: "I saw ba-en-pet fall from the sky . . ."

Paramesse stood next to Horemheb and nodded his head in agreement with Horemheb's words.

"I—" Tut's voice rang out in a shrill, cracked voice, and with sheer embarrassment he shut his mouth and waited for the laughter to ensue.

Small smiles pressed themselves onto a few of the men's lips, but at the cold stares of Horemheb and Paramesse, who stood behind Egypt's Pharaoh, the smiles died quickly.

"Take a deep breath, and then go on," Horemheb coached again.

Tut filled his lungs with the campfire air and tasted the sea salt in its mixture. *These are my men. They follow me. I am their Pharaoh. Act with courage, have courage. Act as a full man, be a full man.* His thoughts raced as he built up his voice behind his closed lips, until the words burst forth.

"Today, I saw ba-en-pet fall from the sky. A gift from the gods!" Tut yelled, pointing up. He knew that technically it was no longer *today*, but he hoped the men would forgive him and continued on. "They are . . . glad with me—Pharaoh—who sits on the throne. I mean, they are pleased with Pharaoh, who invited them back into the people's homes and who . . ." Tut stopped, his mind completely frozen.

"Brought worship to them again," Horemheb coached a third time.

". . . brought worship to them again!" Tut yelled almost immediately after Horemheb's whisper. "Today's victory means . . . they are again pleased with Egypt."

Encouraged by the nod of heads, he continued on.

"We shall . . . we shall . . ." Tut lost his words a second time.

The eyes that fell upon him ate at his courage to speak and filled his mind with thoughts of mockery and pity regarding his young age and, most of his all, his crippled nature. He looked down to his foot and closed his eyes. "I can't do this," he muttered under his breath.

"Look at the people, Pharaoh," Paramesse suggested in a kind but firm voice.

Tut obeyed.

"Tell them we shall be victorious again against the Hittites, just as we were with the Libyans. Pharaoh is the defender of Egypt," Horemheb whispered, still looking out to the men.

Tut raised a fist in the air, but paused, trying to remember the words Horemheb had just told him to say. "We shall . . . have victory!" He raised his fist higher still. "Victory against our enemies, as we did against the Libyans. *Pharaoh* defends Egypt! *You* defend Egypt! The gods honor us!" He shook his fist in the air with every word.

He didn't know what to say next, but the men erupted in victorious yells and dance, and so Tut kept his mouth shut and lowered his hand to his side. *I must have said what I needed to say,* he thought. Then he turned to look at Horemheb and smiled. *Maybe he truly isn't out to kill me after all. Maybe . . . maybe Pawah misunderstood some things.*

EVEN THOUGH THE BATTLE CLAIMED VICTORY, WAR HAD NOT. Battle raged on until the next harvest season came and Egypt forced the Hittites into a temporary peace treaty. Horemheb suggested to Pharaoh Tutankhaten that he leave a majority of the army in the north as insurance if the Hittites or Libyans chose to cross their border again. Tut made the order and only half the army that came with him from Aketaten were to return home with him.

The night before they were to journey back to Aketaten, Tut slept in his tent, and Paramesse and Horemheb walked around the camp making sure things were in order. When their garrison overseers and troop commanders began executing their orders, Paramesse turned to Horemheb and opening his mouth to say something, but instead pressed his lips together and narrowed his eyes.

Horemheb noticed Paramesse's hesitation out of the corner of his eye. He turned to face the Commander. "Say it, friend."

"I will miss you, comrade. Be safe in your travels to Aketaten." Paramesse straightened his back. It would be the first time they were separated since coming into command roles years ago.

Horemheb placed a heavy hand on his friend's shoulder. "Keep the army in order. I will try to persuade our Pharaoh to name a Master of Pharaoh's Horses soon, and perhaps the newly appointed can take your place here in Canaan."

Paramesse nodded. More questions lingered behind his eyes, and Horemheb saw the inquiry.

"What else, my friend?" Horemheb asked, and dropped his hand to his side.

"You seem to do well with our young Pharaoh. He listens to you."

"Just the other day he thought I was conspiring to murder him," Horemheb whispered with a chuckle, and shook his head.

"What?"

"It isn't his fault." Horemheb looked off in the direction of Aketaten. "There are those who would taint his mind against those loyal to the throne."

"Ah," Paramesse said, knowing exactly the man Horemheb referenced. "I'm not surprised after he murdered Phar—" Paramesse cut his words short, but their meaning hung in the air around them.

Horemheb's gaze fell to the ground. "Yes," he whispered, not wanting Paramesse to remind him. That day already haunted his every waking and sleeping moment; every moment he was alive meant she was not with him.

"I'm sorry, Horemheb," Paramesse whispered. "She died of illness," he said, to recount the lie they were supposed to cling to as truth, "and I know you miss her."

No more than a slight glisten adorned Horemheb's eyes. With a set jaw, he turned to Paramesse. "Almost more than I can bear."

Then he walked away toward his tent.

"General!" Paramesse called after him, and took a step.

But Horemheb waved his hand, signaling he didn't want him to follow.

Paramesse watched as Horemheb entered his tent and then whispered, "Amun, be with him." Then, with a heavy heart, he went into his own tent.

ONCE INSIDE, HOREMHEB LOOKED AROUND HIS SPACE, HIS COT, his makeshift basin, his table, his reed brush and papyrus. He felt lost in that moment, as if his life were as empty as that room. He remembered writing a letter to Nefertiti after their walk in the garden when he first broke his rank to speak to her, to comfort her. She had asked him to write her. He had written several drafts of that letter, each one with less and less emotion until his letter ended up being a few professional lines: *In peace, Pharaoh Coregent. The situation with the Libyans appears less than that with the Nubians. I,*

Commander Horemheb, expect, at most, one season's time to settle this dispute. He knew messengers may read the letter—or, if it fell into enemy hands, he couldn't jeopardize the throne in the view of the people. He scoffed at it now and remembered the first draft of his letter, wherein he told her how much he thought of her and missed her and couldn't wait to lay his eyes upon her perfect face again. He should have sent that; then maybe he could have been with her more years. He could have had more time. But she was Pharaoh Coregent, he the Commander.

He pressed his hands to his temples. "Stop," he whispered to himself. "Nefertiti is gone. None of that matters now." He rubbed his head and pulled his wig off. "The past is the past. Miss her in the present, but don't dwell on things you cannot change anymore."

With his last statement, a surging guilt overtook his chest and he sank to his knees. Nefertiti's face came into full view, her face as she died.

"I should have been there. I should have saved her."

He felt like ripping his skin from his head or pushing his skull until he heard the crack, until finally the headache became too much and his hands dropped to his sides as if bricks were tied to them. His shoulders, which had risen to his neck, fell down his back and his chin rested on his chest.

"I'm so sorry, my love. I failed you."

He opened his eyes and saw the corner of Nefertiti's letter sticking out of his shendyt. He closed his eyes and shook his head. It was not yet a dark enough night for him; he would read it when it seemed as though another day would not come.

He rubbed his arm; the spear had sliced through his skin near the wound he'd received from Pawah's dagger that night Nefertiti died. He rubbed that scar and remembered her last scream to warn him of Pawah's hidden weapon. She had saved his life when he had promised to save hers. His digits trembled as his eyes grew itchy and his ears grew hot.

I should have saved you, my love, he thought as his face jumped from a grimace to a scowl.

With no release, he only flattened his fists onto his thighs and took a deep breath. "Scars," he whispered. "Learn from them, hide them, display them, repeat them." He curled his lip. "I already let her die . . . there will be no repeating." The bitterness in his mouth made his teeth feel like rot.

Egypt, you take much, he thought, *and give so little in return. How is it that loyalty to you remains so strong?*

Horemheb crawled into his cot and covered his head, rubbing Nefertiti's gold-and-blue lapis ring that still adorned his pinky finger.

"Please," he begged of his heart, "let me see her. Let me touch her. Let me hold my son. But please . . . no more of her death."

And his body fell heavy from the day's exhaustion and sleep crept over his eyes.

CHAPTER 8
THE TIME OF AMUN

Tut, Horemheb, and Horemheb's divisions traveled back to Aketaten, visiting various cities on the way to proclaim Pharaoh Tutankhaten's victory against the Libyans and the Hittites and to announce that the gods sent their gift of ba-en-pet to show their approval of Pharaoh. Their stop in Men-nefer made Horemheb nervous, for Men-nefer was one of the three key cities where the People's Restoration of Egypt lived. He surveyed the populous of Men-nefer, watching to see who did not shout in favor of Pharaoh's victory. He estimated that about half were loyal to the throne, the other half possibly with the People's Restoration of Egypt, and thus Pawah's supporters.

"We will change that," Horemheb muttered to himself.

His estate was not far from where they were in Men-nefer, and images of his wife, Amenia, came into view; but even though he missed her company, he realized he did not love her. He debated leaving Pharaoh so that he may at least show his face to her while he was here, but decided to not leave the young boy vulnerable.

"A good husband would send a letter," he reasoned with

himself, and so that night he sent word to his wife that he was in Men-nefer but they were to leave in the morning and would not return for some time, and he was sorry to have missed her. He sealed it and called for a messenger.

"It'll do," he whispered.

———

THE NEXT MORNING, AS TUTANKHATEN BOARDED HIS ROYAL barge, Horemheb motioned for him to turn around. When he did so and looked out, his eyes faltered in the rising sun's shadow. He saw his army kneeling, bowing their heads, with their fists over their hearts to him. His jaw fell ajar as he glanced over to Horemheb, who dipped his chin to his chest.

"They respect you, Pharaoh," Horemheb whispered. "You are their fearless leader, divinely appointed by Amun-Re to rule this great land."

Tut turned back to them. "What do I do?"

"Hold your hand out above your head, and say to them, 'Defenders of Egypt, arise and go in peace.' "

Tut did as Horemheb advised and the army stayed on their knees until Tut's barge left the dock.

"Keep your hand high as you pass by them," Horemheb whispered, as the barge passed along the multitude of men on the shore. "You give Pharaoh's blessing to them for their honor. You follow in the footsteps of your grandfather."

Tut smiled. Pride swelled within his chest, and even though his arm ached, he kept his hand raised until the last of the men could be seen on the shore.

———

A FEW DAYS LATER, AY STOOD NEXT TO PAWAH ON THE DOCK of Aketaten's palace as they awaited the royal barge to come into the bay.

Pawah smiled and turned his head to look at the old man, observing the small sags of his face and the creases in his forehead. "I can't say I'm glad to see you are still alive, Ay."

Ay only smirked at the insult, turning to meet the man's gaze. "The gods grant me a long life to give me time to see my daughter avenged."

Pawah lifted his chin and peered down at Ay over his nose. "Ah . . . so we are playing a new game, then, are we?" He laughed. "Age versus time. I hate to tell you, old man—time always wins. Your years are numbered. How many do you think you have left? One?"

"You underestimate me." Even at sixty-three years of age, Ay still had his strength and his health. "I have at least another ten years left in me. Battle has made me lean, strong, and life as an official has let me eat well." He eyed Pawah's frame. "Life as a priest gave you a soft body."

Pawah sneered, but then laughed and shook his head. *Dimwitted old man.*

The royal barge docked, and Ay and Pawah bowed as Tut exited. Pawah knew that if Ay's days were not numbered, the boy's certainly were. His supporters, at the first moment Ay and Horemheb left him, would push the boy from his balcony. Pawah planned to have the crown by the next day. The weight of the crown upon his head neared him. He could almost reach out and touch it. The thought alone caused his heart to beat with anticipatory victory.

"I see you fared well in your first battle, Pharaoh." Though Pawah smiled, it was strained; the throne would have been far too easy to take had he died in the north.

"Yes. It seems Amun has divinely appointed me to lead his Egypt." Tut placed his cane on the dock, attempting to stand again on the solid ground. The barge, although smooth, still rocked a bit as it came up the Nile. "We saw ba-en-pet fall across the camp."

Pawah's jaw let loose, but he shut it immediately.

Ay interjected, saying, "Yes, Pharaoh, we received it at Waset from the troop sent to deliver it. I ordered only the finest smelters to work the ba-en-pet into a dagger for Pharaoh." He looked at Pawah, smirking, as if to say, *Compete now for the throne.*

"Good, good." Tut nodded and tapped his cane on the ground to make sure it wasn't going to move.

Horemheb exited the barge and saw Pawah standing there. His nostrils flared as he stood behind Pharaoh Tutankhaten. Ay found his gaze and Horemheb nodded his head, answering Ay's unspoken question about the boy: *Did you turn Pharaoh against Pawah?*

Ay and Pawah bowed to Tut again as Pawah offered him the lead in walking to the palace. Tut accepted, careful not to trip and fall in front of his viziers. Horemheb fell in line behind Pawah, who followed Pharaoh, Ay beside him. Horemheb licked his lips as he envisioned hacking off Pawah's head with his khopesh. It dangled on his belt—he could easily end him within a few moments.

With a subtle gesture, Ay knocked Horemheb's bicep with the back of his hand and pointed to something off in the Nile, appearing to feign interest in something on the horizon but at the same time finding Horemheb's eyes and shaking his head. He mouthed the words, *Not now.*

Horemheb's jaw clamped shut as he peered at Pawah, again wishing he could inflict the same pain upon him that he felt in his heart for taking away his love and his son. Curling his lip under, he looked back to Ay and narrowed his eyes. Ay was right. There would be a time and a place, and it was not this day. Ay had not been there to keep Pharaoh's

LAUREN LEE MEREWETHER

influence. Pawah had been in charge in Aketaten, and supporters could be lurking behind every corner. The only reason Ankhesenpaaten was still alive—if she was—was because Pawah willed it. Horemheb decided, despite his tiredness, that he would force himself to stay awake so that he may guard Tut's door tonight; who knew what lies Pawah spread during the greater part of the year they had been gone?

Aketaten, Horemheb cautioned himself, *is now the home of the enemy.*

He swore to Nefertiti's ka that he would not fall asleep at Tut's door as he had done with her.

TUT SAT ON HIS AKETATEN THRONE THE NEXT MORNING. HE rubbed his hand over the precious gold in the throne's arm as Ay and Pawah gave their reports. Horemheb stood off in the shadows where General Paaten used to stand. His head bobbed every now and then, tired as he was after staying awake all night. He had sharpened his dagger throughout the night while he eyed the new royal guard, Amenket, positioned outside of Tut's bedchambers until morning.

Ay's old but strong voice forced Horemheb back into the present. "One important aspect I have learned, my Pharaoh, is the people associate this place, the city of Aketaten, with the tyranny of your father and his half-brother. We must move back to Waset to show the peo—"

"Nonsense," Pawah exclaimed, throwing up his hands in exasperation. "Is this not your home, *my son?*" Pawah hissed. Tut's eyes lit and his face beamed at Pawah. "Is this not where you were born and learned to walk? This is where you lay your head. This is your *home.* Your Vizier of the Lower speaks lies to you. You have the people's trust now that the gods have sent ba-en-pet! Pharaoh should stay in Aket—"

"Pharaoh," Ay interrupted. "Pawah does not know what the people of Waset think or believe. Aketaten is isolated from the rest of Egypt. The people associate Aketaten with hunger, poverty, and spiritual sickness. You must leave this place if you at all want the full trust of your people again. This place spits in the face of Amun-Re. We must disown it."

Ay's mouth turned into a scowl. Horemheb knew his thoughts, as they mirrored his own: he wished he had known what he did now, so that he could have proposed the same to his Nefertiti.

Pawah came near to Tut and placed his hand on his shoulder. "*My son*"—he jiggled Tut's shoulder—"do the wise thing and stay in this palace your father has built for you until Malkata is ready for your return. All of your things are here."

Tut was about to say yes until he saw Horemheb in the shadowed corner. The sun overhead that flooded over him in the throne room brought back the memory of Horemheb saving him in battle and the words he told him. *Pawah wants the crown.* It was enough to give pause to the young King.

"What do you suggest, General?" His voice came out like a squeak under Pawah's hard stare.

Horemheb stepped forth into the light. "I have come to love the people of this place, but they are no longer here, and to stay for selfish reasons does not lend to a wise Pharaoh. In my humble opinion"—Horemheb dipped his chin—"we move to Waset and show the people your full divine right to rule."

"Then Pharaoh sa—" Tut started, but Pawah bent down and whispered in his ear. Tut's eyes grew wide. His eyes darted back to Horemheb in accusation. "You loved Pharaoh Neferneferuaten, the woman who tried to kill me?"

Horemheb clenched his jaw and stared at the young boy, whose admiration for him dwindled at Pawah's revelation. He took a deep breath and gathered his strength to speak with a calm voice. "I love Egypt and whoever the divine ruler is, as I have told you before."

Pawah bent down again, but before he could speak Ay stepped forward. "Pharaoh, enough of Vizier Pawah's empty distractions. Two of your three council strongly propose we move to Waset for your and your family's safety and to ensure your lineage and legacy."

Tut nodded, his eyes darting between Ay and Horemheb, all the while ever conscious to the weight of Pawah's hand on his shoulder.

"Move to Waset," Ay urged, his hands and chest emphasizing his words. "Change yours and Ankhesenpaaten's names to honor Amun. You will gain much favor with the people who have so long been neglected in lieu of worship to the Aten disc. Amun lives in Ipet-isut of Waset. Go there. Go to where the divine has appointed you. You should leave tonight. Show the people your urgent dedication to the true gods of Egypt."

Pawah squeezed Tut's shoulder, but Horemheb's words gave Tut strength: *Act with courage, and you will have courage.*

"Pharaoh says we shall move to Waset . . . and my name shall no longer be Tutankhaten, but Tutankhamun." He said it, said the words, even though his voice was quiet and broke at least three times during his statement.

"And your wife?" Pawah asked with an uptick to his voice; he wrenched his fingers tighter on the boy's shoulder, as if trying to deflect a defeat.

Tut thought about not changing her name so the people would not find favor with her, but a nod from Horemheb made him question why he thought she was out for his life as well. He peered over at Pawah and then looked to Horemheb.

Pawah had never saved him . . . but Horemheb had multiple times, despite Pawah's accusations. Tut's gaze dropped to the floor. His wife's mother did try to kill him, and if Pawah said she knew about it and even participated in it, then there had to be some truth to it, even if Pawah was wrong about Horemheb. His mind debated over and over again, until Pawah's grip on his shoulder began to hurt, and he rolled out from under the vizier's clawlike grasp. Tut looked to him and fell mute under Pawah's stare, but at the throat-clearing of Ay, he was able to break Pawah's glare over him. Tut took a deep breath and decided to give Ankhesenpaaten a second chance . . . maybe. At least in a sense.

"Furthermore, Ankhesenpaaten will be known as Ankhesenamun."

"You are very wise, Pharaoh," Horemheb said, and the three of them bowed to him, although Pawah lingered to stand for a moment before he forced his head down. "Thus Pharaoh says."

CHAPTER 9
THE TIME OF MALKATA

So it was known. When the boy King neared twelve years old, the royal household began the move to Malkata, the palace of the great Pharaoh Amenhotep III, in Waset. It took almost a year to fully move the royal household after Pharaoh and his chief royal wife moved back the day after his return to Aketaten. The dagger made of ba-en-pet was presented to him, and on the advice of Vizier Ay, he wore it on his belt daily.

Once the royal household had fully moved, a messenger came to the great throne room of Malkata and bowed low, "Pharaoh, I bring news of the death of Simut, the First Prophet of Amun. The people are in need of another First Prophet. Who shall you appoint?"

"Pharaoh shall . . ." Not knowing who to appoint, he finished, "decide tomorrow."

The messenger left and Ay and Pawah stood nearby. Pawah looked to the servants of the palace and shook his head angrily to himself. He had not thought to bribe these servants. He had thought they would be locked away until he sat on the throne, and then they would blindly follow him.

He sighed at his own lack of foresight. His grip on the boy, both literally and figuratively, had loosened since the time the boy spent with the General, and even more so, now that they had moved to Waset and lived in Amenhotep III's palace, Malkata. And so for the past year, he found his opportunities to kill the boy disappearing.

Ay came near to Pharaoh's side while Pawah was lost in his thoughts observing the servants. "Pharaoh, I suggest Wennefer to be the First Prophet of Amun. He is a little progressive, but he is loyal to your throne and is already among the ranks of the priesthood. He will still hold clout with the people because of his mediation for them."

Tut nodded. "Thank you, Vizier. I will name him tomorrow."

"What's that, my son?" Pawah came up behind Ay. "Who will you name as First Prophet?"

"Wen—"

"Have you considered *me*? I have previously served as Fifth Prophet, and seeing as the original prophets higher than me have now passed on, it would only be wise to name *me* as First Prophet." Pawah pressed his fingers together in front of his chest. If he could be First Prophet, he would have even more influence than solely a vizier; with both positions he could garner much support.

"And who would take *your* place?" Ay asked, folding his arms and staring Pawah down.

"Why, I could also serve as vizier, of course," Pawah said, dropping his hands and glaring at Ay.

"Pharaoh, he failed to serve as Vizier of both the Upper and the Lower for Pharaoh Smenkare, showing us that it is too much for one man. Now he wants to be First Prophet as well? He would collapse from the weight of responsibilities due him," Ay reasoned, turning his head toward Tut.

"No, this is not true. I have *lived* for this moment," Pawah said to Tut, and dropped to a knee beside him, placing a hand on Tut's arm. "Do you not want to make me proud, my son?"

"I do," Tut stammered. He melted every time he heard Pawah call him *his* son, but Horemheb's warning still rang through his head. "But I don't want you to collapse from all the responsibilities."

Pawah chuckled. "An old man like Vizier Ay would collapse, but I would not."

"The choice is yours, Pharaoh, but what will happen if Pawah begins to neglect his duties when one role overburdens the other? What would the people say? Would they turn against you?" Ay asked as he stood straight and tall in his dutiful position. "It would be wiser to appoint one man to each role."

"Yes, I agree. Two roles on one man seems harsh. I will keep you as my vizier," Tut said to Pawah, and smiled at him. Then he nodded, agreeing with himself again.

"Fine." Pawah pressed his lips into a forced smile and stood up. He glowered at Ay, and then looked back to Pharaoh Tutankhamun. He dipped his chest in a hurried bow. "If I can be dismissed, I have other matters to attend."

"You are dismissed," Tut said, and as Pawah left, Ay glanced at Wenamen and nodded toward Pawah. Wenamen nodded at the unspoken order and followed Pawah out at a distance.

"Pharaoh, speaking of two roles . . ." Ay said carefully. "General Horemheb needs a Master of Pharaoh's Horses. Would you consider Nakhtmin as your appointed in my former position? He has been one of my commanders for a long time and has proven himself loyal to the throne."

"Yes, I appoint him, and I will appoint Wennefer tomorrow," Tut agreed, and nodded as he rubbed the gold on the chair's arm some more before he saw the next messenger.

"You are a wise Pharaoh," Ay whispered, and stood behind his throne, ready to help him with attending matters.

Tut smiled up at him. Even though he was the father of Pharaoh Neferneferuaten, Ay didn't seem as though he wanted to kill him. *Maybe Pawah is being overprotective. He does think of me as his son,* Tut reasoned with himself.

———

"THAT CURSED BOY!" PAWAH MUTTERED UNDER HIS BREATH AS he dragged his fingers along the stone wall. He noticed a servant, mindfully wiping stone to a clean polish, following at a long distance, so Pawah kept silent until he turned the corner into his wing and repeated, "That cursed boy!" He hit the wall with his fist. "I should have just done away with him the same night as Nefertiti." His hot breath burned his chin as he spoke his hate. "I could have leveraged the rumors. They both caught the same disease. Ah, it would have incited panic about the plague returning." His whispers burned his lips as he shook his head and began to pace his quarters. "At least *all* of Aketaten came to Malkata." He placed his hands behind his back. "I have my loyal subjects still." But then he slammed a fist into the stone wall again. "Although they pale in comparison to the sheer number of servants in this place!"

He stopped upon hearing quiet footsteps in the hall and whipped his head around to find that same servant still cleaning stone. "Servant, what are you doing in this wing? I know the servants who serve my wing, and you are not one of them." He eyed him, knowing he couldn't have cleaned that much stone so quickly to have kept up with him.

"I am taking the place of Merka this evening," the servant causally stated as he bowed to the vizier, holding the rag in his hand. Pawah lunged for it and ripped it from his hand.

Upon examining it and finding nothing out of the ordinary, he threw it at the servant's chest.

"If Merka is sick, then I do not want anyone to take his place. You have your leave, servant." Pawah shooed him away.

The servant bowed again and left the vizier's wing.

Watching him walk away, Pawah shook his head. "It doesn't matter," he whispered, wondering to himself how much that servant overheard. "I've got time to get the boy to name me Hereditary Prince, next in line to the throne. I must keep him from having an heir in the meantime."

Satisfied the servant had left, Pawah sulked to his room. "I must undo the bond Horemheb made with the boy. How to make him see that Horemheb does not care for him as I do?"

Pawah laid down on his bed and rubbed his temples.

"Why couldn't you have just died at birth?" he asked his next victim. "I would be the next in line for the throne after Nefertiti's death. On second thought, I could just kill him too. It would be easy to hold him down and stab him, blame a guard I paid, or pay off his guards like his father. Sneak some poison." He laughed, but then shook his head at the obvious, dismal outcome. "No, no," Pawah growled in his frustration. "We are at Malkata now. Why didn't I think to bribe the Malkata servants? They would never do it now—there is no reason to. They have their gods, they have their economy. They have their work and health now."

Pawah sat up and stared out into his own private courtyard. "It only means I have a lot of persuading to do with that boy. I'll start with the weakest relationship he has: his wife, Ankhesen*amun*." His lips hated her new name. It symbolized his failure—a little one, but still a failure. He thought he had put a deep wedge between the boy and her, but it just meant he would have to work a little harder at that. "Then I'll sever the bond with Ay, and then the strongest bond of all . . . Horemheb."

Pawah sneered and tapped his fingers together as he thought. *That cursed Horemheb. If he had not stayed outside Tut's door on their return to Aketaten, I would be crowned Pharaoh by now! I just needed a few more nights for Amenket to finish his task. Now, Amenket has been demoted to one of the many throne guards.*

He let out a heavy heave of air and then smirked.

"No matter. I will isolate the boy . . . and then I will strike."

CHAPTER 10
THE TIME OF LIES

TWO SEASONS LATER, THE ROYAL GUARDS HORI AND INENI escorted Queen Ankhesenamun to the throne room per Pharaoh's request. At first her spirits lifted, thinking Tut wanted to see her, but then she soon found out that her grandfather Ay had convinced Tut to send for her only as a signal to the people that she was their Queen. As she walked the long, brightly painted corridors to the throne room, she realized her heart longed to see her friend, her husband. What would she say? What would she do? Stay silent? Say she missed him? Her shoulders slumped with the worry that he still thought she manipulated him, taking part in her mother's plot to kill him, despite General Horemheb and Vizier Ay's statements otherwise; he had refused her since they were married and even more since his return from the northern border; he avoided her at all costs since they had moved to Waset.

Feeling the large presence of Hori and Ineni walking slightly behind her, she didn't feel safe. Her bedchambers, as large and spacious and elegant as they were, seemed to be a prison these last two seasons. She only left to eat with Hori and Ineni by her side. Ineni seemed to be distracted, or something else she couldn't quite place her finger on, but Hori seemed to be alert and made sure she was safe, offering unsolicited advice as a whisper in her ear. She had wanted to see Sennedjem to keep up her skills, but he had advised against it. He never gave her a reason, but perhaps he of the two was loyal to her—or maybe he was not and wanted her to fail when he attacked her at Pawah's call. Either way, loneliness became her friend as she practiced Sennedjem's teachings in the candlelight at night when her servants were gone and the door to her bedchambers closed. The longer she went being cast off by Tut, the more fear she held in her heart that Pawah's deal, one way or another, would come to fruition. He would most likely believe Pawah over her and thus seal his fate and her own . . . unless she could make him believe her. Somehow.

Ankhesenamun bowed to her husband upon entering, then made her way to her own throne beside him. Tut ignored her as she stopped beside him.

She took a shallow breath as she thought of what she would say to him after all this time. "Pharaoh, my husband . . . my friend . . . I have missed you so."

Tut stared at the great doors to his throne and bit his lip, not responding to her.

Ankhesenamun waited a moment longer, looking down to Tut, before adding in a whisper, "I could have left with Nefe and General Paaten, but I chose to remain to keep you safe from Pawah." It was now or never.

At this, Tut's gaze snapped to meet her own. "You stayed to take the throne, you conniving—"

"I do not deserve to be spoken to like that," Ankhesenamun said through her teeth. "I have done nothing to you to deserve the way you speak to me." Her jaw clenched; she sensed it was probably not the best time to bring up Pawah again, and regretted her mistake.

Tut narrowed his eyes at her.

Ay cleared his throat. "Pharaoh, your Queen has done nothing wrong."

Ankhesenamun glanced to her grandfather and was glad he was there. At least he held some sway over Tut. Perhaps in time, with the both of them and Horemheb, they could keep Tut from Pawah's grasp, and she could still find favor with him as his wife.

Tut turned to Ay. "I know what Pharaoh Neferneferuaten's servant almost did to me. She almost killed me. I saw the evidence myself. My guard told me what she did that night."

Ay closed his eyes, bringing his fingers to his lips as he appeared to think, and then met Tut's gaze, lowering his hand back to his side. "My Nefertiti was in a bad place . . . she was not herself. If she ordered her servant to kill you, it was out of desperation, and she was wrong to do so. But your Ankhesenamun has done nothing wrong and had no such knowledge. Please know this, my Pharaoh." Ay bowed before standing straight again.

Tut leered at Ankhesenamun for a moment longer. His scowl almost released itself from his expression, but then Pawah entered the throne room.

Ankhesenamun glowered at this man who took everything from her.

"Ah, is it not the Queen of Deception!" Pawah greeted Ankhesenamun.

Her jaw tightened even more as her hatred for him burned in her gaze. Words caught in her throat, but her grandfather came to her rescue.

"Curse you, Pawah!" Ay said, and stepped toward him. "*You* are the *Master* of Deception!"

"Sit down, old man." Pawah chuckled and came to a knee in front of Tut. "My son—Pharaoh—I have not told you of your wife's indiscretions while you were away at battle, have I?"

"No," Tut said, and leered again at Ankhesenamun, whose cheeks and ears boiled red.

"I'll have your head for the lies you spread—" Ankhesenamun went to slap Pawah, but Tut held up his hand to stop her.

Pawah just smiled and said, "She spent every day with Sennedjem, Overseer of the Tutors. I heard they got quite . . . *intimate*. He even disrobed her once."

Tut's nostrils flared.

"That is not true!" Ankhesenamun yelled, and even though her dagger stayed safely wrapped in her belt, her hand struck out in memory of Sennedjem's teaching, leaning her whole body into the thrust, and hit the vizier square in the chest, knocking him to his behind.

Her eyes enraged at his betrayal of their deal. She had stayed silent for the year Tut had been home from war. Yet now he still accused her! Unless . . . her stomach dropped . . . unless he had meant that he would eventually tell this to Tut whether or not she agreed to the rules of the deal.

"You fool," she muttered under her breath, more speaking to herself in believing Pawah's halfwit deal.

Pawah laughed as he stood rubbing the middle of his chest, his eyes obviously hiding the pain of her punch. "She vehemently denies it." He smirked at her as he caught his breath. "And yet she knows the skills of the tutor! You saw with your own eyes, my son! Where would your sweet wife have learned to hit like that? And yet there are servants and guards who would say the opposite of her . . . that she was intimate with Sennedjem!" He shook his head as his hand still rubbed his chest and let out a *tsk-tsk*. "Pharaoh's wife being had by the tutor."

The dagger felt too close not to use, but where would it leave her and Tut if she killed him where he stood? If defending herself physically was not going to get her anywhere, she thought begging might be a better approach, so she fell to her knees at Tut's arm. "Please, Pharaoh, these are lies! No man has been in my bed! Pawah lies."

"Bring Sennedjem to me!" Tut yelled, and stood up, yanking his arm away from Ankhesenamun.

"Pharaoh, Vizier Pawah fills your head with untruths," Ay pleaded, but Ankhesenamun could see the rage already set in Tut's thirteen-year-old mind. It was the same rage he'd always had, ever since he was a boy. There was little hope to get him to calm at this point.

"Bring Sennedjem to me!" Tut yelled again.

"Vizier Pawah, where are your witnesses? Bring them forward!" Ay yelled as if in a desperate attempt to call out Pawah's lies.

Ankhesenamun's eyes grew wide; Pawah would call on his supporters! She quickly turned to Hori. Would he tell the truth?

Ay must have seen her, so instead called solely upon Hori. "Royal guard!" Ay said, pointing to Hori. "You were with the Queen in Aketaten?"

Ankhesenamun hoped to Amun that Hori was loyal to the throne and would answer Pharaoh's questions before Pawah could call upon his known supporters.

"Yes, Vizier Ay." Hori bowed with his shoulders.

"And what did you see?" Ay asked, leaning forward as if desperate to hear the truth.

Ankhesenamun had told her grandfather everything that happened in Aketaten and knew he hated himself for having to leave her with that monster Pawah. She held a trembling lip as her breaths came out shaky through her nose. She had done nothing wrong, but her honor teetered on the next words spoken by the guard she didn't know if she could wholly trust. The true test of loyalty awaited him.

Hori looked to Pawah, then to Ay, then to Pharaoh, and lastly his Queen.

Pawah licked his lips where a small smile rested.

Ankhesenamun watched Pawah out of the corner of her eye as her gaze locked with Hori's.

"Well?" Tut asked, as if not sensing the unspoken battle in the air.

"It does not matter what I saw," Hori finally said, and Pawah's smile vanished. "The Queen says she did nothing wrong. I saw nothing to refute her statement."

Ankhesenamun felt herself breathe again.

"You liar!" Pawah pointed a finger at him. "Did she bed you, too, to keep your silence?"

Hori's hand wrung on his spear, his knuckles going white as he glowered at Pawah. "I did no such thing."

Pawah sneered. "Perhaps you lie to keep your head—"

"Enough!" Ay said, and stepped nose-to-nose with Pawah. "Leave this throne room, and take your lies with you."

"Oh, they aren't lies, my Pharaoh," Pawah said, looking around Ay to Tut. "Ask *this* royal guard what he saw." Pawah gestured to Ankhesenamun's second guard, Ineni.

"What did you see?" Tut asked Ineni before Ankhesenamun or Ay could refute.

"Does it matter?" Ay asked, turning to face Tut. "We have already heard from one!"

"I want to know!" Tut yelled, and then glared at Ineni. "What did you see?!"

"Pawah does not lie." Hori's gaze fell to Ineni, who continued to speak. "We escorted the Queen to the training yard every day, and one day, Sennedjem took off her belt."

Ineni's matter-of-fact tone enraged the red of Tut's ears. Ineni looked to Pawah. "Royal guard Hori and I were not there, as the training-yard guards took over once we escorted her to and from her bedchambers. She was there almost all day, every day. If Vizier Pawah has witnesses who say she and the tutor Sennedjem were intimate, I cannot refute them."

Tut's eyes snapped to Ankhesenamun.

She took a steadying breath and said, "Pharaoh, I took off my belt."

Hori nodded as if in agreement, and then glared at Ineni. Perhaps he was loyal to her.

"Why?" Tut's eyes cut into her own.

Ankhesenamun's eyes darted to Pawah and then back to Tut. "So I could hide something." She didn't want to tell Pawah she hid a dagger, but it looked like her hand was being forced.

"Hi—" Tut began, but Pawah interrupted.

"What is in your belt?" Pawah's voice boomed over the throne room. "A gift from a lover?"

"No, a gift from a loyal subject of the throne," Ankhesenamun spat back.

"A gift that needed to be hidden?"

Ankhesenamun felt her chest rising and falling with a seething air that burned her lungs.

Now is the time. There is no more hiding.

The dagger was her last defense against the man, and now he was forcing her to reveal it.

The room waited for the Queen's response.

"It was a weapon to protect—"

"A weapon to kill your husband when the two of you are all alone?" Pawah's eyes lit. His hand dropped from his chest. "Finish what your mother started?!"

"No, you monster. I would never hurt Tut."

Ankhesenamun squared her shoulders to the vizier.

"Pharaoh," Tut snarled at his wife, and slapped her arm. "You will call me *Pharaoh*."

Ankhesenamun took a step back, a hitch in her breath. Her hand went to the spot where Tut had hit her. Tears glistened behind her eyes as she surveyed the room's inhabitants, and then she saw Pawah's mouth grow into a broad, close-lipped smile as he watched Tut. He'd won this battle: planted the seed of doubt, rooted it deep in Tut's mind. Then her eyes turned and fell once again on Tut.

"Why can't you see the truth, Pharaoh?" she asked him in a whisper.

Tut yelled and threw his cane at her.

"Get out!"

The air rushed through his throat, causing his voice to break. She saw the pink hue that came over Tut's cheeks before he threw his hands up in the air.

"Leave!"

He looked to the guards and then to Ay and Pawah.

"Everyone! Now!"

His screams were accompanied by his waving arms. He balled his hands into fists.

"Get out of my throne room!"

He sat down and slammed his fists into the golden arms of the throne and yelled at the top of his lungs, *"GET OUT!"*

The servants scurried, and Ay pushed a smiling Pawah out of the room. Hori and Ineni escorted Ankhesenamun away. The throne doors closed, and soon items could be heard smashing against the wall.

Ankhesenamun saw Ay nod to the steward, Wenamen, mouthing *General*. Wenamen nodded in understanding and went to find General Horemheb. She prayed maybe Horemheb might talk some more sense into Tut. Maybe Horemheb would be the one to finally sway him against

Pawah's lies. Her eyes locked on Pawah, his lips upturned in a victorious smug, as Hori and Ineni ushered her back toward her bedchambers—her prison of sorts.

WENAMEN LET HOREMHEB IN THROUGH A BACK ENTRANCE, SO Pawah and the others could not see him enter. Horemheb picked up Tut's cane from where it had fallen after he threw it at his wife and lightly stepped to the front of the throne, where Tut had fallen to his side.

Sensing someone there, Tut spat, "I said to *leave*." He buried his head in his arms and stayed on the floor.

Horemheb sat on the step below him and held out Tut's cane for him. "I will leave if you want me to leave." Horemheb's deep voice calmed the young man's sobs.

"Why did you come?" Tut asked, still not looking at him.

"I heard your cries," Horemheb said, placing the cane down on the step.

Tut only dug his head deeper into his arm. The flush of his cheek told Horemheb he was embarrassed that others could hear him yelling.

"Pharaoh . . ." Horemheb started, but then scratched his chin, not knowing what to say.

At thirteen years old, the boy was almost a man; but he'd had a lot taken from him, and manhood was thrust upon him at an early age. If he had merely been born of a noble household, marriage would still be two or three years off for him, and certainly no eleven-year-old would see battle. Horemheb placed a finger on his lip as he continued taking in all that this young boy had been through: he had lost both parents, his friends . . . Pawah turned his trust against his entire household . . . his foot, his leg, his back, his step-mother . . . Horemheb paused, and a heaviness set in his heart. He pushed Nefertiti to the furthest reaches of his mind for now. She was gone, and the dead could wait.

"You are ashamed of me," Tut mumbled at Horemheb's long silence.

"No, anything but ashamed," Horemheb said, and almost put his hand on Tut's slightly misshapen spine, but decided against it. "Will you tell me why you have locked yourself inside the throne room?"

Tut pushed off his arm and sat curled, wrapping his arms around his legs, facing the wall. "I don't know who to believe. Ankhesenpaaten doesn't love me. Why would she? She could have any man, and yet she said yes to me? Why? Unless Pawah is right and she and her mother were trying to kill me for the crown. Now Pawah tells me she was with other men while I was in battle. Not just any other men, but Sennedjem! My tutor! My teacher, my trainer . . . I thought he was my friend. Then Vizier Ay tells me Ankhesenpaaten is innocent."

Horemheb didn't try to correct Pharaoh at the use of Ankhesenamun's old name, but sat and listened. "It sounds like you must be wise and find out who tells you the truth."

Tut shrugged his shoulders and shook his head, debating all the facts he thought he had known to be true. He finally turned to Horemheb and whispered, "Why did you save me? It would have been easier to just let me die."

Horemheb let out a breath and leaned his weight on his elbows. "I saved you because you are Pharaoh and my loyalty lies with you."

Horemheb just barely caught the light dwindling in Tut's eyes as the boy sighed and said, "Oh," and his shoulders dropped.

Horemheb rubbed his finger with his thumb and bit his tongue, knowing now that Tut had only wanted him to say he saved the boy because he liked him or saw him as a friend or maybe even loved him.

"I would never lie to you, Pharaoh," Horemheb said after a few moments.

"I know," Tut said, and he dropped his head into the space between his knees. Then his head popped up as a memory came to him. "Did you really mean it when you said Pawah only wants my crown?"

Horemheb licked his lips before responding. "Yes, Pharaoh, I did."

Tut clamped his overbite twice. "But what he said made so much sense to me. Am I an ignorant fool for believing him?"

Horemheb snorted and shook his head. "No, you are not. Many people have been fooled by him. Wise men before you have swallowed his lies without their tongues ever detecting a foul taste."

Tut stared at Horemheb for a long time. "How do I know you aren't fooling me now? And you just saved me so you could deny fooling me?"

Horemheb kept Tut's stare. "You don't know." His head shook and his shoulders shrugged. "That's the curse of ruling. Who to trust? Who to love? What to do? You have all the luxuries of royalty, but all the restrictions of freedom."

"I don't want to be Pharaoh." Tut shook his head and wrapped his arms tighter around his legs. "Not if I have to doubt everyone who is supposed to be helping me."

"There was a time when Pharaoh did not have to doubt because there was a fear of going against him. But now . . . now that fear is not what it used to be." Horemheb stared off at the wall. "I'm sorry you have to go through this now. But I would give my life on the assumption that you can trust me, your Vizier Ay, your Commander Paramesse, and your wife Ankhesenamun."

"What if she did . . . ?" Tut took in a deep breath. "What if she and Sennedjem did become intimate?"

"Can you blame her?" The words just came out; he tried to suck them in, but it was no use.

Tut's brow furrowed. "Yes."

Horemheb pursed his lips. "Pharaoh . . . she is five years older than you and she is childless—and not at her own doing. She thinks you want nothing to do with her. She thinks you hate her."

This caused Horemheb to think of his own wife, Amenia. He had always assumed she'd had another lover, just as he had his Nefertiti, since he was away much of the time. There would never be a child with the barren Amenia—no proof. He had long since forgiven her if she ever stepped out of their marriage; but maybe she had not. The feeling ate at his stomach, but he never loved her as he had loved Nefertiti.

"She is still my wife," Tut said, and dug his chin into his knee and then turned his cheek to face Horemheb.

At Horemheb's head-shake, Tut's brow softened.

"Was there a time, Pharaoh, that you ever felt love toward your Queen Ankhesenamun?"

"She was my best friend," Tut replied. "Before Pawah told me *why* she was my friend."

Horemheb let out a sigh. "She is still your best friend. Pawah lies."

"How can I trust you?"

Horemheb only smiled, not wanting to get back into their cyclical conversation again. "You must be wise. As far as your wife goes? Start over your friendship with her. Don't let Pawah influence it."

Tut thought it over and hung his head. "I don't know who to believe."

Horemheb didn't know how to answer, and rubbed the scar on his arm where the Hittite's spear sliced it.

Tut took notice and pointed to his scar. "Why do you help me, General? Truly, why did you save me?"

Tut's eyes pleaded for the answer Horemheb knew Tut's heart longed to hear. But instead, Horemheb studied the scar and took note of the one below it. He remembered his words to Nefertiti: *You can hide scars, display them, learn from them, or repeat them.* Was he to repeat his mistake of loving someone? Tut saved him because, he believed, the boy cared for him. But he could not bring himself to feel the same for the boy. There was too much heartache in it. It would be denying his own son and replacing him with Tut. He had promised himself his own selfish fears would not trump Tut's needs, but as Tut's question lingered between them, Horemheb knew Tut only wanted to belong and to love—just like Nefertiti, and look where it got her.

Perhaps it is better for royalty to stay alone. They make unwise decisions when love blinds them.

In that justification, he readied his response: "You are my Pharaoh."

The words were true and Horemheb steadied his brow to not give away the whole truth, as Tut longed for something more. Before Tut could respond, Horemheb handed him his cane and helped him to stand.

"You are a wise King—you will know what to do. You will know who to believe when the time comes."

"You have more faith in me than I do," Tut said, and took his seat again.

"That just shows you how much more faith you need in yourself."

A KNOCK CAME AT ANKHESENAMUN'S DOOR A FEW DAYS LATER. Hentmehyt answered it and bowed low in Pharaoh's presence. He hobbled in on his cane. "Leave us," he ordered, and the servants hung their heads as they exited Ankhesenamun's bedchambers.

She stood and bowed at the waist to her husband and then stood straight, waiting for the berating to begin. For a long time, they stood staring at each other in silence.

Tut ran his eyes over her face and body, trying to note any last remaining twitches of guilt before he spoke. "Ankhesenamun, I do not have evidence of your betrayal—"

"I did not betr—"

"Let me finish." Tut drew his eyebrows together and took a deep breath. He wished Horemheb were here; the man truly had a way with words. "That's not what I meant."

He hobbled over to her bed and sat on the edge. Ankhesenamun remained standing but turned to face him.

"I meant . . . whether you did or not, I do not know. You say you did not. This time, I will believe you. I know what your mother did, but I only have Pawah to believe for your hand in it and your motives in marrying me—"

"What motives?" Ankhesenamun asked, and put her hands on her hips.

Tut dropped his jaw and shook his head. "Let . . . me . . . *finish.*"

Not another word came from his wife, but her hands stayed on her hips.

Tut chewed on his unspoken words while deciding how best to talk to her. It seemed more difficult now than when they were children. Her face was more slender, and her hips had curved since their marriage. He looked to his own boyish body, and doubt entered his mind again.

"Why, Ankhesenamun? Why did you agree to marry me? I know your mother ordered our marriage, but why did you agree to it before, when I asked you? Would you have agreed to it now?" Tut asked her, and he lost control of his cane as it fell to the floor. "I cannot even walk. I still have a nurse. I am—"

"Pharaoh." Ankhesenamun held up her hand to stop him and let out an unwavering breath before sitting next to him. He debated asking her to call him Tut, but as he was thinking, she responded, "I agreed to marry you because you were my best friend."

"You say that. Why was *I* your best friend?"

"We did everything together. We were always together. You, me, and Nefe." Ankhesenamun's smile tired as she thought about her sister. "What did Pawah say happened to Nefe and General Paaten?"

"They . . ." Tut started. He hadn't thought to ask. "They died, didn't they? We entombed both of them."

"No. I told you they left Egypt per my mother's wishes. Their tombs are empty."

Tut squinted, not believing her, and slowly shook his head.

"Then don't believe me. Believe your vizier." Ankhesenamun stood up and faced him. "Put me to death for betraying your bed. Burn my body, so I'll never have eternal peace."

"I cannot do that," Tut said, unable to lift his eyes to her.

"Why not? That's what a Pharaoh would do if his wife had betrayed him."

"Because . . ."

"Because you might believe me?" Ankhesenamun leaned her body toward him as her tone turned sour. "Why don't you figure out what you want to believe and then make a command to align with it—"

Tut looked up, tilting his head, one eyebrow raised. "What if I did punish you for betraying me?"

Ankhesenamun's face fell slack. "Then you would be wrong."

Tut bit his bottom lip, then, pointing to his leg, blurted out, "Wouldn't you rather be with a full man?"

Ankhesenamun stared at him. "Tut, I never saw it before. I mean, I *saw* it, but I didn't care. You were always my friend. You were the one who made it bigger than it was." She sighed, and after a slow blink and shake of her head, she whispered, "I'm sorry. I meant . . . Pharaoh."

Tut slumped. His distress made Ankhesenamun sit next to him again. "At some point you are just going to have to trust someone, whether it is me or Pawah."

"I trusted your mother," Tut finally muttered. "And she tried to have me killed." Before Ankhesenamun could protest, he turned to her. "I know what I saw."

"My mother went through . . ." She chewed her lip. ". . . horrible things with our father. She told me she saw you as her failure."

"*Her* failure?" Tut looked to his wife, not sure what she meant.

"Yes, and I don't know if she ordered it or someone else, but if she did . . ." Ankhesenamun squinted her eyes shut for a moment before continuing. "If she did, it was because she loved someone else and did not want to marry you, and could not marry the man she loved and did not want to marry a Hittite. She was trapped in her position. She lost her way. I don't know all the reasons, if indeed she ordered her servant to do away with you. I can only guess from the struggles she told me."

Tut stayed silent and cracked his knuckles.

"You know, I came to her when you threatened me on our day of marriage. You know what she told me?"

Tut shook his head bitterly. "What was her sage advice?"

" 'All you can do is love Tut, live truthfully, and pray he one day opens his eyes.' "

Tut dropped his head.

"I've never betrayed you." Ankhesenamun put her hand on Tut's shoulder. He thought about jumping or pulling her hand away, but it was warm and soft—unlike Pawah's hard and cold hand clawing at his shoulder. "It's true, though—I went to the training yard to train with Sennedjem every day. I was afraid in Aketaten."

"Why were you afraid?" Tut looked to her, letting her leave her hand on his shoulder.

"My mother was murdered in Aketaten, despite what the rumors were. I know what *I* saw: my mother's body with a stab wound to her chest." Ankhesenamun blinked back the tears. "I was afraid. I needed to know how to defend myself. I learned to fight with training sticks and with a dagger."

Ankhesenamun untied her belt and unwrapped it to show Tut the blade. "Sennedjem knows why I came to him every day. He is nothing more than my tutor, just as he is to you. I did not betray you, Pharaoh."

"But why would someone kill Pharaoh Neferneferuaten?"

"There are those who want the throne. My mother kept us from it to protect us when Pharaoh Smenkare died. Only keep close the company you trust. There are those who would kill to call the crown their own."

"You said before that Pawah killed her."

"I did not lie."

Tut grabbed his cane and stood up, refusing to believe the man who thought of him as his son would lie to him. "I don't know who to trust."

Ankhesenamun stood up and rubbed his arm. "Pharaoh, I know it is hard. My mother trusted the wrong people, and look what happened. She was killed."

Tut's eyes had a wave of panic behind them. "I don't know who to trust!" He rolled his arm to fling her hand away.

"Trust *me*." Her fingers gripped her linen dress over her chest as she pleaded.

It seemed so easy to do. After all, she had just professed her love and loyalty. But could she just be saying that to gain his trust and set him up for failure? Why would she love *him*? He was broken, disfigured—even his own father knew that and discarded him from his life, and the only mother he had ever known tried to kill him. Why was Ankhesenamun any different?

Ankhesenamun put her hand under his chin and lifted his head to meet her eyes, since she stood taller than he. "What fills your mind, Pharaoh?"

"Nothing," he said, and yanked his jaw from her hand. He then realized they were too close and the thought of kissing her gave way to fear, so he stumbled backward.

"What's wrong?" Ankhesenamun asked as she took a step closer to him.

"You . . . I can't trust you. Not right now."

He wanted more than anything to believe her, but to believe her meant to accept that Pawah had lied to him. Pawah was like a father to him. He was like a son—he even called him that, *my son*. He was proud of him and all he had done.

Who tells the truth?!

Tut shook away the question and decided to think about it later. It was too much for one day. He left her standing with her arms fallen to her sides.

When the door closed, Ankhesenamun debated telling him what Pawah did to her at Aketaten. But she thought that if she did, it may put him over the edge or make him think she was lying even more so than he already assumed. Now was not the time to try to turn him against Pawah. It was the time to try and get him to trust her again. At least for her own sake.

And for yours, my Tut, she thought.

THAT NIGHT, TUT DREAMED FIRST OF HIS WIFE'S SLENDER FACE and curved hips and then of a kiss between them. The kiss lingered, and then, as she pulled away, Ankhesenamun began to laugh uncontrollably and pointed at him, unable to speak. Laughter gripped her knees and pulled them to the floor as her arms wrapped around her shaking belly. "You think you can be with me?" She could barely speak through her laughter. "With your face and your leg?" She pointed as the laughter continued. "With your back and your *cane?*" She wiped tears from her eyes. "You?!" Then, all of a sudden, Sennedjem appeared—older, taller, more fit, more a man. He pushed Tut aside and wrapped Ankhesenamun in his arms. "See how it is done, Tut?" he mocked, and then took his place, running his hands over her body. Ankhesenamun's pleasurable groans filled the room, invading his ears, as Sennedjem kissed his wife in front of him.

"You're right," Tut whispered, and opened his eyes, revealing the darkness of his bedchambers. "You're right . . ."

He looked to the candle. The small candle barely held onto its life on the table next to his bed, gave almost no light. Tut drew in a shaky breath.

"She could never love you," he told himself, "and if she did, she would only laugh."

The ache in his legs pulled his mind from his dream. He sat up and rubbed them. "How wonderful." He spoke his thoughts aloud since no one was around to hear him. "My left leg now jumps to my right. Soon, I will not be able to walk at all." He pounded his legs with his fist to force the pain away. "Curse me, and curse my birth."

Hot tears came to his eyes as he thought about his dream. "She is a woman, and I a boy." His heart still beat heavy in his chest. "I will never be a full man."

His glare, he thought, would certainly set fire to his nearby cane, but his tears put out the spark. Tut pressed his lips into a scowl as he wiped his face with his arm and took a deep breath.

"She lies when she tells me she loves me. No woman would *ever* love me the way I am." He nodded to himself. "So what is her motive for her lies? Pawah says she wants to kill me. But now that her mother is gone, why would she want to be another woman Pharaoh? Could she even be? Wouldn't the crown just fall to my uncle Pawah?" He let out a breath and put his hands on his head and squeezed. "I don't know . . . I don't know!"

He lay back down, trying to ignore the pain in his legs; he was too prideful to call in his nurse, Maia, to rub them for him.

Turning on his side, he huffed, "You are a stupid Pharaoh." He buried his head into his arm. "Father," he spoke to his father's ka, and hoped he was there listening to him, "did you not love me because of my leg? Why did you not think me worthy enough to take your place?"

He waited as if his father would answer him. Only the gentle breeze of the evening passed through his window.

"Did you think me frail and weak and ill in the head? Did you want a son who looked like you and could walk without a cane? Well, I'm sorry, Father." Tut's voice cracked as he whispered. He rubbed his throat and wished his voice would make up its mind on whether it wanted to be deep or high. "I'm sorry," he continued, but struggled with his next words. "When I have a son . . . he will be loved. I promise you that. I will show him I love him despite what he looks like or how he talks. I promise you, Father. I am worthy. I am. I *am*."

He repeated those words, trying to force himself to believe them, but the absence of his father continued to drown any self-confidence he awarded himself.

"I am."

His whisper breathed through the tears that fell from his eyes as the dark, cool night finally lulled him back to sleep.

CHAPTER 11
THE TIME OF REBUILDING

OVER THE NEXT YEAR AND TWO SEASONS, TUT GREW A LITTLE less than a cubit in height and two hundred debens heavier. His neck thickened and his shoulders grew broad and strong from having to walk with a cane. His cheekbones rose and his jaw became defined in his previously boyishly round face. Although his left foot did not change much, his feet did grow, as did his hands, and he enjoyed seeing his muscles form some definition.

He looked to his General Horemheb and smiled. *One day, I will look as he,* he thought.

He envied the General's muscular physique, knowing he would probably never attain that level of definition due to his foot, but his boyish looks were gone and he even stood taller than Ankhesenamun now. His voice had decided to stay deep, but not as deep or as powerful as Horemheb's. Tut shrugged his newly broad shoulders as he sat on his throne. It was good enough. He at least resembled a man now, even though his deformed foot and leg still made him cringe.

His belly rumbled; he looked forward to the next of his nightly dinners with Ankhesenamun. He felt as if he had been granted a second chance with her—although he often debated whether or not she had been fully truthful about her stay in Aketaten when he was away. Pawah was adamant she had betrayed him and was only using him. There was no reason for him to lie . . . except Horemheb's words always came back to him: *Pawah wants the crown.* He had been too afraid to ask him about it, and always wondered if his uncle really killed Pharaoh Neferneferuaten. For him to do such a thing seemed too cold and heartless. It mustn't be true . . . which only made him question his wife further. But even though they were not as carefree as they had been when they were children, somehow it felt as if he had regained his friend. He smiled at the thought.

The day ended. Vizier Ay approached Pharaoh as he stood from his throne.

"Pharaoh, may I have words alone with you?"

"Of course, Vizier," Tut said, and sat back down.

General Horemheb nodded to the two and left them be.

"What is it that you wish to speak?" Tut asked.

His chest puffed; he felt good about his work that day and the past year. He had helped the Mitanni by sending them gold and grain for their efforts to defend against the Hittites, and he hoped they were on a course to mend that foreign relation. The Egyptian vassal states felt supported again, and relations were confirmed that very day to be restored.

Ay knelt and bowed his head to Pharaoh. "Your father and grandfather would have been very proud of you."

Tut nodded in agreement. "I have done well, I will say that." He admired the gold in his cane and took a deep breath. Then he looked out over his grandfather's throne room, nodding again, for once in his life thinking, *I can do this.*

"One thing that still needs to be done . . ." Ay's voice teetered.

Tut's gaze fell upon his vizier and his mouth held a pensive smile, waiting.

"Forgive my boldness," Ay said, and looked upon Tut, "but as your vizier I am obliged to state this: your wife remains childless, and you have no heir."

Tut swallowed and then vented a slight cough; he felt the gold on the arm's chair and became intent in his study of its ornate elegance. He knew eventually he would need to face Ankhesenamun in such matters, but he wasn't expecting it today. Tut nodded and let out a breathy whistle. "Yes, I know, Vizier."

"That is all," Ay said. "You have done well, my wise Pharaoh." He stood up, bowed, and then left the throne room at Tut's dismissal.

The royal guards entered to escort Tut to the dining hall, where his wife awaited him.

THEY ATE IN SILENCE THAT NIGHT. TUT WENT OVER THE vizier's statement again in his head. His wife was childless. His mind raced back to his conversation with General Horemheb when Pawah first accused Ankhesenamun of betraying his bed: *Can you blame her? She is childless—and not at her own doing . . .*

Tut took a deep breath as he brought the goat meat to his mouth, but lowered it; he had lost his appetite—not something that usually happened these days.

"Pharaoh, may I ask what is wrong?" Ankhesenamun's soft voice burst through his thoughts.

"Uh, no . . ." Tut dropped his meat as though she'd shot it from his hand.

"Pharaoh—" She leaned forward and put her elbows on the table. "What is it?"

"Oh . . ." He dipped his fingers in the water bowl and shook his hands, then nodded to the servant to take his bowl. "I—"

But his eyes darted around at the servants who tended to them while they ate. His heart pounded as he saw his second course coming. *I don't want any more,* he wanted to say, but his mouth stayed shut. The plate of sweet cream bread landed in front of him. *Well . . . I'll take dessert.*

He began to pull apart the bread, but then lowered it again, his mind drifting to his dreams of Ankhesenamun, pointing and laughing at him. In a trance, he brought the bread to his mouth and ate with one slow chew at a time.

"Pharaoh?" Ankhesenamun giggled. "Did something happen today? You haven't said a word all dinner. I'm starting to think you just don't like my company." She ran the rim of her wine goblet back and forth across her lips as she watched him.

At his silence, she cleared her throat and he jumped. Tut finally met her eyes and said, "What is it?"

She smiled at him. "I've asked you several times if something is wrong. You haven't said one word to me since we sat down to eat."

Tut let out a captive breath and curled his bottom lip under his overbite. *I want to tell you, but you would laugh at me.* He looked at his stomach, imagining not the slender frame of a man that it was but his former round belly of a boy.

"Pharaoh?" Ankhesenamun asked again.

"I'm thinking." His head shot up to her, but his eyes went wide at the curt strain of his voice.

Ankhesenamun tilted her head and dipped her chin. "Well, then I suppose I will eat the remainder of our dinner in silence." She leaned back, crossed one arm, and continued to sip her wine, staring at Tut.

Tension built in Tut's shoulders as he stared back at her.

He swallowed a ball of nerves down his dry, cracked throat. He reached for his wine goblet, knocking the water bowl so water splashed onto the table. He pulled his hands back under the table to hide their slight tremor. He found Ankhesenamun's eyes again.

Tut looked to the servants in the room and ordered them gone. As soon as the door closed, Tut continued to look at Ankhesenamun, who stared back, sipping her wine, waiting for him to finish thinking.

Just ask her if she wants to have a child with you, he told himself, and cleared his throat. *Wine first.*

He tightened the muscles in his arm to control his hand as he picked up his wine goblet to make sure he would not act so clumsily as he had with the water bowl. He let out a breath after setting the goblet back down. "Well," he began, but stopped.

"Well," Ankhesenamun repeated.

"I . . . I think we should have a child." Tut's heart beat within his chest, half hoping she would reject the notion, and he wouldn't have to hear her laugh at him when he tried to kiss her.

Ankhesenamun's eyes widened, and a smile came over her face. "I'm glad you think so," she offered. "But you seem hesitant . . . ?"

His face remained expressionless and his body sat unusually still. Tut hadn't expected a smile—all of Pawah's mutterings for the last seven years came back to him at once. "I don't understand you, Ankhesenamun."

"What do you mean, Pharaoh?"

"Ankhesenamun . . ." Tut shook his head. "Why are you married to me?"

"Pharaoh . . . we've been through this time and time again."

Tut shook his head; it still wasn't enough for him. He

could not understand why she wanted to be with him, despite what a good job he had done on the throne—he still needed a cane to walk and could never attain the physical stature of Horemheb or Sennedjem . . .

Sennedjem. His mind went blank as he remembered his dream.

"But someone like Sennedjem is—"

"I never betrayed you with Sennedjem." Ankhesenamun raised an eyebrow and tapped her finger on the table.

"I just don't understand why you love me. It makes me think you are lying for some reason." Tut dipped his fingers in the water bowl again and shook off his hands then pushed away his bowl. There would be no more eating tonight.

"Still?" Ankhesenamun narrowed her eyes. "All this time, and you still think I am lying to you?" She slammed her goblet down, making the wine swish and spill. "What have I done—what have *I* done to make you still believe this?"

Tut squirmed in his seat. "Ankhesenamun, I hear so many different stories. It's hard to know who is telling me the truth."

"You still hear stories? From who? Pawah?" She propped her head up on her fist. "Do tell. What does he say about me this time?"

Tut shook his head. *You won't understand.*

"Well, when you decide I am telling the truth, I'll be in my bedchambers." She got up to leave, looking at Tut, who remained seated with his fist tapping his chin. "I don't know why it is so hard for you to believe your wife."

Tut glared at her. "Look at me! That should be reason enough." He tore his gaze away, mad at himself for his outburst.

Ankhesenamun looked to the roof and took a deep breath. After a moment's pause, she walked over to him and hesitantly put a hand on her husband's shoulder. Tut felt her smooth skin against his and noticed her soft caress of his rounded shoulder muscles.

At least my cane made my arms stronger, he thought.

She bent down and whispered in his ear: "I have never seen what you see in yourself. This I want you to believe because it is the truth." She gently squeezed his shoulder and kissed his cheek. "I will be in my bedchambers, should you want to stay with me tonight."

Tut heard the door open and close. An excitement quickened his heart at the thought of rubbing his hands on her body . . . but then he pictured her laughing at him. Turning to stare at the closed door, he chewed the inside of his cheek.

I need an heir.

He tapped his cane on the floor, and the *tap-tap-tap* reverberated through the ornate dining hall almost in line with the throb of his heart.

Ankhesenamun is my wife.

"She said she didn't betray me," he whispered. "At some point, I have to make a decision on whom to trust."

His stomach twirled in on itself as he began walking toward the door, not sure whether to fear the coming night or to embrace it. As he neared the barrier between him and his decision, he whispered to himself: "I love my wife. She tells me the truth. She will not laugh at me." He stepped up to the dining room door, first taking a breath meant for a god, and then opened it to go to his wife's bedchambers.

Tut stood in front of Ankhesenamun's bedchambers, took a deep breath, and decided to knock first instead of just open the door. Hentmehyt answered and then bowed low. Tut stepped inside and found Ankhesenamun being undressed by her servants. A slight blush came to his face, but then a blank mind followed a rush of anticipation.

"Leave us tonight," Tut said after a few moments of silence, and Hentmehyt ushered the servants from the room and closed the door behind her.

Ankhesenamun met him in the middle of the chamber, her linen dress half draped on her body. She peered up at him, for he had grown tall. She placed her hands on his chest and leaned into him.

"What made you come to me, Pharaoh?"

His mind raced. *You are my wife. I need an heir, and I don't have another wife.* Tut pushed those answers away; he was only fifteen almost sixteen, but he knew not to say that. He placed his hand over hers. "Call me Tut . . . like you did before."

Ankhesenamun smiled. "What made you come here, Tut?"

Part of him still feared her laugh as he looked to her lips. "You are my wife . . . I needed to decide whether or not I believed you."

"Have you?"

The question lingered. He just knew Sennedjem was waiting outside her door to burst in at the moment he heard her laugh at his attempt to please her. He must have looked to the door, because Ankhesenamun cupped her hand on his cheek and moved his gaze back toward her.

"Have you?" she repeated.

He debated telling her his fears. If he did and she did not laugh, would it be because she was trying to gain his trust for some underlying motive? He would never know, so he lied.

"Yes."

As if someone gripped Tut's beating heart, he froze, waiting for her laugh to burst forth. His eyes darted from hers to her nose, to her lips, to her high cheekbones, to her bare shoulders. The distance between them diminished to nothing as she pressed into his chest. Her eyes stared back into his, soft, dropping to his lips every now and then. He heard her laugh echo in his mind as he stood, still frozen, straight and tall, until Ankhesenamun rolled to her toes so their noses almost touched and their eyes locked. Tut licked his lip, wanting to kiss her, but his thoughts raced.

She will laugh. I am too young. I am only fifteen. She is five years older. What if she did become intimate with Sennedjem? He is better than me. I can't do this. I need to get out of here before I embarrass—

Ankhesenamun placed a light, feathery kiss on his lips, knocking his thoughts into silence. They locked eyes as Tut remembered to breathe. She rolled back to the flats of her feet. Tut's lips followed hers, wanting the same wave of warmth to once again grace his body. He wrapped his arm around her, wishing he could do the same with his other, but still he held onto his cane. Her lotus blossom scent filled his airway as he leaned forward, pressing her into him. Her lips moved with her soul as he opened his mouth to receive more of her. He moved his hand to her face, where the backs of his fingers traced the outline of her cheek and her jaw and down her neck and shoulder.

As their kisses became longer and more intense, he realized she wasn't laughing. Her fingers did not point mockingly at him but instead gripped his body as she tried to press herself closer to him and her breathing matched his own. He smiled as he kissed her and felt her do the same, and so forgot about his cane.

———

THE NEXT MORNING CAME, AND AS ANKHESENAMUN'S CHEEK rested on his chest and her hand in his, he kissed the top of her head. The birds sang their sweet tune as the morning sun began to sprawl into their room. For once, he felt whole and the world was good. There were no doubts, only a peace within himself.

Even his cane that lay next to the bed didn't give him heartache.

CHAPTER 12
THE TIME OF HAPPINESS

MUT ACCOMPANIED HER FATHER, VIZIER AY, TO MALKATA THE day after Pharaoh Tutankhamun and his Queen announced they were expecting a child. Mut found Ay's gaze and saw the sadness in his eyes. Mut dropped her gaze to the floor, knowing the sadness lay in the fact that at only seventeen she had been married and divorced.

It is not my fault Menna decided to find another woman. She gritted her teeth as her hands hung by her side. *Who am I fooling?* She never tried in the marriage, always looked for a way out, and almost every night did not let him touch her. She didn't love him, but going beyond the typical age to marry scared her, so she married him, unfairly, at fourteen.

They had divorced quietly—no legal proceedings, just a simple farewell. Menna paid her for the portion of the household she was entitled to, so that he may stay there with his new wife, a beautiful woman named Ahset, while she left and arrived back on her father's steps the day before last. Ay had said nothing, but her mother had not let her sleep without knowing how disappointed she was in her.

Ay's hand touched her back and she nearly jumped out of

her skin. "I'm sorry, Father. You startled me." Mut's gaze lifted only slightly before dropping again.

Ay touched her chin and guided her face up to look at him. "My daughter, I saw your sister in her unhappiness."

Unhappiness? Mut had to keep her breakfast from rising to the top of her stomach. *How much unhappiness did she have, Father? Beloved by you and Mother? Queen and Pharaoh of all Egypt? Six beautiful daughters . . . I am divorced at seventeen with no children. When she was my age, she had three daughters and was the Queen of Egypt. And yet you still compare me to your lotus blossom, your Nefertiti?*

Mut's blank stare appeared to cause a mist well in his eyes. Her jaw clenched at the contradiction between her thoughts and how she should feel toward her murdered half-sister. It seemed to Mut that, in the years since Nefertiti's murder, her father took a renewed interest in her happiness —as if he were trying to right a wrong with his precious lotus blossom—and in a way it kept her from truly grieving her sister.

Please do not remind me of my unhappiness and compare it to hers, Father. I am not her. I am not her replacement.

"I do not wish unhappiness for you. Please smile."

"It is hard," Mut whispered, and pulled his hand away.

"What would make you happy?" Ay whispered back.

Mut winced and rubbed her arm. A slow shake of her head accompanied her response: "Nothing."

Her marriage failed because she loved another man. What would make her happy? Him. Horemheb. Her mother told her every night that she was childish, that her infatuation would pass. If he wanted her, he would have written. Yet, to Mut, he was the one who had shielded her from the blood and the death in that council room. He had come to her side while her father clutched her sister. There was no one else she would ever share that bond with. Before she agreed to marry Menna, she'd accepted that Horemheb would probably not even remember her. Her mother was right, but even now, she had found no one else who could compare. Was she doomed to love a man who didn't love her, who would *never* love her? What else would make her happy? She truly didn't know.

"Mut," Ay began, ending her self-reflection as he pulled her into an embrace. "I know you did not love Menna. I should have said something to you, but you and he agreed to set up a house together, and who was I to stand in your way?"

"Please, Father, I . . . I don't want to speak of it." Mut pushed him away.

Everyone but Menna knew I didn't I love him.

"Mut." Ay grasped her arm and turned her toward him. "I'm sorry."

Mut's mouth contorted into a frown as tears welled in her eyes, and then she allowed her father to hug her. She made herself not cry, though. She held in those tears. "I should have children by now, like all the other women my age."

"Don't compare, Mut. The one for you might still be waiting." Ay pulled her away and looked into her eyes. "Promise me something."

"What?" Her voice fell low and lifeless.

"Promise me you will not marry until you find love and you find someone who wants to make you happy." Ay wiped his hand on her cheek and settled his grasp on her neck. "Please."

"What if I'm an old woman? What if I never—"

"Mut," Ay whispered. "There is that possibility, but I never want to see you settle for something or someone you can't see yourself with. Marriage is supposed to be for life. If you can't see yourself with anyone, then live alone. Be happy with yourself. Be happy in your trade, your hobbies, your passions . . . help younger women, become a priestess, become a physician. You are learned. You have been a scribe—you can read and write. The whole of Egypt is waiting for your talents." Ay pushed back a stray hair on her wig. "Whatever you do, Mutnedjmet, live and be happy."

A slow smile crept along her face as she looked into her father's beaming eyes. It seemed his words were genuine for once; and for once, he was talking to her and not about Nefertiti. He was proud of her; despite being divorced and childless, her father was proud of her.

"Thank you, Father," she whispered, and she could no longer hold her tears back. She rushed into his arms again and squeezed.

***

Mut entered the royal harem and found Ankhesenamun in the courtyard garden. She waved her father off as he attended to business and bowed to her sister's daughter.

"Mut!" Ankhesenamun threw her hands in the air. Even though Mut was her aunt, she felt like a long-lost younger sister to Ankhesenamun, who wrapped her arms around her and whispered in her ear. "I am so, *so* happy to see you!"

"As I am you, my Queen." Mut smiled, but her eyes did not.

Ankhesenamun searched Mut's face. "What is it?"

"Nothing." But under Ankhesenamun's stare, she gave way. "I will not burden you with my troubles."

Ankhesenamun chuckled and patted her back. "When we were young, we could tell each other anything: Nefe, you, and me." Her mind lingered for a moment, wondering how her sister fared in Canaan with General Paaten, her mother's steward Aitye, and the one who called himself Atinuk, friend of her father's royal wife Kiya. The last she saw of them, they were shadows climbing over the palace wall in the pre-dawn lights, only moments after she'd heard her mother scream and die from their safe place within the palace tunnel. General Paaten had promised her mother to take them to safety, away from Egypt, if anything were to happen to her. He kept his promise, but Ankhesenamun had chosen to stay and protect Tut from her mother's killer: Pawah. Her heart had dropped—sank, rather—into her stomach upon realizing she would never see Nefe again. She wanted to write a letter, but to where would she send it? Would it seem odd that the Queen of Egypt writes to a young woman in Canaan? Would it raise questions as to whose body was laid to rest in Nefe's tomb? Maybe her sister had written letters, but the only palace she knew of was Aketaten, long abandoned. Would General Paaten allow her to write a letter? Or would he consider it a liability to their location? How would they know if she lived or died at Aketaten? He would probably think the letter would prompt Pawah's henchmen to come after them. They were in hiding; they were starting a new life.

The spark in her eye dimmed a bit as she wondered. She was happy Nefe lived away from Pawah and safe with General Paaten, of course, but sad she would probably never see her sister again. She might as well be dead to her.

"I know you miss your sister." Mut stroked Ankhesenamun's arm.

"As I know you miss yours." Ankhesenamun pulled Mut into an embrace.

Mut licked her lip and her gaze fell. "Yes."

Ankhesenamun shook her head and whispered, "Enough of the past. What of the present?"

Mut shuffled her feet and then finally lifted her chin. "I only wanted to come and wish you well while you are with child. May the god Bes and goddess Tawaret take care of you. May Hathor—"

"Mut," Ankhesenamun put her hand on Mut's shoulder. "Thank you for your blessings . . . but there is something you want to tell me. What is it?"

Mut chewed on the inside of her cheek before responding. "Well, it's just that . . . I am past the age of marriage. I wait for someone, but I don't think he remembers me. I . . ." Her voice trailed off and she lost her gaze to the courtyard's flowers. "My marriage ended because I am in love with another man. Or maybe it is as my mother told me —a childish infatuation." Mut turned back to look at her Queen. "I am but a silly girl," she said, repeating her mother's words from the night before.

Ankhesenamun opened her mouth to speak, but she did not know what to say.

"I assume I am jealous of you." Mut chuckled, a hard block in her throat. "You have a husband whom you love and loves you back. And now even with his child." Mut floated her hand above Ankhesenamun's flat stomach but dropped it before she touched her.

"Oh, Mut . . ." Ankhesenamun grabbed her hand and looked Mut in the eye. "My life has not been worthy of envy. You last saw me when we were in Aketaten, when my mother was alive. We had it good then." She chuckled and shook her head at her own past naïveté. "Now you see me after all the hardship. You see my smile, but you don't see the tears that led to it."

Mut stroked Ankhesenamun's arms. "I know, but I feel so . . . lost."

Ankhesenamun whispered, "You will find your way." She could tell her words were not what Mut was looking for. "Mut . . ." Her face pulled back into a grimace, not finding the right words to comfort her.

Mut nodded, but a sorrow sank into her shoulders.

"If you love someone, go to him. Ask him. If you never do, you'll never know."

"If he remembered me, he would have asked me to marry him by now." Mut patted Ankhesenamun's hand. "Or, at the very least, sent a letter to see how I was doing." Mut let go and threw her hands in the air, keeping her elbows close to her side. "No, I already know. My heart won't let me move on with my life."

"What is there to lose, Mut? Just find him and ask him." Ankhesenamun played with Mut's wig. She missed Nefe, but she was glad at least Mut was still here, a memory of her sister. Mut let out a breath and Ankhesenamun lifted her chin. "I think you need closure. Find him. Ask him. And if he says no . . . then you will truly know. But he may choose to court you."

Mut's eyes lit at the possibility.

"I think you are in love with the unknown—not knowing what or if he may love you in return. Maybe you dream of this life you have built up for yourself. But if he says no, then you have nothing left to wonder, nothing left to dream about with him. Then you can look beyond him."

"You are a wise Queen." Mut's lips held a polite smile; then she laughed. "So you agree that I have a childish infatuation."

A smile crept on Ankhesenamun's face as she slowly blinked. "I am not the one who said it." She wasn't going to insult her only friend.

CHAPTER 13
THE TIME OF DOUBT

AY LEFT THE THRONE ROOM SMILING, AND TUT, WITH A BEAM
on his face, sat in his throne. He drew in a deep breath,
knowing he had done well today under Vizier Ay's direction.
He had made wise choices. But ultimately, the reason for the
smile on his face was the simple fact that Ankhesenamun
held his child in her womb. He hoped for a boy, but would
love a daughter just the same. He felt the cool gold under the
palm of his hands and squeezed before he grabbed his cane
and stood up to retire for the evening. His royal guards came
forth to escort him, but just as he reached the throne room
doors, Pawah showed his face.

"In peace, my son, my Pharaoh." The man's words caused
Tut to stand even straighter. "I heard of the great works you
have done today. I am *so* proud."

Tut felt his chest puff and a pleased grin graced his lips.

Pawah put a hand on each of Tut's shoulders and
squeezed, looking him in the eye. "Your father and
grandfather are proud of you."

Tut finally burst at the seams: "Vizier Pawah, I know I did
a good job today. Today I felt like Pharaoh."

"Well, you are Pharaoh," Pawah said, and then, with a downcast gaze accompanied by a sigh: "but . . ."

"But what?" Tut said, his eyebrows falling with his countenance.

"I have heard a rumor," Pawah said, drawing the corners of his mouth into a frown. "One that you may not want to hear."

Tut's face fell slack and the color drained. "What is it?"

Pawah hid a smile as he dropped his chin to his chest. "It is only a rumor . . . but every rumor has a bit of truth, does it not?" His eyes lifted to find Tut's.

Tut swallowed a forming lump in his throat. "I suppose."

"Rumors I have heard in my dealings around Malkata say that the father of Queen Ankhesenamun's child is not Pharaoh," Pawah whispered, "but rather someone else . . . perhaps a certain tutor?"

Tut rolled one shoulder out from Pawah's grasp. "No, that is a lie!" Tut's brow furrowed. "The child in Ankhesenamun's womb is mine."

Pawah only nodded, feigning to listen. "Are you certain?"

"I-I am—" Tut stammered.

I have been with her every night. She has been in my bed.

And then: But during the day, she is not beside me . . . well, most days she is, but today she was not. Where was she? Sennedjem? Why would there be rumors? Why would she do this to me yet again? Do I not make her happy? Of course not! I am such a fool. I could never please her the way a full man could. I was foolish to think she loved me.

As the silence grew, so the seed of doubt again took root in Tut's racing thoughts.

"Well, if you are certain," Pawah cut through Tut's reflection, "then the rumors must not hold any truth."

"Yes . . ."

Tut's thoughts drifted. *Every rumor is seated in a bit of truth.*

What truth did this rumor hold?

Is the child mine? Ankhesenamun promised me she has not been with anyone else.

"As your vizier, I wanted you to be aware of the happenings around the palace. I hate to bring bad news on such a day as this." Pawah placed his hand over his heart and hinged at the waist. "But such is my responsibility to you."

"Yes . . ."

Guards escort her everywhere. Whose child would it be if not Sennedjem's? Where and when was she alone with a single man? Is one of her guards the father? What is the truth?

"Well, it is only a rumor." Pawah stepped back, watching Tut get lost in his own mind. He smiled and then sulked away down the corridor.

"Yes . . ." Tut said again, still lost in his thoughts.

Who can I trust?

TUT CAME TO ANKHESENAMUN'S BEDCHAMBERS AND CALMED his thoughts before entering. He came up to his wife and rubbed his hand on her near-flat belly, but they both knew a child grew there, for the barley and wheat seeds sprouted after she relieved herself over them. Then his smile fell as he looked into Ankhesenamun's eyes. He opened his mouth to speak, but thought otherwise and dipped his chin again.

Ankhesenamun took note of his odd behavior and peered up at him. "What troubles you? Is there ill news that came to Pharaoh today? Have the Hittites attacked again?"

"No," Tut's answer came softly. He lowered his head and lay his lips on hers, all the while afraid another man's lips had been there.

Ankhesenamun chuckled and kissed him fully before pulling away. "Then what bears on your mind, Tut?"

"There are rumors about the palace . . ." Tut chewed his tongue.

They can't be true. She loves me. Or is she playing me a fool? No, she couldn't. She wouldn't! His gaze dropped to his leg, and the amount of weight he placed on his cane became ever present. *Maybe she would.*

"What rumors?" Ankhesenamun found his eyes and wrapped her arms around his waist.

Tut brought his hand to cup her cheek, but stopped short of her face, instead rolling his fingers into his palm and dropping his clenched fist.

"Is the child mine?"

He spoke in a low whisper so that the servants would not hear, but Hentmehyt heard and looked away, closing her eyes.

Ankhesenamun's brow furrowed and she pursed her lips. "Yes, the child is yours." She shook her head and withdrew her hands from his waist to put them on her own. The servants now looked on, very aware of the conversation. "Must you even ask?"

Tut ordered the servants gone at the sudden surge in Ankhesenamun's voice. At the close of the door, he grasped her shoulder and placed his forehead to hers. "Today I received word that the child was not mine. It was suggested Sennedjem is the father. Tell me, is it true?"

Tears welled in her eyes as her voice constricted, seemingly along with her heart. "Tut, why can't you believe me? You have been the only one in my bed."

"Then why are there rumors, Ankhesenamun?" Tut pulled back and dropped his hand to his side. *Someone other than Pawah said this. Many people.* "There is truth in every rumor."

"Who told you this? Was it Pawah?" Ankhesenamun's hands fell into quaking fists. Her body shook as her voice grew thick. "I've told you he killed my mother. He wants the crown. What better way to get the crown than to have Pharaoh disown his own child? There is no heir then."

Tut shook his head. "He isn't that cold-hearted. He wouldn't do something like that. He is my uncle."

Air rushed through her flaring nostrils. "And I would? Am I your cold-hearted wife?!"

Tut clenched his jaw and clamped his teeth, rethinking what he said. His voice lowered along with his chin. "You put words in my mouth." But his mind replied: *If the father is someone else, then yes, you are.*

"No, Tut, *you* put your words there." Ankhesenamun stepped forward so she stood toe to toe with him. "Do you believe the child is Sennedjem's? I have not been to the training yard since you have been home. I have not seen or spoken with Sennedjem since we moved to Malkata."

"Well, what about another man?" Tut asked with a shrug, trying to find a reason for the rumors.

Ankhesenamun let out a frustrated sigh; her eyes gazed upward and the flats of her palms pressed against her temples.

"Is the child mine, Ankhesenamun?"

"Yes," she said, still holding her gaze up. "There is no one else!"

"There is truth in every rumor."

"No, there is not." She dropped her head and hands. Tears welled again in her eyes. "These rumors are lies. Lies are absent of truth!"

Tut stood and chewed his lip as his eyes ran over her face and body.

Tears began to fall down her cheeks. "Why are you still wary of me? What have I done, Tut, to make you question me? Why is it so hard for you to believe me when I tell you that you are the only one?"

"Because—" Tut's face burned as his anger flamed inside,

anger at himself for making his wife cry. "Well, look at me!" He threw the tip of his cane in the air and balanced on his good leg. "Look at me!"

"I'm *looking*!" Ankhesenamun yelled. The vine of desperation wrapped her lungs.

Tut lowered his cane and tried to calm his breath. "I should have known you would never be satisfied with me."

"You're right," Ankhesenamun snapped as she crossed her arms.

Tut looked at her as his back slumped. *I knew it.*

"I'm tired, Tut." She spoke through her tears and then chewed her lip before continuing. "I'm tired of defending my honor with you. You are the father of this child, and whether you choose to believe me or not, it doesn't change that fact."

Tut nodded, trying to keep back his own tears. "I don't know who to believe," he whispered, and turned to exit her bedchambers.

I cannot believe her. Why? Why do I have so much doubt? Because Pawah told me many people are saying she was with other men when I was gone. Her guard even said she was with Sennedjem—I heard it from his own mouth. Does she lie or do they lie? I cannot think about it now.

Ankhesenamun followed in step with him. "Why? Why are you doing this? Why do you push me away?"

Tut stopped, but then continued walking out her door.

ANKHESENAMUN STARED AT THE CLOSED DOOR. SHE THOUGHT she was past this. She thought she had won Pawah's game. Her heart sank. No. The game would never just go away. It was either going to end with her execution or Pawah's exile. It wasn't going to stop anytime soon.

"Curse that Pawah," Ankhesenamun spat as hot wrath swarmed her face.

Her shoulders rose to her ears as she remembered Pawah's hands about her neck in Aketaten. With his words in her memory and Tut's latest Pawah-induced accusation in her mind, her head swirled with rage and she clutched the air, wishing she could use the dagger in her belt on Pawah, the man who threatened her life and now continued to drive her and her husband further apart.

"The child is *Pharaoh's*," she told her servants who came back into her room once Tut left. "I have never been with another man."

Her servants bowed to her, but said not a word. She had spent a majority of her time at the training yard in Aketaten, and no one could be sure if there was a forbidden romance between them. The servant halls seemed quiet, but behind the doors, gossip and rumors spread as Pawah snuck his supporters in to plant tarnish against the Queen.

Hentmehyt stepped forward. "We know your majesty would not stray from Pharaoh's bed. Come, Pharaoh's chief royal wife." Stepping forward, she tucked her fingers behind Ankhesenamun's arm, and led her as if she were an alabaster statue. "You are with Pharaoh's child. You mustn't get angry, or the anger will seep into the child." She waved her hand over Ankhesenamun's belly. "Lay down and rest."

"Why can't he trust me, Hentmehyt?" Ankhesenamun's voice lost its life as her arms lay limp by her sides. "Why can't he see the child is his? I have not been to the training yard since Aketaten. I have not even been alone with a man since we have come to Malkata." She shook her head and shut her eyes. "He will never believe me. I will always be the liar to him. I will always be the one he thinks wants to do away with him. He will always see me as a greedy, conniving woman. I can't do anything to make him change his mind." She looked to Hentmehyt. "What do I do?"

"There, there, my Queen," Hentmehyt said as she guided Ankhesenamun's head to the headrest. "Here is a wine to drink to help take away the grief and anger. You need your sleep for the child." Hentmehyt's eyes glistened as she handed wine to Ankhesenamun after the cupbearer Ipwet had a sip.

Ankhesenamun brought it to her lips, but stopped. "Why the tear, Hentmehyt?"

Hentmehyt quickly brushed it away and took a small breath. "I am sorry, my Queen, for your current struggle. All of us," she said, gesturing to the servants in the room, "feel your sorrow."

Ankhesenamun gave a half smile. "You are too good to me, Hentmehyt."

Hentmehyt forced a smile in return and said nothing as Ankhesenamun drank.

"This is very bitter, Hentmehyt," Ankhesenamun said, pulling her lips back, and then her eyes darted to Ipwet, who had sipped her wine before her. She saw Ipwet taste the wine herself.

Could it be poisoned? Ankhesenamun's shoulders tensed as her eyes grew wide, but Ipwet only stood tall, her emotionless face staring back at her. Ipwet wasn't reacting as if she had been poisoned.

Hentmehyt's hand guided the Queen's chin to face her. "It is good for you and the baby," Hentmehyt said, nodding. "There is boiled poppy in the wine. It will help you sleep and take your pains away."

Ankhesenamun looked to her steward, feeling her shoulders relax a little. "Thank you." She looked into the wine and swirled it. The bitterness of the poppy grew on her tongue and slowly transformed into an unusual sweetness as it mixed with the wine's flavor. It made her want to take another sip. She looked once more to Ipwet to make sure she gave no reaction to a poison that may lay in her cup. Her gaze dropped and she shook her head at herself. She let out a breath and took another sip, and then another. Hentmehyt ordered the remaining servants to leave. By the end of the drink, Ankhesenamun's eyes rolled around in her head and the cup fell from her hand as a deep sleep overtook her.

———————

HENTMEHYT PICKED UP THE GOBLET AND BROUGHT IT CLOSE to her chest, trying to calm her own breathing. Grasping Ankhesenamun's hand, she closed her eyes and then placed it next to Ankhesenamun's body on the bed.

Ipwet stood by the table, watching them, stifling a yawn.

Hentmehyt stood up and tossed the goblet to Ipwet. "Tell him"—her voice sharp—"I will need one every night until it is finished."

Ipwet shrugged. "Yes, head steward." Then she turned and left the royal bedchambers with a slow, steady gait, as if there were no burden in the world to hurry her.

A shaky breath escaped Hentmehyt's lips as she brought her hand to cover her mouth. "Forgive me," she whispered, and then dropped to her knees and put her head on Ankhesenamun's arm, not knowing how much longer she would have to give her the wine. "Forgive me, my Queen."

CHAPTER 14
THE TIME OF HEARTBREAK

THREE MONTHS PASSED, AND ANKHESENAMUN WAS SIX MONTHS with child. Every night since Tut had left her, Hentmehyt gave Ankhesenamun one goblet of wine with boiled poppy, until a deep ache contorted Ankhesenamun's lower abdomen as she slept. The second ache turned to pain and woke her from her slumber. The thick throat of sleep held tight to her vocal cords as another wave of pain overtook her body. Finally it passed, and she propped herself up on her elbow and called out to Hori.

The light from the corridor entered her room as he opened the door.

"Yes, my Queen? Is all well?"

"Get me Hentmehyt!" Ankhesenamun ordered, as another wave fell upon her body and sucked her breath away. She pressed a fist to her lips as her body crumpled in on itself.

Hori ordered Ineni to go retrieve the steward and her servants, then opened the door fully and lit the alabaster torch in the room. Its amber glare fell upon the Queen in her bed, grasping her hard ball of a belly. He swayed from side to side, rapping his fingers on his thigh in indecision. A grimace appeared on his face as he went and brought the water basin near her bed. He dipped the towel to dab her head as they waited for Hentmehyt.

"What is happening?" The shaky words flowed past Ankhesenamun's lips.

"My wife woke from pain in her slumber before she delivered my son . . ." Hori said, and gestured to Ankhesenamun's belly.

But it is so soon.

Sweat beaded her brow as pain descended onto her torso again. When it subsided, her thoughts drifted to her mother—

How did she do this six times?

—but then to her father and then to Tut. Her mother told her that at first her father had been there for each one, even when it was not customary for him to be, and then it had become days and days before he would come to see his child. Ankhesenamun held her breath and her brow furrowed.

Will Tut come see me, or will he assume the child is not his?

"Hori," she whispered, uncaring about titles. "Do you think he will come?"

Hori flinched at her question, but only dabbed her brow again with the damp cloth.

"Please answer me." Ankhesenamun winced as another pain coursed through her body. She waited for it to pass, holding her breath and clamping her teeth. Her head rolled and her shoulders met her ears as she endured the pain.

Hori waited until her fist relaxed and he heard her breathe again. "I do not know, my Queen." He dabbed her forehead a little more.

She realized the gentleness of his touch upon her brow and locked eyes with him. "Are you loyal to me, Hori?" Her chest yanked air into her lungs. She longed to know where he placed his loyalty . . . especially since she had questioned it while they were in Aketaten. She longed to not be alone. Not now. Not again.

Hori's shoulders rolled back and he bowed his chest and head to her. "Forever on my life am I faithful unto death to Pharaoh and his family."

Ankhesenamun knew she might never be alone with Hori again; she needed to ask him the questions that had haunted her while she lived in Aketaten. She had to know, had to ask, before the next pain began its surge.

"Do you know of Pawah?"

The question lingered between them as the pain began its upward climb.

"Yes," Hori whispered, and wrung out the cloth after letting it soak in the water. "He is Pharaoh's vizier."

"No—" Ankhesenamun's color drained from her face. "*About* him?" she forced out.

Hori only looked into her eyes.

She clenched her jaw in agony and shut her eyes, wondering how she would get through the paralyzing pain that gripped her body.

Hentmehyt entered. Hori's eyes darted to the side at the sound of footsteps and quickly bent down and whispered in Ankhesenamun's ear, "You are safe with me."

He came to standing as Hentmehyt approached. He offered her the rag and appeared to searched Hentmehyt's eyes for some reason behind the pains, but Hentmehyt only yanked the cloth fully from his hands and turned her nose up at him.

"Leave, guard. This time is for women only." Hentmehyt averted her stare from the large man to Ankhesenamun, who lay holding her breath and clenching her stomach. She snapped the cloth at his arm, and he turned to go, but his stare lingered at the steward before he finally left.

Hentmehyt knelt next to her Queen and counted between

Ankhesenamun's pains. "We do not have time to go to the pavilion." Hentmehyt left her side and told Ineni to call the midwives and servants to the royal bedchambers, then returned to Ankhesenamun.

"Hentme—" Ankhesenamun started, before a groan stopped her words.

"*Shhh*, my Queen." Hentmehyt stroked her face. "If you stand it will be easier."

Ankhesenamun balled her hands into fists and her shoulders rose as the pain came again. Tears came forth from her eyes. It felt as though someone were ripping open her insides.

"My Queen," Hentmehyt said, soothing Ankhesenamun's shoulders down and flattening Ankhesenamun's hands against her chest. "They are less painful if you stay calm."

"But they are so soon," Ankhesenamun cried, knowing a woman with child is pregnant for at least two seasons. "Why are they so *soon*?"

The pain ripped through her body again and Hentmehyt kept smoothing her shoulders down. Ankhesenamun leaned her head upon Hentmehyt's bosom as the pain subsided.

This is too soon. Our baby will not survive. Will I survive?

She winced.

I'm such a selfish mother. My baby is coming too soon and I'm worried for my life?! Maybe the gods know I will not be a good mother and so take my baby away from me.

She shook her head as tears of pain, tears of sorrow, fell from her eyes.

"It is too soon," she whispered.

How will Tut love me after I lose his firstborn? How will we survive this? My child is coming too soon, and yet I worry about Tut's love for me? How can I be so selfish? Please, Hathor, Bes, Tawaret, Aten, Amun . . . whoever be with my child!

Hentmehyt's eyes hid the truth in the dim light. "There is

still hope, my Queen. You have been with child six months—there is still hope."

"I only pray—"

Ankhesenamun went to tighten her fists as the pain came again, but Hentmehyt flattened them. Ankhesenamun's mind went blank as her breath hitched and her toes curled.

"Breathe in, my Queen. Ten, nine, eight, seven . . ."

Ankhesenamun did as she was told and her mind focused on the next number in the series.

"Now, breathe out, my Queen. Ten, nine, eight, seven . . ."

The wave seemed to pass quicker than it had previously.

The servants entered along with two midwives, carrying a birthing stool. The servants came with towels and heated water, the last servant girl with the small statues of the god Bes and the goddesses Tawaret and Hathor.

"Let us get you to the birthing stool," Hentmehyt said, and helped Ankhesenamun to stand. A warm drizzle of blood trickled down her leg, and Hentmehyt chewed her lip and then called the midwife over.

"We need to get you on the birthing stool," the midwife crooned, and took her Queen's hand to help her stand on each of the stool's foot placements. She placed the bucket of heated water under her so that the vapors might help ease the delivery.

A servant midwife in apprenticeship stood behind Ankhesenamun and held a Bes amulet over the Queen's brow, all the while chanting spells: *"Make strong the deliverer's heart, and keep alive the child coming . . ."*

Noticing the amount of blood, the midwife told the servant girl, "Bring me the delivery aids." The midwife mixed together a mixture of sea salt, emmer wheat, and Nile rushes and spoke to a moaning Ankhesenamun as she mixed: "This will aid you, my Queen, in your birthing of the royal one." She then rubbed the plaster over Ankhesenamun's belly, and it seemed the Queen's contractions became more intense and quicker.

Ankhesenamun let out a groan of agony as servant girls on either side soothed down her shoulders and fanned her. Hentmehyt, standing behind the midwife, counted breaths for her Queen. Glistening tears formed in her eyes as she watched Ankhesenamun, and her hands wrung behind her back.

Hours passed, it seemed, and finally, a limp, silent baby girl emerged from her mother.

Tears filled Ankhesenamun's eyes after the laborious delivery, tears at seeing a tiny version of herself; but then a slow dread overtook her heart, taking the color of her face with it.

"Why . . . ?" she began, trying to catch her breath. "Why is she not crying? Why is she not moving?" Her mouth contorted into a grimace and concern covered her eyes as she stared at her daughter, who was only a little longer than the hand of the midwife.

She is so small. She's not moving. Is she dead? She is. I know it. The gods took her from me. They knew. I knew. She shook her head and tried to roll forward to her daughter, but the servants held her back so she would not fall from the birthing stool. *No, she just needs food. She needs air.*

"Are you going to feed her?" Her eyes searched the midwife, looking for some tell of happiness, some indication her child was alive.

The midwife opened her lips to speak, but no words came out as she performed the duties to help remove the afterbirth from Ankhesenamun's womb. The servants on either side of Ankhesenamun grabbed her when Ankhesenamun's legs gave out. They laid her on her back against the piled cushions behind the birthing stool.

Sweat poured into her lips; she licked it away and tried to find her breath again. "Why . . . why isn't she crying?"

No, please, my daughter. Please cry. Please let me hear you just once. Please, Amun. Please, Aten. Please, Bes, Tawaret, Hathor!

The midwife cut the cord from the baby girl and cleaned her off, handing her to the wet nurse with a slow shake of her head. The wet nurse wrapped her and offered her breast, but the child only lay limp in her arms.

"Why isn't she crying?" Ankhesenamun asked again. She turned to her side and looked up to the wet nurse with her lips pressed together, not knowing whether to scream or to cry.

The wet nurse knelt down to her Queen and offered the small child to Ankhesenamun as the servant girls propped her up with pillows. "My Queen," the wet nurse said as Ankhesenamun took her child in her arms, "your daughter did not survive the delivery."

The pains of her labor paled in comparison with the pain of the new weight that fell into her stomach as she stared into her daughter's perfectly formed red face. Her tiny fingers pressed to her chin from the nurse's tight wrapping. Ankhesenamun's body inhaled but had forgotten how to exhale as the vision of her baby blurred from the tears in her eyes, until finally she let out a guttural yell.

"WHYYY?!"

She pushed her daughter as close as she could to her chest, wrapping her whole body around this tiny child. Indecipherable moans took the place of her words as she clutched her daughter even tighter.

I did this. I am your mother. I caused you to die. My body should have been enough for you. I'm so sorry, my sweet girl. I should have not been so angry at Pawah! My anger killed you. My anger did this. I am responsible. Please, Aten, the sun who hides his face—please, Amun—please, Bes, Hathor, please, no! No. Don't do this to me.

Ankhesenamun rocked back and forth, holding her daughter pressed to her chest, tears flowing down her pained face.

Hentmehyt closed her eyes as she stood listening to Ankhesenamun's cries. The tears she had held back finally came to fruition and ran down her face. She bent over to the midwife and whispered a choked "Make sure our Queen is physically well before you leave for the night."

The midwife nodded and wiped her own tears.

Hentmehyt went to the door and asked for a messenger to tell Pharaoh Tutankhamun that his wife bore him a daughter who did not survive the night. Hori nodded and let his head drop before carrying out the order.

"You knew this was going to happen, didn't you?" Ineni whispered to Hori.

"No." Hori shook his head. "This is a horrible thing. I would never wish it upon any woman . . . or father," he said, thinking of his own children, especially of the two he had lost.

THE NEXT MORNING, THE SUN ROSE UPON TUTANKHAMUN sitting on the edge of his bed. He wrung the cane in his hand. The news of the death had come to him in the middle of the night. He stared at the door of his bedchambers as he muttered to himself, unaware that his words echoed his wife's.

"This is my punishment." A grimace crumpled his pale face. "Gods punish me for being born this way. The gods knew I was never to have children. I am nothing!" Sorrow fell over him as he felt his heartbeat in his own ears. "My father knew it. That's why he had nothing to do with me. That's why Pharaoh Neferneferuaten tried to kill me." Tut nodded angrily. "Nothing good happens, and if the gods grant it, it is taken away." His chin trembled as he lowered his head. "I have failed my child. I have failed Ankhesenamun. If she had married a full man, they would have had a living child."

And then, worst of all: *I should have been there with her.*

A soft rap came at his door.

"Leave me!" Tut yelled, and threw his cane at the door.

The door opened, and Pawah appeared in the shadows. Silently, he closed the door behind him, picked up Tut's cane, and came to Tut's bedside.

"My son, I heard about the child. I am so sorry." His voice held a mystique to it, as if it hovered over Tut's heart, protecting him from the outside world. "If only chief royal wife Ankhesenamun's body could handle such a feat, I'm sure the baby would have survived."

Tut looked to him. "What do you mean? The gods punish me for not being born whole."

"No, my son." Pawah knelt before him, placed Tut's cane on the bed, took Tut's hands in his own, and leaned against Tut's knees. "The woman's job is to carry the child. There must be something wrong with her body, or else the gods punish her for her transgressions against you."

"She promised me she was never with another man," Tut said, shaking his head. "No, this is my doing."

"And yet you have not been in her bedchambers for months? So you do believe something about the rumors is true," Pawah said. "She can say many things to make Pharaoh believe she is the mother of the heir to the throne, to keep her name and her legacy as the mother of the Pharaoh to come."

Tut rolled the thought over in his head, chewing on

Pawah's words. *She promised me. But what if my uncle is right?* His heart beat faster as he pictured her with Sennedjem, the older and more capable man—more *attractive* man.

"No!" he yelled, and tried to push the image from his mind. His eyes narrowed at Pawah. "Leave me!"

"Pharaoh, Pharaoh," Pawah whispered, and stood and put his hands on Tut's shoulders. "Why do you take your anger out on me when *she* was the one who betrayed you? Are you certain the child is yours?" He chuckled. "Is there even need for you to be upset at the child's death?"

Tut slumped and swallowed his confidence as his gaze fell to the floor. "I was so sure." A slow, disbelieving head shake followed his whisper. "I don't know."

"You may never know, my son," Pawah said, and sat next to him, wrapping his arm around his shoulders. "But such is life. I only know what my informants have told me in my position as Vizier and your Regent while you were at battle with the Libyans and Hittites. It is her word against many, but it is up to you to believe. She *does* have a pretty face . . ."

Tut's cheeks swelled and he bit down on his bottom lip.

"She is a smart woman. She *is* Nefertiti's daughter. It is such a shame to waste such beauty on such a temptress as she. Her mother was the same way. No one can blame her." Pawah squeezed the ever silent Tut. "I just don't want to see you hurt, my boy. You were a threat to Nefertiti, and she almost got her wish and had done away with you."

Pawah peered at Tut through the corner of his eyes. Tut sat with a slumped back, two fists in his lap, staring straight ahead. Not noticed by Tut, one corner of Pawah's mouth curled into a smile.

"And yet, you poor orphaned boy—well, young man now —have fallen in love, dare I say, with her daughter . . . and, perhaps, lean unwisely upon her father?"

Tut shook his head and grabbed his cane from the bed. "But Egypt is flourishing again with the help of Vizier Ay."

Pawah blinked hard as his next words came out quickly. "Ay helps you because he is setting you up to fail." Pawah gestured to the roof with his free hand as he came up with his impromptu response. At Tut's silence, he asked, "Why do you think he helps you so?"

"Because I am Pharaoh."

"No," Pawah wagged his head from shoulder to shoulder in a grandiose disagreement. "Ay helps you to ease his own conscience. His daughter tried to kill you. His granddaughter betrays you. Do you think Ay has your best interest in mind? You are nothing to the old man, my son. He is living his last days to set you up to fail."

Tut resisted still. "I have not failed yet under Vizier Ay's guidance. The gods grant him a long life to help me."

"And most his age die very soon." Pawah stopped and examined him.

Tut's neck hurt from his clenched jaw and tight shoulders. His eyes focused on the door in front of him. Tut's knuckles grew white as they gripped his cane across his lap. "Why did you come here, my uncle? Vizier Pawah?" Tut said through his teeth. "To worsen my pain?"

"No, my son!" Pawah threw his hands in the air as his feet shuffled into a solid, wide stance. "No! No! No!" His head shook like a horse with every *no*. His brow furrowed as he placed two hands on Tut's shoulders and commanded Tut's focus from the door. Pawah locked eyes with him. "I came because I care for you. I heard the news of the child, and I wanted to assure you the child was not yours. I came to lessen your heartache, my son. *I* have your best interest within my very soul. I am the only family you have left. The rest are merely relation by a late step-mother who ordered your death . . . and Ankhesenamun—even though you share the same father, she truly is her mother incarnate."

Maybe you have my best interest at heart, but . . . Tut began to wring the cane in his hands. *You are only relation by marriage, too, you know,* he wanted to say—but he dared not insult the man who called him son.

So many questions came to him. Why would Ay help him so much? Had he not already apologized for his daughter? Ay seemed to care about him. And as for Ankhesenamun . . . he wished Pawah would use her title, but he was too afraid to bring it up; she was Egypt's Queen, after all. And, well, Ankhesenamun seemed to care about him too. Unless the rumors were true and Pawah told the truth. But Pawah wasn't as truthful when it came to Horemheb. Horemheb seemed to care about him, or at least enough to protect him. But he remembered that odd look he gave Paramesse in Libya after he had fallen amongst the sea of dead men. It always made him wonder in the back of his mind. Why would Horemheb wait all these years, though, and why did he sacrifice himself to save him from the Hittites? It wasn't like Horemheb knew he would save him in return.

Pawah's eyes bore into his own.

What would Horemheb say? What would he do? What would Ay do? What would his grandfather and father do? What would *Pharaoh* do?

They would fight. They would ask the questions that came to them. They would demand an answer. So, instead of staying silent, he decided to defend his honor.

"What if the child was mine? There is a chance, you know." Tut dipped his chin and felt foolish for even saying that last part, but he charged onward. "I am capable of fathering children."

"I do not doubt it," Pawah snapped back almost too quickly, "but there is also question, given eyewitness accounts, that another could be the father," Pawah whispered, and patted Tut's shoulder.

Tut shrugged him off. "Tell me who saw her with another man. *Who* saw her in his bed?" Tut asked, his eyebrows drawing more together with every word.

"I have a list of names. I can give the list to you if you would like." Pawah's voice was smooth but did hold a hint of pity.

Tut drew in a deep breath and a grimace grew on his face. If he found Ankhesenamun to be a liar, he would have to either execute her or exile her; but he wasn't quite ready to do this—even though he had not been by her side the past few months, he did care for her. But what if he found out she truly mocked and laughed at him behind closed doors? It would be the realization of all his fears.

"I will send by way of messenger in the evening time," Pawah suggested, and then patted his shoulder again. "My son, don't you worry. *I* am here for you. You can always trust me to tell you the hard things when no one else will. *I* will always tell you the truth."

Tut squinted at that word: truth. "The truth," he whispered.

Such a hard thing to know. Everyone's a liar, he thought. *My father, my mother, Ankhesenamun, Ay, maybe Pawah, and even . . . and even Horemheb. They are all liars. No one tells me the truth. I can't trust anyone. Can I?* Tut shook his head. *I don't know who to trust.*

"Yes, the truth," Pawah whispered back. Then he stood up. "Now don't you be too upset at the death of another man's child." His bottom lip formed into a pout. "Vizier Ay and I will be waiting for you in the throne room when you are ready to attend to the day's matters." He bent down and placed his forehead to Tut's and gave another squeeze of his shoulder. "The gods grant you wisdom, my son. You will see that *I* speak the truth."

Tut watched Pawah leave and realized his hands ached from gripping his cane. "I don't believe you, uncle. The gods abandon me. They blind me. I trust no one. Was the child mine? I don't know, not anymore." But Pawah was gone. He spoke to no one but himself. He laid back down in his bed and never felt more alone. "I still mourn the child nonetheless."

An hour later, Tut slowly opened his door, having refused his servants to dress him that morning. He took a slight step backward upon seeing General Horemheb at his door alongside his three other royal guards.

"What are you doing here?" His voice sharpened and his eyebrows fell heavy over his lids.

"I came to help escort you to the throne—" Horemheb began.

"I don't need your help."

Tut pushed past him and began to walk with the three royal guards, but at not hearing Horemheb's heavy footsteps behind him, he stopped and peered over his shoulder. Then he hung his head as he motioned to his guards.

"Leave us."

The guards looked to each other and then went a ways off.

Horemheb came up behind Tut.

"What was the real reason you came? To comfort me for the loss of my child?" Tut's voice held a certain roughness to it, and his eyes darted from Horemheb's feet to his own.

"If that was what you wanted, yes," Horemheb whispered.

Tut sensed the pity in his voice and cringed. He turned to face the older man. "Pawah already came to comfort me this morning." Then his gaze fell back to the floor.

Horemheb's gaze hardened, but his lips stayed sealed.

"He . . ." Tut trailed off, not wanting to admit to Horemheb what Pawah had said—that he had proof, eyewitness accounts, that his wife had been with other men. His cheeks blushed.

Horemheb pursed his lips as he studied Tut and knew then Pawah was no comfort to him. *Do I tell him of my son? Do I tell him about my loss?* He swallowed, and then his whisper cut the silence between them. "I know what it is like to lose a child."

Tut looked up. *You?* his eyes asked. Horemheb only nodded to Tut's silent question.

Tut's gaze fell, along with his shoulders. "How did you know the child was yours?" His voice almost inaudible.

Horemheb let out a breath through his nostrils and looked off to the courtyard and saw the bright sun's rays falling over a rather beautiful scene. It didn't seem fair that a day such as this could boast such beauty in such a sorrowful time. He remembered Nefertiti's touch and her laugh and the way her lips pressed against his.

"Does she love you?" he asked, and turned his face toward Tut, who still looked to the ground.

Tut let out a heavy sigh before asking, "How would I know?"

Horemheb felt Nefertiti's breath against his neck, felt her pain as his own, felt the way she had jumped in his arms, the way she said his name, the way she touched his face and gazed into his eyes.

"It's something you know. The way . . ." He took a deep breath, trying to keep his sorrow from leaching into his words. "The way she looks at you, the way she wants you. The way she kisses you, talks to you, encourages you, touches you." Horemheb bit his lip before continuing. "It's different than a harlot or a woman out for lust. There is meaning behind your woman's kiss."

Tut's eyes grew wide, and then he scrubbed his hand over his face and averted his gaze from his General.

Horemheb cleared his throat as he observed Tut and guessed he had never been with another woman. "But even if no harlot or second woman has been in your bed, it's just something you feel." He pictured Nefertiti smiling at him, apologizing for hitting him in the chest and hurting her hand that night in Aketaten's palace garden. The corner of his mouth turned into a smile as his gaze fell inward.

Tut's eyes once again darted between Horemheb's feet and his own. He licked his lip before saying anything. "You must love Amenia, and she must love you. You are a lucky man."

"Yes, I do." Horemheb said with a slow nod. Tut didn't need to know Nefertiti was the mother of his child and the woman he truly loved. "I never knew my son. He died in the womb." Horemheb blew out a breath to settle his nerves, thinking about the rage he held for Pawah. "If you need comfort, my Pharaoh, know this: if the Queen fights for you and her, she is loyal to you. If she is hurt by your words, truly hurt, she cares for you. If she feels joy and sadness with you and helps to carry your burdens, she loves you. A woman who does not love you will use you without a second thought. Your words mean nothing, and you are nothing to her."

Tut didn't smile, but mulled over the General's words, thinking back to his first night with Ankhesenamun. There was something behind her kiss; he knew he felt it.

But, he debated, could he trust himself?

AFTER THE DAY IN THE THRONE ROOM, TUT WENT TO Ankhesenamun's bedchambers. He stood outside the door for a long time debating whether to knock or to open the door—an act which was in his right to do so and which he had done every night he had slept in her room. But tonight she was without child. Without *his* child? Did he dare bring it to her attention again? He half believed that Sennedjem or the true child's father already came to comfort her as he should have.

"Pharaoh, she is in a great deal of pain," Hori whispered to Tut, noticing how long he stood in front of her door.

Tut nodded, then stared at Hori for a long time. *Were you the father?*

Hori looked much more of a man than Sennedjem— taller, bigger, stronger. Tut shook his head and let out a breath, looking to the doors again. He finally opened both and walked inside.

Even though the sun had not yet fallen behind the horizon, the room was only dimly lit, due to a curtain that had been pulled in front of the window. The light from the corridor fell in from the open doors behind him. The heat was almost unbearable and the room stunk with the smell of blood. Tut thought back to the battlefield but quickly shook the image from his mind, not needing or wanting those images in his head. Not right now.

"We had a daughter," a quiet voice came from the bed.

Tut noticed no servants, no midwives; not even Hentmehyt was in the room.

"I dismissed them," Ankhesenamun answered when she saw Tut looking about the room.

Tut closed the doors and walked to where his wife lay. He still didn't know what to say as he lit a candle next to her bed.

Ankhesenamun rolled away from the candlelight. "Don't look at me." Her voice cracked.

"Why?" Tut finally said in a breathless whisper.

"Because," Ankhesenamun said as tears clogged her throat, "I lost our child." She let out a shallow, hitched breath. "I lost her."

Our child? he thought. *Even in grief, she clings to her truth. Maybe she does tell the truth . . . and so, perhaps, should I. But Pawah has a list of names, people who have seen her with at least one other man. Are they all liars?* Tut pursed his lips as he thought. *There was something behind her kiss . . . but how do I know she loves me?* He looked to his cane. *She said she doesn't see what I see. She said she loves me. She says the child is mine. Why would she lie? But why would the list of people lie? There is no reward for them. Either way, she lost her child, and if the child was mine, I also lost my daughter today.*

"Have you gone?" Ankhesenamun whispered at the room's silence.

"No, I'm here," Tut said, and sat at the edge of the bed. He put his hand on Ankhesenamun's back. He still had no words for her. He had no words for himself. The candle burned half its length before Tut asked, "Are you well? Did the midwives take care of you?"

"Yes." Shame weighted her whisper. She rolled her back away from Tut's hand. "I am fine." Her words leaked self-hatred.

Tut's gaze fell to her body. He placed his hand on her back again but kept silent, knowing his words may only aggravate her emotional state further. But after a few moments, he could no longer suppress his question: "Where is our daughter?"

Ankhesenamun finally turned to face Tut, her cheeks streaked with kohl and burning red, and held out to him his wrapped baby: her fingers still by the lifeless chin.

She had his eyes and straight nose. Finally, his heart settled. This was his child. At that realization, a weight bore upon his shoulders and down his spine; he could no longer breathe as he held the dead thing, *his* lifeless baby girl. The heat and the stench of the room crashed upon him in a bewildering rush of loss as he let out a wordless cry and pulled the child close to his chest.

Two hands came upon his shoulders as Ankhesenamun pressed her forehead against his neck. The heat of her breath against him caused him to melt even farther into the baby.

"My child . . ."

His whisper filled the room with a deafening sorrow. Feeling his wife's tears upon his back, he closed his eyes.

I should have come to her this morning, he thought. *I should have been here with her. I should never have doubted her.*

"I'm sorry, Ankhesenamun. I should have—"

"Pharaoh does not apologize." Ankhesenamun wiped her tears, streaking the kohl further, and lay back down. The day, the heat, the emotional drain—exhaustion overtook her.

Tut turned to his wife. "No. The gods punish me."

"I am a woman. I bear children, yet I could not do it." She closed her eyes. "I could not sustain life."

Tut looked back to his daughter. "No, Ankhesenamun. You are with me and so are punished with me. There was a reason I was born this way. I was not meant to have children." He studied his daughter's red, opaque skin . . . her perfectly formed face.

"But you survived. You beat all odds against you. You are strong. It is me. I am to blame." Ankhesenamun began to cry. "I thought since we had gone back to the gods of our country, they would be merciful to us." Her face contorted as she cried harder and harder. "But I see they want our first child to pay for the transgressions of our father. He turned his back on them, so they turn their back on us."

Or the Aten is truly the only god. Tut gazed upon his daughter's face, wondering. None of his father's children had died at birth. But then he thought of his own mother—she died during childbirth. *Perhaps, there are no gods. Perhaps I am just cursed. Someone Ankhesenamun should not be with. I have only done her harm. I doubt her. I accuse her. She will want me to go, especially since I did not come when she needed me.*

Still holding his daughter in one hand, he stood on his good leg and grabbed his cane.

"Please leave her with me," Ankhesenamun pleaded, grasping the edge of his royal shendyt.

Tut's heart dropped, knowing she did not ask for him as well. He looked to his daughter and handed her back to Ankhesenamun. He kissed his wife's forehead and turned to leave.

"Tut."

Hearing his name in her broken voice almost brought tears to his eyes, so he did not turn to face her but stopped walking.

"Will you stay tonight?"

Tut dropped his chin. "Hentmehyt can stay with you." His ears begged to hear her refute his suggestion, to show him some indication of forgiveness.

After a moment, Ankhesenamun's broken voice answered his silent plea: "I want you to stay with me. I need you, Tut."

A small, relieved smile crossed his lips. "Even after I did not come this morning?"

"Yes." She reached out and touched his hip. "Please . . . stay."

Tut felt the tension leave his body. He placed his cane on the bedside table, turned and lay down next to his wife, their baby girl between them. They each longed for her cries, but only the soft flickering of the candle adorned their ears until they both, exhausted from the day, fell asleep and the candle died out.

CHAPTER 15
THE TIME OF MEN-NEFER

HOREMHEB WENT TO HIS ROOM THAT EVENING. HE ORDERED the servant to prepare a bath. As the servant gathered the heated buckets of water to pour in the overhead water trough, Horemheb untied his shendyt and leaned against a table, pulling his wig from his head.

He rubbed the kohl from his eyes as he let out a captive breath, then felt the stubble regrowing on his chin. He felt something flutter down his leg, and when he looked, he saw the folded papyrus on the floor. That letter punched him in the stomach again as he stared at it.

Did Nefertiti know about our son? he thought. *Is that what this letter tells me?*

He reached down to pick it up, and as he turned it over in his hand, her seal's ridges shadowed in the candlelight.

On an especially dark night, he thought. *I told myself I would read it.* He shook his head. *Once I have finally read it, though, I will have nothing more from my love. She will be gone.*

He placed it, wrapped in his clean shendyt, on the table. He blew air from his mouth and bowed his head.

"My love," he whispered to her ka, hoping she wrapped her arms around him as he mourned her, as he missed her.

"General," the servant said, breaking him from his thoughts. "It is ready."

The servant had taken his position behind the wall partition so that he may let the water out from the trough and refill as necessary. Horemheb took a breath and went and stood under the water trough.

"Begin."

His command could have sliced through the stone wall. As the hot water fell on him, he felt his muscles tinge in the warmth. He pressed his hands against the partitioned wall and let the water flow down his back. When that was done, he began to clean and shave himself. When he finished, he let the water run until it only dripped from overhead.

"General, I can send for more water," the servant's small voice squeaked from behind the wall.

"No. I am finished." Horemheb turned and began to dry himself.

The servant came from behind the wall partition and saw him drying his own body. "I can send for someone to—"

"Leave me." Horemheb's eyes bore into the innocent servant.

"Yes, General." The servant bowed slightly from the waist and left Horemheb to his solace.

Horemheb went through the daily motions, applying oil to his skin, lining his eyes with kohl, using his myrrh-infused powder to keep his odor to a minimum in the desert heat. He kept his mind purposely numb, so that he may last as long as he could stand without reading Nefertiti's last letter to him. He at last stood looking into his expressionless reflection in the polished copper mirror, and then he closed his eyes as he remembered her last words to him.

You made me feel alive.

"I'm sorry, my love," he whispered to her ka. "I failed you. I failed you when you needed me the most."

He opened his eyes to his reflection and noticed the scowl on his lips and his flared nostrils. "Ah!" he yelled, and punched his reflection again and again until his hand ached and the copper dented, showing a marred and distorted reflection of his face. "If I had spent more time trying to end Pawah than I did trying to be with her, she would still be alive." He clenched his jaw. "Even if it meant not loving her, I would rather her be alive. I would not have failed her. I would never have failed her." He looked at the distorted cheekbone in the reflection, but his eyes remained perfect in reflection as they bore into his own soul. His reflection screamed at him, *You let her die!*

He couldn't bring himself to turn away from the reflection, but instead leaned closer. His eyes yelled at him louder and louder until he ripped the mirror from the wall and threw it across the room.

"I know!" he yelled.

The clang of its drop sent guards into his room.

"General?"

"I said leave me!" he yelled, standing, staring at the cursed mirror, every muscle in his body strained and tight.

They paused to look at each other, eyebrows raised in confusion.

"Yes, General," one said, and they both left the room.

His chest rose and fell rapidly. *I prefer the battlefield, so I don't have to see myself,* he thought. He fell to his knees and his body reverberated on the stone floor, all the way through to his stomach. He saw his reflection again from the mangled copper mirror lying on its side.

"You won't leave me, will you?" he whispered to his reflection. "Always a reminder of my biggest failure."

He fell to his hands and became the master of his breath

again until he was able to stand. He walked over and pulled his clean shendyt to his waist and caught Nefertiti's letter as it almost fell to the floor again. He turned it over again as he sat on the edge of his bed.

Finally, as if Nefertiti's ka willed him to open it, he broke the seal and began to read.

My dearest Horemheb,

He lowered the letter and covered his mouth with his other hand, pushing back the water that welled in his eyes. Taking a deep breath through his nose and sucking the tears back from whence they came, he gathered himself.

"Be gentle, my Nefertiti," he whispered as he exhaled, and then began to read again.

I hope this letter finds you in peace. I am so happy you are in my life and for the moments we have shared, but I have had a dream where I have seen the end of Egypt, should I not marry the Hittite —and with no husband already. I must marry, and I must marry soon. My father said he would fight a war if I refused the Hittite with no husband.

But, my love . . . I carry your child.

He stopped breathing. "She did know. She never told me. Why would she?" he whispered. "As she lay dying in my arms? She did not want to double my pain."

He closed his eyes and shook his head, debating whether he should continue. There was still much to read. He opened his eyes and forced himself to continue. The shaky pen strokes told him this letter was either written hastily or with much indecision, uncertainty.

His heart fell at the next lines.

Thus, I have resolved to marry Tut, so the people may think it is his child, so our child may not be outcast or his life endangered as a potential threat to the throne's heir. If it is a daughter, perhaps Tut will allow you to take the child to Amenia. My one request is that Amenia allow me to know this child, that I may redeem myself as a mother. If it is a son,

"A son," he said to her ka. "Our child was a son, my beautiful one."

His hands gripped the letter as he read now.

Tut may want to claim him as his own, should he have no other sons.

I am sorry this has happened, but please admire your son from afar while staying near, and should Tut have a son of his own, I don't know what will happen.

Horemheb thought, *Tut lost his child today . . . and now he knows the pain.* His jaw clamped shut as he imagined life watching his son being claimed by another man and never being able to tell him "You are my child."

All I know is this: I love you and wish our lives had been different so that we could have been together.

Our time dwindles. I saw my death in a dream, and Pawah waiting for me to die.

"Pawah will die for making your dream a reality," Horemheb whispered to the paper.

If this is a vision from Amun, my love, I make final requests:

He sucked in a breath. What would she ask him to do? These words that were never spoken, words she never had time to speak as she died. What was he to do to redeem some of his utter failure?

He read on:

Make sure Pawah will never get the crown. Once I'm gone, he would only have to get in close with Tut and then push the poor crippled child down the stairs. With no heir, Pawah ranks as the next male relative and takes the throne. Akhenaten might have put Egypt through torture, but Pawah as Pharaoh would be the end of Egypt altogether.

Horemheb thought, *I will kill him when the time is right. He will never know the crown. I will take my revenge for you, my Nefertiti. I will avenge you, for what little consolation it will bring.*

His hands gripped the letter, but when he saw this left ridges in the thick papyrus, he smoothed out his grip, not wanting to ruin this last remnant of his Nefertiti.

Please take care of Mut for me. She is a woman now. I ask you to request marriage to her and keep her safe in one of your houses. Be good to her, as you are to me.

He dropped the letter, unable to continue reading.

"Marry Mut?" he whispered.

He stood after picking it back up and paced in front of his bed.

"Marry *Mut*?" he repeated, shaking his head. "I will keep Ankhesenamun safe, but I cannot marry Mut. She looks too much like you. I will never love her for her. She will remind me every day of my failure to you."

He clenched his jaw as he paced some more.

"Why this request? Why, Nefertiti? She is safe in your father's house. She is more safe not with me. I failed you,

Nefertiti. What makes you think I won't fail her too? No one is safe with me."

He put the letter on the table and lay on his bed. Rolling to his back, he took in a deep breath.

"Marry Mut?"

He looked to the empty space next to him and imagined Nefertiti lying next to him. She pleaded with her eyes.

"Marry Mut?" he asked her ghost.

She reached out to touch him but vanished with his imagination as he realized her hand would never grace his skin again. He closed his eyes, remembering her lotus-blossom scent and the warmth of her body against his. He put his hand where her cheek would have been.

"I miss you." His vision blurred. "I'm sorry I let you die. I let you die."

He repeated his whisper until the exhaustion of the day overtook his eyes.

———

THE SUN FILTERED IN THROUGH THE WINDOW'S TRANSLUCENT curtains, but Horemheb lay in his bed awake long before the sun, looking to the roof, his hands clasped over his stomach. The gentle breeze fluttered through and embraced his body. A tear drizzled from the corner of his eye as he remembered such a morning with Nefertiti next to him, asking him to marry her, asking him if he would want every morning to be like that one. He had rejected her proposal for the better of Egypt. He clenched his jaw and felt the scars on his hands, his arm, his leg; but there were no physical scars from his failure of his Pharaoh, of his love, save the small one from Pawah's dagger.

The scars I can't see hurt the most.

"I was wrong," he whispered to himself. To Nefertiti.

I should have taken you as my wife, come what may. What I would give for a morning with you again. Why did I refuse? For Egypt . . . ?

"For Egypt." His whisper was full of sorrow, with a hint of regret wrapped in resentment. "Egypt takes much from us. From me. I'm sorry, Nefertiti. I wish we could have known our son. I wish I could have . . . no—*would* have . . . taken you as my wife."

Without breaking his gaze upward, he reached his hand over to the table next to his bed and grabbed Nefertiti's letter to him. He brought it up to his eyes and settled his mind before he continued reading.

Please take care of Ankhesenpaaten and Nefe, should General Paaten fail in his promise to me. Keep them all safe from Pawah and Beketaten.

Where I have failed them, teach them about Amun.

"I will try, my Nefertiti."

Horemheb knew that if he could keep Tut safe then Ankhesenamun would be safe as well, for Pawah wouldn't go after Ankhesenamun without first going after Tut. But doubt lingered in his mind.

I couldn't even keep you safe. Why entrust me with the safety of your daughter?

As for Amun . . . he thought. *She is being taught by the Amun priesthood now—but I will be there for her, should she have any questions.*

He continued reading.

Counsel my mother and father in their sorrow. They have many children, but my father only has me from my mother, whom he loved greatly. Should I die, my death will be hardest for him.

Horemheb took a deep breath. Ay and Tey—how would he counsel them? He knew Tey probably never wanted to speak to him again, and Ay, well . . . there were no side talks in the corridors as there had been before. No more words exchanged in candor or in friendship. The only words exchanged between them now only concerned Pawah and Tut.

He leaned his head into his hand. "I will try, my love," he repeated, resolved to fulfill her last requests.

I have so much guilt, my love. It weighs on my heart. Pray for Ammit to not devour it when placed upon the balance in the afterlife. Eternal unrest is more than I can bear.

His heart weighed with her burden and her fear.

Ammit will not devour the heart of Pharaoh, my love. The gods know what we did to Pharaoh Akhenaten, as horrible as it was, had to be done.

He shook his head. Had Pharaoh Akhenaten not become lost in his zeal for the Aten disc, he would never have known Nefertiti as he did, and perhaps the whole royal family might still be alive. Pawah would never have been able to garner such rebellion from the people, never have killed three successive Pharaohs. Tut would not be in danger.

Tut. His mind wandered and his heart ached for him. *In his reign, maybe he would have let me be with Nefertiti. I'll never know.*

His eyes fell again to the letter, and cords wrapped his throat as he realized only a few more sentiments remained . . . and then his Nefertiti would be gone forever. There would be no more remnant of her. He debated closing the letter—but these were her last wishes.

"Amun, give me strength," he whispered, and read the last of the letter.

No matter the outcome, I will wait for you in the afterlife. You have given me joy and happiness in this time of darkness. I will always remember your caring touch, your patience, your taking of my burdens, your protection,

Horemheb put the letter down.

"Protection." He bit his lip and shook his head. "I failed you, my love. I did not protect you. I should have been there."

He pulled the letter back once more to see what other lies she told him.

your loyalty, and your love. I loved Thutmose, but it was a young love. I loved Akhenaten, but it was more because I needed to feel loved. However, the love I have for you, Horemheb, is mature and selfless—one I will never forget. Every night as I go to sleep as Tut's wife, I will remember you and dream of life as yours and yours alone.

Love,
   Your Nefertiti

He wished there was more. He wished he could continue reading forever just to feel close to her again. He read the letter twice more in its entirety, then turned to his side and placed the letter in the empty space next to him on his bed.

"I will take care of Mut and Ankhesenamun," he whispered to her. "And the boy, our Pharaoh." The breeze on his back felt good in the growing heat of the morning. "I must first go visit with Amenia to discuss another wife. How will I leave Tut, though?"

Malkata is safe . . . I thought Jabari safe too, but he led Nefertiti to her death. I have to go to Amenia. Taking a second wife should not be done through a letter. He needed her approval, or they would need to agree to a divorce. He didn't want divorce for Amenia; her infertility would only make her live alone or as a concubine. He didn't love her, but he did care for her.

"I will have to tell her I have been unfaithful, for she won't understand why I take another wife."

His stomach curdled at the guilt of infidelity, but Nefertiti's last wishes decided what he would do. He promised her ka that Mut and Ankhesenamun would be safe from Pawah.

"I have failed you once . . . I will not fail you again, my love."

He lay there for a while longer until a knock came at his door.

It opened and a messenger said aloud, "Pharaoh needs you at once."

Horemheb waved him away. After the door closed, he went and picked up the mirror and placed it back in its place. He found his distorted image, and reapplied his powder and his kohl, his mind numb.

He grabbed Nefertiti's letter and hid it in his shendyt before leaving to Pharaoh's throne room.

NEFERTITI'S FIRST REQUEST WAS TO TAKE CARE OF MUT BY WAY OF marriage, Horemheb thought as he bowed before Pharaoh Tutankhamun.

Tut raised his hand and dismissed all in the throne room. Then he stood and hobbled to Horemheb, who stood on the step beneath the throne platform.

"The child was mine." The young man's voice filled with a shake that made even Horemheb's knees wobble. Tut's gaze fell to the floor.

Horemheb wanted to ask him why there had ever been

question, already knowing the answer, but decided to leave Pawah out of the conversation when he saw Tut's shoulders slump and noticed the dark circles under his bloodshot eyes.

"I'm sorry, Pharaoh."

Tut opened his mouth to speak, but no words came out. Horemheb studied the boy—well, now a man, at sixteen years of age. "Don't pity me," Tut whispered with a curt spew, upon noticing Horemheb's stare.

"I'm not pitying you, Pharaoh." Horemheb found Tut's gaze. "I'm grieving with you."

Tut's jaw fell slack, and he looked to Horemheb again, as if longing for him to embrace him. Tut's eyes welled with tears. "How did you help Amenia through your son's death?"

Horemheb thought about the question for a second. *Amenia is barren—what is he talking about?* Then he remembered. He had let Tut think Amenia was the mother of his child that died in Nefertiti's womb. He slowly shook his head, thinking it would be the same story except for the name of the mother, so he wouldn't be lying to him.

"I didn't." He turned his face away from Pharaoh. At Tut's silence, he continued, "It is something I will always regret. I failed her."

"If you could go back, what would you do?"

Horemheb turned to face Tut again. His mind warned him to not let Tut get too close; for if he failed him like he failed Nefertiti, the pain, the guilt, would be too much to bear. He took a step backward and bowed his head. "I would have been there."

Tut seemed to accept his answer and nodded. Then he hobbled past him and toward the door. He stopped upon reaching the wooden giants. "General," he said, turning to Horemheb. "Go see Amenia. I will spend this time with Queen Ankhesenamun."

Horemheb bowed as Tut left him alone in his throne room. He kept his head lowered as he straightened. Perhaps the gods were in fact telling him to honor the last requests of his love and go to Amenia for approval to marry Mut. He took a deep breath and hoped Pawah would not strike while he was gone.

He planned out what he needed to do before he left. He would need to tell Ay he was leaving for a month. He knew that Ay had built a network of loyal supporters to keep Tut and Ankhesenamun protected. Now was the time for Ay to put it to work.

Then, as Pharaoh requested, Horemheb would go see his wife in Men-nefer.

AFTER TWO DECANS OF TRAVELING DOWN THE NILE TO REACH Men-nefer, Horemheb stepped into his estate and looked around the courtyard and up to the main house. He bowed his head in the heat of the sun and walked up to his door.

The door flung open and Amenia rushed into his arms, rising on tiptoe so that her head could fall on his shoulder. "My Horemheb!"

His arms slowly found their way to her back. He squeezed as he forced a smile to his face. "Amenia, it is good to see you." He pulled back from her to look her in the eyes. He wished it were Nefertiti who greeted him at his estate, and yet at seeing Amenia's face, his guilt of putting his wife aside rushed over his heart.

She studied his face and the gleam in her eye diminished. "You must be tired. I did not know you were coming." Amenia hooked her arm in his as they walked over the threshold. "I will have Menhet prepare food and drink." She turned to gesture to Menhet.

"Yes, Mistress of the House," Menhet said with a bow of his head.

"It is not necessary." Horemheb waved a dismissal to the servants, who lined the inner corridor. He felt he didn't deserve food. Food was for the faithful. Food was for a man who did not fail those around him.

"Is all well?" Amenia asked. Her eyes still searched his.

Horemheb looked around at his estate. Amenia did such a wonderful job keeping things in running order; she was a good wife, and seeing how she welcomed him, he figured she looked forward to their evening together, as she did every time he came home. In contrast, he was a horrible husband; he had not seen her in years and had only kept in touch via a letter every now and then. He had fulfilled his responsibilities—gave her a home, gave her clothes, gave her food—but had not stayed faithful, had never loved her. He'd only married her because their fathers, his especially, desired it.

Part of him wished she had been unfaithful, too, since they both had only stayed married for convenience: she had a luxurious estate to live in and did not have to live as a concubine or in her father's house as a sterile woman, and he had someone to take care of his estate and to not incur the wrath of his own father.

Her hands never left his body as she showed him around his estate, pointing out all that she had changed or maintained in his absence. The longer her fingers lingered on his skin the more he realized she had not been unfaithful. But his mind could only compare her with Nefertiti. Amenia's touch was firmer, her voice higher; her skin was darker and her body larger, her eyes smaller, nose less straight, eyelids less hooded; her scent of cinnamon contrasted with Nefertiti's sweet scent of lotus blossoms.

She took him to his storehouse and showed him the grain

she had brought home from her employment at the temple as a Chantress. As she went on about her role in the temple, she beamed, and he nodded, pretending to listen as his thoughts continued to race in his mind. Amenia did have a beautiful singing voice; it appeased the gods. If ever someone bought her as a concubine, it would have pleased him as well, but Horemheb had stayed married to her so she would not have to live that life.

Evening came and he lay down on his back next to his wife, who rubbed her hands on his chest and pressed herself next to his body. "I missed you," she whispered in his ear.

Not hearing her, he looked to the roof as his thoughts filled his mind: *Nefertiti is dead; Amenia is your wife. How will you explain wanting to take another wife without telling her that you've strayed? Maybe you do tell her you've strayed . . . maybe she has, too. We both knew this was a sham marriage. Right? We stayed together for her benefit. Right? She would have been forced to live as a concubine or live alone in her father's house after her sterility became known. Maybe she wouldn't care what I did.*

"What are you thinking?"

Her question went unanswered for some time as Horemheb thought.

How will I marry Mut? How will I convince Amenia to let me bring a second wife? How will I tell her I loved another? Do I tell her? I would have to . . . there would be no sense in bringing a second wife. But how? O Nefertiti, why do you ask me to do this? Perhaps I tell her and she tells me she also loves another, and then we can divorce and she can be with her lover and I can marry Mut and be without Nefertiti. At least then, Amenia may be happy. She has been a good wife to me, and I . . . I have not been good to her. How do I tell her? How do I ask her? What do I say?

Amenia cleared her throat, throwing Horemheb out of his thoughts and into the present. He swallowed and looked to her. *Did she say something?*

"Is there something that takes your mind from me?" she asked, stroking his shoulder and bicep.

He snatched her hand and sat up, pulling her up with him. He faced her and took a deep breath. "Amenia," he began, but that was all he had. He didn't know how to proceed, and despite all of the thoughts of the day, his mind went blank.

She placed the tips of her fingers under his chin and lifted his face to hers. "You don't need to speak if you don't want to," she said, and pulled his lips to hers.

Horemheb, for a moment, thought it felt good to kiss a woman again. With the hungriness of her kiss, he found it difficult to disengage; but he would not use her, so instead he placed his hands on the sides of her arms and pulled his lips from hers.

"No, I need to say this," he said, but then remained silent, trying to think of what to say. Her eyes searched him and nearly found his soul. He finally spoke: "We both know this marriage was not what we wanted, and we stayed married to make it easier on us."

"What are you talking about, Horemheb?" Amenia shook her head and drew her eyebrows together. Her head tilted in confusion as she dropped her arms. "What do you mean? This marriage wasn't what we wanted? Easier on *us*?"

Horemheb's head and shoulders fell as a thick lump grew in his throat. It was as if the sword of an enemy sliced through his stomach, causing his chin to tremble. Had he been wrong? All this time? His cheeks burned as he spoke the truth he had made himself believe for almost two decades. He lifted his head, but he couldn't look Amenia in the eyes.

"Yes . . . I didn't want to divorce you and make known your infertility. It would only curse you to live the rest of your life in your father's house or as a concubine."

Amenia's eyes welled with tears. Horemheb silently

prayed they were tears of relief, not of sorrow, but his prayers were not granted.

"The only curse was not being able to have children with the man I love. But if that is how you feel . . ." She pulled away from him. "I would have preferred to live my life as a concubine. At least then I could live in luxury and never be cut off for being unable to bear a child. I could have sung every day and lived carefree"—her breath became hot —"instead of managing your entire estate in your absence."

Horemheb shook his head, feeling the complete weight of what he had done to his wife be cast upon his shoulders, now as he realized the fullness of his horrible mistake. "I'm sorry, Amenia. I thought it was best for you. I didn't want you to have to . . ." He trailed off, seeing her cover her eyes with her hands.

"Why do you tell me this?" she whimpered with a breaking voice.

Horemheb wanted to disappear as he sank his nails into his arm. He had assumed wrong all this time, and now, even though he didn't love her, he was responsible for her pain. He had hurt her. She cried because of him. One more woman he had failed. "I—"

"I want the truth, Horemheb." She looked up at him, her kohl streaked down her cheeks.

Horemheb swallowed and slumped even further. *I am so sorry, Amenia.*

"I have been with another woman—" He stopped as her shoulders crumpled, but he continued. "I loved her, but she is now gone to be with Re."

"And why do you tell me this now? How long? Do you still love her? Did you ever love me?" Amenia's questions came out with one breath, but before Horemheb could answer any of them, she waved her hand. "No, don't answer. I don't want to know."

"I tell you this now, because her last request was for me to marry her—"

Horemheb stopped. He couldn't say it, couldn't say *sister*, because then she would know who the other woman was and thus potentially jeopardize Mut and the throne. So he paused before he continued with another half-lie.

"—her friend." He swallowed a lump in his throat. "She wanted me to take care of her friend. Her friend is very young, and she feared for her well-being. So I have come to Men-nefer to ask if I can grant her last request and marry her friend."

Amenia pursed her lips as her hands fell to her lap. She looked him in the eyes.

"Horemheb, you've already done what you pleased. Do whatever else you want." Her voice was cold and monotone.

She got up from the bed and walked to their window overlooking the courtyard.

"Amenia, I'm—"

"Don't apologize, Horemheb!"

She spun to face him.

"You know, I assumed as much. That you were with other women." She nodded her head. "You haven't come home for years, but I did all of this: ran your estate, took care of your home, all of it for you. I thought at least you still loved me." Her voice gave out as she calmed her hitching chest. "I thought I was the only one who held your heart. I hoped for all these years that when you came home and saw what I had done, you would come back to me." Her hands clenched into fists. "And it turns out *I* am the fool!" She chewed on her lip as her tears streamed down her cheeks. "Another woman held your heart. Another held your love. All of this"—her hands opened toward the courtyard of his estate—"was in vain."

"Amenia," Horemheb began again, but she threw up her hand to halt him.

"And now," her voice spewed with hate, "I find that the woman you want to bring into this estate is young, so you can have many children with this one. You rub my infertility in my face forevermore!"

"No, Amenia." Horemheb jumped from the bed and came to stand in front of her, hoping at least to alleviate some of her pain. "I don't plan on having children with her."

"Then you punish her like you do me!" She shoved him in the chest. "A lifetime of solitude and false hope!"

"No, I will take care of her," he refuted, and then she slapped him in his face.

"Just like you take care of me? Taken care of but not loved? Don't subject that girl to this life. If you take her as your wife, you love her. Don't treat her like me. Don't treat her like your estate steward!"

Spittle landed on his cheek. At his silence, she hit his chest.

"I hate you!" she yelled, and banged her fist on his chest again. "I hate you!" She hit him with her other hand until she was beating on his chest. "I hate you for leaving me! I hate you for betraying me! I hate you for marrying me! I hate you for loving someone else!"

Guilt crept through his stomach as he accepted her blows. He stood there with his chin dipped, his eyes open, letting her beat his chest raw as she screamed how much she hated him. He deserved it . . . in so many ways, he deserved it. The pain he brought her summoned tears in his eyes. He did not love her, though he did care for her.

Her arms and tears tired until they ceased to run. She looked at his red chest through her blurry vision and then whispered, "I know you left me because I could not have children."

Horemheb shook his head. He didn't know if that was why he chose not to love her, or if he just never did love her. Maybe if he held a job that didn't require him to always be somewhere else, he might have fallen in love with her—whether or not they had children.

"No, Amenia, that is not the reason. I should never have married you." His voice kept low and calm. "You deserve better than me. You deserve someone who loves you unconditionally. I never have truly loved you—"

The last words he spoke were like a knife to her heart as her labored breathing stopped. His eyes grew wide. He had never meant to speak that last sentence.

"I'm so sorry. That—" He tripped over his words. "I—I didn't . . ."

But it was too late. He'd already spoken the truth. He had added more than she could bear to hear in one night. His voice tangled with the thick air in his throat as two tears fell from his eyes. Her gaze slowly fell to the ground as he finally found his breath and, therefore, his voice.

"I'm sorry."

She only nodded. He tried to reach out for her arm to comfort her in the truth as she walked away, but she stood rigid at his touch. He let his arms fall and she went and lay down in their bed, facing away from him.

He pulled at his neck as he watched her, unmoving, and scratched his chin.

Why did you say that? You could have just left it alone. You ignorant fool!

His feet shuffled. He didn't know how to make it better. He wanted to make it better.

Her soft whisper came to his ears. "Leave."

He rubbed his temple, debating what to do. Eventually, he went to her and kissed her cheek and whispered in her ear, "I'm so sorry, Amenia." She held no response. He only wished for her forgiveness, but knew it would not come that night. He had failed her, just as he failed all those in his life. "I hope one day you can find it in your heart to forgive me."

She closed her eyes and whispered, "Please leave."

Horemheb bit his lip. He longed to soothe her pain away, but staying would only cause her more. And so he stood up and left with a gentle close of the door behind him.

HE SLEPT IN THE SECONDARY BEDROOM THAT NIGHT. IN THE morning he left before Amenia awoke, leaving an apology letter to her. At the end of it he wrote that he had made a promise to the other woman, and should her friend accept his marriage proposal, a second wife would come to his Men-nefer estate until he could set up another estate for her in Waset. And if she wanted a divorce, he would give her all that she was entitled and more.

He hoped she understood despite the pain he had caused her, though in his heart he knew it would not be so.

CHAPTER 16
THE TIME OF SWAY

PAWAH REQUESTED A PRIVATE AUDIENCE WITH PHARAOH. UPON seeing him, he threw his arms around the crippled boy and said, "My son!"

Tut pressed his lips together in a thin line. Only after a moment did he return the embrace.

"How do you fare after Ankhesenamun losing your child?" Pawah asked him, looking him up and down with practiced concern, eyebrows knitted together and eyes searching Tut's face.

"I fare as best I can," Tut responded, and pulled his back straighter. He still feared requesting him to use Ankhesenamun's official title, but they were in private audience, so he brushed it aside. "After you made me believe the child was not mine, I found her. She is my daughter. Was. I don't know who is on your list of eyewitness accounts, but Ankhesenamun's child was mine."

Pawah pulled the corners of his mouth into a grin. "Of course, my Pharaoh." He bowed. "I only tried to make sure she did not hurt you. I am glad the baby girl was indeed yours, for both of your sakes. As Vizier, I only tell you of happenings that may affect you in some way."

Tut jutted his bottom jaw forward so it aligned with his overbite as he narrowed his eyes at his uncle. "Yes, I suppose so."

"I still have the list should you want to see it." Pawah patted a piece of papyrus tucked into his shendyt.

Tut looked to his hand and became cognizant of the heavy air coming from his nostrils.

"I can see you want to know," Pawah said, and pulled out a rolled-up piece of papyrus. He began to unroll it.

Tut's eyes found Pawah's. "No. I don't."

"Do not be unwise, Pharaoh. Can you imagine the uproar of the people if they found out Pharaoh's wife had been with anyone other than Pharaoh? Can you imagine the weakness of the throne in their perspective? You are Amun's divinely appointed! No one touches your chief royal wife!" Pawah thrust the list at Tut.

"No one does touch her." Tut leaned forward. "Your eyewitnesses are liars." He put his hand on Pawah's and lowered the papyrus from his face.

Pawah began to roll it back up. "Ah . . . I see." He shook his head and knocked his teeth with his tongue. "Well, when it becomes known, I will not say I told you so, my son."

"There will be no need." Tut noticed a red tinge growing in Pawah's ears and his cheeks.

"One man can lie, but so many with the same lie? For what do they gain?" After seeing Tut think over the question, he smiled and added, "No matter. If you trust her, then I trust her."

Tut tried to calm his breath and slow his heart as he nodded in agreement with his uncle.

"But what to do if you are like your father and have no son with your chief royal wife? What would you do then?"

Tut stared into Pawah's eyes and blinked. He remembered when Pawah had to bend down to speak with him; now he looked him square in the face, even while leaning on a cane. Tut's jaw twitched as he tried to come up with an answer.

Pawah said, his voice steady, "You could name me Hereditary Prince . . . ?"

The question filled Tut's ears as his mind raced to Horemheb's words: *Pawah wants the crown.*

At Tut's silence, Pawah continued. "Indeed, I could—"

"I have time for a son, uncle." His new courage lifted his chin. "I'm not going to die anytime soon. I still have a whole lifetime ahead of me."

"Of course you do, my son." Pawah placed his hands on Tut's shoulders. "But in the meantime, it is wisest to name me Hereditary Prince, in case Ankhesenamun cannot bear you an heir or proves to be unfaithful to your bed as the eyewitnesses say."

"I do not doubt my chief royal wife." Tut stood as straight as he could under Pawah's heavy hands, but still a small part of him did not fully believe his own words. His mind only remembered her kiss—there was something there, even if he had no other woman's kiss with whom to compare. He remembered feeling her pain, seeing her raw sorrow at their child's death, and it gave him a dash of confidence in his statements to Pawah. "As you said—if I trust her, then you trust her. She will bear me an heir. She will bear me a child."

"Thus Pharaoh says." Pawah's half smile slid easily onto his face. "In time, you may reconsider."

Pawah bowed his head, finally removing his hands from Tut's shoulders, and stepped back. The young Pharaoh needed his space. But Pawah knew for a fact Ankhesenamun would bear no heir. Just a little more time, and then Tut would grant him the title of Hereditary Prince, and after a quick little accident, the throne would be his—and, for good measure, he'd marry the poor widowed Hereditary Princess. He felt so close, he could taste the gold of the throne under his hands.

———————

NEWS OF TROUBLE AT THE SOUTHERN BORDER MADE ITS WAY TO the throne room only a few decans later. A messenger troop bowed before Pharaoh Tutankhamun.

"Nubians have attacked again. The southern border troops request Pharaoh's Armies to put down the attack."

Tut gripped the arms of the chair and then dismissed the messenger. He looked to Ay and then to Pawah, each standing on either of his sides. Fear rendered his voice mute —he had no desire to go back to war.

"Pharaoh, you should go with your army to resist the Nubians," Pawah cooed.

Ay turned to face him. "The decision is yours, Pharaoh, but know this: You are needed in Waset. The country rebuilds itself. The relations with the Mitanni need the trust rebuilt. The Hittites constantly attack."

"Nonsense." Pawah waved at the old man, who still stood strong. "Leave your bidding to me, and I will ensure the relations between Egypt and her foreign allies are rebuilt."

Tut shook his head, letting Ay respond to Pawah in Pharaoh's place. "If Pharaoh were to leave, those responsibilities would fall to his chief royal wife Ankhesenamun. Do you try to take away her right as King's daughter and King's great wife yet again?"

Pawah narrowed his eyes. "You see, Vizier Ay, in Aketaten she busied herself in the royal harem, in the training yard, with a certain tutor." His eyes dropped to Tut, whose gaze fell to the floor. "I *had* to step in her place, or else the matters needing decision would fall to the wayside."

"I'm sure you gave her reason to busy herself in the royal harem," Ay replied.

Tut looked to Pawah, clearly not fully trusting his Vizier of the Lower anymore. "Vizier Ay, would it be good for me to go to the Nubian border?"

"I believe Pharaoh in attendance with his army will only further validate Pharaoh's divine position," Ay said. "Your grandfather did such a thing. But the relations with the Mitanni are shaky at best, so you are also needed here."

Tut looked to his hands. He did not want to hold a weapon again; although he liked the strength that surged through him when he carried his dagger made of ba-en-pet around his waist, he knew his chances of being lethal with it were slim. "Where am I needed the most?"

"Nubia," Pawah said immediately.

Tut's shoulders fell.

"General Horemheb will need to go to Nubia, since Commander Paramesse is in the Lower," Ay said, and folded his hands behind his back. "He could do your bidding there."

Tut sat up a little straighter. It was a solution, yes, but he didn't want General Horemheb to go without him.

Pawah took a step toward the throne. "But the army always is victorious when Pharaoh accompanies them."

Tut's eyes darted to Pawah and then back to Ay. "Then I am needed in Nubia."

Ay closed his eyes and let out a heavy sigh.

Tut wished he did not need to make this decision, but at least, he hoped, with the General he could be safe from Pawah's striking distance.

A smile crept over Pawah's face until Ay asked Tut, "Who do you leave in your absence?"

"My chief royal wife has the responsibility. Queen Ankhesenamun shall rule in my absence."

Pawah's face fell. "But my son—"

"I am Pharaoh." Tut looked to Pawah and narrowed his eyes at him, silencing his tongue. "If I trust her, then you trust her."

Pawah shut his mouth. That evil sorceress had worked her curse over him. He would have to make sure he severed the tie between him and his wife for good. The old man should surely die soon enough . . . and then there was Horemheb. The hardest one to take down. What doubt should he put in the boy's mind about his new mentor?

Pawah bowed as the thoughts raced through his head and muttered, "Thus Pharaoh says."

CHAPTER 17
THE TIME OF SURROGATE

THE DAY AFTER PHARAOH TUTANKHAMUN AND GENERAL Horemheb left for the Nubian border, Ay watched as Ankhesenamun walked the halls of the royal harem—her shoulders slumped, her step heavy, her eyes dim. Ay came to her and wrapped her arms around her.

"I would give anything to see you smile again."

"There is nothing you can give me, grandfather." Ankhesenamun shook her head. "If you could grant me a body that could provide for a child, then I would be happy."

Ay chewed his lip as he held her. "Your grandmother could not have children either. She died shortly after delivering your mother to me . . . and now both are gone." He stroked Ankhesenamun's shoulder. "My Temehu asked for the same, and it cost her life. Perhaps a weak body is passed down."

"Mother had six children," Ankhesenamun said, looking her grandfather in the face, her voice defiant.

"It could skip generations." Ay shook his head. "My concern is that you will pray for this as we did, and you will lose your life. Please consider a surrogate mother. If Nefe were here, you could ask her. Ask Pharaoh to have a child with another woman, and then you can claim the child as your own."

"I could never do that!" Tears welled in her eyes.

"Yes, you can. Many have done so when they have not been able to have children."

"I don't want Tut with other women. He is my husband."

"My Nefertiti said the same about her husband. She lived in fear of your father being with other women, and when he did behind her back while she was with child, she was never the same. Don't let it tear apart your happiness. He is Pharaoh, and Pharaoh usually has many wives."

"Officials usually have many wives, but you have only Tey. Horemheb has only Amenia."

Ay ignored the comparison to Horemheb, knowing his love for Nefertiti. He smiled and put both of his hands on Ankhesenamun's cheeks. "Yes, I do. It is my choice. Tut has to make that choice. To save his wife from potential death in childbirth, would he not consider another woman to bear his heir and name you the mother?"

"Tut thinks I have not even been faithful to him. He thought, for half of my pregnancy, that he was not the father. Pawah has told him lies. He could care less if I die."

"Ankhesenamun, you speak your own truths, but maybe not *the* truth. I believe Pharaoh cares for you a great deal. If another had doubts about his wife, there would be a divorce —if *Pharaoh* had doubts about his wife, there would be no question about exile or execution. Yet you still remain alive and married and in Malkata even. Pharaoh cares for you. I believe he would not want to trade your life for a child's."

She closed her mouth and pressed her forehead into Ay's chest. After a few moments, she looked up to her grandfather, who had pulled away slightly.

"Think about my words?"

She nodded in agreement. "Who should I ask?"

"Probably a friend who you can trust with your motives and who will not want Pharaoh to name her the mother of the heir. Someone of noble blood. No servants."

"I am not so lucky in friends these days," she muttered, and looked away, not bearing to see his pity.

Ay rubbed her back and lifted her chin to him. "You will find someone."

"If you could go back and tell Temehu the same, do you think you would have chosen her over my mother?"

Ay hesitated. "After knowing your mother, Tey, and knowing you and your sisters, and having so many children with Tey . . . I cannot say. I miss my first love, my Temehu, every day. I wish she were still here, but I cannot imagine life without any of you either." He let out a breath. "I told Temehu exactly what I am telling you, and she chose to try one more time. It took her life away. I do not wish the same for you."

Ankhesenamun smiled sadly. "Thank you."

He cupped her cheeks and guided her forehead for his kiss. "I will be looking for a suitable surrogate for you as well."

IT HAD BEEN ALMOST TWO AND ONE-HALF SEASONS SINCE Ankhesenamun and Mut had last spoken. But at the request of Queen Ankhesenamun, Mut came to Malkata, and they walked the royal shore of the palace lake.

"You have been quiet today, chief royal wife," Mut said as they walked.

"Call me Ankhesenamun when we are alone," she whispered. They had left Hori and Ineni at the other side of the lake.

Mut smiled. "What bothers you, Ankhesenamun?"

Ankhesenamun stopped and looked to the Nile just to the east, enjoying the breeze on her face. "I was wanting to see if you had accepted marriage or had spoken with the man you wanted to marry?"

Mut looked off into the Nile too. "I think he does not remember me, and I am afraid to approach him. He has another wife."

"Oh?" Ankhesenamun said, snapping her head back to Mut. "This I did not know."

"Yes, I know. Stupid Mut." Mut shrugged her shoulders, and her eyes darted between Ankhesenamun and the ground. She remembered her sister's words: *Don't ever be the second wife.* Nefertiti's advice still haunted her actions and froze her will to speak to General Horemheb.

"No, that is not what I meant. I just didn't know."

"Why do you ask?" Mut felt heat rush up her body to her cheeks.

Ankhesenamun paused. "I cannot have children. My body is too weak. Your father came to me and asked me to find a friend who may step in my place and have a child, and let Pharaoh name me the mother." Ankhesenamun kept her voice low in case the wind carried it to the wrong ears. "Would you do this for me before you marry? It would be in secret."

"I don't know, Ankhesenamun . . ." Mut rubbed her own arms and shuffled her right foot behind her left. "He is your husband. What if it became known? I would have to be his concubine, and I don't want that life. I can't even play an instrument. I don't sing. I don't even dance well or do anything that concubines do."

"It can be a good life. I will make sure of it." Ankhesenamun squared her shoulders to Mut and grabbed her hands and pulled them to her chest.

"I don't—"

"You will never go hungry, you will have the luxuries of royalty, you can bathe and lounge all day, you will—"

"I will never have children, never be loved for me, never have peace." Mut grimaced at that future. "I am sorry, Ankhesenamun. That life is not for me. I want to be loved. I want to have children. I want my own husband."

"Even as a second wife?"

Ankhesenamun looked as if she regretted the words, but it was the truth. Mut knew she was almost eighteen now and not yet married.

"A concubine is better than living alone. Better even than a second wife."

Mut looked at her with one eyebrow raised. "I see what you are doing."

"What?" Ankhesenamun asked, wide-eyed.

"You are comparing the life I want with the life you are offering. You want Pharaoh to marry me?"

"If you want a husband?" Ankhesenamun rose her shoulders to her ears and then let them drop. "It is not a bad life, and you would share at least one of your children with me."

Mut shook her head. "I don't think so." Tut was no Horemheb, and if she did not want Menna to touch her, she did not want Tut to touch her. She still saw him as the seven-year-old boy who her, Nefe, and Ankhesenamun were all friends with. There would never be anything between them. There would never be love. "And please do not command me to."

Ankhesenamun shook her head. "I would never command you to, Mut." She rubbed her own arms too as they both looked to the Nile.

"So what will you do?"

"I don't know." Ankhesenamun took a deep breath. "What will *you* do?"

"I don't know."

"Go to the man, like I said before," Ankhesenamun advised, grabbing Mut's hand. "If you will truly be happy as the second wife, then just go to him and ask. If he says no, then please consider my offer."

"Maybe . . ." Mut said at last.

"Maybe what?"

"Maybe I'll be Tut's wife and you can have some of my children." Mut squeezed Ankhesenamun's hand and they locked eyes.

"Why the change in mind?"

"The man I want will not want to marry me. I would never be happy either way, so which would you pick?" Mut's eyes searched hers for an answer. She still felt so lost.

"I cannot make the decision about your life for you, Mut."

"You are a good Queen and a good friend." Mut squeezed Ankhesenamun's hand a second time.

They began walking around the lake to get back before dark.

"Some friend . . . I have only spoken with you twice over the past years."

"For some friends years can pass, but it only seems like days." Mut shrugged. "I don't have many friends."

"Neither do I."

Mut was silent, her mind numb, not wanting to think, until they were almost back to the guards who stood waiting for the Queen. Ankhesenamun dropped Mut's hand, and Mut looked to her. "I will think on it, my Queen." Mut knew to use her title now that other ears could hear her.

"Thank you, Citizeness Mutnedjmet."

CHAPTER 18
THE TIME OF APPOINTMENT

TUT AWOKE IN HIS TENT SHORT OF BREATH. HE'D HAD A DREAM of his father tossing him from the window and laughing as he lay dying on the ground below. Tut shook his head and then sat up. Swinging his feet to the floor, he let out a moan.

A few months had passed since he had left for war. He'd injured his leg in battle a few days prior, and Horemheb had told him to stay in the camp to let it heal. He did not think any bones were broken, but as a precaution, Horemheb suggested he not fight until he was able to move without pain.

He huffed. *I am never without pain.*

He hit a fist against his leg. "Ow." He hung his head and pulled his hand away from his leg. He lay back down and rubbed his eyes, remembering how he had injured himself. Again, he had charged the enemy, attempting to lead by example by being brave and courageous, only to fall, again, from his chariot. He looked to his crown on its stand and his dagger made of ba-en-pet beneath it.

"Some divine appointment. Some gift of the gods. Some *blessing*. General had to save Pharaoh a third time," he whispered, lifting his legs one at a time back into his cot. "Right in front of the whole cursed army."

The sun had gone down for the evening, and he listened to the sounds of the army returning to camp. There were no victory chants or yells; he assumed this meant fighting would begin again in the morning.

A messenger came to Tut. "General Horemheb requests an audience with Pharaoh."

Tut nodded, and a few moments later Horemheb entered Tut's tent. Before he could speak, Tut blurted, "I guess you can accomplish much more when you don't have to watch out for me." He turned his back to Horemheb, shielding him from his legs. He didn't want his General to see him lying there like an invalid.

Horemheb approached and said nothing for a moment. He chewed the insides of his cheeks, scanning the hunched back and motionless legs of his Pharaoh. Looking to his own legs, he let out a heavy sigh and then dismissed the servants with a nod of the head. Once they were alone, he jutted out his chin and scratched it as he went and sat on the edge of Tut's cot. After a long day, his feet and legs ached. He peered over at Tut, recalling the same image from years before. This latest fall seemed to cause Tut to regress back to the small child on the Libyan battlefield.

Tut didn't bother to move or to rebuke him for sitting on his cot. He didn't even move.

Horemheb sat there for a moment and then wiped some blood spatter from his bronze armor that he had missed when he cleaned himself before approaching Pharaoh's tent. He stretched out his leg and flexed his foot, then let it drop and did the same with the other. The *thud* of his heel on the ground with each drop of his foot reverberated up into the cot on which Tut lay, but still the lad did not speak.

"The army waned without your presence, Pharaoh," Horemheb finally said.

"Why? They didn't need to keep me safe while also fighting a battle." Tut hugged his head closer to his chest, and his voice came out as a murmur.

"You are a symbol of the gods' blessing on them and on their endeavor." Horemheb paused and watched as Tut mulled over his words. "I was wrong to suggest you stay at camp. Tomorrow you should come, but direct your soldiers from a distance. At least then the men would see you and be inspired to fight with the gods' blessing."

"I don't inspire anyone, General." Tut clenched his arms tighter round his chest, as if he were trying to disappear. "Even my chief royal wife may have not been inspired by me," he whispered, his eyes darting to Horemheb.

"What do you mean?" Horemheb found his gaze.

Tut looked away as soon as they locked eyes and sucked his bottom lip into his mouth. "Nothing," he said after a few moments. "I believed her for the most part, but . . ."

Horemheb stayed silent.

After a few moments, Horemheb's stare must have sat heavily enough on Tut's back for him to take a deep breath and continue. "Pawah says he has a list of eyewitness accounts of her with other men. He thought my daughter was not mine." He kept his gaze locked on the wall of the tent in front of him.

"Pharaoh—"

"I wouldn't blame her, as *you* said. I mean, look at me. I am not a full man. Why would she want to be with me? I am almost five years her junior. I can't even stand in a chariot. Can't walk like a normal man. I'm tall, but I'm crippled. I haven't been to her bedchambers all that much since . . ." His voice trailed off as he lifted his head. "The only reason she agreed to marry me all those years ago was so she could be chief royal wife." He slammed back down into his cot.

"She was already a Queen of your father's," Horemheb pointed out. "She had nothing to gain by marrying you. She married you because at one time you were her best friend, and now she loves you."

Tut snapped his head to Horemheb. "But the list—"

Horemheb's voice boomed in response, "If your Vizier Pawah told you about this list—" He took a deep breath to calm himself and lowered his voice. "Whatever Pawah tells you, I would take with skepticism."

"Because he wants the crown?"

"Yes." Horemheb's jaw clenched and his hand turned into a fist; he knew to what ends Pawah would go to in order to get it.

"How do you know that?"

"He . . ." Horemheb knew he had agreed with Ay to not tell what Pawah did to Nefertiti, but Tut should know. Maybe Tut would appoint a new vizier and Pawah would lose his status even more; or, in contrast, it may give him the backing he needed to garner more supporters, for how could the son of the blasphemous King do such a thing to Pawah, their savior? He chewed the insides of his cheeks as he debated.

"Well?" Tut demanded.

Horemheb's shoulders dropped the tension in his neck as he finally decided to go against Ay and speak the truth. He locked eyes with Tut with a turn of his head.

"Pawah killed Pharaoh Neferneferuaten and arranged the murders of your father and Pharaoh Smenkare."

Tut's eyes bulged and his body grew rigid. "Why?" was the only word he could force from his lungs.

Horemheb squinted. "You know why. I have already told you."

"Then why didn't he kill *me*?" Tut sat up and crossed his arms over his chest. "My uncle may not be as trustworthy as I originally thought, but a *murderer*?"

A pounding in Horemheb's ears accompanied the image of Nefertiti lying dead with Pawah's bloody dagger next to her. A vein throbbed in Horemheb's neck. But as he clenched his teeth, he thought, *The boy is just another victim of Pawah. Pawah fills his head with nonsense. I cannot blame Tut.* His pulse settled and his jaw relaxed.

"The only reason he did not kill you is because the Libyans and Hittites took you away from him, and it was better for him if you fought the battles and he could gain more support while you were away. Now he does not strike, I assume, because we are in Waset, not Aketaten. His control is weaker away from Aketaten, and you have turned from the Aten disc and now worship Amun-Re, which gives the people less anger against you and your family."

Tut lowered his chin. "So did Ankhesenamun tell me the truth?"

"What did chief royal wife Ankhesenamun tell you?"

Tut slumped and his arms, although crossed, loosened across his chest. "That Pawah killed her mother."

Horemheb looked Tut in the eyes. "She did not lie. I was there. I was too late, but I was there." His jaw clamped shut to prevent a whimper as his chest again constricted around his heart.

Tut grew silent for a moment and avoided eye contact with Horemheb as his eyes darted from one side to another, bouncing between the two versions of the truth he had been told. "Then it is true . . . Pawah lies to me."

Horemheb looked forward to the tent door and then dropped his chin. He licked his dry, cracked lips; he longed for beer or wine—at this point, he'd even chance illness from drinking water from the Nile. Looking back to Tut, he forgot about his thirst and instead he let out a deep breath.

"I believe Pawah has always lied to you. I don't know entirely the reason why he has not struck to kill you yet. As I said, I only assume based on what I know and can surmise."

"What should I do?" Tut's voice wavered.

"What would you do, Pharaoh? Do not ask me. When I made that decision for Pharaoh Neferneferuaten, it cost her life. I was not there to save her from him." Horemheb looked to his hands, his calluses blistered from his khopesh. The day had been a hard fight. Yet the day waned in his memory, replaced with the image of Nefertiti dying in his hands. *You made me feel alive.* He clamped his hands shut to rid himself the image. He looked to Tut again.

"If what you say is true," Tut said, "I should exile Pawah . . . ?"

"I do not know, Pharaoh. I thought I knew what to do, but Ay says Pawah's supporters are indebted to the man. If you exile him, he will surely have you killed. If you *kill* him, he will be a martyr . . . and martyrs cannot be silenced. The people may associate you with your father, leaving us with the same problem as before. I just don't know. Like I said, the last time I advised a Pharaoh in this regard, she ended up dead." He shook his head at his own defeat and let out a huff through his nose. "The one thing I do know is this: I promised Pharaoh Neferneferuaten to keep all of you safe from Pawah. It was her last request."

"Pharaoh Neferneferuaten wanted *me* to be safe? She tried to kill me!"

"My Pharaoh, she was not in a good place for a long time." Horemheb wet his lips. "Years of turmoil sat upon her mind and shoulders. But when her time came, she saw clearly."

Horemheb hung his head. She had felt backed into a corner and did not know where to turn with the Hittite prince coming, Pawah at her door, and the people yelling for Tut. His heart hurt for her. He had proved unable to save her from any of it.

"So . . . that is why you protect me? That is why you save me in battle? To fulfill my predecessor's last request?" Tut crossed his arms again and leaned away from Horemheb, as if to shield himself from the answer.

"No."

As he looked upon Tut, Horemheb envisioned his own son questioning his love for him, and in that moment, he remembered his own father. He had worked all of his days to try and earn his father's approval, but he always seemed to fall short.

"You are Pharaoh." His half-lie made his eyebrow twitch. He silently cursed himself—he hadn't focused as much to keep it steady, with his thoughts on his own father.

Tut noticed the tic. His stare intensified upon Horemheb. "You act much more than General. Why do you protect me? Why are you sitting here with me? Why are you telling me all of this?" Tut uncrossed his arms and leaned toward Horemheb, glaring at him with what looked like hope. Hope for affection. For that one word: *son.*

"Because," Horemheb said, his mind racing, "because I don't want to see you hurt like your father, your uncle, and your step-mother. They all fell to Pawah. I failed them all. I will not fail you."

There was more, but Horemheb held it in. He could not accept him as his son, though he knew that was what the boy wanted to hear. But if Horemheb accepted him as this, as *son*, and then failed him like he'd failed the others, the pain and guilt would be more than he could bear. And now Tut was no longer a child. He could withstand the neglect of his own father; he no longer needed a surrogate father. He didn't need his General's love.

Tut's eyes searched for more, but when Horemheb did not say more, his shoulders slumped. "I am just a responsibility to you, then."

His whisper gripped Horemheb's heart, making him rethink his decision. "Pharaoh . . . I am your friend, too. I do not want to see you in pain. I do not want you to struggle."

Tut nodded, but that was clearly not the answer he needed.

Horemheb brushed off the current conversation, accepting his original reasoning—Tut was a man now; he could handle it. So he changed the subject back to the situation that placed them in Pharaoh's war tent. "I think you could make a good archer," Horemheb said, letting out a breath to calm his mind. "The khopesh and the chariot may not be the best for you."

"What?"

"For the rest of the battle with the Nubians. Maybe you should learn from the archers and be an archer without a chariot—an archer on land." He knew Tut could not walk and shoot an arrow, and even if he could he would be slow and an easy target. Without a chariot, an archer was only good in the beginning of battle. But perhaps that was where Pharaoh—*this* Pharaoh—needed to be.

In the ensuing silence, Tut thought about Horemheb's words. His eyes analyzed his General; clearly Horemheb no longer wanted to discuss the past. But still—Tut was determined. He would prove himself to Horemheb, and even if Horemheb lied to him, he would not let Horemheb save him a fourth time.

"No," Tut finally said, his voice quiet and somber. "I want to learn from you."

"I—" Horemheb began, his voice rising with an excuse—*I am not a good archer*—but then he shook his head and said instead, "Thus Pharaoh says. We will begin in the morning on the battlefield."

Tut smiled as Horemheb rose from his cot and bowed at the waist, waiting for Pharaoh's dismissal.

"Thank you, General, my friend." Tut nodded and signaled him to leave.

Horemheb nodded to him as well. "Pharaoh, my friend."

Once Horemheb was gone, the full weight of the conversation fell upon Tut. Pawah . . . Tut shuddered at the thought of being killed by his last living male relative, his uncle, the man who had called him *son* from so early on. He flinched at that thought. He'd considered the man his father. He'd been foolish, had thought someone cared about him. His forearms trembled and then grew taunt and his body fought between picking something up and chunking it across the tent, ordering Pawah's immediate death, and crawling into bed to wonder if what he had just been told was true.

Could he believe his General? Or was he just another who wanted the crown, filling his head with lies? The General was smart; he knew how to strategize. Pawah had said, many years ago, that Horemheb loved Pharaoh Neferneferuaten. Was all of this part of his strategy for the crown? Save Tut, comfort him, advise him, encourage him? He had studied Horemheb's face, but found no deception. Out of all the people here in the battle, he was going to have to trust him for now. The man had never given him any reason to doubt except that one look he gave Paramesse in Libya. What did it mean?

THE NEXT MORNING CAME AND HOREMHEB SENT HIS TROOP commanders to the battle line with the army as he and Tut stayed behind the range of the Nubian archers. He taught him to string a bow, Tut kneeling so he wouldn't need his cane. Then they used some wooden planks as target practice. Tut excelled at letting the arrow fly whilst kneeling, but when it came to standing, his foot would not support the weight needed for him to shoot the bow.

"This is why I will never be a full man!" Tut yelled, and threw the bow to the ground. The quiver of arrows still slung around his back, Tut grabbed his cane from the ground. "This," he yelled, waving the cane in the air, "will be what always sets me apart, sets me *back*, and I wouldn't be surprised if it kills me one day!"

Horemheb, with a calm hand, picked up the weapon. "Pharaoh, men train hard their entire lives to be archers in your army. You will not master the art in one day." He handed the bow back to him.

Tut sank in his outburst and could not look Horemheb in the eye. He reached out his hand to receive it back. His eyes focused on the sand and rock beneath his feet.

"We will modify for the weight distribution," Horemheb suggested, and ordered a nearby servant to go fetch a medical stabilizer used for broken arm- and leg-bones.

When the proper tools arrived, Horemheb made quick work of his improvised solution. Binding the stabilizer with a spear broken to the length of Tut's leg, he situated the moon-shaped cradle of the stabilizer under Tut's buttock and forced the handle into the ground.

"Lean on this," he whispered to Tut.

Tut shifted his weight to the wooden seat and felt his crippled foot go limp as his weight settled onto the stabilizer. He smiled at Horemheb and then lifted the bow, notched his arrow, and let the arrow fly. The *thud* of the arrow piercing the wooden plank put an even bigger smile on Tut's face, just as the sun went down for the evening.

"I am ready for battle tomorrow," Tut said as he went back to his tent. He motioned for Horemheb to follow him.

Horemheb nodded. "Thus Pharaoh says."

They made it back to Pharaoh's tent and Tut turned and plopped down on his cot.

"Tomorrow morning, then?" Horemheb asked him.

Tut nodded. "Thank you, my friend. You have always been good to me."

Horemheb smiled. "A man is always good to his friends."

"No," Tut said, and shook his head. "Not always. But you —you have shown me care and wisdom. I never thanked you for saving my life both at the northern border and here. I would not be where I am without you." Tut placed his cane across his lap, taking a deep breath, and studied Horemheb's face. "I always wanted a father who loved me for who and what I am." Tut smiled and wrapped his hands around his cane, twisting the smooth polished wood between his palms. "But I am glad I have a friend like you instead."

Horemheb pulled his bottom lip into his mouth; he did not know what to say that would not be overstepping his role as Pharaoh's General. Instead he remained silent for a moment, thinking. He held together the barrier he had placed around his heart with a fragile thread. Finally, he said, "I am glad I have a friend like you, too, Pharaoh."

The two looked at each other for a long while, Tut hoping for something more, Horemheb longing to call him *son* but too afraid.

"I will go see how the army fared today," Horemheb said, and waited for Tut's dismissal.

Tut stood instead and stepped toward Horemheb. "I will go with you."

"Thus Pharaoh—"

But Tut took a step without his cane and fell into Horemheb's chest with his arms thrown around him.

Horemheb closed his eyes and wrapped him in a strong embrace.

———————

THAT EVENING, HOREMHEB LAY IN HIS COT AND THOUGHT about Nefertiti's last request. He pulled the letter from his shendyt and read it again, focusing on the part where she asked him to marry Mut, as it seemed the most daunting to him.

"My love," he whispered, "why marriage? I could make sure she was taken care of in other ways. I could ensure the man she married did not beat her, and if she needed a divorce I could help her with expenses. She is only two years older than Pharaoh—twenty years younger than me. She reminds me too much of you, my Nefertiti. Marriage would not be fair to her or to me."

But he reread the letter a second time; it was her last request: to marry Mut and keep her safe. He had already told Amenia to expect a second wife; he scratched his chin, wishing he had not, wishing he had not told her anything.

"I'm sorry, Amenia," he whispered, and shook his head at his having failed her as well.

He laid the letter on his chest and detected a small trace of Nefertiti's perfume from the porous papyrus. He brought it closer to his nose so it laid on his neck and closed his eyes, imagining her with him.

"For you, Nefertiti," he whispered. "I will marry your sister if she has me, but regardless, I will keep her safe."

———————

AFTER A SEASON OF FIGHTING, THE NUBIANS FELL INTO retreat and the battle ended well for the Egyptians. Tut, at the very end, managed to shoot a few lethal arrows at the enemy. A smile accompanied the young Pharaoh as he journeyed back to Waset, his General by his side, his army—who now gave him their complete loyalty, being shown he was a Pharaoh who stood behind them and supported them, unlike his father—at his rear.

Upon Pharaoh's return, Pawah met him in his throne room before Vizier Ay had the chance to get there. "Ah, in peace, my son! I'm so glad you have returned home safe and sound."

Tut went to cut him off after he called him *son*, but remembered Horemheb's warning—this man wanted to kill him. And so he let Pawah have his statement. "Yes, General Horemheb and my army kept me safe."

"No, no. The *gods* keep you safe. Not the General."

Tut nodded agreeably, lest he give the man any more motive to kill him.

"Say, my son, have you given any more consideration to whom you shall name Hereditary Prince?" Pawah stepped closer to him and bowed his head, placing his hands on Tut's shoulders.

Tut thought about what to say. He did not want to name Pawah Hereditary Prince. Horemheb said he killed his father and had planned to kill him too. If he named Pawah Hereditary Prince, would Pawah kill him to get to the crown? Time would not be on his side if he did, and if Ankhesenamun could not bear him an heir, he did not want a liar—and possibly a murderer—to take his throne. But if he didn't, then what would Pawah do? The answer escaped him.

"Yes, I have thought about it."

"And?"

"And I will make a decree later. I am tired today."

"Thus Pharaoh says," Pawah said, and patted his shoulders, his eyes dancing. "I know you will choose the man who has been most loyal to you and loved you like a son." He locked eyes with Tut and gave a slow nod of his head.

Tut smiled at Pawah and simply nodded in return, letting him believe it would be he whom he named.

THAT EVENING, PAWAH WAS IN HIS BEDCHAMBERS DRYING himself from his bath. *This is the way to do it. No blood shed. Just a simple decree,* he thought. *I am such an honorable man. I love my country.*

A messenger entered Pawah's bedchambers and bowed low, afraid to speak.

"What is it?" Pawah said, rubbing his towel over his face and head.

The messenger straightened, his hands and voice slightly trembling. "Pharaoh has decreed that General Horemheb be named Hereditary Prince."

The statement lingered in the quiet air as Pawah stopped, frozen, as his anger melted the shock. *"What?"* Pawah lowered his arms, letting the towel drop to the floor.

The messenger cleared his throat and repeated in a less shaky voice: "Pharaoh has appointed General Horemheb as Hereditary Prince."

Pawah clamped his mouth shut, and with the rage of a thousand men, sent his hand flying across the messenger's cheek, knocking him to the floor.

"Get out!"

The messenger, holding his face, scrambled to his feet and didn't bother bowing as he left the room.

Pawah yelled and threw his table to the floor. Faience figurines shattered on the floor. He let out a guttural scream that attacked the stone walls and came back to pierce his ears. He fell to his knees.

"I will kill them both." His whisper burned his chest, but his threat fogged with doubt in his mind. "I do not have the support I had under Pharaoh Akhenaten. Why did I ever cut a deal with Nefertiti? I should have just led the rebellion and taken the crown by force!" He beat his chest at his own poor foresight. "I should have just killed the entire royal family in one fell swoop, and not left Amun's divinely appointed to chance. Now, the loyalty is not as strong. The economy and people's faith flourishes again. There is nothing to give grievance against the new Pharaoh." He threw his fists against the stone floor and yelled out again in his regret. "I must continue to pit Tut against those he trusts and make him dependent on me so that he changes his decree."

How to undermine Horemheb and Ay?

He smiled. He already knew what he would do with Ankhesenamun.

She was too easy.

CHAPTER 19
THE TIME OF PROPOSAL

As soon as General Horemheb returned from Nubia, Mut asked a messenger to bring her to him. They found him poring over maps of upper Egypt in one of the many libraries in Malkata. Mut waved the messenger to leave.

Horemheb had aged since she had last seen him, but he was still as handsome as ever. His arm muscles bulged as he placed his weight on them to lean on the table. Mut licked her bottom lip and took a breath of courage.

Will he remember me? What do I say? "In peace, General Horemheb, I've dreamed about our marriage and life together since I was a child"? No, stupid Mut. Just see if he even remembers you.

She stood a ways off. If he lifted his head, he would see her, so she stepped closer. "In peace—" Her voice was nowhere to be found, so she tried again. "In peace, General."

He looked up and his face went white, as if he had seen a god in human form. He stood up and froze, looking at Mut with wide eyes.

She walked to the table and looked across it at him. "In peace, General Horemheb," she said again.

He let out a breath as his face regained its darker hue. "I

apologize, Citizeness Mut." He shook his head. "You look too similar to . . ." His voice trailed off and his eyes dimmed. He cleared his throat and shook his head again. "How may I help you?"

Mut's heart quickened—he knew who she was after all. She smiled; her eyes gleamed. "I know it has been many years since we last saw each other, but I have come to ask your advice." She cleared her throat and rubbed the back of her neck, thinking to herself, *Yes, yes. I will just go from here. At least I didn't sound like a blabbering child!*

"Anything," Horemheb said, and motioned for her to join him on nearby chairs.

"Well, if I ask you"—Mut's fingers tingled as she realized she was purposely keeping her breaths shallow so Horemheb wouldn't think something was wrong with her—"you must promise what I am about to say stays between us." She bit her lip and noticed herself blinking more than usual.

"I promise," Horemheb said.

Mut noticed a smile rested on his full lips. She had to swallow first and avert her gaze as she felt her former nine-year-old self gush upon looking at him. She tried to keep the heat from rising to her cheeks, but it seemed to want to stay, just as it did ten years ago.

"Queen Ankhesenamun has asked me, since I am her friend and am not married . . ." Her cheeks blushed at her own foolishness. She should have either just stayed married to Menna or said yes to Ankhesenamun. She never should have come here. But she charged on: ". . . she has asked me to marry Pharaoh and bear children for her—"

"No," Horemheb said, quite bluntly.

"No . . . ?" Mut asked after a moment of silence. Her brow contorted. "Just no?"

Horemheb clenched his jaw, not even noticing the blushing of her cheeks, lost in his own thoughts. *I can't let her be the mother of the next heir, because then she will be involved in all of this too. Nefertiti asked me to keep her safe. Pawah will want his hands on her and her child. I can only help Ankhesenamun so much, for she is already married to Pharaoh, but I can help Mut much more. Nefertiti wanted me to marry her. Do I ask her? She looks so much like my love . . .*

He averted his eyes from Mut, not able to look at her anymore. *Nefertiti's last wish was for me to marry her and take care of her. And now here she is in front of me. The gods once again provide me the path I should take.*

He bent forward, resting his elbows on his knees, and summoned the strength to look Mut in the eyes once again.

She is not Nefertiti, he reminded himself.

"I don't mean to sound as a dictator to you, Citizeness Mut. You have your own life. You make your own choices."

Horemheb leaned back and scratched his chin before placing his hands behind his head, silently wishing he could lead her away from both paths: as Tut's wife and as his own. He finally perceived Mut's admiring gaze as it lingered at his arms, and he quickly dropped them.

I cannot do this, Nefertiti. He realized that Mut must still admire him as she did when she was a child. *It will not be fair to her. I can never love her the same as she loves me. I cannot disappoint her like I did Amenia.*

"You don't sound as a dictator to me, just someone giving their advice." Mut paused. "But may I ask why the curt 'no'?"

Horemheb took a deep breath, hesitant to ask her to marry him, but he leaned forward once more. As a final yes to Nefertiti's last request, he grabbed Mut's hand.

"Because, Citizeness Mut, I have stayed away all this time knowing you are much younger than me. I assumed you would marry someone closer to your age, but now that you are older and have not married, I want to ask you something."

He forced his expression still so as to not give away his lie. He could feel Mut's hand become clammy and the pulse of her heart quicken from his touch on her wrist.

This is not fair to her, but Nefertiti asked me to take care of her through marriage and now the time has come. My hand is forced.

His shoulders loosened, and his chest fell. "Before you make your decision to marry Pharaoh . . . would you consider marriage to me? As an alternate to bearing the next heir to the throne?"

He did it. It was done, and he felt sick to his stomach.

"You want . . . to marry me?" Mut asked, as if in a daze. But then, as her smile drifted into a line and her eyebrows pulled together, she let out a short breath. "Even after all this time not speaking with me or writing me?"

"With the death of Pharaoh Neferneferuaten, I did not think you would want to marry me." His voice dropped. "I failed to protect her."

Mut nodded, accepting his response, and half smiled before she changed her tone and furrowed her brow. "We mourned her, but I do not blame you." She released her face and smiled fully. "I will marry you, General Horemheb."

He felt a polite smile cross his face, and he nodded, swallowing a lump that had built in his throat. "Good." He hit his knee with his hand. "Good." He hit his knee with his hand a second time.

AS THEY MADE PLANS AND SET A DATE FOR HER TO MOVE TO Men-nefer, her eyes sparkled and her soul danced, but a small doubt darkened her sudden happiness—self-doubt. Her mother's words pushed themselves to the forefront of her memory: *Mut, you have a young girl's infatuation. . . . Let go and move on with your life. That is what your sister would have wanted.*

"Nefertiti," she hummed as she dwelt on her mother's words. Mut realized the looks he gave her now were not the same as those he once gave her deceased sister. She debated asking him if he ever thought more of her sister than of her —or if he even thought of her at all—but reminded herself that he had said he'd wanted to write her.

Twenty years . . . she thought. *But twenty years is not that unusual of an age difference when the man is as established and rich as Horemheb.* She brushed aside her doubts. *And it is what I've been dreaming of and waiting for. I am just being silly: silly thoughts of a jealous girl, nothing more. Why else would he ask me to marry him? Wife of General Horemheb, Mistress of the House, Mutnedjmet: I can already imagine our lives together, filled with children and happiness even as the second wife.*

She smiled and looked to her auspicious future.

AFTER LEARNING OF THE MARRIAGE PROPOSAL, AY, WITH THE rose of his cheeks burning in the shade of Malkata's rooftop, found Horemheb.

"You!" Ay jabbed a finger into Horemheb's shoulder. *"You!"* He jabbed again, spittle forming at the corners of his mouth.

Horemheb knocked Ay's hand away. "What?"

"I know what you are doing." Ay's old voice boomed from his chest.

" 'Doing'?" Horemheb's eyes narrowed as he clenched his jaw. *Old man, do not test me.*

"Do not play the fool. I know you loved my Nefertiti, and now you take her sister, my Mut? Why? To fulfill some fantasy with Nefertiti? Mut will never be out of Nefertiti's shadow in your eyes. I want her to have better than that. I want her to be *happy*! She will never be happy with you! Have your senses scattered, you coward?"

Horemheb's muscles strained against his skin, resisting the urge to punch the old man for his insult. Mut did deserve better, but he did this for Nefertiti, as her last request. "Ay," Horemheb spat through his teeth, "listen to me. Your granddaughter, Queen Ankhesenamun, has asked Mut to bear Pharaoh's children for her. Pawah would surely come after them both at some point, especially the child. Is that what you want?"

At Ay's silence, Horemheb continued. "This here, this is the letter from Nefertiti." Horemheb pulled the papyrus from his shendyt. "The one you handed me after she was murdered . . . at the docks. Do you remember?" He unrolled it. "Read what it says."

While Ay read, Horemheb spoke. "It was the only way I knew to keep her safe and honor Nefertiti's last wishes."

" 'Keep her safe'?" Ay's words were harsh as he ripped Nefertiti's letter in half. "You couldn't even keep my Nefertiti safe, and now you want me to entrust *Mut* into *your* care?"

Horemheb gritted his teeth as he watched the last remnants of his one love fall onto the floor. Then, with the burst of a thousand spears, he leaned forward into Ay's face. "You were Master of Pharaoh's Horses! *You* ranked higher than *me!*" His voice grew more bold and deep as the veins in his neck bulged. "You didn't save her either!" His breath grew labored as he continued, despite Ay's fierce glare. Horemheb beat his bronze armor with his fist. "*You* were her father. She had no living husband. *You* should have kept her safe. I know I failed her—do *you*? Or do you still blame others for your failure?"

Ay leaned forward, so the two men could feel each other's breath on their noses. Ay poked his finger into

Horemheb's chest. "You keep Mut safe, and you treat her like a queen." Then he wrapped his fingers behind Horemheb's corded neck and pulled his face as close as he could come without touching. "If you hurt her or neglect her in any way, I will curse you to an eternal death." Ay narrowed his eyes. "And you had better pray Pharaoh has an heir, *Hereditary Prince*. Do *not* involve my Mut with the turmoil of the throne. You will *not* fail her like you did my Nefertiti."

Horemheb jerked his head away and out of Ay's grasp. "You will not threaten me." His eyes narrowed, glaring right back. "I *will* take care of Mut."

Ay spat on Horemheb's armor. "You can forget about Nefertiti's other requests. My wife and I do not need or want your counsel in our sorrow." The sneer on Ay's face curled up to his nose. "And *I* will make sure Ankhesenamun is safe." He jabbed a finger into Horemheb's chest. "And *I* will teach her about Amun." He jabbed again. "And *I* will make sure Pawah never takes the crown." And again. "*I* am Nefertiti's father. She should have asked *me* to take care of *my* family! Not you!" He jabbed a finger in Horemheb's chest a final time. "*You* are just some disobedient, unskilled coward who couldn't even kill Pawah when given the chance and then lucked into the position of General! Rewarded after failure! Despicable!"

Every muscle in Horemheb's body strained as Ay turned and walked away.

AT THE TURN OF THE CORNER, AY STOPPED AND WATCHED Horemheb gingerly pick up the two pieces of papyrus. His old heart wished his daughter had written him a letter, something he could have held—but no, Horemheb had stolen her from him. If he had no letter, then Horemheb could live with a torn one.

He wished Mut would have just stayed unmarried or found someone else—anyone else but that man. He shook his head at her decision; but it was her decision. He had tried to tell her; he had pleaded, but Mut had just simply said, *I thought you wanted me to be happy!* How could he argue with that?

But that man . . . Horemheb had stolen another one of his daughters.

CHAPTER 20
THE TIME OF HOPE

TUT KNOCKED BEFORE ENTERING HIS WIFE'S BEDCHAMBERS. A great smile crossed her face at the sight of him, and his lips tingled with excitement. He wanted to run to her and wrap her in his embrace, but knew he might only look a fool—what if he fell and the servants, still in the room, were to see?

"Leave us," he ordered, his heart pounding.

He wet his bottom lip, as he waited for the servants to leave. She had told him the truth. She did love him.

I've been so ignorant. I will beg her forgiveness. All this time she loved me . . . and I left her to fight a war, tempting death.

Ever since Horemheb had said the same as his wife, a weight had lifted from his shoulders, knowing she had spoken the truth. His doubt of her loyalty waned as Pawah's list shrunk in importance in his eyes.

"Tut!" She ran to him and threw her arms around his waist, pressing her cheek into his chest. "I am so glad the gods brought you home to me."

He let out his breath. *If I cannot run to her, my wife will run to me.* A slight tear formed in his eye as he laughed and stroked her back. He pulled away, looking into her eyes.

"I have missed you, Ankhesenamun. I hated to leave you when you were still not well."

"I have healed," she said, but the light in her eyes dimmed.

Tut took notice of her fallen smile and the lack of luster her skin held just moments before. He cupped her cheek in his hand and stroked the fingers of his other hand down her neck and arm, letting the cane fall and allowing his wife to support his weight.

"We will heal together."

Our daughter would have been so lucky with you as her mother.

Ankhesenamun's luster came forth again before he lowered his head to place a soft kiss on her lips.

"I have missed you, Tut." She swung her arms around his neck and kissed him again.

"I became an archer," Tut whispered to her. "I was able to fight alongside my army like a full man, and I will be training with a master bowman to help me should I ever need to go to war again." He failed to hide a prideful smile.

Ankhesenamun beamed at him. "You always overcome. You should be proud. *I* am."

"No," Tut said as he took her arms from his neck. "Don't be proud of me."

His smile fell. *How to apologize? Where to start?*

He cupped her cheek, kissed her forehead, and found her eyes again. "There is something I need to tell you, for it weighs on me."

"What is it?" A slight quiver came to her lip, but she forced her smile to stay.

"I doubted our daughter was mine until I saw her face," Tut admitted, and his gaze fell to the floor lest he see her hurt. "But Pawah told me he had a list of people who said they saw you with other men."

"Tut, I never—" Her voice broke.

"I know." Tut looked to her again and put his hand on the side of her face, his fingers tracing her temple to her cheek. "I know now. General Horemheb told me about Pawah. He told me to not believe what Pawah says. He told me the same as you, and that is how I know you tell me the truth."

"I'm glad you believe me . . ." Ankhesenamun said, and let her phrase hang in the air.

"But?" Tut stuttered after a few moments of silence.

"But I wish you could believe me without the word of your General." Her body slightly fell away from his, her shoulders slumped.

"I believed Pawah over you," Tut said, wrapping his arm around her waist and pulling her closer again. "I took his word over yours. Forgive me. I am sorry, Ankhesenamun."

"Pharaoh does not apologize," she mumbled, and pressed her forehead to his chin.

"Look at me," Tut pleaded, and she reluctantly obeyed. "To the only woman who has ever truly loved me . . . *I am sorry.*"

A smile took over her slack features. She kissed him softly. He felt her breath as a cleansing breath. The sparkle returned to her eye as she spoke.

"All is forgiven. Always, Tut."

———

A FEW MONTHS LATER, IT WAS DECLARED THAT QUEEN Ankhesenamun was with child. The people gave offerings to Bes, Tawaret, and Hathor for safe delivery of this babe. The people rejoiced with Pharaoh and his chief royal wife.

However, it was not long before Hentmehyt began to offer wine again to Ankhesenamun. Tut even lay next to her as the steward brought the wine to her Queen.

"The stress of the day wanes. Hentmehyt is good to me,"

Ankhesenamun told Tut after her steward handed her the goblet. Ipwet, the cupbearer, stood off to the side, having drank some herself.

Hentmehyt's gaze fell as her fingers left the goblet. She bowed and said that she would return with another goblet if the Queen desired.

The servants left Tut and Ankhesenamun in her bedchambers.

"May I have a sip?"

Ankhesenamun offered it to Tut, who knocked his tongue against the top of his mouth after taking a sip.

"It is quite bitter."

"Yes," Ankhesenamun said. "I noticed, but the taste has grown on me the longer I drink it."

"Pharaoh's wine should not be bitter," Tut said, shaking his head, and rubbed his tongue over his teeth to remove the taste.

"Oh stop!" Ankhesenamun laughed and cast a playful hit on his chest and drank again.

"How can you drink that?" Tut grabbed the cup from her. He smelled it and then ran his finger in the cup itself. A gooey sap was at the bottom. "What is this . . . ?"

Ankhesenamun looked and her eyebrows rose. "I don't know." She wiped her finger in it, too, and tasted it.

"Don't do that," Tut said, grabbing her hand. "What if it is poison?"

"If it were poison, Ipwet would be dead. And poison is tasteless," Ankhesenamun said. "This . . . it is sweet and . . . sharp?" Words to describe the taste eluded her as she rubbed her eyes. "Sleep with me now. The day has tired me so." Ankhesenamun rolled into Tut's chest, her six-month belly rolling onto his thigh.

Soon, soft snores came from his Queen, and Tut, realizing she wasn't going to die of poison, took the goblet and examined it. Again he tasted some himself. It was indeed sweet and had a quick bite at the end. He would ask Vizier Ay in the morning.

He reached over and placed the goblet on the table and blew out the candle so the room only filled with moonlight. Tut caressed Ankhesenamun's face. "I love you." He traced her cheekbones in the moonlight. "And I'm glad you didn't drink poison."

She murmured in her sleep. He kissed her forehead and when she didn't wake he wrapped her in his arms and dozed beside her.

THE NEXT MORNING, TUT ASKED VIZIER AY ABOUT THE SAP AT the bottom of the wine goblet, but Ay did not know. He suggested it may be a type of honey; honey was used to sweeten bitter food and drink, after all. Tut seemed to accept Ay's answer, admitting that the wine was indeed bitter when he had sipped it. He would have sent it back for new wine, he explained to Ay, but since his wife enjoyed it, he let it be.

After Tut had left the throne room, Ay called Wenamen to him. "Try to find out the source of the sap. I don't trust anything anymore."

"Yes, Vizier," Wenamen responded. "I know a servant in the winery who is loyal."

A DECAN CAME AND WENT AND WENAMEN RESPONDED BACK to Ay, "The servant I know who is loyal to the throne has said the wine is poured from the main amphora and sent with Ipwet to the Queen's chambers every night. I even asked him to pour some into his hand to make sure it held its gold color. It did. There is nothing additional in the wine. I tasted it. It was fine."

Ay rubbed his chin. "Tell them to throw that amphora away, and to inspect all the amphora for this sap."

"Yes, Vizier Ay." Wenamen bowed and left to carry out the vizier's order.

Ay looked out to the courtyard, thinking, *I do not like this.*

CHAPTER 21
THE TIME OF HERITAGE

HOREMHEB RECEIVED A LETTER FROM HIS ESTATE JUST TWO months before his marriage to Mut. He read it in his bedchambers and then stumbled backward, sitting down at the edge of his bed and letting the letter fall to the floor. He closed his eyes and covered his mouth, hiding a grimace. As he let out a heavy sigh, he leaned his elbow to his knee and rubbed his temple.

"Amun-Re," he prayed, his eyes upward and a warble in his voice, "do you punish me for going against your appointed? Do you punish me for my part in Pharaoh Akhenaten's and Smenkare's murders?" His eyes squeezed shut again as his head fell into his chest. "Do you punish me for my love for Nefertiti? For my unfaithfulness to Amenia?" He rubbed his neck and then let his hands fall into his lap. "How much more? How much *more*? Forgive me. I cannot bear any more of this." His whisper reverberated within his chest.

The letter stated that Amenia had perished in her sleep. She had refused to eat, the steward wrote, due to heartache.

Despite the heat of the bedchambers, a sudden cold grew

within his chest. "I caused her death." He lay back on his bed, his arms open to either side, ready for the great goddess Ammit to take his heart. "I have failed Amenia as well."

A wave of guilt crashed over his body as he remembered telling her about his infidelity with Nefertiti.

My Nefertiti . . .

He remembered her face and the scent of her lotus-blossom skin.

Amenia is the one who died, yet I mourn and remember Nefertiti at the news of my own wife's passing. Curse me. I am not worthy of either of them. It grew harder to breathe. *I should have loved Amenia. I should have loved my own wife. Why does failure follow me like a bad stench? Why can I not save those under my protection? I am General of Pharaoh's Armies. I should never fail. I am sorry, Amenia. I am sorry, Nefertiti. I am sorry, my son.*

Tears did not fall, but numbness took their place. "Forgive me. Hear me. Please. I cannot bear any more."

———

HOREMHEB SPARED NO EXPENSE IN HIS WIFE'S BURIAL. IT WAS the least he could do. Her brothers seemed to be pleased with the elegance and wealth of her tomb, given Horemheb's status. His father sent his regards but could not attend due to his own deteriorating health.

Once the shaft and tomb were closed, Horemheb stood at the entrance. He dipped his chin and prayed that she would find peace in the afterlife and that he could make up for his transgressions against her.

His mind raced back to Nefertiti's words in her final letter: *I have so much guilt, my love. It weighs my heart. Pray for Ammit to not devour it when placed upon the balance in the afterlife. Eternal unrest is more than I can bear.*

"As do I," Horemheb whispered to her ka. "As do I." His

words barely floated from his mouth.

He left for his father's house. Before he stepped foot in his estate, he took a deep breath, not sure what to say or what to expect. *I haven't seen or spoken with my father in a very long time.*

When the servants showed Horemheb inside, his father was in his room on a chair next to his bed.

"In peace, my dear son," his father said with a slow nod of his head. He pressed his lips together, as if he wanted to say many things, but only sympathies came forward. "I am so sorry to hear about Amenia. A wonderful woman she was. I wish you two were able to have children so you could have some remnant of her still."

Horemheb only nodded and swallowed a lump in his throat.

"She died so young. Was she ill? She would come to me every now and then and help me, keep me company." His father looked out the window and touched a dried rose on the bedside table.

Horemheb closed his eyes and dropped his head, his guilt further weighing on his shoulders. "She was a better daughter-in-law than I was a son."

His father chuckled with a sadness in his eye. "Yes, she was." He touched the dried and fragile petals with a tenderness. At Horemheb's silence, his father repeated the question. "She was ill?"

Horemheb did not know what truth to give him. He seemed much more relaxed in his old age than he had been when Horemheb was a youth. Horemheb's thoughts drifted to his childhood and his father's constant berating: *You'll never amount to anything. You won't even make Troop Commander like me. Try harder, son. I don't accept anything less than perfect. If you can't attain perfection, you'll never be a good son—*

"Son?" His father's words pierced his thoughts.

"Yes?" Horemheb lifted his head and looked him in the eyes.

"Was she ill?"

"She was . . ." Horemheb let out a breath and determined that his father might as well know; it would all come to light in a few months when he married Mut. "She was ill of heart."

His father shook his head. "What does that mean?"

Horemheb's gaze dropped to the floor as he pressed his lips tight, now too embarrassed to admit to his father what he had done and how he had treated Amenia all these years. Maybe if she had not loved him, as he had always assumed, his treatment of her would not weigh so heavily on his heart.

"Son, what did you do?" His voice was no longer kind, but cold and harsh.

Horemheb pinched a smile and crossed his arms. *That's the father I remember.* Tension strung along his neck and shoulders and he narrowed his eyes, focusing on the wooden floor beneath his feet. "I loved another." His voice matched his father's.

"You *what?*" his father asked.

Horemheb lifted his chin and peered down at his father. "I loved another woman," Horemheb stated again. "I told Amenia that this woman's dying request was for me to marry her young friend and take care of her. Amenia was heartbroken—"

"Of course she was." The same flat look that stared at Horemheb in his youth stared back at him now. "All these years of looking in on me, even when her own parents were still alive, bless their journey to Re. Do you not think she told me of her despair and work in earning your love?" Then he spat, "You have achieved nothing!"

"I have achieved *General* of Pharaoh's Armies." Horemheb's voice boomed throughout the small room. "I cannot go any higher in Pharaoh's army, but with Pharaoh Tutankhamun naming me Hereditary Prince, I may someday be King of Egypt if he has no heir. I cannot go any higher than Pharaoh. What more do you want from me, the son"—Horemheb jabbed a finger in the direction of his father—"of a *commoner?*"

"I wanted you to be a good man."

The statement stopped Horemheb's tirade and rippled through his insides.

"I *am* a good man." Horemheb stood up straight as he looked down at his father, now old and crippled.

His father only nodded and pulled his lips into a pressed smile. "Hmm . . . you say you are a good man." He found his son's eyes. "Yet you allow your wife to believe she was loved when you loved another?"

Horemheb's chest grew tight, constricting his throat; he shut his mouth and swallowed before beginning his defense. "I did not know Amenia loved me. I thought I did what was best for her, given her . . ." He paused; his father had never known about her infertility—but she was gone now, and it mattered little if he knew or not. "Given that she was barren."

"Son, I knew that." His father folded his hands in his lap. "She told me a long time ago. You failed to realize that what was best for her was to *love* her, regardless of whether she could or could not have children. She was your *wife.*"

Horemheb threw his fist to his side and began to pace. *All this time, he knew? Did her parents know? The whole reason I did not divorce her was so she would not have to make her infertility known. She was my wife . . . but I did not love her.*

He stopped, looked out to the courtyard, and shook his head. "They are both gone now. I cannot change anything."

His mind turned to the polished copper mirror on the wall above his water basin, and again he saw his face looking back at him. *Your father is right. A good man would have loved his wife.* He wanted to punch it until he no longer recognized the failure of a man in its reflection.

"You can marry that girl, the friend of your lover. Love her as you should have loved your wife with the same love you gave the other woman."

Horemheb hung his head. "You do not understand."

I cannot love her the same way. She is her sister. She looks so much like her. I just can't.

"I raised you to be a good man. A good man honors his agreements. A good man loves his wife. You could have been a stone mason or a goldsmith, I would not have cared."

Horemheb spun around. His chin quivered. "You wanted me to take after you! You raised me to be in Pharaoh's army! I had to leave Amenia for seasons at a time, years even—"

"At first, yes. But after I saw what your mother had gone through, it was not what I wanted for you." His father shook his head and then let out a deep breath. Tears actually came forth in the old man's eyes. They had never graced his face when Horemheb was a child. "But when I tried to tell you, when I tried to make you see, when I proposed marriage between you and Amenia, you did not take my advice."

"What advice? I was never good enough for you. *That* was your advice. You pressured me into the marriage. I never loved Amenia the way a man should love the woman he marries."

"Then you should never have married her. But you did. When you chose to marry her, you should have honored your word to her." His father's eyes were cold. "But you were determined to go all the way to the top. You went in the opposite direction I wanted for you. But yes, I suppose you did it." His mouth held a slack grimace upon his hollowed cheeks. "You achieved more than ever I did in Pharaoh's army, and at such a young age." His words were as flat as his feet.

"Father, I thought you—" Horemheb shook his head as his shoulders slumped. "I thought you wanted me . . ." He trailed off.

Was his entire life one big miscommunication? One big failure? Could he have had happiness with Amenia, adopted children, lived his life as a goldsmith or a stone mason doing hard labor on the gods' temples? He would never have known Nefertiti, never felt such sorrow at her death. He would never have lost a son before knowing him. He would have saved a lot of heartache, but . . .

But doubt still lingered in his mind. He didn't think he would have ever loved Amenia the same as he had loved Nefertiti, but had he even given Amenia a chance for his love? Finally, the question that he had wanted to ask his father since he became a man came to the front of his lips. He paused before they spilled out.

"Then . . . am I failure in your eyes?"

His father only sat back in his chair, and his gaze fell. "I'm tired, Horemheb. Please let me sleep."

Horemheb clenched his jaw and sagged his body against the wall for a moment before he stood again to leave.

"Horemheb," his father called, just as Horemheb opened the door.

Horemheb looked over his shoulder.

"A good man loves his wife. If you marry that young woman, the friend, love her. Love her, and then all of this will matter not. You have your past, but it is up to you what you do with your future. I learned that lesson too late in my life. Your mother—your poor mother—she took the brunt of it. Do not be like me, Horemheb. You will die alone—a failure where it means the most."

Horemheb lowered his head for a moment. Before leaving, he said, "Get some rest, Father."

CHAPTER 22
THE TIME OF MARRIAGE

HOREMHEB STOOD ON THE VERANDAH OF HIS MAIN HOUSE, waiting to bring Mut into his Men-nefer estate in marriage, as they'd both agreed. When Mut crossed the threshold of his estate, she would be his wife. He'd lost sleep as this day approached, and now his stomach tumbled within his core as she came with her boat full of things and her own two servants, Raia and Tener, ready to move in.

He looked at her; everything, down to her wig—although less ornate—gave her the same shape as Nefertiti. Or rather, Nefertiti when she was not wearing her crown. Mut's long, slender frame held her long neck the same as her sister. The only perceivable difference Horemheb could find was how Mut's face took a slightly more round shape. She was almost as an apparition to him.

Horemheb smiled at Mut as she walked to his main home through the courtyard of his estate, her servants following behind with her items. Horemheb blocked her path to the entrance, standing with his hands by his sides. He wished Nefertiti were walking to him, and in a haze he imagined Mut as her; for a brief moment, he found peace again.

Mut's words broke him from his trance. "Horemheb, won't you let me in?" She dipped her chin and lifted her eyes to his.

His smile lessened when he heard Mut's voice instead of his love's. After a quick race of his pulse, knowing that Amenia had died because of his behest that he marry Mut and that Nefertiti was gone, with this as her last request, he stepped back and let her walk across the threshold of his home. He followed behind her.

She went to grab his hand, but he pulled away. She looked to him with an eyebrow raised, and it filled him with dread. He would leave her tonight to settle, knowing eventually he would have to consummate the marriage, lest she divorce him. Without her in his home, he would not be able to keep her safe. But he couldn't, not tonight. She pulled her hand back and her smile disappeared.

This marriage isn't fair to her, he realized upon seeing her confused expression. Amenia was right; my father was right. I will be a good man. I must make it fair to her, he thought, *but I don't know how. I love . . .* He sighed. *I loved Nefertiti, and Mut is her sister. I can't be with her. . . not now, not tonight.*

The servants who had worked under Amenia's stewardship now sneered as Mut walked through the entryway. Horemheb had gathered them to meet their new Mistress of the House. Their whispers filled the hall.

"She's so *young* . . ."

"She's younger than *me.*"

"He wanted *this* over Amenia?!"

Horemheb, in his deep, battlefield voice, boomed, "Silence! This is my wife, Mutnedjmet. You will respect her as you did Amenia. You will keep her safe in this household. That is my command as owner of this estate. If you cannot abide by this order, you are free to find employment elsewhere."

The silence in the house grew maddening until Horemheb was satisfied of their understanding.

He showed Mut around the estate most of the day, and as evening came, they shared a meal in awkward silence. They retired to the bedroom, Mut entering first and followed by Horemheb, who left the door open.

Mut looked to him again with a raised eyebrow. Then her face relaxed and she lifted her shoulder to her chin. "Are you afraid of me?" A half smile arose on her face.

"No, Mut. It's—" He dared not tell her about her sister, his love for her and her final request. He did not want another to die of heartbreak. "It's just that I am tired. You bathe and sleep here tonight. You must also be tired after your long journey here. You will be safe here—" Mut looked to him as her posture loosened and her hand stroked the base of her neck. Horemheb hurried through his speech. "Sleep well tonight. I will sleep in the secondary bedroom."

He did not give her a chance to respond as he stepped into the hallway and closed the door. He leaned back against the wood and let his head fall back.

What have I done? He thought. *She looks so much like her sister . . . O Nefertiti, why this? Why marriage? I cannot do this. It tears my soul each time I look at her. She reminds me of my failure. She reminds me of you. She reminds me that you are gone.*

He closed his eyes and pushed off the door to go to the secondary room to bathe and sleep. He planned to rise early and leave a note saying he was called to Malkata. He would be home at an unknown time. He knew it was dishonorable for a man to leave his wife—especially the day of marriage—but he could not bring himself to touch her.

MUT STOOD IN HER NEW ROOM, LOOKING OUT TO THE courtyard and to the Nile beyond.

"Well, it is a beautiful view," she told her two servants in a quiet voice. "At least I have a nice bed all to myself with a nice view of the trees and the Nile." She wiped a tear from her eye, and her servants drew near to her. She spun around to face them and spoke, her words breaking. "Am I fool for marrying Horemheb?" she whispered to them.

"No," Raia said to her. "He is only tired, as he said."

"Do you think he truly loves me? Or do you think this was arranged between my father and him? He said I would be *safe* here. What an odd thing to say. Is there something happening in Waset? Father wanted me out of harm's way, so Horemheb only married me to move me here?" She held her breath and bit her lip.

"We have heard of no such thing."

Tener shook her head to Raia, as if to confirm she had not heard anything either.

A heavy sigh came forth from Mut's chest, and her hands raised to cover her face for a moment. "He barely spoke to me all day. He just showed me around. Didn't touch me. Said nothing to me about how happy he was or that he wanted me here. He almost didn't even let me inside. He hesitated when I asked if he was going to let me in. Again I ask you: Am I a fool?"

She leaned toward her servant girls, wanting them to refute her and tell her they saw no such thing. That they had heard him say to another servant that he was *glad* she was there. Something . . . *anything*.

Suddenly, the door flew open with no knock and two of the original servants under Amenia came in. They pressed their lips into a polite smile and narrowed their eyes at the three women. They then threw the linen sheets on the bed, not bothering to wrap the mattress or the cushions for the headrests. Without acknowledging Mut or waiting for her dismissal, they walked out and shut the door with a loud *thud*.

"Something tells me they don't like us," Tener said to Raia and Mut, smiling wryly.

Mut stared down at her empty hands, chest caved. "I wish my mother were here," she whispered.

Her mother's words came to the forefront of her memory: *You will not be happy waiting for Horemheb!*

She brushed those words aside, wincing. Her mother may be right, but she wasn't going to give up. Not yet.

Tener and Raia nodded, but Raia spoke up: "You are now the Mistress of the House and head of General Horemheb's estate. You need to show them you are the master now."

Mut nodded and wiped her nose. "Maybe tomorrow." She looked to Raia. "I think I will bathe now."

Raia nodded and went to heat the stones for the water.

Mut turned to look out to the courtyard again in the growing dusk. She could not get Horemheb's statement out of her mind: *You will be safe here.*

"Do you think Horemheb is just keeping me safe? Then, whenever the danger is out of Waset, he will divorce me? Or, even more embarrassing, this is all a fake marriage set up by my father?"

Tener remained silent.

"I just thought he wanted to marry me . . . it seemed he did. It was all I wanted." Mut's whisper made her breath hitch. "Do you think I am a fool to marry him?"

"No."

"Do you think he loves me . . . ?" Her voice fell low near the end of her question, not wanting to hear the truth.

"He is twenty years your senior and had not spoken with you since your sister's death." Tener wound her fingers in front of her chest and kept her voice low. "If you don't mind me speaking freely."

Mut stared at Tener. "So you do think I am a fool."

"I never said that." Tener clenched her hands and dipped her chin, avoiding Mut's eyes.

Mut bent forward on the window sill and lay her head on her arms. "But you meant it."

"Mistress of the House, I trust your judgment. You would not have married him if you did not think he would take care of you, meet your needs and treat you well."

Tener rubbed Mut's back, just as she had seen Tey do when Mut needed comforting. Mut stood up, her arms crossed over her chest. They found each other's eyes, and Tener's hands fell to her sides.

"I suppose. I just had hoped he loved me as well." Mut wiped a tear from her eye as she walked with a heavy step to her bath.

Tener stood and looked out, admiring the stunning courtyard view. "We cannot get everything in life," she whispered to herself. "Though it appears she got most of it."

CHAPTER 23
THE TIME OF DEATH

WHEN THE TIME FOR ANKHESENAMUN TO GIVE BIRTH DREW near, Pharaoh held a feast in honor of his coming child.

"Don't you think it is a little early to celebrate?" Ankhesenamun whispered to Tut. They sat at the royal table, on a platform above the festivities.

"No, of course not," he said as he rubbed her nine-month belly. He kissed her stomach and then her lips.

"Tut," Ankhesenamun whispered, and her eyes darted to the guests. "Not here. You are Pharaoh."

The Amun priests and the stewards of Malkata had told them about the strict formality of Pharaoh's actions and words. Pharaoh was not to show any affection. He was to command the utmost respect from all, just as his grandfather had. He was to be on a level above all others, and when he wanted to show affection or speak without the convention of Pharaoh, he was to dismiss all so that they would not see or hear him do so. It seemed they wanted Tut to bring back the former respect for the throne of Egypt, the respect his father had diminished.

His gaze fell to her lips and then back to her eyes as his

smile grew broader. "I have been so happy, and I know *our* child will only make me more complete."

Ankhesenamun smiled back, but not as fully. A fear lurked in the back of her mind; she remembered the birth of her first daughter so vividly every day. "I have been happy as well."

Tut wrapped his arm around her shoulder. "But what else is it, Ankhesenamun? Anything you ask you will receive." Tut held her hand and ran his thumb over her fingers.

She hesitated as her breath wavered, still afraid of what the guests would think of his prominent affection toward her in the open hall, but more so, she feared losing this child too. "It's nothing, Tut."

He rubbed her hand amid the feast as his guests drank and ate to their content and then stroked her arm. "Tell me."

She looked down at her belly and rubbed what felt like a foot on the side of her stomach. "What . . . what if our baby dies like our first child?" Her hand dropped and tears welled in her eyes. "What if my body cannot provide for a living child?"

Tut lifted her chin and found her eyes. "Then we shall mourn this child like we did the last and then try a third time and a fourth and so on." He guided her lips to his and then rubbed her belly. "Many offerings and prayers have been given for this child—by all the people, all the priests, all the slaves and servants. Prayed for since we knew you were with child. The gods will surely hear our prayers and accept our offerings. We have returned Egypt to them, we rebuilt our foreign relations, our borders are finally at peace, and I have the most beautiful woman in all the lands as my wife and the mother of my children. Egypt is flourishing again, and I have condemned my father's ways. The gods are pleased with us. They will surely grant us a child."

Ankhesenamun smiled at Tut's infectious touch. "Surely, a living child."

A lurking doubt held in Ankhesenamun's mind. Other noble women talked of children moving while in the womb, but she had never felt her first child move . . . nor had she felt this new child move for some time. When speaking to the midwives and other noble women, she had only smiled and agreed that the feeling of movement was wonderful, not wanting to acknowledge that maybe she had done something to her children.

After taking a sip, Ipwet placed a goblet of wine in front of Ankhesenamun. She bowed and walked to her place to await further goblets. There was a short, passing glance between Ipwet and Pawah as Ankhesenamun took a sip of her wine.

Vizier Ay, his wife, Tey, their daughter, Mut, and her husband, General Horemheb, came forward to the royal table and bowed before Pharaoh and Ankhesenamun. They brought gifts of frankincense, myrrh, and kapet for them to burn in the morning, the day, and the evening as an incense in their worship. Mut brought a blanket that had been her sister's. She came forward and bowed to Ankhesenamun, handing her the folded linen and wool.

"My Queen, this was your mother's, my sister Nefertiti. It was passed to me, but I wish for you to have it."

Horemheb chewed his lip as he watched the exchange.

"This was my mother's?" Ankhesenamun asked, and pressed her nose into the faded blue and white threads. She looked to Mut with tears in her eyes. "Thank you, Mut. This means more than you know."

Horemheb lowered his head and his eyes.

Mut smiled. "I thought she would want her grandchild to have it."

Ankhesenamun lowered the blanket to her swollen belly and smiled. "She would."

Tut rubbed the back of Ankhesenamun's neck and kissed her cheek at the sound of happiness in her voice.

THE FEAST WANED AND THE GUESTS WERE DISMISSED. PHARAOH and his Queen thanked each of them for coming.

Ankhesenamun pulled Mut from view and wrapped her arms around her. It had been a long time since Ankhesenamun had seen her, and yet Mut was just as sweet as she remembered her. "Thank you, Mut. Please come by again when our baby is in my arms. I want her to meet her great aunt."

Mut smiled and dipped her chin. "I will."

Her eyes held something, Ankhesenamun thought, but she was too tired to ask, and it seemed Mut did not wish to discuss. A good friend would ask, she chided herself as Mut stepped away. Perhaps another time.

THAT NIGHT, ANKHESENAMUN WAS AWAKENED BY PANGS OF labor.

"Tut . . ." she whispered as her nerves jittered.

It was the right time for labor—not months early like her first child—but fear still gripped her heart as she remembered her first daughter's limp body.

"Tut," she said a little louder.

He stirred from his sleep.

She poked him in the arm. "Tut!"

He awoke with a start and looked to his wife, his eyes wide in the dark. "What's wrong?"

"The baby—" A deep pain locked her body, making her gasp.

Tut leapt out of bed and fell to the floor, remembering his bad foot too late. He crawled up the bed and grabbed his cane. "Don't worry, Ankhesenamun!" He quickly lit the candle and made his way to the door. Opening it, he yelled to Hori and Ineni, "Get Hentmehyt and the midwives!" Hori smiled and bowed as Tut shut the door. "Ankhesenamun!" he cried as he came back to her side. He sat on the bed and kissed her forehead and ran his hand down her arm. "We are going to have a beautiful baby!"

His wide eyes held an awe and excitement in them that caught the candlelight. She remembered his words: *All of Egypt has prayed for this child. Surely the gods will grant us a living baby.*

She pushed her fears to the back of her mind. His contagious energy helped her get through the pains, remembering Hentmehyt's wise words of advice in her last labor: open hands, long breaths, think of anything else besides the pain.

Hentmehyt and the servants came and helped her walk to the royal pavilion set for her birth. "This is where your father was born," an elderly female servant whispered to Tut.

Tut smiled, looking around. "The next King might be born here as well," he said as he watched the servants help Ankhesenamun with her labor pains.

"Pharaoh, if you will leave us?" Hentmehyt asked, looking at Tut. She was smoothing out Ankhesenamun's hands against her shoulders while another servant ran her hands down Ankhesenamun's lower back.

"If the Queen desires it, I would like to stay," Tut stammered, and stood awkwardly in the midst of all the women.

They were all silent as they looked to their Pharaoh;

Ankhesenamun's groans were the only sounds filling the vicinity.

"That is a most unusual req—" Henmehyt began, but Ankhesenamun interrupted her.

"Please stay, Pharaoh—" She lost her breath as pain coursed through her body.

Tut smiled and lifted his chin.

When the time came for the baby's arrival, the midwife knelt in front of Ankhesenamun and the servants held her arms on the birthing stool. Blood ran down her legs and Ankhesenamun saw the midwife glance to Hentmehyt, pursing her lips.

Is this normal? Is it happening again? she wanted to ask, but the pain in her lower abdomen and bottom kept her words at bay. Ankhesenamun grimaced as she pushed, hoping, *praying* for a living child.

The priestess behind her chanted in a stronger voice, building upon itself as she held the Bes amulet over Ankhesenamun's brow: *"Hathor will bless her in this amulet of health! Horus will save her! Make strong the deliverer's heart, and keep alive the child coming!"*

The baby's head and then arms and then legs came forth.

"It's a girl!" Tut exclaimed, and kissed his wife on the side of her head, somewhat knocking the servant from her position. His smile grew from ear to ear as they looked into each other's eyes. "You did so good, Ankhesenamun," he whispered to her.

The servant tried to move back to her position to hold her Queen on the stool.

Through her labored breaths, Ankhesenamun smiled, but her eyes darted to the little body now in the midwife's arms.

Please cry. Please make a sound, she begged her daughter. *I cannot bear it again. Please. Please, Amun, Hathor, Bes, Tawaret. Please.*

The midwife turned the baby on her stomach and rubbed and patted her blue back.

"Why isn't she crying?" Ankhesenamun grimaced; she had asked the same question about her first daughter.

The midwife looked to the Queen before drawing a slow breath. "Sometimes, we must work to get newborn babes to breathe," she said, and continued to work the baby's back, but shook her head.

Tut only stood with his hands by his side, his face draining of excitement the longer the midwife worked.

Ankhesenamun's whimper came forth again: "Why isn't she crying?" Tears streamed down her face, as she already knew the answer to her question.

Hentmehyt's eyes watered as she gestured to the wet nurse to go to the midwife; then she stepped back with a hard stare in her eyes and a rigid lock on her jaw.

HENTMEHYT ENSURED ANKHESENAMUN'S HEALTH BEFORE leaving to find Ipwet. The royal couple's cries of grief followed her into the corridor as she went straight to Ipwet's quarters. She threw open her door, pulled her from her cot as she slept, and slapped her awake.

"What is it, Hentmehyt?" Ipwet asked, blocking her next slap.

"You tell that worthless piece of dung"—Hentmehyt held Ipwet's shoulders with both hands—"I will no longer be a part of his doings, even if he does choose to murder me and my family. I can see the Queen hurt no longer. Her second child has died."

Ipwet shrugged off Hentmehyt's hands and yawned. She shifted her weight and her head lazed to the side. "Babies die. Mothers die. It is the danger of childbirth. No one will blame us. No one will know." Ipwet rolled her shoulders back, forcing her eyes open even more as she spoke. "We agreed to do this, Hentmehyt, to save our own families. Pawah was our savior when Smenkare's purging came. We didn't see his ruthlessness until he came asking for payment. He threatened to burn our families. Would you condemn all your family to eternal nothingness? They would have no body to return to in the afterlife. You should reconsider."

Ipwet waited for Hentmehyt's response, but none came, so she let out a sigh.

"Hentmehyt . . . the Queen is fine. She will live. It is better this way."

"*You* don't have to see the Queen's tears . . . hear her cries . . ." Hentmehyt crossed her arms tightly over her chest and shook her head. "I don't care what happens to me. My heart cannot take it anymore!"

"What about your family, Hentmehyt? The child grew to full gestation. It almost didn't work," Ipwet said, rubbing her eyes. "We had to give her a full dose of silphium at the feast. Next time—"

"But her second baby still died!" Hentmehyt threw her hands in the air. "There will not *be* a third time. The third time she will deliver a healthy baby, untouched by the silphium's sap."

Ipwet took a deep breath and sat down on her cot. "I do not wish to die, nor do I wish for my family to die . . . What if we asked Pawah if we could give her silphium every day instead, not just after she has become pregnant?" Ipwet suggested. "That way she would never become with child. That way the silphium would never force death upon a third."

Hentmehyt threw her hands on her hips as she paced in front of Ipwet. "I already suggested that to Pawah, and he did not want it that way. He wanted her to become with child first, *before* he supplied the silphium to us to administer to her. That was when I truly knew how cold-hearted and cursed he is. To kill Pharaoh's child . . ." Hentmehyt's voice trailed off and she stopped pacing. "Using us . . . using me. We killed Pharaoh's child." Her hands ran down her face and she looked to the ceiling, letting her arms fall to her side.

Ipwet gave Hentmehyt a hard look. "Just do what he says and everyone you love will be safe."

Hentmehyt looked to Ipwet. "Everyone except the Queen and her children. I'd rather her just not be able to become with child than to do that to her again."

"As would I, but if we were to keep her from becoming with child, we would need more of the silphium, and it comes from Pawah. You said yourself he did not agree to it."

"But . . ." Hentmehyt wagged a finger as a thought appeared in her mind. "We could do it without Pawah's knowledge . . . and then we save ourselves and our families and I will not have a third child's life on my hands."

Ipwet raised her eyebrows as Hentmehyt continued to speak.

"We are in Malkata—the plant grows in abundance at the northern border. We can buy it ourselves. No one will think twice."

"And when it becomes known *we* supplied and administered the silphium, Pawah looks innocent. At least now, if we are found out, we can also point to Pawah and his threat of our families. We may come away with our lives, but execution awaits us if we do it on our own."

Her face drooped with each word Ipwet spoke.

"If she becomes with child again," Ipwet said, offering another alternative, "I will stock it up and give one full dose early in her pregnancy so it appears she only miscarried."

Hentmehyt shook her head. "I cannot bear it again. If she

becomes pregnant a third time, we dispose of the silphium and the poppy, and we only give her the wine. Nothing more added. We can tell Pawah it didn't work, and hope he believes us."

"Silphium always works . . . Why do you think they grow it in abundance?" Ipwet shook her head. "Pawah will not believe us. He has many supporters all over the palace. We don't know who would tell him they saw us disposing of his silphium and poppy, but if they do? *Then* he will carry through on his threat, that I am sure."

"Then what do we do?"

"What Pawah commands."

A long pause. Stillness overtook the two women until Hentmehyt finally shook her head.

"No. We will *say* we will carry out his plans, but we will not."

"I am not risking my afterlife for Queen—"

"You are a steward of Amun's divinely appointed and for his Queen. We all made a vow to do whatever it takes to protect them, even if it means having no afterlife!"

Ipwet scoffed and shook her head. "Strong words from a woman who has killed both of the royal children of Pharaoh Tutankhamun and his Queen."

Hentmehyt clamped her hand over Ipwet's mouth and pushed her backward. "You will watch your tongue."

Ipwet pushed Hentmehyt off of her. "Or what?"

"Should you not forget: I am the Queen's steward, and I have authority to remove you from Malkata, and your reputation will proceed you. You will die from hunger in the streets."

Ipwet had realized she could lose her position, of course, but it had never occurred to her that in being removed, she would never be employed again. Which was worse: certain death from hunger in the streets, or the chance of having no afterlife? She closed her mouth, narrowed her eyes, and nodded, making her decision.

"I will do whatever it is you order," she said through tight lips and clenched teeth.

"Good." Hentmehyt adjusted the wig upon her head. "Then it is decided. Should our Queen become with child again, we will dispose of the silphium and the poppy when received."

CHAPTER 24
THE TIME OF ACCUSATION

NEWS OF THE DEATH OF PHARAOH'S SECOND CHILD SPREAD throughout Malkata and then to the rest of Egypt, and all of the kingdom mourned the deceased princess save for one. The people prayed a third child come soon.

But Pawah did not need a third child to drive the final wedge between Tut and his wife. A few decans after the death of their second child, Pawah requested a private audience with Pharaoh. He did so after Ay had gone to Mennefer, to take Mut home while Horemheb stayed with his divisions in Waset, so that the old man would not be around to meddle. Tut reluctantly accepted Pawah's request, making sure that his guards lined the throne room should Pawah try anything.

"My Pharaoh." Pawah came and bowed before Tut. "My son, I come with grave news."

Tut's fingers curled at being called *son* by this man.

"Of course you do," Tut said, adopting a hard tone, and then took a deep breath, ready to hear what else his uncle had to say. "Is my wife seeing other men again?"

"No, my Pharaoh, but she commits an even more heinous

crime, and this I know for certain." Pawah bowed again before approaching the throne. His fingers glided on its golden arms. He then placed his hand on Tut's shoulder. His eyes lingered on the gold until he drew out of Tut's peripheral vision, standing above and behind him, his hands firmly on the younger man's shoulders.

"Oh, what is it this time, Vizier Pawah?" Tut rolled his shoulders from underneath Pawah's grip and continued looking forward—at the position where Pawah *should* be talking to him. He tilted his head away from Pawah.

Pawah smirked and leaned to whisper in his ear: "Ankhesenamun *kills* her children . . . the third child, should she conceive again, will not survive."

Tut's body went rigid, his neck stiff, before he let out a heavy breath. "That is the most ridiculous notion I've ever heard." Tut turned his head to face Pawah. "Begone with your lies." He threw his hand up to dismiss him.

"Ah, Pharaoh . . ." Pawah dodged Tut's wayward hand and came and knelt in front of the throne. "I do not lie."

"You have not seen her tears nor heard her cries." Tut shook his head and stood up to peer down at Pawah. "I know your accusation to be a lie."

Pawah dipped his chin and closed his eyes. "I overheard Hentmehyt, the chief royal wife's steward, admit it to the cupbearer. The Queen asked for wine with boiled silphium."

Tut shrugged. "So?"

"Do you not know, Pharaoh?" Pawah lifted his chin, his shoulders hunched in submissiveness like a good official of the King. "Silphium is known to prevent one becoming with child . . . but also to cause children already in the womb to die."

Tut stopped breathing for a moment. His mind raced back to the sap he found at the bottom of her wine goblet. His eyes darted as he tried to remember if Ankhesenamun had mentioned silphium. This was the first he had heard of it.

"You already know?" Pawah asked him, taking a step back.

Tut's hand clenched into a fist. "No, it is not true." He sliced the air with his other hand to sever his doubt. "And even if I were to believe you, there is no reason for her to do it!"

Pawah pursed his lips. "Well, she could be wanting you to name her Coregent . . . like her mother did with your father. You would not do that if you had an heir, I believe."

Tut's ears boiled, and he spat through his teeth, "You lie."

"Go ask her head steward, Hentmehyt," Pawah urged. His eyes narrowed. "She has no reason to lie. If you do not believe me, go hear it from the source."

"I will," Tut seethed, "and when I find you to be a liar, I will disown you, Uncle."

Pawah bowed. "I am no liar."

Tut pushed past him, his thoughts racing. Just when he thought he knew the truth, Pawah found a way to put doubt in his mind. Would it ever end?

TUT FOUND HENTMEHYT IN MALKATA'S ROYAL HAREM. He stepped close to her, removing any personal space between them, and looked her straight in the eyes.

"Tell me now: Did or did not my wife kill my children by asking for silphium?"

The surprise showed in Hentmehyt's eyes. But before the truth could fly past her tongue, Pawah caught the corner of her eye, lurking in the harem's shadows. She closed her eyes and hung her head, realizing her will had failed her—she was not fit to be the Queen's steward nor hold any position in Malkata. She disgraced herself as her lips spoke.

"Yes, my Pharaoh. My Queen asked for wine with boiled silphium."

The half-truth stained her tongue. The Queen had asked for wine, yes, which was harmless, but she had no knowledge of the boiled silphium, and half the time did not know even about the boiled poppy which made her crave wine every night.

Tut's nostrils flared as he lashed out and hit Hentmehyt with his cane. "And you gave it to her?! You worthless servant!"

He hit her until she scurried off in tears, not because of the cane's bruising slaps but because of the immense lie she told and the immense pain the lie brought.

"You disgrace Pharaoh and his name!" he called after her, his eyes filled with rage. Tut yelled in agony and in anger as he paced the hallway. His anger built upon itself, coming out in whacks to the stone and loud yells and punching of the air as he paced.

Pawah watched from a distance and all but smiled as he turned the corner.

TUT THREW OPEN THE DOORS TO ANKHESENAMUN'S bedchambers and marched in with his eyes aflame.

"Ankhesenamun!"

He stood with cane and foot planted to the floor, his free hand clenched in a furious fist by his side. The servants looked up, fearing for their Queen. He looked and did not see her.

He stared down a servant until she squeaked out, "She is bathing."

"Leave us!" Tut yelled, and the servants scurried out.

When the door closed, Tut marched straight to Ankhesenamun's bath chambers. He found her naked in her tub with lotus blossoms floating around her. She had her hands on her belly, and had not yet washed her face, as the kohl streaked her cheeks.

"Ankhesenamun!"

She held a vacant stare; her eyes, lined with dark circles, were red and swollen. Their daughters' lifeless faces haunted her sleep without end. Her body was as fatigued as her soul, and her voice was as numb as her heart.

"Why are you so angry, Tut?"

"You will call me 'Pharaoh.' "

She sat up in her tub and leaned her arms on the stone rim, wincing at the pain in her bottom. "Why are you mad—again—*Pharaoh*? Did Pawah tell you something *again* that you have chosen to believe?"

"No. Your steward, Hentmehyt, told me you ordered wine with boiled silphium."

Ankhesenamun curled her lip in disgust. "I did no such thing." Her voice enunciated every word and her fingers gripped the stone rim of the tub.

"You kill your own children?" Tut looked down to her with cold eyes.

All of the pain and loss and grief surged through Ankhesenamun as she let out a guttural roar, shooting up out of the water with such a force the water overflowed the edges and washed on Tut's feet. "I would rather *die* than kill my own children!" Her muscles strained against her skin. "And if you don't believe me over Pawah, then *you* never knew me!"

"Hentmehyt, Ankhesenamun, not Pawah! Hentmehyt told me so. Why would she lie? She has nothing to gain by lying!

She has nothing to lose either!" Tut's fist clenched, his eyes wide.

Ankhesenamun's ears pounded. "I don't know why she would lie—"

"You are the *liar!*" Tut pointed his cane at her, then quickly lowered it, needing it again. "You killed my daughters!"

She threw her hands in the air and then gently eased herself back into the tub again. She licked her lip and took a breath to settle her heart. Tears welled in her eyes as she swallowed her passion. Her voice, barely a whisper, spoke again.

"You were my friend once, and up until this moment, I loved you with every fiber of my heart."

Tut came near to her in a rage as she spoke, her voice growing stronger.

"For you I came back to Aketaten, knowing Pawah killed my mother. For you I put my life in danger. For you I have endured your unending accusations of betrayal—and now murder!" She spoke as a charging horse. "But I can see I am nothing to you, you hot-tempered fool!" She pounded the water. "They were my daughters too! I would *never* kill my own children! *Never!*"

"I want you gone by the end of the month." Tut sneered and turned to leave.

"Fine," Ankhesenamun said, her jaw clenched. "If you want to believe others over your wife, then so be it. But when you find out I have told the truth, I will *never* be yours again."

Tut stood there, his chest rising and falling as quickly as the changing winds. He peered over his shoulder. "You are not to leave your bedchambers except to the royal harem."

Ankhesenamun released a bit of tension in her shoulders, seeing he did still care for her—a little, at least—but disgusted he would think she would do such a thing.

He marched out, slamming the bedchambers doors behind him.

"You blind fool . . . you cannot see the truth," Ankhesenamun spat through her teeth. She took a heavy sigh and shook her head. "I will deal with Hentmehyt later."

She lay her head back in her tub, wishing she had left with General Paaten and Nefe all those seasons ago. She prayed blessings on them, and then cried, knowing her husband thought her a murderer and a lying, conniving demoness.

But most of all, she wished her mother were here with her.

CHAPTER 25
THE TIME OF ALLEGIANCE

A FEW DAYS LATER, ANKHESENAMUN LEFT HER BEDCHAMBERS and dismissed her royal guards, as she wanted to walk the halls of the royal harem alone. She found a seemingly empty corridor and slid down its stone wall. She looked up and down and saw no one—no servants, no guards—and finally she felt her heart scream, though no sound escaped her lips. She buried her head in her hands and curled her knees to her chest. Knowing she could not make a sound, for fear of someone finding her, she sobbed into her linen dress. Her life was an utter mess.

She heard footsteps and hoped they would pass on. She buried her head deeper, hoping the person would not recognize her, since she was not wearing her crown. Her gold-lined dress, collar, and wig gave her status away, however, for a familiar voice asked:

"My Queen, are you all right?"

She did not even look up. After spending so many days together in Aketaten, Ankhesenamun could pick his voice out of a crowd, but she feared him now. Someone might see them alone together and twist what it was into some perversion of a relationship to Pharaoh.

"Overseer of the Tutors . . . Sennedjem . . . please leave me in my lonesome."

"I cannot leave my Queen alone. Even though we are in Malkata, there could be danger around any corner."

He is right, Ankhesenamun thought. *But I don't want to be found alone with him. And then a realization hit her like stone: Maybe he was the one spreading the rumors . . . maybe he wanted to brag about how he bedded the Queen amongst the servants and officials. But no: Or maybe Pawah just made it up to have Tut distrust me. Sennedjem had nothing to do with it.*

She lifted her head. Her makeup ran with her tears, soiling her dress.

"Why, Sennedjem?"

Her thoughts raced with questions of why. Why both of her children died, why her husband believed she killed them, why she did not run away with Nefe. But Sennedjem answered a different why—why he would not leave her alone in a seemingly forgotten corridor of Malkata.

"Because even though you are Pharaoh's chief royal wife, you are still Pharaoh Akhenaten's daughter. There are some who do not like you, and wish you harm. I will not stand by while my Queen is vulnerable."

"Please . . . leave me. There are worse things than death." Her arms clutched her body, holding herself together in front of her subject.

"My Queen, please . . . do not make me leave you."

His voice lowered as he took a step toward her, erasing the distance between them. He reached out his hand to her but pulled it back when he saw her flinch away. She looked up and found him looking to her. They locked eyes. His firm, intense gaze upon her told her he was serious: he was not going to leave. It was the same look of determination as the day he found out she could be in danger at Aketaten with Pawah in Pharaoh's throne.

"Pawah still lives here," he whispered; a slight flush overcame his face and neck.

"I know, and he takes my husband from me. He lies to him about me and you, and the latest . . . I apparently have killed my own daughters." More tears welled in Ankhesenamun's eyes.

"What do you mean, about *me?*" Pink hued his cheeks. He shifted his weight and, seemingly unsure of what to do with his arms, he crossed them over his chest.

"Pawah has told Pharaoh that he has eye-witness accounts of you and me together," Ankhesenamun said, shaking her head.

"We were together every day in Aketaten," Sennedjem said, and tilted his head.

"No—together in bed," she clarified.

Sennedjem stepped back, his eyes wide. He dropped his arms as he stammered, "I do not know . . . what to say."

"Say nothing and leave me, before anyone else gives reason to Pharaoh. I'll assume the next thing he will do is have both of us executed."

"Pharaoh, he loves you, no? He would not execute his love. Maybe me, if he truly believes the rumors, but never his Queen."

"You have more faith in his so-called 'love' for me than I do."

She shook her head and gave a hollow laugh then shut her mouth—she was saying too much to a servant. But Sennedjem knew the truth about Pawah; he could be trusted, couldn't he? He was even, perhaps, a friend.

Sennedjem took in a deep breath and slid down the wall next to Ankhesenamun. "I know what I'm doing right now could get me exiled or punished, even executed . . . but I want you to know something, my Queen Ankhesenamun." He peered at her over his shoulder. "I would die for you. It is the oath I took a long time ago, and so I speak to you as a friend, if I can be so bold as to call myself your friend."

Ankhesenamun hesitated and swallowed what she could from her dry throat. She found his eyes and knew he meant what he said. She gave a slow nod for him to continue.

"Remember when we were training while Pharaoh was away to war? You kept dropping your guard, and I was able to tap your shoulder every time."

Ankhesenamun shook her head and closed her eyes. "Is this how you make me feel better?"

"No, no, hear me." He leaned his shoulder toward her. "Do you remember?"

"Yes, I remember. I never was good at the fighting sticks." Ankhesenamun's voice was muffled, her head buried in her arms.

"But you improved every day. You endured through the heat and the training, day after day. You were determined. You never gave up. When I realized you trained for your life, I realized you are a warrior at heart. You have what makes great men great, and you are our Queen!"

A small smile crossed Ankhesenamun's lips as Sennedjem continued.

"Pharaoh is blinded by Pawah and his schemes, but you will endure. Keep true. Even if it is at the very end, he will see his folly."

Ankhesenamun's smile faded. "But I'm so tired, Sennedjem. I'm tired of fighting."

"Even the fiercest warrior needs rest," Sennedjem reminded her.

She looked at him and whispered, "Thank you."

Sennedjem nodded.

After a few moments of silence, looking between each

other, unsure what to say next, Sennedjem finally slapped his thighs and stood up.

"Well, what shall it be, my Queen? Are you to fight? Or are you to run away?"

She wiped her tears with her fingers. *I endure,* she told herself. *I am a warrior. I do not give up. I only rest.*

Standing up, she kept her gaze locked with Sennedjem's. "I will fight."

"My good and honorable Queen." Sennedjem bowed to her. "Do you still possess the dagger I gave you?"

"Yes." Ankhesenamun patted her belt.

"If Pawah attacks you, do not hesitate to use it. I will come before Pharaoh on your behalf if he sees you in error." He dipped his head in servitude.

Ankhesenamun lifted her chin. "I will not hesitate."

ANKHESENAMUN WENT TO THE COURTYARD TO GATHER flowers, escorted by Sennedjem, who would not leave her by her lonesome. He had sent for Hori but, at Ankhesenamun's command, not for Ineni. Given Ineni's blunt account of her whereabouts at Aketaten, she decided she did not trust him.

Hori came and eyed Sennedjem, who gave furtive glances to the Queen as she picked some white acacia blossoms and intertwined them with the vibrant yellow sesban blossoms. Sennedjem noticed Hori's stare, so he turned to look around the courtyard to make it seem as if he were only studying the surroundings.

Ankhesenamun finished picking her flowers and turned to the two men. "Do you think he will like these?"

"He?" Hori asked.

"Pharaoh." Ankhesenamun twisted the stems together so they would survive their journey to the throne room.

"Very nice," Hori said, and Sennedjem nodded in agreement.

They escorted her to Pharaoh's throne room, and when she entered, Tut's eyes fell on Sennedjem and never left him, even as his Queen spoke to him.

"Pharaoh—" She bowed to her husband, suddenly realizing she had left the royal harem and her bedchambers against his direct command. Hopefully he would not reprimand her for it. "I have brought you a gift." She took a step up to the platform and stopped, seeing that he looked past her to Sennedjem.

"Why is *he* here?" Tut asked with a clenched jaw.

"He did not want me to be alone."

"Alone?!" Tut spat at her, spinning his head to face her. "You were alone with *him?*" His accusatory finger pointed at Sennedjem.

"Pharaoh, was I to grieve with my royal guards, my servants? I *wanted* to be alone. Sennedjem, who feared for my safety, would not leave me alone when he came upon me in the corridor. He sent a messenger to Hori to come at once, so they both could escort me. He is your loyal servant. He has never touched me. Please, if you believe nothing else, believe this," Ankhesenamun pleaded. Her daughters were already taken from her; it would do no good to have another innocent life taken as well.

Pharaoh ignored the both of them and looked straight to Hori. "Is this true?"

"From my account, yes, it seems it is true. I have never seen Overseer of the Tutors Sennedjem act improperly toward your chief royal wife." Hori looked Tut straight in the eye as he spoke and bowed his head afterward to signal he was finished speaking in the presence of Pharaoh.

Tut's nostrils flared. His jaw loosened and he chewed on the insides of his cheeks. *If there are those who refute Pawah's list, then I can believe Ankhesenamun never betrayed my bed, right? But did she kill our daughters? Hentmehyt said she did. O Amun, why can't the truth be plain?* He peered to Ankhesenamun. *I love her, but can I trust her? General Horemheb said I could. Pawah—if it is all true, he is the threat. But why would Hentmehyt lie?*

"Leave us."

All the servants left and when the throne room doors closed, Tut stood to face his wife.

"You have gone against my direct command."

Ankhesenamun's face drooped. "I'm sorry, Pharaoh." She looked to him with tears in her eyes. "But I am hurting. They were my daughters too." Her gaze fell to the flowers she held in her hand.

Compassion began to claw its way through Tut's angry barrier. He set his jaw, reminding himself of Pawah's words, of how they were confirmed by his wife's own head steward. *I need to find the truth!*

"Then why would you kill them?" he asked.

"I didn't, Tut." She touched his chest as the dam failed and tears rushed down her cheeks. "I never requested silphium." Her hands ran up his shoulders as she pressed her head into his chest. "Please . . . please . . . believe me."

His free hand almost came to rub her back; instead, he clenched his fist, placed it by his side, and stood unmoving against his wife's cries.

"I feel as though I have lost my friend. Where did you go? I want my friend back. I want my husband back."

He grasped her wrist, pulled her hand from his shoulder, and guided her to step backward. He studied her face for a long time; there was no sign of deceit, no sign of lying . . . but Hentmehyt told him she had asked for the wine with boiled silphium. He let go of her and then cupped her cheek.

"Why do so many say differently than you?"

Ankhesenamun covered his hand with hers. "Pawah bribes many."

He pulled away from her and then sat back down. "I don't know who to trust."

"I am your wife." She fell to her knees at the side of his throne as more tears appeared in her eyes. "What more can I do to gain your trust? What more can I do to show you the truth?"

Tut gritted his teeth and shook his head. "I do not know, Ankhesenamun. Everything Pawah says is supported by others—"

"Whom he has *bribed*." Ankhesenamun's fist hit the throne's arm.

"You know this?"

Ankhesenamun took a deep breath. "I know he bribed those in Aketaten. He told me himself. He attacked me and the servants did nothing because they were bribed. The whole city was corrupt. He planned to kill you, but if I stayed silent, he said he would let you live a while longer." Tears fell from her cheeks. "But I think he now plays a different game. He wants you to believe him over me and name him as your successor, and if you do not, he said he would kill you and make me his wife so he could become Pharaoh. I have stayed silent because he told me he would kill you immediately." Her breath hitched as she spoke. "Tut, please . . . you have to believe me."

Tut hummed and scratched his chin, as he had seen Horemheb do on occasion. What Ankhesenamun said did go along with what Horemheb had told him, but he just didn't know. Pawah had a long list, and Hentmehyt—what did all of these people have to gain?

Her hand fell to his thigh. "Please."

Does she tell the truth? Why, then, did both of my daughters die? Was it because of me as I originally thought? Was it because the gods punished her for being unfaithful? Was she even unfaithful? She denies it. Sennedjem denies it. Hori gave no indication it was the truth. Was it because I am the son of the Pharaoh who turned his back on the gods, and I am enduring their wrath? But one question lingered more than the others: *Did she kill my daughters? One death is common enough, but two subsequent deaths?*

Tut let out a heavy sigh. He grasped her hand and debated what to do—throw it away in his anger or, enticed by the smoothness of her skin, kiss it? In the end, his impulse took over. He kissed the back of her hand, then turned it over and kissed her palm.

"Ankhesenamun, I love you . . . but I cannot fully believe you right now."

Ankhesenamun's face contorted as if he had stabbed her in the heart.

He kissed her palm again. "Please leave me until I can figure out what is the truth."

She held back her tears and nodded, unable to speak, and then hurried down the platform steps toward the doors.

Tut watched her, tears welling in his own eyes.

As Ankhesenamun—escorted by Hori and Sennedjem— neared the royal harem, she stopped and turned to the two men, looking Hori in the eye. Her brow furrowed.

"Do you believe me?"

"You are my Queen. You have my loyalty," Hori said with a nod of his head.

She leaned forward, staring him down. *"Do you believe me?"*

Hori pressed his lips into a half smile. "I believe you would not do as Pharaoh thinks."

Ankhesenamun drew in a long breath; with her exhale, her shoulders slumped. She went to sit on a bench on the courtyard path in front of the royal harem.

"I have never touched our Queen in the manner of the rumors," Sennedjem whispered to Hori, his voice steady.

Hori eyed him and nodded. "I assumed as much, though you stare too long at her beauty. Even in Aketaten, you watched her leave your training yard every day."

Sennedjem frowned, looking at Ankhesenamun. "Yes, I did, and maybe I do stare too long. But she needs someone." He turned his focus back to Hori.

Hori knew he spoke the truth. She had been isolated, and now no one stood by her side. He also knew the Queen trusted Sennedjem enough to let him tie a dagger in her belt, for he had seen that day in the training yard.

"If you speak to her in private, I will not tell," Hori said, and put both hands on his spear. "I will keep watch."

Sennedjem smiled grimly. "You are an honorable man."

Hori nodded. "As are you."

Sennedjem took a deep breath. "In peace, royal guard Hori."

Then he went to his Queen's side and knelt by the side of the bench, still keeping his status as a servant, as Overseer of the Tutors.

Gazing into the flowers she had picked for her husband, Ankhesenamun whispered, "Do you believe I would do—"

"My Queen," Sennedjem interjected, "it matters not what we believe. We know you. We have been with you for most of your life. If our beliefs are of importance to you, then we do not believe the lies." Sennedjem spoke with his head bowed.

"Then why can't *he*? I am his *wife*!" She squeezed the flowers and gave them a hard shake as she spoke.

Sennedjem stayed silent for a moment as he watched a few petals fall to the ground. He lowered his voice. "Pharaoh has much for which he is responsible and much to make up for his father. He wants to be wise, and Vizier Pawah does have such a hold on him."

"But we have told him, all of us, that Pawah lies." She dropped the bundle of flowers and leaned her elbows on her knees, balancing her head on her hands.

"But Pawah has others to validate his words. Pawah only needs for him to doubt." As he whispered, Sennedjem picked up the flowers and placed them next to Ankhesenamun.

"I wish I had run away. I'm not what you think I am," she said, and wiped a few tears that had escaped her eye.

"That is not who you are. My wife, may she find eternal peace, held the same values. She was going to stand for right and never run away, nothing to ever compromise herself. You are the same." He gave her a nod and a smile.

Ankhesenamun let his words sink in for a while, then spoke: "I did not realize you were married. I should have assumed, but I never think of anyone else having a family. Was your wife as selfish as I?"

Sennedjem half smiled and gestured to the seat on the bench. Ankhesenamun nodded. He took a seat beside her, keeping a respectable distance between them. "My wife was not selfish, and neither are you. You have a lot more to worry about than she did. A lot more to fight for."

Ankhesenamun studied Sennedjem, who looked out into the courtyard admiring the breeze. "Do you miss her?"

He hung his head. "There are days still where it is unbearable to be without her, and yet there are other days I rarely notice she is gone." His gaze seemed to turn inward as he reflected on his life with her. "She died in childbirth. I never knew if we had a son or daughter, for our child never came into the world." He let out a breath and covered his mouth. After some time, he dropped his hand. "I cannot believe eight years have passed."

"Eight?" Ankhesenamun asked, raising her eyebrows. "You did not want another wife or children?"

"I do," Sennedjem said. "But I just wanted her. I became a tutor in Pharaoh Akhenaten's royal harem and worked my way to Overseer. I put my time into training and fighting. I thought about staying in Pharaoh's army, but the prestige of such a position did not seem worthwhile anymore. I did not want to . . ." His voice trailed off.

"You did not want to what?"

He shook his head. "It doesn't matter. I tell you all this because no matter what happens, we will support you. I will go to Pharaoh myself, even if he kills me, and stand by your side against Pawah. You have nothing to fear. Hori and I do not fear death."

Hori turned, peering over his shoulder, and nodded to the Queen in acknowledgment of Sennedjem's words.

"We are with you to the end." Sennedjem picked up the flower bundle between them and handed it to her.

Ankhesenamun dipped her chin as she accepted her flowers. "I thank you," she whispered, and ran a light finger over one of the blooms. "It is good to know I am not alone."

"You are never alone, Queen Ankhesenamun."

There lay a sweetness, she noticed, in the way he said her name.

She smiled at him. "You are a good tutor," she said, and they both chuckled.

Hori, having heard the conversation, smiled with them.

———

A FEW DAYS LATER, AY CAME AND BOWED BEFORE PHARAOH and then approached the throne, coming to Tut's side. Wenamen trailed him, but knelt at the lowest stair of the platform of which Pharaoh's throne resided.

"Pharaoh Tutankhamun," Ay began in a low voice. "Malkata's high steward, Wenamen, has found the identity of the substance in Ankhesenamun's wine goblet."

"I know what it is." Tut sulked deeper into the throne's seat. "Silphium."

Ay's head titled to the side. "Yes. But it was not in the wine amphora."

"I know. Ankhesenamun asked for silphium to be put in the wine." Tut gritted his teeth and fixed his gaze upon the throne room's entrance ahead of him. "Pawah says she killed my daughters. Hentmehyt confirms she asked for wine with boiled silphium."

Ay stood up. "To what end?"

"She wants me to name her Coregent." Tut shrugged. "Per Pawah."

"And you believe Pawah?"

"No." He shook his head. "But I believe her steward, Hentmehyt. She said my wife asked for wine with boiled silphium."

Wenamen cleared his throat. "My Pharaoh," he began, knowing he should not speak until invited to speak; but what he had found which at first seemed of no importance now seemed worth risking a chiding. "Hentmehyt's family owes Vizier Pawah a debt."

Tut's spine peeled off of the throne as he gripped its arms. "What debt?"

"Pawah protected several families from death when they chose to worship Amun during the reign of Pharaoh Smenkare. Hentmehyt's family was among them."

Ay looked to Wenamen and then back to Pharaoh. "I also came to tell you, Pharaoh," Ay said, "that a container of silphium plants was delivered to the servant of Pawah's steward two decans after Queen Ankhesenamun announced she was with child."

Tut's eyes darted between Horemheb and Wenamen. "How do I know you are not telling me this to make me believe Ankhesenamun's lies? You are her grandfather! You would tell me anything to keep me from believing the truth."

Ay's hands folded in front of his belly and his voice dropped again. "The truth is as I have spoken, Pharaoh: the sap in Ankhesenamun's drink was silphium, but the orders of this plant came at a very suspicious time to *Pawah's* servants —not Ankhesenamun's servants. Wenamen has offered the true and suspicious information that the steward who told you Ankhesenamun ordered wine with silphium owes Pawah a debt equaling her and her family's lives."

Tut sat back in the throne as he pursed his lips and his eyebrows gathered over his eyes.

Ay dipped his head. "Pharaoh is wise enough to draw his own conclusions, and to believe what he wants to believe." Then he backed away from Tut and descended the platform steps.

Tailed again by Wenamen, Ay left the throne room, leaving Tut to mull over the new facts presented to him.

CHAPTER 26
THE TIME OF DISMISSAL

A MITANNI MESSENGER BOWED BEFORE PHARAOH Tutankhamun, sitting in his throne.

"From King Tustratta of the Mitanni," he began, and read from his papyrus scroll:

" 'King of Egypt, my brother, I hope your throne is well, your household is well, and your wives, nobles, warriors, and horses are well. It is not well with me. I hope you do not follow your father's footsteps and neglect our friendship, and I pray you will rekindle our alliance to the strength it was with your father's father, my brother Amenhotep III. Behold, I have sent one male servant and one female servant to you along with iron swords for your best soldiers and vats of perfume and jewelry. I only wish to gift more, but in my present state of affairs, I cannot. Please return gift for gift. I do not need more servants, but I am in need of Egypt's aid. The Hittites yet again tear down our borders and march ruthlessly through our lands, slaying our women and children, burning our cities to rubble. Please send your army to help us defend against the Hittite King Suppiluliuma I.

Brother, send your message back so I may receive your army in good company.' "

The messenger lowered the scroll, rolled it back up, and then bowed again to Pharaoh Tutankhamun.

Vizier Ay stepped forward and leaned in to whisper in Tut's ear. "The Mitanni were shown to be a good ally to your grandfather. They provided many goods and gifts to our people. They have sent wives to your grandfather to show their commitment to the alliance." Ay stopped, straightened his aching back a moment, then leaned over again. "If the Hittites take the Mitanni lands, then we will need to reinforce our northern border tenfold, as the Mitanni also border Egypt. We would be ripe for invasion from the Hittites. It would be in Egypt's best interest as well to help the Mitanni defend against the Hittites."

Tut pushed his jaw to align with his overbite as he considered the old man's words. "Vizier Ay, do you think it is wise to fight another country's wars? We could make preparations at our border for when the Mitanni fall. Why shed more Egyptian blood?"

"You ask wise questions, Pharaoh. The decision is yours alone. Should the Hittites attack our borders again, we may need to call upon the Mitanni to reach our border first, before our army could arrive. We also must defend against the Nubians and Libyans. We cannot keep our army concentrated to the north at all times."

Tut nodded and wished in his heart that he did not have to make this decision.

So many lives. So many men. So many families.

He chewed his lip, closed his eyes. "More bloodshed now for less bloodshed later," he whispered, and Ay nodded along with his logic as Tut opened his eyes to the messenger. "Egypt will send aid." He turned to a nearby Egyptian messenger. "Send word to Commander Paramesse to move to north of the Mitanni capital of Washukanni to aid in the Mitanni's defense of the Hittites."

The messengers bowed and left together for Mitanni.

THAT EVENING TUTANKHAMUN TOSSED AND TURNED IN HIS bed. He rubbed his leg; it was causing him much pain tonight in particular, but he was still too proud and embarrassed to call a servant to rub it for him. Finally he threw his sheet from his body and sat up. He felt the weight of the world in that sheet. Rubbing his bald head, he let out an exasperated breath. His father, Pawah, the Mitanni, Ankhesenamun . . . they all weighed heavy on his mind—especially tonight, as he had just ordered Egypt's soldiers to the aid of a former ally.

"There must have been a reason my father severed their alliance," he whispered, but shook his head, remembering the tales of his father's negligence. "Or no reason at all." He lay back down, closed his eyes. "No reason at all," he repeated, but his mind continued to race.

Maybe all this time I have been thinking my father saw me as nothing because of my foot . . . but the truth was the same: really just no reason at all. I have been trying to prove myself to my father—prove I can be a wise ruler, prove I am a man—when he had no reason at all to think differently. He chose Smenkare in my place . . . for no reason at all.

His mind wandered. "Hentmehyt has no reason to lie," he whispered, recalling his words to Ankhesenamun. "No reason. Unless . . ."

His eyes popped open. He swung his legs to the side of the bed, grabbed his cane, tied his royal shendyt, and left his bedchambers.

Escorted by his royal guards, he walked all the way to Hentmehyt's bedchambers. He thought about knocking, but in the end he decided she was but a servant. His leg ached. He longed to sit, but determination to find the truth motivated him onward. He had his guards push open her door.

"Steward of the Queen! Hentmehyt!" he yelled, and he heard her stir.

"Pharaoh . . . ?" she murmured, and rubbed her eyes from the firelight streaming in from the corridor. "Pharaoh!" She jumped from bed and bowed to him. "What may I do for you?"

"Tell me the truth," he ordered her. "Did or did not my wife, Ankhesenamun, ask for wine with boiled silphium?"

Hentmehyt fell to her knees. Tears began to stream down her face. Her arms came to her chest as she cried, "Pharaoh, be gracious!"

"The *truth*, Hentmehyt!" Tut's eyes focused on her own, trying to calm his breath. Already he knew something was not right with her response.

Maybe she did have reason to lie.

"I only ask for protection from Pawah and his wrath!" Hentmehyt bowed prostrate on the floor in front of Tut. "For me and my family." Her forehead touched the stone floor. "Please."

"Tell me the truth!" Pharaoh said a third time.

Vizier Ay and Wenamen were right. Pawah had his hand in this.

Ankhesenamun was right.

He held back his heartbreak as his words to her rushed over him like a sandstorm.

"Pawah threatened to send his supporters to kill my family and me, as well as the cupbearer Ipwet and her family, if we did not do as he commanded. He said he killed many and would not hesitate to kill us—"

"Do *what*?" He tapped his fingers on his cane's handle. His patience grew thin.

"We were to take the wine and mix it with boiled silphium and boiled poppy. The poppy to make her want more wine, make her ask for it every night. The silphium, in small doses, would eventually kill the child." Her tears ate at almost every word as she stayed with her head to the stone floor. "Forgiveness, Pharaoh . . . please . . . grant to me Pharaoh's forgiveness."

He clenched his jaw. *Forgiveness.* Such an impossible word. Such a hard gift to give. This woman had poisoned his wife, had killed his two daughters. This woman had lied to him and caused him to almost exile Ankhesenamun. This woman had drugged his wife with poppy and silphium. Yet she begged forgiveness?

Looking down, he saw his white knuckles wrapped around the handle of his cane. *Forgiveness.* The word repeated in his mind. He needed forgiveness from Ankhesenamun. In that moment, he decided to show Hentmehyt grace, and hoped the gods would be with Ankhesenamun to grant him the same.

"You will have your life." His words came monotone and empty. His chin quivered as he took a breath to settle his anger. "Pawah will no longer be a member of Pharaoh's family or council. You have nothing to fear from him. But you will be gone from Malkata by sunset tomorrow, or else I will have you thrown in Pharaoh's pit for the rest of your life."

Hentmehyt covered her head with her hands. "Thank you, Pharaoh, for your generosity. Thank you for your care of this steward."

He turned and the guards closed her doors behind him.

He stood with a straight back—as straight as its crooked nature permitted—and chewed inside his mouth.

He turned and told a guard to deliver the same fate to Ipwet, the cupbearer. Both women had killed his daughters. Both women had drugged his Queen. She should be extended the same mercy as Hentmehyt; the same exile.

The guard bowed and left. Three guards remained as they escorted him to Ankhesenamun's bedchambers. Hori and Ineni stood guard, and at Pharaoh's presence, they bowed and opened Ankhesenamun's door.

Pharaoh entered and had them close the door behind him. The moonlight fell on her bed and outlined her body in its shadows under her sheet. He walked to her bedside and watched her sleep, hating himself for pushing her away and not believing her. A weight fell upon his body. A wave of nausea gripped his stomach as he thought about what he had said to her, what he had done to her. Tears welled in his eyes as he slipped into her bed, wrapping his arm around her waist and kissing the back of her neck.

She stirred. "Tut . . . ?" she whispered, and touched his hand over her stomach.

"Yes, my Queen," he whispered back, and swallowed a lump in his throat.

She rolled to face him. "Why are you in my bed?" Her words drew out with a sigh as she opened her eyes, adjusting to the moonlit darkness of the room.

"I have come to tell you I have found the truth." Tut's voice cracked as he gazed into her eyes, and his chin quivered.

"And you believe me now?" she asked, her eyelids heavy and drooping.

He noticed the dark circles under her eyes. *She has not been sleeping,* Tut thought. *Because of me and my treatment of her. Our daughters died and all I did was make it worse for her. I hate myself. I don't deserve you, my love.*

"I will never doubt you again, my Ankhesenamun."

"I have never lied to you, Tut," she whispered, her eyes slowly blinking.

"I know this now." He nuzzled her neck with his nose; his lips brushed her collarbone enough to leave a soft kiss. "I am sorry I did not believe you. I am sorry I hurt you. I am sorry, Ankhesenamun . . . with every thread of my being I am sorry." He pushed his forehead into her shoulder. "I am so sorry." Two tears ran down his cheek and onto her neck.

She rubbed her hand down his clean-shaven head and back. Her body lay unmoving. "Pharaoh does not apologize."

"I am not Pharaoh tonight. Only a man who has hurt his wife in the most horrible of ways." He kissed her shoulder and pulled back. Looking in her eyes, he lingered in the dark abyss for a moment, that one impossible word echoing in his mind—*Forgiveness*—before the whisper came forth: "Will you forgive me?"

His heart beat faster as he worried she would not. After all he had done and said to her, Horemheb's words came back to him: *Can you blame her?*

HIS TEARS ON HER NECK, HIS HEARTBEAT AGAINST HER CHEST, Ankhesenamun was speechless.

Forgiveness . . . ?

Her jaw clenched as she thought, but then her face relaxed and the tension of the past left. In the moonlight, in these sheets, she found her friend and husband again. Her heart gripped itself, not wanting to endure another round of doubt from him; and yet she couldn't help the thought of pushing him away from crossing her mind.

As if reading her thoughts, Tut whispered: "I shall always believe you, my wife. From now until forever. No matter who or how many people tell me differently. You are my wife. You I will always believe. I love you." He caressed her face. "Please forgive me."

She kissed him, keeping their eyes locked. Then she caressed his face with her hand, and whispered, "Always."

CHAPTER 27
THE TIME OF DECREE

THE NEXT MORNING, PHARAOH CALLED PAWAH TO HIS THRONE room.

After Pawah bowed and ascended the platform steps, he shook his head. "I have more ill news, my Pharaoh. I heard a certain Queen was in the company of the Overseer of the Tutors, a certain Sennedjem, again."

Pawah's whisper crawled over Tut's neck and bit his ear.

"I saw him escort her with Hori, the royal guard," Tut said, and peered at Pawah. "Do not twist the truth to me, Pawah. I—"

"My Pharaoh." Pawah chuckled and laid a hand on his shoulder. Tut's gaze fell to Pawah's hand and then back to Pawah's eyes. "I do not twist the truth. What I say is true— there are even those who validate what I say. Have I ever lied to you?"

Tut almost stood up to punch him square in his jaw, but knew it probably wouldn't do any good and would only speed the time it took for Pawah to decide to kill him.

Pawah smiled at him, oblivious to the thoughts racing

through Tut's head. "My son, I only have your best interest at heart."

While Pawah continued on with some other lies about his wife, Tut wondered how to protect himself, but snapped back when Pawah called him that word again—*son*.

"I am not your son," Tut whispered, and rolled his shoulder from his hand. "I am the son of Pharaoh Akhenaten."

"Something I would not say too loudly these days," Pawah warned, and shook his finger in Tut's face. Tut wanted to grab it and break it off of his hand, but resorted to just clenching his jaw instead.

"Vizier Pawah . . . Uncle . . . have you lied to me all my life?"

"Absolutely not!" Pawah shook his head, and his brow furrowed at the accusation. "Why do you think such things?"

Tut shrugged. "You seem to think everyone is out to kill me or hurt me."

"I only know this from experience. People are only nice to Pharaoh because he has something they want." The man's smile overtook the falsity in his voice. "My son—"

"I—am—not—your—son," Tut repeated, each word emphasized.

"Nonsense! I know you are not my son. But as the last male relative, *I* am your *only* family." Pawah pressed his palms together in front of his chest and hinged at the waist. "The most loyal of family."

"You are not my only family. I have my wife, Ankhesenamun, and my step-mother's father, Vizier Ay, as well, and even his wife and his daughter, the latter of whom is married to General Horemheb, my Hereditary Prince." Tut sat up straight and leaned back into his throne, his feet planted on the floor, his hands on the throne's golden arms. His nostrils flared at all the years of Pawah calling him *son*.

Horemheb! He is more a father than you will ever be!

"Your step-mother tried to kill you," Pawah said, and walked around to face Tut. "I cannot believe you would consider the old man, Ay, to be family."

"Ay has been more loyal to me and more helpful to me in my duties as Pharaoh than you have ever been." Tut held his head steady, his muscles tightening.

"Because," Pawah began, "he rules *for* you—"

"No." Tut's voice grew deep and firm.

"My son, he—"

"I am *not* your *son!*" Tut grabbed his cane from across his lap and shook it at Pawah. "Begone, Pawah! Take your half-truths with you. You are no longer my vizier, and you are no longer my uncle. Leave Malkata. Leave Waset. No! Leave *Egypt*. Never show your face to me again."

Pawah's smile fell. "Pharaoh, I do not understand. Have I ever led you astray? Has anyone ever not validated what I said? Tell me who." Pawah feigned his pleading as his brow furrowed in thought, searching for something to sink his hook back into, something to make Tut recant his command.

"Begone, Pawah." Tut lowered his cane and sat back, nodding to the nearby guards to carry out his order.

"It is General Horemheb, is it not? He poisons your mind against me." Before Tut could respond, Pawah followed with another question. "Did he tell you he loved Nefertiti?"

Tut closed his mouth. Pawah, seeing the visible shake of his jaw, smiled in victory. A small peace settled his panicking heart.

"The only reason Horemheb wants you close is to kill you in revenge for keeping him from his true love. You know he helped kill your father. Your father died at his and Nefertiti's hand. He wanted to be with her, but she would have had to marry you." Pawah shook his head.

"Lies. General Horemheb loved Amenia. They even . . . almost had a son together. See how much you know? You tell so many lies, you cannot keep your own—"

Pawah laughed. "And you believed him? That it was Amenia?"

Tut was silent; his ears boiled red.

"Amenia was barren, child," Pawah said. "He had no son with her. She could never bear children!"

"He said she did." Tut's words held no emotion. His uncle's charade had ended. The lies held no sway over him.

"Then he *lies!*" Pawah spat, and his finger jabbed like a snake's bite.

"You tell me many lies, Pawah, and you dare to bring my father into it? You *coward.*" Tut did not smile nor scowl. "Begone and never return to Malkata. You are to leave Egypt! You are no longer my own, and you are disowned from Pharaoh's family."

Tut pointed to him and the royal guards stepped forth from the pillars and grabbed Pawah by each arm.

"Throw him from the palace doors!" Tut ordered, and they began to drag Pawah out. "Make sure he crosses the Nubian border in exile!"

"LET ME GO!" he yelled, and yanked his arm away. Once out of their grip, he dusted off the imagined residue of their hands and turned his nose up at Pharaoh. "Fine, boy, let the General prove his worth to you as he did to your father. See where you end up. I'll leave you to find out who is truly loyal to you."

"You will call me *Pharaoh* or risk your life." Tut's hands gripped the gold-covered arms of the throne as he leaned forward, as if daring Pawah to call him *boy* or *son* once more.

Pawah narrowed his eyes at his once-puppet child and clenched his fist. "Thus Pharaoh says," Pawah spat from his teeth. He took one last look at the boy King and marched with heavy feet from the throne room, the guards close on his heels.

"You will pay for this," Pawah whispered under his breath.

CHAPTER 28
THE TIME OF ALLIES

ANKHESENAMUN HAD ACCEPTED HIM BACK INTO HER ARMS, and into her bed, but Tut could not remove the guilt from his heart. It seemed peaceful between them when she had learned of his decree against Pawah almost a season ago, but still an ache sat in the pit of his stomach, knowing he had wronged her in such horrible of ways. He'd apologized, but he felt it wasn't enough. His eyes never left her even as they ate breakfast, for he was forever afraid she would change her mind.

"What is it, Tut?" she asked in a whisper, her eyes searching his face as she sipped her wine.

He blinked, not realizing how long he had been staring at her. "I love you," he said, and then dropped his head, ashamed to look at her more.

She giggled. "I love you too."

He lifted his eyes to her.

A grin spread over her lips. "Now, what truly is it?"

He thought about his decrees of the past month. Several had been in honor of his wife, but one really stood out. It was finally ready for her to see.

"I have built a monument for the both of us to show all of Egypt that we are united forever."

Her jaw dropped. She beamed, her eyes sparkling.

"I will take you to see it today!" He smiled. "I hope you know this is only a token of my appreciation, Ankhesenamun. I will do much more."

"Tut, you don't need to—"

"I want to, Ankhesenamun, my wife."

His lips pressed into a small smile. Often over the last season since he'd exiled Pawah, he'd gathered flowers from one of Malkata's many courtyards and presented them to her. He'd even taken the role of the servant at times, dismissing the servants so that he may dress her and bring her food. But he never felt it to be enough.

Her eyes narrowed a little before they regained their sparkle. "Well, thank you," she whispered, and went back to finishing her meal.

THAT DAY THEY WENT TO IPET-ISUT AND TUT PROUDLY revealed the statue of himself and Ankhesenamun.

"It's beautiful, Pharaoh," she whispered, staring up at herself.

Tut gazed at her. "Now you will have your own legacy in stone, to forever be remembered." He gestured to the wall to the side of the statue. "Your name will always be spoken by the people of Egypt."

She read the writing on the wall and let out a small breath. She turned to face him and her eyes misted. "Thank you," she whispered.

He nodded toward the back of the statue. They walked around and Tut looked up at his statue's shoulder.

Ankhesenamun's stone hand lay in a protective resting position upon it.

She grinned and furrowed her brow at the odd sculpture. "Why is my arm depicted that way?" she asked, peering up at Tut.

"Because . . ." He half smiled as he looked at her. "You are the one who has protected me from the very beginning, even when I doubted you so harshly. You never left me."

"And I never will," she whispered.

His lips smiled, but his heart faded. How could he ever be worthy of her?

"I know," he breathed.

They traveled back to Malkata, and instead of asking the royal guard to escort Ankhesenamun back to her bedchambers or to the royal harem, he grabbed her hand.

"Will you sit next to me in your throne?"

She nodded with a gleam in her eye.

And so it was known that for the next season, Pharaoh Tutankhamun ruled with his chief royal wife, Queen Ankhesenamun, seated by his side.

ONE MORNING SOON AFTER, TUT OPENED HIS EYES IN THE growing dawn light that filtered in through the window. He stroked her arm as she held to his chest, stirring awake. He felt undeserving as he kissed the top of her head.

When she fully awoke, she lifted her face to him and smiled. She yawned and kissed his lips before rolling over. He watched her slide out of bed with grace, her long, slender, well-oiled body beautiful, yes, yet still pale compared to the beauty of her heart. She walked around to him and rubbed his chest.

"Are you ready to dress for the day?" she murmured.

He grasped her wrist as he sat up and guided her into his lap for a long embrace. There had been no tension in his shoulders since he disowned Pawah, yet this morning had brought some. His dream the night prior was of a different path, one where Ankhesenamun had cast him out of her life instead of forgiving him. The loneliness he felt in his dream had followed him out of sleep in the form of a heavy ache in his chest and a thickness in his throat. He touched his forehead to Ankhesenamun's and stroked her cheek as his eyes prickled with tears.

"What is on your mind, Tut?" she whispered, rubbing his chest and neck.

He held her gaze for a while before he spoke. "I do not deserve you, Ankhesenamun." He swallowed, trying to make his words more audible. "Nor have I ever deserved you. But I will spend the rest of my life earning your forgiveness."

"You already have my forgiveness," she whispered, and squeezed her arms around his waist. "As I have told you many times before."

His eyes shone in the morning light as he rubbed her back. "No—I hurt you. I accused you of horrible—" His voice cracked. "I do not deserve your forgiveness that you give so freely to me."

Ankhesenamun's cheeks glowed and her eyes beamed. "Tut, no one who asks for forgiveness ever really deserves to be forgiven. But I forgive you because I love you."

He kissed her and ran his hand down her back and shoulder. "But I have been so—"

She cut him off, hovering her mouth over his. "You were influenced by people who wished you harm, who wanted you to fail."

"No." He shook his head. "I was too blind to see your importance to me. *I* should have protected you, believed you, trusted you, not spat in your face. So, my wife, my love, I will spend *every day* proving to you how much I love you and how important you are to me."

She only bit her lip and smiled.

"I am devoted to you, my Ankhesenamun," he whispered.

She leaned in to kiss him once more. He kissed her with his whole self, pressing her into his body and running his hands down her back—

"Tut—" A giggle burst through her whisper at the touch of his hand on her backside. "We will be late in hearing the messengers." She half-pushed his chest away from her, but her eyes tempted him.

"I am Pharaoh, and you, my Queen!" He smirked and pulled on her arm so she fell back into his chest. "Egypt can wait."

TUT SAT ON HIS THRONE, HAPPY, HIS WIFE NEXT TO HIM. HE even held her hand as he ruled, not wanting to break contact from her smooth skin.

One day a messenger came forward and bowed to the royal couple. "Pharaoh Tutankhamun, Commander Paramesse asks to send reinforcements to the northern border in the defense of the Hittites. The Commander's men are spread thin along Egyptian and Mitanni borders in aiding the Mitanni. Egypt's border forts are vulnerable and may not withstand a full attack from the Hittites."

Tut pressed his lips together. His Master of Pharaoh's Horses, Nakhtmin, was in upper Egypt defending against the Nubians, and several troop commanders defended against the Libyans in lower Egypt. General Horemheb was the only logical choice for whom he should send, but part of him did not want to send Horemheb to a potential death. He wanted him close; he wanted him safe.

Vizier Ay stepped forward and repeated what Pharaoh was already thinking. "The only one to send is General Horemheb and his divisions."

"Or we pull Egypt's forces out of the Mitanni land," Tut whispered, his eyes studying the messenger who stood awaiting his command.

Ay nodded. "Doing so, you will ruin any relations with the Mitanni. They are a powerful ally to have," Ay whispered back, but then took his place again, leaving the decision to Pharaoh.

Tut felt he was sinking in his gold throne. He wrinkled his nose as he searched within himself to find the wisest command. Tapping his finger on the throne's arm with one hand and rubbing Ankhesenamun's hand with the other, he took a deep breath.

"Send General Horemheb to the northern border," Tut ordered.

He looked to his Queen, remembering Horemheb's words: *The army wanes without you, Pharaoh. You are a symbol of the gods' blessing on them and their endeavor.* He licked his dry lips as Ankhesenamun locked eyes with him. She squinted her eyes, as if trying to know what he thought. *If I can go with them, then they will be victorious and less Egyptian blood will be spilt. The quicker we can all come home.*

Tut looked back to the messenger. "Pharaoh will join General Horemheb and Pharaoh's Armies."

Ankhesenamun gripped his hand and mouthed *No.*

Tut dropped his gaze, but only for a moment. "Messenger, you are dismissed."

The messenger bowed and left with the command to General Horemheb.

Tut could feel Ankhesenamun's stare upon his cheek, but he couldn't turn to her. He only whispered, "I'm sorry, my love, but it is what I must do for Egypt."

He heard her breath hitch, but she stayed silent.

———

THAT EVENING, AS ANKHESENAMUN ORDERED THE SERVANTS to leave, Tut sat on their bed. Dinner had been consumed in silence. They said not a word to each other for the first time since Pawah's exile.

The sound of the door closing prompted Ankhesenamun to spin around to face Tut.

"Do not go!"

Tut only rubbed his neck as his chest caved. He lifted his chin and found her eyes. "I don't want to go, but—"

"Then don't!" Ankhesenamun dropped to her knees, pulling her hands around Tut's waist. Her eyes filled with tears as she grabbed his shendyt in her fists. "You are Pharaoh, you don't—"

"*Because* I am Pharaoh the army needs me."

"Please, Tut . . ." She knelt between his legs, her head buried in his chest. "You told me you were devoted to me."

Tut wanted to run his hand over her wig and back and tell her he would stay, but the weight upon his shoulders was too great. A second "Please!" came from his wife, and he squeezed his eyes shut and clamped his jaw. He placed his hands on her shoulders and she began to cry, as if she already knew he was not going to stay.

"I am devoted to you, my love. I love you more than my own life."

He paused. How to go back on his word? They had become so close in the past two seasons. They had rebuilt their relationship. They were best friends again. To throw it all away? Would she forgive him yet again? To say Egypt required this of him when it went against the wishes of his wife? How to make her see this was the only way to save

Egyptian blood? How to ensure this would not tear down all they rebuilt together?

"It has been a year of fighting, Ankhesenamun. The army needs their Pharaoh with them to invigorate them, to show the gods' blessing upon them. If I go, they will be victorious, and the faster we can all come home. Think of the blood saved, my love." He caressed her face as his own eyes filled with tears. He kissed the top of her head and felt her tears on his thighs. At her silence, he continued, "I am sending Egypt's army to die for another empire. I must be there with them."

Her whimper was barely a whisper: "To die?"

His heart sunk. Yes, death was a possibility. But he had to be strong for his wife. He placed his finger under her chin and lifted her face to his.

"I will come back to you."

"How can you be sure? You are going to war. You are going to lead your armies into battle. Please do not leave General Horemheb's side." Ankhesenamun pulled up into his lap and draped her arms around his neck.

"I am sure of it," Tut told her, his voice firm. "Whether or not I stay by General Horemheb's side."

He knew if he were to be an archer, he would either be in the chariots, which gave him pause, or on the back lines with the longbow archers, and the General would stay with the infantry. But he had survived Nubia. His army was loyal to him now that Pawah was gone.

"Please stay by his side," she begged, nuzzling her nose in his neck.

"Do you not think I am an effective warrior on my own?" Tut asked, his gaze falling to the floor.

"No! It is just easier for me to know someone who is loyal to you guards your back."

Ankhesenamun pulled his lips to hers. The taste of her tears filled his mouth as they ran down her face.

"Please stay by his side," she whispered again, pulling away.

"He is my Hereditary Prince, Ankhesenamun. We cannot fight together. If I were to—" He stopped, not wanting to continue his sentence at her widening eyes. "If something were to happen, the throne would be empty."

Her eyes closed, pushing tears from them, and a grimace fell upon her lips. "Would that not be reason to stay?"

"Ankhesenamun, I must go. I am sending our men to die for the Mitanni. General Horemheb told me the army wanes without me, and they have been waning long enough."

After a few more moments of silence, she pressed her forehead to his.

"What if you don't come back to me?" she asked.

"As long as I have your love, I will die the happiest man in all of Egypt." He stroked her cheek. "And if I die, I want you to find blissful happiness, and I will regret every day in my journey to Re that I will not be able to feel your touch, kiss your lips, grow old or have a child with you." Tears fell down his own face as he spoke. "And when I complete my journey, know I will bless you and the Hereditary Prince Horemheb. I want you to be happy, Ankhesenamun."

"I don't want to marry Horemheb. I don't want anyone else but you," she cried.

"Please, my love—" His heart broke watching her grieve him. "I promise, I will come back to you."

But as he kissed her, a deep fear set in. What if he didn't?

CHAPTER 29
THE TIME OF CONSPIRACY

PAWAH SAT AT HIS TABLE, HIS HEAD RESTED ON A PROPPED-UP fist, drumming the fingers of his other hand on the wooden surface. He looked around his new abode and rolled his eyes at its averageness when compared to the grandeur he had fallen from. But it wasn't his fault. It was that boy's fault.

I should have killed him when I had the chance.

At least he'd had the foresight to threaten those cursed guards into releasing him in Waset instead of the Nubian border, and at least here in Waset he could still have a hand in the happenings at Malkata. He had waited far too long to let the throne slip from his fingers now.

He sneered at the undeserving family who had occupied this home before him. He had saved them while under Pharaoh Akhenaten's reign, and they owed him as much to leave for a while so he could regroup; and with his threat of burning them while they slept, they happily repaid him. Their neighbors also knew to be silent, as the same threat would befall them should they speak about his whereabouts.

He chuckled at what people would do for their faith, for their precious afterlife. There was no such thing! But if they believed it, then it was to his advantage . . . and he made sure to take advantage.

In the meantime, he'd had his gold and grain stored away and brought to this new house while he cultivated a new plan. But he had to be careful with how he spent his wealth now. There would be no replenishing from the royal treasury anymore.

At least not until he took the crown.

He sat back in the chair as Merka went about his duties and brought him food for the evening. Beans and bread . . . it reminded him of his wretched childhood. He eyed Merka.

"Couldn't spare an extra shat of copper for some fish?!" His voice rose with every word until he slammed his fist on the table.

Merka let out an audible sigh and shook his head at his master. "You told me to—"

"Get out!" Pawah waved him off. "Make yourself useful and clean the bath chamber."

When Merka sulked away, Pawah muttered, "Only *one* bath chamber in this house." Then he ate like a beast of the field until his pushed his empty plate away and slammed down the beer in his cup. "I have come too far to end up back where I came from . . ." His voice trailed off as he remembered the nights going hungry, with only bread and beans and beer, as a child. "I have come too far."

A knock at the door came, and a messenger stepped inside.

Pawah crossed his arms and leaned back in his chair. "Well? Are you going to speak? What have you found out?"

The messenger cocked his head to the side and raised an eyebrow in disgust. "I cannot believe I am still doing as you say."

"Because you love your family." Pawah grinned. "And you

do not want Pharaoh to know of your hand in killing his father and uncle." He shook his head with a *tsk-tsk*.

Why must I always remind these people why they still obey my command?

He let his hands fall to the chair's arms. "Now, what goes on in the world?"

"Pharaoh and General Horemheb, the Hereditary Prince, are joining Pharaoh's army at the northern border to aid Egypt's allies, the Mitanni." He sulked and his eyes glared at the former vizier. "Pharaoh thinks you gone, so he is taking royal guards with him as well, so as to end the fighting with the Hittites sooner."

Pawah narrowed his eyes at the mention of Horemheb as the Hereditary Prince, but brushed it aside as a new plan formulated in the very moment the messenger quit speaking.

"It seems sometimes the gods actually answer a prayer or two," Pawah mocked, lifting his hands in a façade of praise.

The palace will not be as heavily guarded? Perfect. Now to plow my way to the throne. Who should do my bidding?

Then he snapped at the messenger, making his decision, for he'd had one man in mind for a long time. "Bring me Sitayet, Captain of the Troop."

As the messenger turned around and slammed the door behind him, Pawah's smile grew.

"For Sitayet has a debt to repay." His voice sung with excitement. "And he just so happens to be in command of over a thousand men, at least a hundred of whom owe debts to me as well."

He stood up and grabbed the rest of the loaf from the preparation table and bit into it, not caring that some of it was meant for Merka. His teeth ripped into it, and as he chewed the grainy bread, he dreamed of the smooth, honey-soaked bread he would have in the palace.

"So close," he whispered after he swallowed, and took another bite.

A few hours later Sitayet appeared at the door of Pawah's main house of his estate. "What do you want, Pawah?"

"You will call me by my title," Pawah ordered as he gestured him inside his home.

Sitayet huffed. "The last I heard, Pharaoh disowned you. You have no title except *Citizen*, like the rest of us."

Pawah narrowed his eyes at him. "I see." He calmed the rage within. He would get what he wanted soon enough, and then, if Sitayet survived the task he was going to give him, he would make sure Sitayet paid for that comment when he married Ankhesenamun and became Pharaoh.

Pawah sat down, not offering Sitayet a chair. He popped his knuckles. He had lost a good amount of control over his former supporters, and had resorted to blackmail and death of their families to get his way.

Every night he dreamed of his regret at not rebelling on the night Nefertiti took Akhenaten the hemlock-poisoned wine. Why did he strike a deal with them? Ah, because back then he was still compassionate—still *naïve*—and did not want to spill any more Egyptian blood. He should have had the entire royal family slaughtered, every single one—*then* he and his Beketaten could rule Egypt. Now, in his new temporary home, he would set out to do whatever it would take to seize the crown. The gods had presented a perfect opportunity to finally strike out the royal line and his so-called successor, Hereditary Prince Horemheb.

Sitayet crossed his arms and took a wide stance, his feet firmly planted on the floor. "Are you going to say something or just sit there in silence, *former* Vizier Pawah?"

Pawah's nostrils flared again, and he forced himself to calm his desire to use the man's dagger against him. "I will talk when I am ready, Sitayet, conspirator in the murders of

Pharaoh Akhenaten and Pharaoh Smenkare *and* Pharaoh Neferneferuaten." Pawah's words flowed easily from the lips; he smiled as he watched Sitayet flinch. "Sit down, my *friend*."

"I am not your friend," Sitayet grunted, but took a seat across from Pawah nonetheless.

"I heard Pharaoh and General Horemheb will be taking Horemheb's divisions to the northern border. Are you one of the Captains of the Troop selected to go?" Pawah asked, and leaned in, his fingers interlacing in front of his chin.

"Yes. So?"

"I want you to kill for me," Pawah said, his eyes boring into Sitayet's.

The man's jaw dropped. "You want me to kill *who*?" He crossed his arms even tighter, seemingly already anticipating the answer.

"Pharaoh and his General. I have a list of names, men in your troop who owe me, as do you. And to sweeten the deal, I will give your families one hundred containers of grain."

"One hundred?" Sitayet's eyes grew wide at the large amount of grain. But then he shook his head at the notion. "I will not murder Pharaoh Tutankhamun and General Horemheb for you. You will not bribe me."

"Then I suppose I should submit the letters you wrote to me regarding rebellion and hemlock to Vizier Ay and Pharaoh Tutankhamun. Such letters would surely incriminate you and the other conspirators against Pharaoh Akhenaten and his brother, Smenkare. What do you think Pharaoh will do to you once he finds out you were responsible for the death of his father and uncle?"

Pawah's threat ate the air around Sitayet. They both knew the penalty for conspiracy against Pharaoh—execution by impalement and possible burning after death, which equaled no afterlife.

Sitayet finally spoke. "You will be killed as well."

"Actually, I was quite discreet. All of your letters are addressed to my deceased wife, whom, I will assure Pharaoh, never told me any of her dealings." Pawah smiled. "I am clean in all of this. And regardless, as far as Pharaoh knows, I am no longer in Egypt for such matters, for Pharaoh has exiled me."

Sitayet pounded a fist into the table. "Curse your heart to Ammit!" But he sat back—clearly he knew Pawah had him— and took a deep breath as he considered his options.

Pawah watched him. *So weak.*

"When I become Pharaoh, you and your family will be set for life."

"Yes, but the catch is obeying your every order," Sitayet mumbled.

"Let's go over your options, shall we?" Pawah hummed and drummed his finger on the table. "On one hand, you die a horrible and painful death—most likely never to see the afterlife because of your dealings in Pharaoh's father's and uncle's murders—and I get to live. Or, you do this one thing for me, and you and your family are set for life. But yes . . ." Pawah chuckled. "You will need to follow my every command, now and once I seize the throne."

A grimace overcame Sitayet's face as he thought.

Pawah grinned all the while, letting him try and fail to think of a way out of his task. "So you agree to kill Pharaoh and General Horemheb?"

Sitayet's silence grew as he stared at Pawah.

"Oh, and"—Pawah smirked—"if you do not kill Pharaoh and General Horemheb as I ask . . . I will personally take a knife to your children while you are away fighting a needless war."

Pawah sat back as Sitayet's eyes grew with the question of whether or not Pawah would actually do it. To confirm this he said, "I killed three Pharaohs, Sitayet, and I would not blink an eye at killing your worthless children. The same goes for you and this list of names I have here—let's see . . ." He snatched a papyrus from the table. "Ebana, Kenamon, Mahu, Yuf . . . and so on and so forth."

He rolled up the papyrus list and tossed it across the table. "There are over a hundred names on this list. Pick the men who will help you kill Pharaoh and General Horemheb, and leave some to desert the army and bring me word back before the palace receives the news of Pharaoh's death."

Sitayet did not move, did not look at the list; only at Pawah, still weighing his options.

Pawah placed both hands on the table. "Do we have a deal?"

Sitayet stayed silent.

Pawah leaned forward. "Do you remember when your family would have died of starvation? When your family could have been executed for your crime of worship? But I saved you. I gave you grain. I filled your bellies. I hid you from Pharaoh Akhenaten's and Pharaoh Smenkare's wrath against your worship of Amun-Re. I returned to you your faith."

He stood, towering over Sitayet.

"This is what I desire in return! There is no such thing as a free meal!"

"What you gave us—our faith, food, our lives—you now seek to take away. To kill Amun's divinely appointed!" Sitayet shook his head. "We might as well give up our faith."

"Well, it is your choice . . . and I suppose you make the decision for your men on that list as well. I have their names in letters as well, listing them as conspirators to the throne. You all can die. It is up to you." Pawah motioned to the papyrus roll on the table. "Or you can keep your faith and die by impalement, and after you are dead, I will still take a knife to your worthless families and then set them all on fire . . ."

Pawah put his hand over his heart and feigned sorrow. " 'Oh, it was a horrible, horrible accident, the whole house burned down! Killed all inside . . . poor, poor family.' " His hand dropped to the table and a sneer replaced his façade of sorrow. "Who will be left to entomb your ashes, Sitayet? How will any of your family have an afterlife with no body for their ka to return to?"

Sitayet sat frozen, numb. Finally, he spoke: "I know you would do it too."

Pawah nodded, sitting down. "I promise you on my life, I would."

Pawah smiled to himself. Sitayet could not respond. Would he condemn his whole family and the families of the men on that list to eternal death?

"So, we have a deal?" Pawah asked after a few moments of silence.

"What choice do I have?" Sitayet finally answered.

"Oh, there's always a choice, my dear boy." Pawah laughed. "There's just always a *better* choice."

Sitayet shook his head as he peered at Pawah. "You are evil. One day I hope they kill you. I hope you endure the same threats you cast upon me."

"Curses don't become you, Captain." Pawah chuckled and then took a breath as he leaned forward on the table. "So we have a deal?"

Sitayet released a shaky sigh from his lungs and muttered a breathy "Yes."

CHAPTER 30
THE TIME OF ASSASSINATION

AFTER THE LONG JOURNEY TO EGYPT'S NORTHERN BORDER, THE battles drew the newly arrived soldiers in without a moment to rest. Tut stayed behind the lines with Horemheb, strategizing in the tents. The days grew long and the battles longer. Men were killed and their bodies brought back to Egyptian land. It seemed the Hittites, with their iron weaponry, outperformed the bronze weapons of the Egyptians. The archers were crucial in keeping the Hittites at bay, but their numbers were falling due to the Hittites' long spears and impeccable aim. As the army waned at the lack of Pharaoh's presence on the battlefield, Tut went against Horemheb's advice that they both stay behind the battlefront, insisting that he instead join the army in the fighting.

"I need to be on the front line," Tut pleaded with Horemheb as he stuffed his dagger made of ba-en-pet into his belt.

"The front line is for charioteers, Pharaoh."

Tut put his free hand on his hip. "I am an archer, and the best archers are in chariots. Have I not studied under master bowmen for the last few years to train for this very moment?"

"Pharaoh, I cannot protect you if you are on the frontlines. I am the General and your Hereditary Prince. Let me go to the frontlines in your place. We cannot both be on the frontlines."

Horemheb hoped he could talk some sense into the lad, but knew Tut had his own reasoning. They had discussed it every day on their journey to the lands north of Washukanni.

A short wave of fear crossed Tutankhamun's eyes, but he pressed his lips together into a smile. "I do not need your protection anymore. I am a man." He was nineteen now, well into manhood.

"You are a man, yes, but you are also Pharaoh. You are our empire's leader." Horemheb rolled his shoulders backward, getting ready for the morning's battle. "If we were to lose you, it—" He stopped, thinking: *If I were to lose you, I would lose myself.*

"I trust my army, General. As you said, they are willing to give their lives to protect me. They are empowered by me." He gestured to his dagger made from the gods' gift of ba-en-pet. "If I am not there, their energy will wane."

Horemheb wanted to punch himself in the face for saying that to him all those years ago. Now Tut threw his words back at him, and all Horemheb could do was shake his head. "Pharaoh, I know you should trust your men, but Pawah—"

"*Pawah* is disowned. He no longer has any claim to the throne. He has been exiled to Nubia. He cannot hurt me now. There is nothing about which to worry, General." Tut chuckled and slapped Horemheb on the side of his arm, but stared at the two scars there.

Horemheb saw him staring and covered them, rubbing them as if warming up his muscle. "I'm not worried, Pharaoh.

I know you can hold your own. You are very good with the bow."

Tut smiled. "I am a man now."

"You've been a man for a while now," Horemheb joked. His eyes held his pride.

Tut laughed.

His life seems to be good now, Horemheb thought. Tut held Ankhesenamun's love. Tut no longer worried who to trust. Pawah held no claim to the throne and no longer lurked in Malkata. Tut's future was bright. Surely the gods would grant him safe passage during this war so that he may return home to Ankhesenamun.

Horemheb's smile dimmed as he became serious. "It's been eight years since your first battle, and you have grown into such a fine man. I am proud of you. I am proud to call you my Pharaoh."

Tut seemed to stand a little taller, and his grin danced between a full-fledged smile and a prideful gleam.

Horemheb took a deep breath and ran his eyes over Tut's matured face. "Please, let me go to the frontlines. Stay with the men at the back. Come out of the tent, but don't engage more than shooting your bow. I am your Hereditary Prince. With you behind and me in front, we will uplift the men's spirits."

Tut only stared at him for a long time.

"Pharaoh?" Horemheb asked finally.

"I never told you thank you," Tut said, and nodded. "Thank you for being my mentor, Horemheb. I should thank Vizier Ay as well. Without you, I would not be here. I would not have even made it past childhood." Tut chuckled and shook his head, remembering his first battle, remembering how he fell from the chariot, remembering his ignorance.

"I would do it again." Horemheb bowed his head. "And will continue as long as you would have me."

"Go with peace," Tut said, and placed his hand on Horemheb's shoulder. "Go to the frontlines."

Horemheb returned Tut's gesture. "Go with peace, Pharaoh," he whispered, and he prayed to the gods that nothing happen to him, surely out of harm's way at the back of the fighting.

They stood there for a moment, then Tut squeezed and let go and Horemheb followed suit.

Be safe, Horemheb's heart spoke through his eyes.

THE NEXT MORNING CAME EARLY, AND HOREMHEB WAVED TO Tut as he led his divisions to the lines behind the charioteers. Tut waved back, lifting his hand to the men with his dagger of ba-en-pet raised high so it glinted in the morning sun.

"Amun be with us!" he yelled, and the men chanted the same in return.

Soon the whole of the army had marched out to meet the Hittites, and Tut was left with fifty of his men. He settled into his stabilizer for his leg so he could shoot his bow. The archers stood with their longbows and drew their arrows and let them fly toward the hoard of Hittites rushing out to meet the Egyptians. They again drew their arrows, hoping to strike the enemy down before their fellow brothers in arms clashed with the enemy and rendered their skills useless.

Tut aimed and let his arrow fly, not noticing the looks between some of the men who stood slightly behind him. He heard the sound of a dagger unsheathing and spun around, only to fall from his leg stabilizer, which got stuck in the mud. He looked up to see a dagger stab where he had been standing. He called out but could not finish his question: "What—?"

Another dagger came whooshing down in the direction

of his chest, but he rolled to get out of the way, pulling his dagger from his belt and stabbing one of his attackers in the chest as he rose to his good foot. The weight of the man's body pulled the sunken dagger from Tut's hands. He looked at his attackers, three of them, at least ten more behind them fighting off the men who remained faithful to him.

"Why are you doing this? I am your Pharaoh. I am Amun's divinely appointed!"

"Forgive us, Pharaoh. The General wants the throne," one told him.

Tut's brow wrinkled in confusion. "Horemheb?"

One lunged at him. Tut parried the attack, but without the use of his other leg he fell and the man fell on top of him. The crack of Tut's bone sent a guttural yell from his mouth. The man reached for his dagger as Tut tried to kick him off of his leg. Another man came rushing to him and held down his arm, and the first man raised his dagger high above his head, ready to sink it into Tut's chest. Excruciating pain radiated from his leg and shot through Tut's entire body.

I need my other arm. I need my leg.

Tut watched as the dagger came plummeting down toward his chest, but with the strength of holding his weight on his cane for so many years, he shot his arm up and grabbed the man's hand right before the blade touched his leather armor just below his golden collar.

Tut yelled to supplement his strength and to ignore the horrid pain in his leg. The man went to put his other hand on top of the dagger, and Tut knew he would not be able to hold the dagger if he could not get his other arm free.

"I am your Pharaoh!" Tut yelled once more in a last attempt to save himself.

In the fleeting moments, he saw Ankhesenamun and her smile. *Forgive me,* he wished to her. *For leaving you.*

Just then, two arrows flew, one penetrating the chest of

the man on his arm and the other penetrating the back of the man who was to stab him in his heart.

Tut rolled out from underneath the bodies, sustaining a small gash from the falling dagger.

Soon, those loyal to him had him surrounded and took him back to camp.

MEANWHILE, ON THE BATTLEFIELD, HOREMHEB SWUNG HIS khopesh and killed one of the last Hittites before their retreat began. As he stood looking toward the retreating enemy, labored in his breathing, he heard his name faintly called from afar. It sounded like Paramesse's voice. Spinning around to see why he called him, he came face to face with a khopesh. He blocked his fellow Egyptian's attack with his own khopesh. Thinking maybe the Egyptian did not know who he was, he yelled—

"I AM GENERAL HOREMHEB!"

—but the soldier continued his attack, and was joined by three other men, quickly surrounding their General.

Horemheb used his wooden and leather shield to block one attack and his khopesh to block another, but the third swing got him in his leg and he fell to his knee. He stood up, wobbly, but continued to defend himself.

"I AM YOUR GENERAL!"

He yelled this again and again, but soon his strength tired and could no longer yell, putting his energy into swinging his khopesh to block his attackers. Blood ran down his knee, and his leg felt as if it had run into a thousand spears. He knew it was only a matter of time before his leg would give out completely. Another swing of an attacker's blow finally broke his wooden shield and the sharp sickle-shaped blade dragged across his back and shoulder. He yelled out before falling forward onto his hurt leg. Pieces of his shield bounced away from him and his khopesh fell only an arm's reach away, but he pushed himself up to kneeling, knowing that with no shield he stood no chance. He looked one of his attackers in the eyes. He steadied his labored breathing.

"May Ammit devour your hearts," he cursed them.

"General Horemheb, I am Sitayet, Captain of the Troop." He dropped his shield and took his khopesh in both of his hands. "Know this: we do this not on our own accord, but because our families are at the will of Pawah and his loyal supporters. He did not follow his exiling as you thought, but instead stays in Waset in secret. When we do this horrible deed, he has promised not to harm our families . . . and then he will take the throne." Sitayet cast his gaze to the ground.

Horemheb shook his head. "If Pawah is Pharaoh, all of Egypt will suffer."

"Egypt is a great country . . . but we love our families more."

"Then Egypt was never your country," Horemheb whispered, refusing to move his hand to his bleeding and agonizing shoulder. He would not show pain in his last moments. "Be quick with it."

He focused his thoughts on Nefertiti and Tutankhamun, envisioning their smiling faces before him. He would have peace in his last moments; they could not take that from him.

Sitayet took a deep breath. "Forgive me, General."

He raised his khopesh and wound it behind him to chop off Horemheb's head.

Horemheb kept his eyes open. This man would remember him.

Just as Sitayet should have let the khopesh fly, an arrow pierced through his back. Paramesse came running with two archers, who corralled the other three men, ordering them to drop their weapons. Paramesse came and put his hand on Horemheb's good shoulder, looking him over.

"They could have done worse."

Horemheb shook his head at his friend, grinning grimly. "You were almost too late."

Paramesse helped Horemheb to stand. "We came as soon as we could. There was an attack on Pharaoh as well."

Horemheb froze as a weight fell from his chest down to his stomach.

"Is he . . . ?" His voice trailed off, unable to ask the question.

His body felt as though it was caving in on itself, every muscle holding his anticipation inside. His mind raced back to the day he held Nefertiti in his arms for the last time, watching as she died . . .

Paramesse's voice cut through his memory. "They broke his leg. It seems pretty severe."

Horemheb's face paled. "Will he live?"

"I do not know. Maybe if we were at Malkata, with the best physicians, but . . . I just don't know."

Horemheb began hobbling, with his hurt leg, in the direction of camp. "I must see him."

"General!" Paramesse stopped him. "What about these three?"

"Kill them," Horemheb said with a wave of his hand.

The haze of the dusty battlefield and the stench of blood almost caused him to vomit as something Sitayet said before he almost killed him rushed to the forefront of his memory: Pawah was in Waset. He had turned Egyptian against Egyptian. He would continue until either he was dead or had the crown.

Horemheb looked to Paramesse with his brow furrowed in thought. Paramesse stood waiting, his hand in the air, ready to give the signal to execute the traitors.

"Perhaps," Horemheb muttered, "we send them back to Malkata to be killed, as examples of what happens when people follow Pawah . . ."

His eyes darted back and forth, trying to take in all that had happened in the last few moments. If there were four men who attacked him, Pawah would be smart enough to keep some behind to send word that both General and Pharaoh were killed, so he could seize the crown when the palace and Ankhesenamun were left vulnerable.

"What if we tell the camp that Pharaoh and I succumbed to our injuries?"

Paramesse's eyebrow raised and he tilted his head at his General's odd question.

Horemheb continued. "Then let the remaining traitors go back to Waset to tell Pawah. Tonight, send our known loyal messengers to Vizier Ay and Queen Ankhesenamun to tell them we have perished." He closed his eyes, trying to stand still and keep the ground from moving. "Because Ay needs to be coronated before Pawah learns of what happened here. Once they receive the news, I believe Ay should then marry Ankhesenamun and keep the throne from falling into Pawah's hands."

"But you are Hereditary Prince," Paramesse stated. "The throne is yours if Pharaoh should die without an heir."

"If Pharaoh lives, he will be seen as a god, Osiris, risen from the dead to the people. It will squash any form of doubt in all the people's minds, and there will be no more threat of rebellion from Pawah's supporters." Horemheb looked to the three men and the dead man, Sitayet. "We can end this now."

"And if Pharaoh dies?" Paramesse whispered, and his eyes squinted at his friend.

"If he dies, then I go back, gathering support at Mennefer and Waset before I reach Malkata." Horemheb looked off toward camp, his face paling even more. He rubbed his fingers and felt the clamminess of his palms. "And then *I* will be seen as Osiris, risen from the dead. We will have set out, finally, what we were to do with Pharaoh Amenhotep and his Queen Tiye: usurp power from the priesthood of Amun and make Pharaoh all-powerful. There will be none who cross him, for who would cross a god risen from the dead?"

Despite the warm blood that ran down his back, his extremities felt cold. A small wave of nausea caused him to clamp his jaw shut.

Paramesse took a step toward Horemheb and reached out an arm to his friend. "Ay is an old man. Do you think he will live much longer?"

"He will live long enough for one of us to get back to Malkata," Horemheb gambled. The ground started to spin, and he grabbed onto Paramesse's arm for support.

"You are losing much blood." Paramesse snapped to a few wayside soldiers: "Take him to camp, bandage his wounds."

As they came, Paramesse whispered to Horemheb, "I hope you are right. For your sake and for Egypt's."

HOREMHEB AWOKE TO SOMETHING WET DABBING ON HIS HEAD and body. His eyes darted around. His vision blurred, but something flickered in his sight. Was he still on the battlefield? Was he dead? His leg felt stiff and his shoulder and neck felt stiff as well . . . restricted.

Torchlight. That was what flickered. His vision began to come back to him. His hand lay beside him and he felt his cot.

"Am I in my tent?"

His lips felt pasty and dry, so he licked them as he continued to look around. He heard a murmur in response, but he couldn't quite make out what the voice said.

"Am I in my tent?" he muttered again, and this time a more clear voice accompanied his vision as it finally returned to him.

"Yes, General Horemheb."

He rolled to his good side and sat up. His leg was wrapped in layers of linen and honey. He sat there for moment, feeling a wet rag on one side of his neck. He wanted to slap it away, but he lacked the strength; instead he felt what was on his neck and shoulder: more linen. The sweet smell of dried honey reached his nostrils. He couldn't quite turn his head, but finally noticed a servant boy dabbing wet rags on his head and body. He must have developed a fever at some point.

"How long have I been here?"

"Fourteen days," the servant boy said. "You lost much blood, but your wounds are healing."

Horemheb put his hand to his face, unbelieving that it had been almost two decans. "Is Pharaoh alive?" The question hovered in the air as Horemheb braced himself for the truth.

After a few moments of silence the servant whispered, "For now. He does not fare well. He fell very ill a few days ago and is not improving. His leg is healing, but his body does not seem to be. He shakes, saying he is cold, but his body is hot to the touch."

Horemheb's heart rate fell to a sluggish pace. He hung his head and winced at the strain of the muscle in his shoulder. Men had died from this evil spirit that now had a hold on Tut. If they were in Malkata, he could call the priests to try and lift the spirit from him; but they were here in this wretched place.

He watched the servant dab the linen cloth on his leg as he thought about Tut lying in his cot, sick and injured, and prayed to the gods that he would pull through. He closed his eyes and leaned on his hand as he tried to get the ground to stop moving.

"Don't move your head too much, General," the servant warned. "The physician had to stitch your shoulder back together. The khopesh went deeper than he thought originally."

Horemheb's hand dropped to his lap, and he let out a breath. "My leg?" he asked, looking at the bandage. He lifted it up and saw that a deep gash had scabbed over right above his knee.

"Your leg is healing. The physician said you should probably be able to regain your full mobility."

Horemheb nodded, but the pain in his shoulder was more than he thought should accompany the motion. He tried to still his head to pacify the growing pain in his shoulder and neck. "How much time does the physician give Pharaoh to become well?"

"He didn't know." The servant stopped talking abruptly so that he may focus on his task.

"What is it? What more is there?" Horemheb asked as he pushed away the cloth.

The servant did not look at him and hunched his shoulders. "I am not to say."

"Tell me. I am General of Pharaoh's Armies. Follow my command." Horemheb's chest tingled as he waited for the rest of the truth.

The servant closed his eyes. "Pharaoh will not become well. The physician said the sickness can take a few days or a few decans. He said he usually sees it take people according to their size—larger people take longer to die and smaller people take shorter."

Horemheb felt the cold chill spread from his fingers into his hands as a tremble reverberated through his muscles.

No . . . no . . .

His breath caught in his throat as he tried to swallow the truth. Finally, he was able to breathe.

If I survive, I will kill Pawah after I make him endure the same agony he has caused me.

"When did Pharaoh fall ill?" His voice wavered with his vision.

"Only four days ago," the servant said, "but he is not a large man."

Horemheb clenched his fist. "It could be any time," he whispered, and set his jaw. He went to stand. "I must see him."

"No, General," the servant said, and touched his good shoulder. "The physician said you need to rest."

"Move, or I will throw you out of my way!"

Horemheb's hard, set stare scared the servant into submission; the boy's hand snapped back and his head bowed as he stepped back. Horemheb stood, despite the searing pain in his leg and back; he shuffled his feet to keep his balance.

Paramesse entered Horemheb's tent. "I thought I heard your voice," Paramesse said, and tried to guide him back to the cot. "You need to regain your strength."

"No, I need to see Pharaoh." Horemheb pushed Paramesse's hand away from his body and shuffled again. He fell to his knee, his injured leg giving out beneath him.

"Then take this, General Horemheb," his servant said, and offered Horemheb a cane.

Horemheb looked at it and realized how much he was going to miss Tut if he did not survive.

Paramesse smirked and shook his head as Horemheb steadied himself to stand. "You never listen to anyone."

"Not when Pharaoh lies dying."

Paramesse took a hard look at Horemheb and breathed deep. "Let me walk with you."

Horemheb nodded, thanking Paramesse for his understanding, as the servant handed him warm water that was boiled for purification. He drank until he became sick to his stomach, but he felt less dizzy. Then he nodded to Paramesse to take him to see Tut. They came to Pharaoh's tent as Horemheb hobbled along, but before Horemheb entered where Tut lay, Paramesse touched his good shoulder.

"Friend, it is likely he will not survive. If you go back to Malkata, you will need to be fully healed and have your strength back to face the people. You will need to stay hidden with a chosen few."

"Have you sent word to Vizier Ay?"

"Yes. They are probably reaching Men-nefer by now, if the path is clear, with the attackers in tow. They will be executed for conspiracy and murder of Pharaoh and the Hereditary Prince. Only your and Pharaoh's servants, my troop commanders, and I know you and Pharaoh are alive."

Horemheb nodded, not really listening, his mind filling with dread at seeing the young man whom he had come to love for one last time.

"Good," he told Paramesse.

Then, after a hesitation, not knowing what he would see and wanting time to stand still so he would never have to say goodbye, he entered Pharaoh's inner tent.

Tut lay there shivering with cold sweat, his body hot to the touch. Servants dabbed him with cool water. Horemheb hobbled over to him, noticing Tut's crown on its stand and his dagger made of ba-en-pet below. A blood-stain cloth lay next to it.

"I got one of them." Tut's whisper broke Horemheb's stare. "But there were too many."

"Please leave us," Horemheb asked the servants, who obeyed. Horemheb shuffled around to look at Tut's bandaged left leg.

Tut struggled to speak as his eyes found Horemheb through his heavy eyelids. "The men who attacked me said *you* ordered them to."

Horemheb's mouth contorted into a grimace, and he could utter but a single word. "Pawah."

"I know," Tut said, nodding his head. "I should have thrown him in prison, or worse."

Horemheb closed his eyes. "And I should have killed him long ago." His whisper paralyzed his stomach. "I have failed you, Pharaoh."

"No. I was the one who wanted to go off on my own." Tut chuckled and swatted the air above him. "I always knew this wretched foot would fail me." He chuckled again through his gasping breaths.

Horemheb pressed his lips into a thin line as he looked down at Tut's leg. He hated himself for letting the boy take the blame from him and place it upon his deformity.

Tut pointed to Horemheb's cane. "It looks as though you will be taking my place."

"Do not jest, Pharaoh." Horemheb smiled, looking at the cane. "No one can ever replace the great Tutankhamun."

Tut laughed as he tried to breathe. "They said my leg is healing, but now I've become sick." He tried to suck in some air through his labored breaths.

Horemheb lowered himself and knelt on his good knee next to Pharaoh's cot. "You will—"

Tut shook his head and put his hand to Horemheb's mouth to silence him. "I know. I can feel it coming."

And suddenly Tut's eyes rolled in their place and he drifted off to a fitful sleep.

Horemheb's brow furrowed as he watched Tut struggle, wishing he could take the boy's place, wishing somehow he could take this away from him; but instead he watched him, helpless and unable to comfort his Pharaoh. He folded his arms and placed his head on them, still by Tut's side, and closed his eyes.

He would stay there until the end. It was all he could do.

AFTER AN INDETERMINATE AMOUNT OF TIME TUT BROKE HIS thoughts.

"I want you to know something—" Tut coughed. "All my life, all I ever wanted . . ." He stopped to catch his breath again, then: ". . . was someone to love me . . ."

His whisper reached Horemheb's ears as he came out of his light slumber next to Pharaoh. Tut didn't speak the remainder of his thought: *as a son.* His teeth rattled and his body shook with the chills of infection.

Horemheb grabbed his hand as Tut took as deep a breath as he could before the aching pain in his abdomen kept him from inhaling any more.

"Please, Horemheb . . . please tell Ankhesenamun I am so, so sorry. For everything." Tut coughed, then forged on with his words. "I want her to be happy more than anything. I want her to find someone who loves her as I do now, someone who can love her more."

"I will," Horemheb whispered, watching Tut try to catch his breath.

He finally was able to get a good breath, and it allowed him to speak: "I was too blind to see those who could see past my shortcomings."

"No, Pharaoh—"

"Please . . . call me Tut," he said through his rattling teeth. Beads of sweat ran down his brow. "I should have asked you to call me by that name a long time ago."

Horemheb placed his other hand on the young man's and closed his eyes.

"Tut . . . you had no shortcomings. You were a child thrust into a man's role . . . a god's role. You are strong. You overcame every obstacle, every failure, every setback. You became *everything* I hoped you would become."

Tut smiled. His hands trembled. "And at the end," he whispered, "I can see what my life could be." He closed his eyes at the irony of it all. "Is that what happens, General—"

"Horemheb."

"Is that what happens, Horemheb?" Tut whispered.

"What?"

Tut clutched his stomach as he gagged, but then settled himself.

"At the end, is that what happens? Do you see all of your mistakes, see the life you could have had if you had done things differently?"

Horemheb felt Tut's words encompass his whole being. "Yes," he said, as two tears pushed forth from his eyes. He put his other hand on Tut's head and wiped the sweat from his face, as a father would his son. "Yes. But Tut," he whispered, as Tut's eyes closed and rolled under his eyelids, "remember this: you grew from all of your mistakes. That is more than most can say. You should be proud of your life, for I am—" His throat closed, prohibiting him from finishing his sentence.

Tut opened his eyes and found Horemheb's gaze. "I am going to die soon?"

Horemheb clenched his jaw. It was a truth he was not ready to accept, but his nature forced him to nod. He leaned forward and placed a kiss on Tut's forehead.

At least I have more time to say goodbye to him than I had with Nefertiti. I will cherish these few moments the gods grant me.

Tut's face drained of color. "Horemheb, I always wanted to tell you something—" He stopped, lacking the energy to speak more.

He cannot breathe. Tell him, Horemheb! Tell him you love him. Take whatever agony comes. It is the truth! he yelled at himself.

Just as the light began to leave Pharaoh's eyes, Horemheb grabbed both of Tut's hands in his and leaned in close. Knowing Tut's time was almost up, he let the tears flow from his eyes as the words flowed from his heart:

"I love you, *my* son."

A small smile and a sparkle in his eyes graced Tut's ashen face. His lips trembled as he mustered the last of his energy. "Remember me," he whispered, "*my* father."

And then his chest sunk into the cot, not to move again.

"Always."

Horemheb placed both of Tut's lifeless hands over Tut's chest, trying to keep the tremble in his hands from overtaking his arms and the tears from turning into sobs. His mouth contorted into a grimace as he laid his head on Tut's shoulder.

Then, after a moment, the realization that Tut would never breathe again hit him, and an agonizing moan escaped his lips as the threads holding his already broken heart were plucked away once again.

SOLDIERS WHO HAD TRAINED AS PRIESTS BEGAN THE mummification process on their King. Paramesse—at the request of a hidden Horemheb—made sure they rubbed black tar on his skin so that he could be as Osiris in the afterlife.

He would rise again. His name would be remembered forevermore.

Many parts of the rituals were not as clean as they could have been, as they performed them in the midst of a battle over the next two months. Once completed, Tut's body began the journey back to Waset, to be buried in his tomb in the Valley of the Kings. But first, his makeshift coffin went through the campground so all could pay their respects to their Pharaoh.

Horemheb watched from his tent as Tut's body passed through the camp. When he could not bear it anymore, he whispered to Paramesse, who stood just outside his tent flap, "I should go back to Waset now."

"You need your strength, friend, if you are to fight Pawah. If you are to take the crown. You need your rest. You need to heal."

Inside, Horemheb knew Paramesse to be right, and so he watched as the men bowed to pay their respects to their young Pharaoh.

When he returned, however, he would have his revenge on the one named Pawah.

CHAPTER 31
THE TIME OF TAKING

ANKHESENAMUN SAT ON THE THRONE IN HER HUSBAND'S place. Her heart both jumped and sank each time the throne room doors opened. Her eyes longed to see Tut enter; her ears dreaded the news brought when it was not Tut who entered. It was no different today when the doors opened yet again. Her grandfather stood by her side as a soldier messenger approached and bowed.

"My Queen," he said, raising his head. "I bring ill news from the frontlines of the Mitanni and Egyptian border."

"Have we lost a vassal state?" Her voice held a deeper fear, as it had with every messenger that had come from the northern border.

"No, my Queen. Much worse news." The messenger took a breath as he looked upon the widowed Queen.

Ankhesenamun closed her eyes and wet her lip anticipating the worse.

His words were quick: "Pharaoh Tutankhamun and General Horemheb have perished on the battlefront. They were killed by men commanded by Pawah. He is in Waset."

The shock held her breath at bay. Even though she had

anticipated the news, she still was not ready for it, especially with the news Pawah still haunted them. The messenger's words hit her as if a stone wall had fallen atop her. The pit of her stomach weighted her to the throne and dragged her shoulders down with it, causing her chin to tremble.

At her silence, Vizier Ay stepped forward from his position behind Ankhesenamun's throne. "Who else knows of this, messenger?"

The messenger stood straight, his eyes not on vizier Ay but on his Queen. "A company of us were disbanded three decans ago to bring word of their deaths. One of our number separated from us in the night. The remaining are outside Malkata's throne room. We do not know where the missing soldier went. Otherwise, our northern army, our company, and now you, Vizier Ay, and Queen Ankhesenamun know of our Pharaoh and the Hereditary Prince's death."

Ay pursed his lips and said with as forceful a command as he could muster, "Leave us." His voice had become less bold than it had in his youth, yet all left—all except High Steward Wenamen, whom Ay had gestured to stay.

Ay turned to Ankhesenamun. "We must assume Pawah knows this by now."

Ankhesenamun stared blankly ahead as tears welled in her eyes. "Tut is . . . dead?" Her voice was barely above a breathless whisper.

"My child." Ay placed both of his hands on her arms and knelt so he was at eye-level with her. "I know the pain. When Pawah killed your mother . . ." He stopped and gathered himself. "I know this pain. But if we are to succeed, we must tend to the throne before we can grieve. We must keep the throne from Pawah. Keep *Egypt* from Pawah."

"Tut is dead," Ankhesenamun whispered again, lost in her grandfather's words.

Ay rubbed her arms as if trying to wake a newborn babe. "Ankhesenamun, please be with me. Here. Now."

She found his gaze as tears streamed forth from her eyes.

"Marry me or marry Pawah. Those are your choices, Ankhesenamun. He will come after you, as you are the last living daughter of Pharaoh Akhenaten. You are the last Hereditary Princess. You must decide now before it is too late."

Ankhesenamun pushed her grief aside and wiped her tears, finally sensing the urgency in his voice. "I . . . I ch-choose you, Grandfather," she stammered through the tears that replaced the ones she had wiped away.

Ay took her hand and pulled her to her feet. "We can grieve later, but now we must make sure the throne is kept from Pawah."

She nodded as more tears streamed down her face. "Egypt must come first."

Ay's eyes narrowed as he thought about the sacrifice his lotus blossom made for Egypt. He would not let the same happen to his granddaughter. "When this over, I will make sure you are happy. Not only for your sake, but for my own debts to your mother."

"How can I be happy again?"

"Time will provide." Ay nodded, then pressed his forehead to hers. "We must now be married, and I must be coronated before Pawah realizes what has happened to Pharaoh Tutankhamun and seizes the throne."

She found her grandfather's eyes and pressed her lips into a straight line. "I am ready."

Ay looked into Ankhesenamun's face, seeing her resemblance to Nefertiti. "You are strong like your mother."

Ankhesenamun smiled. She felt a gentle breeze against her back, and knew her mother went with her to whatever future lay before her.

Ay told Wenamen to send for the First Prophet of Amun, Wennefer, and the others to come to the throne room. Then he took her hand and readied himself to receive the crown.

PAWAH PACED INSIDE HIS STOLEN HOME IN WASET, WAITING TO hear if the fool Sitayet had decided to do what he told him. He knew where each man's family lived, and had enough oil and torches to consume all of their homes. He had dreamed about the thrill of going along at night and setting fires, but he suppressed the urge to do it anyway, for there were more important goals in his life.

A knock came at Pawah's door, jarring him from his thoughts.

"Open it!" he ordered Merka.

A soldier messenger, Yey, bowed with a sneer. "Sitayet was killed, along with all those he ordered to attack Pharaoh. You will keep your promise to their families?"

"Yes, yes, of course." Pawah waved his hand to Merka to weigh out the grain for their families. "And the boy and his General?"

Yey's jaw clenched before he spoke. "Both dead."

Pawah thrust his hands into the air to retrieve his own victory, dancing in a circle. "Years and years of work, and now the crown is mine!"

"Pharaoh Tutankhamun disowned you," Yey said. "How do you have the right to the throne?"

"Ankhesenamun is Hereditary Princess, and she promised herself to me." Pawah sneered and threw a tabletop figurine at Yey, who ducked, and it smashed into the wall behind him. "Do not question me again, or risk your life!"

Yey stood like a scared boy in the corner of the room until finally he nodded. "As you command."

"Good. Glad you can be of some use. Glad for your families."

When Yey left with a slam of the door, Pawah went to where Merka was weighing grain and emptied the scales. "We will not pay them. We have more important matters to pay for."

Merka bowed his head in obedience. "Afterward, then?"

"No! We do not pay those who are no longer useful. Sitayet and the others are dead."

Merka swallowed but bowed his head again.

"Gather my finest linen and jewelry. I shall go to Malkata to be crowned King of Egypt!"

TUT'S BODY HAD NOT YET REACHED WASET WHEN PAWAH heard the news of Ay's coronation a day later, when Yey came back to tell him. Pawah let out a curse, curling his arms over his head. In that moment, he wished he had never killed Beketaten, for now it would have proved useful to be married to a daughter of Pharaoh Amenhotep III—disowned or not. He cursed himself as he ran his nails down his cheek, leaving temporary marks upon his handsome face.

He paced as he began to think up a new plan. He just needed Ankhesenamun to be his bride and Ay dead. He'd already killed four Pharaohs—what was one more? He looked to Yey and an idea struck. One solider was all he needed. Yey could bring him to the palace saying he found him in Waset and arrested him, knowing of his exile. The palace would lack its usual amount of guards, for they had gone north to fight the Hittites. Then he would kill Ay, blame Yey, and, finally, force Ankhesenamun to be his wife. He slid his dagger into the long sleeve of his robe and grinned, envisioning wearing the crown that very night.

And so, under threat of death, Yey took Pawah to Malkata under the guise of having captured him as a prisoner.

After a few moments walking silently down the halls, Pawah turned to order Yey to Pharaoh Ay's bedchambers. Pawah's head snapped in each direction to look for Yey, but he was alone. Yey had slipped away. He let out a small growl.

"Well, he has sealed his family's fate," he muttered.

Quickly, he tried to adapt his plan now that his scapegoat, Yey, was nowhere to be found as he walked to Pharaoh Ay's bedchambers. He would lie in wait—

Or so he thought, until he saw Ankhesenamun exiting the throne room, Hori walking behind her. He thought about killing the old man first, as originally planned, but now there was no one to blame for his death.

He watched Hori and Ankhesenamun walk away from him. Perhaps it would be to his advantage to pull the defenseless Ankhesenamun into Ay's bedchambers and demand Ay to give him the crown? Then he could hit his future wife over the head and strangle the old man . . . and tell everyone he died in his sleep? Yes. That would work. With no one left for the throne, and Ankhesenamun's promise to marry him, they would *have* to believe him and crown him King of Egypt.

So instead of going first to kill Ay, Pawah grabbed a moderate-sized stone statue that stood on a small pillar and snuck up behind Hori.

ANKHESENAMUN WIPED HER EYES AND WALKED WITH HER CHIN down. Her Tut was gone. Still, her eyes narrowed in anger. *Pawah.* The bronze blade pressed against her side, wrapped securely in her belt. She took a shaky breath. Her training with Sennedjem had been a long time ago. Doubt encased her mind—doubt of her abilities to successfully defend herself. But at least the strong and loyal Hori walked behind her, always, as if a shadow. A small, pressed smile arose on her lips. She knew she was safe with him.

Just then she heard a *thud* behind her. She spun around and saw Pawah standing over her protector with a bloody statue in his hand. Before she could react beyond a small yell, he rushed upon her, wrenched her wrists, and pulled her close.

"You will silence your tongue, Ankhesenamun." His breath ate at her eyes as one of his hands released her wrist and pushed on her mouth.

Her jaw clamped shut; he removed his hand from her mouth.

"My grandfather will never let you steal the throne." Her eyes burned at his sneer. Every force in her body wanted to take the dagger from her belt and stab him over and over and over again—for her father, her mother, and now for her husband. She wished she was as the goddess Isis and could bring him back to life only to kill him again.

"Your grandfather is an old man." Pawah thrust her against the wall as he leaned in close. "Ah . . . this is a familiar scene, if I recall the throne room of Aketaten. I give you the same option as I gave your mother, Ankhesenamun: die or be my Queen."

Ankhesenamun's nostrils flared and images flashed in her mind: her mother's dead body on the stone floor of the council room . . . her mother's muffled scream filling her ears . . . Pawah's lips upon hers as she realized, eight long years ago, that he had power over her in Aketaten. Her vision hazed from the rage that rose from her chest, but she matched his smug manner.

"Your ultimatum has little hold now, since you have been disowned by Pharaoh Tutankhamun. My grandfather will never grant you any authority in Egypt. No one will ever remember the man who began his descent as the Fifth Prophet of Amun. I curse you to be erased from all of history."

He only opened his mouth as his ears turned red.

She seemed to have rendered him speechless in the moment, and so Ankhesenamun smiled at him and took her opportunity. As though Sennedjem was right there with her guiding her arms and body through the motions, she slid her arm up and down, locking Pawah's arms against her chest; she took her other hand, curling it into a fist, and she swung and pummeled him against the side of his head.

"No one will remember you—"

She kneed him in the stomach, causing him to huddle over.

"—and after all your tries and—"

She grabbed her hands together, forming a ball, and thrust them down on top of his back, sending him to the floor.

"—attempts and murders—"

Then she kicked him with so much force, she ripped her skirt from the wind-up.

"—you will amount to *nothing*. You will have come so close to taking the crown, and in the end, you will fail. Your entire life was spent on achieving something you will never attain."

She kicked him again in the stomach, but he grabbed her foot and pulled, causing her to fall off balance. He grabbed her by her head as he stood and thrust her back against the wall, gripping her jaw almost to break it. Ankhesenamun let out a whimper as her hand fell to her side. She tried to reach the dagger Sennedjem had given her in her belt, but her fingers could only run along the handle and could not fully grasp it.

Blood trickled from his nose and lip. "You should have called for help when given the chance, you worthless fool," Pawah said as he pushed his hand down hard on her throat. "I don't need you. Horemheb is dead and Ay will be soon enough." He whispered in her ear: "I am still the last living male relative to the throne, and it will be mine."

"The throne room is not yours," Ankhesenamun said through labored breaths.

With one hand she tried to pull away his fingers on her throat, the other grasping the dagger's handle at last. She yanked it, ripping it from her belt. She wanted to bury that dagger deep within his heart, but the wall would not let her get the angle she needed, so she swung her arm up, slicing a long slit on Pawah's chest and chin.

He yelled, stumbling backward and grabbing his face. "You demoness! You daughter of Set! You conniving—"

The narcissistic wretch finally had a stain to his face. Ankhesenamun hiked her dress and kicked him in the head, knocking him to the floor once again, but this time motionless.

"If you hadn't pinned me to the wall . . . you'd be a dead man," she coughed.

As her knuckles went white around the handle of the dagger, she thought about plunging it into his chest as he had to her mother. She pushed the image of her mother's bloody body from her mind. She wanted him to suffer more than just a quick death from a knife wound to the heart.

"You will die a traitor to the throne," she whispered. "And I will relish knowing the pain you suffered every day for the rest of my life."

Hori sat up and let out a gasp as he looked around, blood running down his cheek and head. "Chief royal wife, has he hurt you?"

"He tried to kill me." Ankhesenamun spoke through a

raspy breath as she pulled at her throat, realizing then how hard he'd choked her.

Hori stood, albeit a bit wobbly at first, but then came to kick Pawah himself, the traitor still motionless on the floor.

"You will die for this," Hori spat at him.

He bound Pawah and dragged him into the Malkata throne room for Pharaoh Ay to sentence, Ankhesenamun looking on with triumph.

AY GRINNED FROM EAR TO EAR WHEN HE SAW PAWAH THROWN at his feet.

Pawah awoke and his eyes darted around the throne room.

"We found the former Vizier Pawah attempting to strangle chief royal wife Ankhesenamun," Hori declared, and pointed at Pawah. Blood still trickled from his head, but he stood strong.

"You saw nothing, you pathetic waste of a royal guard!" Pawah yelled at Hori, who promptly struck him in the back with the butt end of his spear.

Ay stood, feeling the coursing rage and racing joy chase each other throughout his veins. His heart thumped loudly in his ears. The corners of his mouth curled up in victory, and a slow escape of air cleansed his body. Eight long years he had waited. Revenge on his daughter's murderer was now within reach. The crown sat upon his head, and its weight felt good as he peered down at the one who had taken everything from him. He had known Pawah would come, for he was too greedy not to. And now, at last, he could watch the cursed man die.

Ay walked down the platform steps and around Pawah—at a considerable distance, knowing Pawah was still in his prime, and he an old man not having the strength to withstand an attack.

"The gods have smiled upon me this day, you traitor to the throne," Ay said, pulling his hands behind his back.

Pawah sneered. "I am no traitor, Pharaoh Ay. I only tried to resist the seductress."

"I grow tired of his lies, Pharaoh," Ankhesenamun's voice resounded off the stone throne room. "He attacked me in Aketaten, spread lies about me to Pharaoh Tutankhamun, and has tried to murder me in Malkata." She walked around to the front of Pawah, where Ay now stood.

"He has done these things to you, my Queen." Ay looked to her, knowing she needed revenge too. Nefertiti was his daughter, but she was Ankhesenamun's mother, and Tut was her husband. "You, my Queen, decide his fate."

Ankhesenamun took a deep breath, as if to soak up her moment of victory. She closed her eyes and lifted her chin. The dagger still dripped Pawah's blood as she held it loosely in her hand.

"There is nothing more I want to do than to kill him myself," she whispered. "But I want him to suffer as the traitor and murderer he is."

Ay nodded and smiled, thinking the same.

"Death," Ankhesenamun ordered. The crisp ring of her voice sounded in the pillared throne room.

"Death it shall be," Ay commanded. "Impalement in front of the temple of Amun-Re for treason and conspiracy against Pharaoh Neferneferuaten, Pharaoh Tutankhamun and Pharaoh's chief royal wife. The traitor's body shall be burned so that he may have no afterlife."

Pawah looked to Ineni and Amenket, the guards, as they stepped forward to carry him out. "Thus Pharaoh says," they both said in unison, and each grabbed an arm.

Hori watched them fulfill their duties without interfering,

but eyed Ineni until he left the throne room before taking his place on the side wall next to Queen Ankhesenamun's throne. He would wait to escort Ankhesenamun to the palace physician.

Ay looked to Ankhesenamun. "Finally." He pressed his forehead to his granddaughter's. "Finally we can rest."

"I miss them," Ankhesenamun said with tears in her eyes. "It still does not bring them back to us."

"No, but at least I can die knowing she is avenged . . . and Mut the widow of a rich man, and you the Queen—free to marry whomever you wish when I am gone. Name your Hereditary Prince, my Ankhesenamun. I will declare him and you can be happy." Ay stroked her face. "I could not give your mother happiness, but I can give it to you."

Ankhesenamun's heart still ached for Tut, and her gaze fell. She opened her mouth to speak, but Ay spoke first, seeing her hesitation.

"After some time for grieving and healing," Ay suggested, and placed his finger under her chin, lifting her face to his.

"Yes." It was the only word she could muster, and knowing Pawah would soon be dead, she finally felt safe, and her heart felt at peace, even in its sorrow.

DOWN THE CORRIDOR AND ALMOST TO THE PALACE DOORS, Ineni and Amenket let go of Pawah. "You will leave now," Ineni ordered. "We have repaid our debt. Life for life. Now begone. Leave Egypt if you want to live. We will be telling the chief royal guard you have escaped in a few moments."

"I still own you," Pawah put a bloody finger in Ineni's face. "Don't you forget, you are traitor to the throne as well, and I keep excellent records. You were among the ones who turned a blind eye to Akhenaten and Smenkare's deaths. You even conspired to kill Pharaoh Neferneferuaten as well. I have supporters that will bring those letters to Pharaoh, and I will not hesitate to take both of you with me to the execution poles."

Ineni's face fell as if he wished he had never made a deal with this evil man. He chewed his lip as his eyes narrowed on Pawah. Then with a sneer, he mumbled, "We will tell them you escaped in the morning."

Pawah patted Ineni's cheek and Amenket's shoulder. "Good." Then Pawah turned to leave. He tightened his robe to cover that girl's dagger strike and hoped no one would notice the blood trickling from his chin on his otherwise perfect face.

Taking in a deep breath of fresh air outside the palace walls, he knew exactly where he was headed: Men-nefer. He had heard a certain widow now resided there. Would the old man Pharaoh die with *two* daughters' lives on his conscience? No, he thought not. Leverage Mut's life for the crown, and then his final goal would be achieved. *Good things come to me*, he thought, *when I take what I want*. Victory tingled his lips as a smile spread over them.

EPILOGUE

THE TIME OF REMEMBERING

His retelling finished, Horemheb fell mute. Silence overcame the room.

His eyes welled with tears as he remembered all that had been lost and would be remembered no more: his love, his Nefertiti . . . his unborn son he had never known . . . the man he called his son, Tutankhamun . . . Ankhesenamun and Ay.

They will all be lost to time, their names never uttered again—a true eternal death here among the living, so unworthy of royalty.

His gaze fell to the feet of Amun's statue.

Forgive me, Tut.

Forgive me, Nefertiti.

"Pharaoh," First Prophet Wennefer spoke. "Will you continue into the night, or shall we reconvene tomorrow?" Wennefer shook his head, as if disapproving of how many more days this Pharaoh would draw out a story soon to be forgotten.

Horemheb knew they all grew increasingly frustrated with these days of retelling. But he ignored this as he lifted his chin once again.

"Pharaoh Ay did what he thought was best—" Pharaoh

Horemheb's voice cracked. He licked his lips and let out a heavy breath, holding his tears at bay. Clamping his jaw shut, he peered to his wife. Ay did at least give something back to his granddaughter.

But he would speak of that tomorrow.

The sun dipped low over the horizon, its shadow cast throughout most of the room. The five prophets of Amun sat with slouched backs, tiring of his tales as their feet waited in eagerness to go destroy the past.

Pharaoh Horemheb looked to the papyrus edict in front of him and the sloshed ink in the well. His eyes darted between the reed brush and the place for his cartouche and seal on the edict.

One more day, he thought. *One more day, and then I will be able to say goodbye.*

His teeth ground together as his jaw clenched tighter.

I only lie to myself. I have already said goodbye, and yet I cannot bring myself to say goodbye again. I will spend the rest of my life saying goodbye.

"We shall meet at first light."

Pharaoh's words hung heavy in the air and his chest drew stiff. He knew he could not go on to a fifth day, as there was no more story to tell after tomorrow. His stalling was becoming evident, and he knew he would have to sign the edict at tomorrow's sunset. Numbness overtook his fingers and toes as a perceived chill in the air enveloped his body and pulled the corners of his contorted mouth downward.

His love, his Nefertiti—her words came back to him in that moment.

Will I ever just have love?

He had responded, *You have my love.*

But he realized now that she meant *peace.* She had wanted peace in this life; and now he understood her unfulfilled desire, for after tomorrow he would never have peace again knowing he erased her memory.

For Egypt, he thought. *Egypt takes much. How much more will Egypt take from me?*

He looked to Mut and his unborn child, and took a long breath as the prophets exited the room. Mut walked to face him and put her hands on his shoulders as he stood. He leaned his forehead to hers.

"I am sorry, Mut, my Queen. This . . . this weighs so heavy on me. I have fought many battles. I have won many wars. But this . . . *this* . . ." He closed his eyes as his ribs constricted his lungs.

"I know," she whispered at his silence. She stroked his cheek. Tears pooled in her eyes as well. "But may Amun be with us and give us strength."

Pharaoh Horemheb shook his head as the next words flowed on his breath.

"No. May Amun grant *peace.*"

THE STORY CONTINUES
SILENCE IN THE STONE BOOK IV

Silence in the Stone Book IV

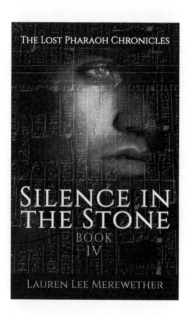

Reborn as Osiris, General Horemheb stakes his claim to the throne and takes his final revenge.

Receiving the crown with his Queen by his side, Pharaoh Horemheb knows all should be well in a flourishing and peaceful Egypt. *Yet* the position of Pharaoh is skirted and dishonored. The Amun priesthood suffers fear and restraint from the people who now know their past corruptions.

How will he do what needs to be done to reestablish the power of Pharaoh and keep authority over the priesthood? And how will he live with his overwhelming guilt?

EXCERPT FROM CHAPTER ONE: THE TIME OF DEPRAVITY

One day was all he needed.

Pawah planted his feet outside the palace doors of Malkata as he peered over his shoulder at the two royal guards escorting him away, Ineni and Amenket.

"In the morning, we will tell the chief royal guard you have escaped." Amenket glowered at Pawah, gripping his spear with both hands. "Then we will have paid our debt."

Ineni nodded, his knuckles growing white from their firm grip upon his own spear.

Pawah leered at the two men. *Your debt will never be repaid.*

Their eyes bore into his own, but Pawah knew he still held the upper hand. He needn't remind them that their letters to him indicted them in the murders of Pharaoh Akhenaten and Pharaoh Smenkare.

Ineni spat at Pawah's feet as they closed Malkata's doors to him.

"Fools," Pawah whispered under his breath, and began to calculate what needed to be done prior to the morning. He stared at the sun in the sky. *Midday.* He wrapped his robe tightly over the bleeding dagger wound in his chest and wiped his chin with his forearm, letting his sleeve fall to cover the blood on his arm. *Curse Ankhesenamun and her dagger.*

He went and stooped at the Nile's edge and lapped up some water to wash his chin free of any smeared blood. His mind raced. *What to do? What to do now?* His plans to take the crown thus far had failed. *First, I need to hide.*

Narrowing his eyes against the sunlight, he made out the barge to take him across the Nile to the city of Waset. He needed to stop by his stolen estate first and gather some needed items before the royal guards came to arrest him. *Do I run? Flee Egypt?* His nose wrinkled in response.

"I have come too close to give up now," he whispered from the depths of his chest.

He began to walk toward the barge.

Blood drizzled from his lip, but his tongue lapped it up.

You will pay for that, little girl.

The barge worker looked the other way as Pawah boarded.

At least I have a few still loyal to me, he thought as he stood at the end. He peered over the Nile to the city of Waset in the east. *I have more than a few. I can always secure loyalty other ways, but my funds are running thin.*

He ran his thumb over his finger pads as he looked into the waters of the Nile. A crocodile sat nearby, waiting for something to be snatched up.

Waiting . . . He shook his head. *I waited too long. I should have seized the crown when I had the chance, when we could have killed all of them in one night, instead of saving Egyptian blood and giving Nefertiti the hemlock-laced wine to take to her husband. Why didn't I let the rebels storm Aketaten and kill the royal family? I would have been King. All of it for naught!*

His fist made contact with the barge's railing.

"No," he whispered. *I have come too far . . . too close . . . but how do I give myself another chance? How? How?!*

He watched as the crocodile's mighty jaws snapped from the water with a fish in tow.

That's what I do. I am done waiting. A frustrated breath accompanied his thoughts as he remembered his long-held motto: strike only when you can win. *But look where that got me. I am out of ideas. Think, Pawah. Ay is Pharaoh. Ankhesenamun is Hereditary Princess—but, unfortunately, I will have to do away with her like her mother. If she only did not refuse me . . . and Ay, he has no sons. Horemheb is dead, as well as that wretched boy Tut, so there is no Hereditary Prince.*

A thought struck him.

Hereditary Prince . . . yes . . . I must make Ay name me Hereditary Prince . . . but how? He won't name me on his own accord . . . and his daughter is dead so there will be no Hereditary Prince by marriage.

A small flash of jealous lust came over his eyes. "Nefertiti," his lips crooned. "Why did you refuse me?" His head slung back and forth; he both hated her and wanted her. "We could have been great, you and I . . . me as Pharaoh, you as my wife." His mind flashed to all of the desires he'd held for her in his own twisted imagination.

Then he stopped as a realization dawned on him: Nefertiti had a younger sister. *What was her name?* He watched the crocodile yet again prey on an unsuspecting fish as the barge moved toward Waset.

"*Mut.*"

He held his chin up and thrust out his chest, standing as tall as the statues in Ipet-isut.

"Mut . . . Horemheb's wife." *His widow.*

He knew then exactly where he was headed: Men-nefer.

Would the old man Pharaoh die with two daughters' lives on his conscience? No, he thought not. Leverage Mut's life for the crown, and then his final goal would be achieved.

Good things come to me, he thought, *when I take what I want.*

Victory tingled his lips as a smile spread over them.

He stepped foot on the other side of the Nile and went straight to his stolen estate.

As he threw open his door, Merka, his servant, dropped his head. "Are you our new Pharaoh?" he asked, his mouth pinched and his voice holding a certain tone of mockery.

"No, you ridiculous buffoon," Pawah said, his prideful beam falling from his face. He slammed the door closed. "Do you think if I was Pharaoh I would come back here?"

Merka pushed his lips forward and shook his head in a failed attempt to hide a smirk.

"Fetch me gold for a trip." Pawah shook his fingers at him to shoo him away. *I cannot deal with you right now,* he added in his mind, *but you will pay for your insubordination.*

"Where are you going?" Merka asked, not moving.

"You do not ask questions!" Pawah grabbed his collar and half pushed, half pulled him in the direction of the estate's treasury.

Merka let out a heavy sigh and went and measured out a few debens of gold.

"Here are ten debens."

Pawah held out his hand, but Merka dropped the linen sack on the table just out of Pawah's reach. Merka's uncaring eyes and finger-tapping on the table almost caused Pawah to slap him.

"Get me twenty more," Pawah said, dismissing Merka again, and then leaned forward to yank the sack from the table.

One copper deben should be enough to make it to Men-nefer, but I may have to leave the country and will need a good stash should I find myself in exile again.

Merka came back, dropping two more linen sacks on the table, both again just out of Pawah's reach.

"You thankless servant!" Pawah growled at his subordinate and then whispered under his breath, "I would have killed you by now if we were in Aketaten."

Merka shook his head uncaringly. "But we aren't." His voice was monotone and flat.

Pawah drew near and slapped Merka across the face. "Do you know how many lives I have taken? As if yours would mean anything to me."

"Then why do you keep me around?" Merka leaned forward so his nose almost touched Pawah's.

Because I am running low in support and those I can manipulate.

But he couldn't admit that. Instead, Pawah wrenched Merka's collar in his hand. "When did you become this way?"

"When you refused to pay the soldiers what you promised. I joined you because I did not want an heir of Akhenaten on the throne. That horrid man we had to call Pharaoh stripped us of food, work, and decency. He robbed Egypt of faith. My only son joined the army ranks and went to Re in one of his border crises because he refused to set up proper defenses."

Merka's breath was hot on Pawah's nose.

"That was why I joined you. You gave my family bread to eat. You paid me to work for you in the People's Restoration of Egypt. You protected us in our worship to Amun." Merka narrowed his eyes. "I've killed for you, helped you to kill several royals, and you aren't even loyal to those who do your bidding." He spit at Pawah's feet. "You left Sitayet's, Ebana's, and the other's families without grain after they died in their assassination of Pharaoh Tutankhamun and General and Hereditary Prince Horemheb. You had promised them their families would be taken care of. You threatened their families' *lives* if they did not do what you asked."

Merka shook his head and pushed off Pawah's hand around his beaded collar. "My mother gave me this collar when I took a wife, and I'll not have you ruin it." Merka leaned past Pawah and grabbed his reed brush to take note of the withdrawal of funds. "Now do you want me to dress you in linens with fewer decorations?" Merka asked, not bothering to peer up at Pawah. "For your travel."

Merka's eyes widened, seemingly noticing the blood stains on Pawah's chest, and his gaze jumped to his chin. "What happened at Malkata?"

"I was . . . caught," Pawah muttered.

Merka snapped his reed brush accidentally. "You were . . ." Merka grunted; his hand crumpled the papyrus as it curled into a fist. "I want no more to do with you, but my hands are as bloody as yours and I am tied to you as you are to me. I know you will not kill me, because you *need* me. I am one of the few you have left."

Pawah went completely still, his eyelids held heavy over his eyes, and then, with the force and swiftness of a crocodile, he swatted the papyrus and brush from Merka's hands and grabbed him with both hands, again by his precious collar.

"You're wrong."

Then he pushed Merka into the wall and bashed his head against the stone until Merka fell to the floor in a seizing heap. Pawah chuckled to himself as he squatted down so he was eye-level with him, watching the life leave his body. He tilted his head, slightly amused at the way Merka's body lay dying and slightly in awe of his handiwork against the stone wall. His gaze finally fell from the blood spatter back to Merka, whose life drained from his eyes.

"I don't *need* you, and I tire of your ungratefulness."

He stood and kicked Merka's body after he was gone.

"Really, you should be thanking me. If someone comes looking for me in the morning, I've just spared you the impalement . . . but mostly, I don't want you to give anyone any details of our happenings."

Pawah burned the papyrus. No more would he have to keep records of how much he had taken from the royal treasury for his own estate to supply the movement once the priesthood's funds had run out so long ago. No more would there even be proof of such a thing.

He peered over to the large chests of gold, copper, bronze, and grain. He would take as much as would fit in his sling. Smiling, he went up to his room on the second floor and gathered up his lists and records of who did what in the movement—

"Pawah, my handsome man," a woman's voice crooned. "Where are you going?"

He twirled around to face his mistress from the night prior as she lay in his bed. "Ah, my beautiful . . . Nile reed." *Because I cannot remember your name. There are so many of you.*

He helped her to stand and slid his hands around her waist, placing a kiss on the base of her neck like he did with all of the women he brought into his bed. This woman was no different. He pulled her close and peered out the window to gauge the time. His lips turned into a scowl.

Not enough daylight left to be with this woman.

"Why is your travel sling packed?" she asked. "Why . . . you're *bleeding!*" Her finger graced the wound on his chin.

He winced. *I don't want to kill you, but if you ask any more questions, I may have to. I can't have loose ends around Waset.*

"My lily flower . . ."

He ran his fingers down the outline of her jaw. *She is naïve enough to believe whatever I say. Neglected wives are so desperate for love.* He titled his head as an idea came to him.

"I must go to Nubia."

"Nubia?" Her eyes danced. "Why? Don't you want to stay here with me?"

"I do," he whispered, and pulled her mouth to his. "But," he said, pulling away, "I have been reinstated as Vizier of the Upper, and Pharaoh Ay needs me to go and reconcile the border disputes. You make plans to divorce your husband and I will bring you to the palace with me."

He gave her his charming grin and got a small thrill at what this brainless woman would do in his absence. Not that he cared, but it was amusing, nonetheless.

"Oh!" She smiled and giggled, her shoulders rising at the possibility of living in Malkata. "That is great news!" She pulled his hands to her chest. "We must celebrate!"

"I want to." He hummed as his eyes ran over her bosom. This was no lie—he certainly wanted to. "But I must be going. I'll let you out the window and down the tree. We don't want you getting in trouble should anyone see you coming from my estate door. I don't think your husband would take too kindly to that." He winked at her. *Nor do I want you to see Merka's body lying in the main room.* He waited for her to object to the window, but she didn't. That was why he kept this one around.

She took a deep breath and nodded. "I am always so careful."

"I know you are, my charming anemone."

She giggled again at this, playing with her wig.

"I shall be back at some point in the future. I'll send you my usual call."

He winked at her as he patted her cheek, then hurried her out the window to let her down. She blew him a kiss and he in return once she was at the base of the building.

He turned back to his room and gave a soft chuckle at the ease of it all. He finished putting the papyrus scrolls in his sling. If he were to be taken in, then he had his records of those who would join him. His very last resort of evading arrest and impalement.

After stitching his chest and rubbing honey into his chin, he changed his clothes to look like a noble. He looked at himself in the polished copper mirror as he thought what lie to tell people.

"I cut myself shaving," he said, his voice dripping with ease and charm, "because I was too entranced with the news of Pharaoh's untimely demise."

He descended back to the first floor, opened the door to his estate, and then yelled to Merka's body, "Make yourself useful while I am gone!" He walked out of his estate with a sneer on his face. A bark of laughter followed, and he muttered under his breath, "When I become Pharaoh, I will return for my gold."

He headed to the nearest dock, his mind focused on one person.

Mut.

How would he get her to let him inside? He could bring word of General Horemheb's death. *No. She probably has already received that news . . .* His mind whirled as his feet took him where he needed to go. *I will be his estate trust, that's it! I need her to sign legal documents for his estate. Yes, she will let me in, and then, once I force her into submission, I will send word to Pharaoh that Mut is ill and needs her father to come at once.*

He laughed at the ease of his plan and then snorted, wishing he had done the same years ago with that cursed Nefertiti. He had been a different person then, but he cared not now for the blood of Egyptians. He cared not for the diplomacy.

I will take what I want at any cost!

He stepped onto the barge to Men-nefer, paying his toll, and looked across the Nile to the grand Malkata.

Ankhesenamun's words hung in the back of his mind from that morning's attack. Had it really only been just that morning? It seemed a life away now. *No one will ever remember the man who began his descent as the Fifth Prophet of Amun. I curse you to be erased from all of history.*

Fear of her curse coming to life began to muddle his vision, so he pushed it aside as he planned out his great victory. *I will be remembered, girl—always. It will be you, Ankhesenamun, who they will forget.*

He looked to the sun and smirked. One day's head start.

357

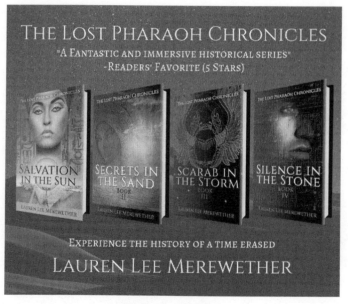

Order each book on Amazon
or sign-up at www.laurenleemerewether.com to stay
updated on new releases!

Go further into the past with the Prequel Collection and find
out how Pawah rose from an impoverished state to priest in
The Fifth Prophet, how Tey came to Ay's house in **The Valley
Iris**, why Ay loved Temehu so much in **Wife of Ay**, General
Paaten's struggle in the land of Hatti in **Paaten's War**, and the
brotherhood between Thutmose and Amenhotep IV in
Egypt's Second Born.

The Prequel Collection

Dive deeper into the story with the Complement Collection
and find out exactly how Pawah transformed the naïve

Nebetah into the conniving Beketaten in *Exiled*, and where General Paaten and Nefe end up in ***King's Daughter***.

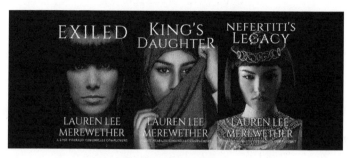

The Complement Collection

Please note the complement collection will contain spoilers if you have not read the series and relevant prequels first.

For *Exiled*, the reader should read book one of the series, ***Salvation in the Sun***, and the prequel, ***The Fifth Prophet***.

For *King's Daughter*, the reader should read book one and book two of the series, ***Salvation in the Sun*** and ***Secrets in the Sand***, respectively; and the prequels, ***The Mitanni Princess*** and ***Paaten's War***.

Sign-up at www.laurenleemerewether.com to stay updated on new releases!

A LOOK INTO THE PAST

As readers may have gleaned from this novel's prologue and epilogue, the account of Pharaohs Akhenaten, Smenkare, Neferneferuaten, and Tutankhamun were removed from history by a later Pharaoh. Only recently, archeologists have uncovered and continue to uncover bits and pieces of what happened during the Amarna period, the period of time this series covers. The author has taken liberties in *Scarab in the Storm,* Book III of The Lost Pharaoh Chronicles, where there were uncertainties and unknowns in the truth.

Scarab in the Storm covers the most famous section of time during this lost period. Pharaoh Tutankhamun is the famed boy King Tut whose coffin was opened in 1925 by Howard Carter, revealing the pristine, golden funerary mask that has come to be associated with Ancient Egypt just as much as the Great Pyramids and Sphinx of Giza. His tomb was completely intact, most likely due to a landslide that occurred, covering and burying the entrance to his tomb. Because his name was also blotted out by a later Pharaoh, his tomb was essentially forgotten until 1925.

In the late third regnal year of Pharaoh Tutankhaten, he

changed his name and his chief royal wife's name to honor Amun instead of the Aten and moved Egypt's capital from Aketaten back to Waset. Additionally, there is no known coregency between Pharaoh Neferneferuaten and Tutankhaten, but there is a theory that Neferneferuaten reigned during Tutankhamun's first three years, since he was only nine, and a coregency did exist. For the storyline of *The Lost Pharaoh Chronicles* to continue, the author made the first two years of Tutankhaten's reign a coregency with Neferneferuaten. *Scarab in the Storm* starts with the beginning of Tutankhaten's first year as sole regent, his third year on the throne.

Tutankhamun probably died in modern-day Syria. His mummification appeared rushed, and his mummy was decorated as Osiris, even with an erect penis as Osiris was depicted, for status of Lord of Resurrection and Fertility. Tutankhamun's mummification was not as polished as other pharaohs, presumably because the priests who usually performed those rituals were not in Syria, and his tomb appeared to be rushed (e.g., the summary of the rebirth instructions for his ka were painted, not carved, on the stone walls of his tomb). His tomb was probably meant for his vizier, Ay, and Ay's tomb, which probably was originally Tutankhamun's, was laid next to Amenhotep III, Tutankhamun's grandfather. It is accepted that Tutankhamun died at eighteen or nineteen years of age after a nine- to ten-year reign due to a break in his leg made worse by the onset of malaria; however, conspiracy theories still exist.

Tutankhaten's children's mother presumably was his chief royal wife, Ankhesenamun, and his half-sister from the same father, Pharaoh Akhenaten. However, the DNA of his children's mother shows no father-daughter relation to the mummy identified as Akhenaten. If the children's mother was not Akhenaten's daughter, then their mother is an unknown, lesser wife of Tutankhaten; if the children's mother *is* Akhenaten's daughter, then Akhenaten's mummy is actually someone else (presumably Smenkare), and Smenkare's sister bore Tutankhaten and not Akhenaten and his sister. In *Scarab in the Storm*, the author took liberties with these DNA studies and wrote Ankhesenamun as the mother of Tutankhamun's daughters and both Ankhesenamun and Tutankhamun as the son and daughter of Akhenaten; however based on DNA results, either one relation is true and the other is not, or they are both false. In addition, there are theories that Tutankhamun's daughters are actually twins, and that they suffered from Twin-Twin Transfusion Syndrome (TTTS), where the blood supply in the womb is unevenly distributed, which would account for their different sizes. One fetus is assumed six months gestation and the other nine months, and both were mostly likely stillborn.

The Ancient Egyptians believed a child lived in the womb, and children were cherished in their culture. This is in stark contrast with other ancient cultures, which would leave deformed or female children to die outside the home. Silphium was a plant that has been farmed to extinction, but was widely used in ancient times as birth control. It prevented a woman from becoming pregnant; one full dose induced menstruation, causing miscarriage early in a woman's pregnancy. There is no record of using small doses of silphium to cause stillbirth in the way it is used in *Scarab in the Storm*.

Many theories posit that after Tutankhamun's death, Ankhesenamun was the one to send the letter asking for a Hittite prince—not her mother as depicted in *Secrets in the Sand*, Book II of The Lost Pharaoh Chronicles—because she did not want to marry Horemheb, the Hereditary Prince, who was most likely born a commoner. However, a few attribute the letter to Pharaoh Neferneferuaten, whom some believe may have been Meritaten, Nefertiti, Neferneferuaten Tasherit, or a joint rule by sisters Meritaten and Neferneferuaten Tasherit. If Ankhesenamun sent the letter then it is believed Vizier Ay sent General and Hereditary Prince Horemheb to kill Zannanza, the Hittite Prince, and then assumed the throne in his absence by marrying Tutankhamun's widowed chief royal wife and assumedly the last remaining Hereditary Princess, Ankhesenamun.

A little peek into the author's mindset:

- It is believed the young Tutankhamun had anger issues based on reliefs depicting Horemheb soothing Tutankhamun's angry outbursts.
- Horemheb was married to Amenia, a prophetess of Amun, who presumably died during the reign of Tutankhamun. They had no children. It is assumed he married Mutbenret during Tutankhamun's reign. (Mutbenret was formerly Mutnedjmet due to a translation error; *The Lost Pharaoh Chronicles* use Mutnedjmet as her name.)
- There are only a handful of named fictional characters in the story. The majority of the main characters are based on and/or named after their real-life counterparts. The author wanted to stay as close to the historical account as possible, yet still craft an engaging story.
- Pawah was a lay prophet and scribe of Amun in the 18th Dynasty noted during the reign of Neferneferuaten, and although his quest to take the throne could have been a possibility, there is no evidence to support Pawah as the villain in *The Lost Pharaoh Chronicles*. The author wrote a prequel

collection for the series, and one of the prequels is the character Pawah's backstory, **The Fifth Prophet**, available on Amazon.

- The author used "Pharaoh" as a title in the story due to the mainstream portrayal of Pharaoh to mean "King" or "ruler." *Pharaoh* is actually a Greek word for the Egyptian word(s) *pero* or *per-a-a* in reference to the royal palace in Ancient Egypt, or, literally, "great house." The term was used in the time period this series covers; however, it was never used as an official title for the Ancient Egyptian kings.

- The term 'citizen/citizeness' is similar to the modern 'Mr.' and 'Ms.'; Whereas, 'Mistress of the House' is what they called a married woman over her household.

- The phrase, 'in peace' was the standard greeting and farewell.

- Ancient Egyptians called their country *Kemet*, meaning "Black Land," but because the modern term *Egypt* is more prevalent and known in the world today, the author used Egypt when referencing the ancient empire.

- Regnal years were not used during the ancient times, but rather used by historians to help chronicle the different reigns. The author decided to insert these references throughout the novel to help the reader keep track of how much time has passed and to have a better idea of the historical timeline.

- Additionally, the people of Egypt seemed not to celebrate or acknowledge years of life; these were included in the story for the reader's reference. The only "birthday" celebration was every month of Kaherka, which is equal to December in the Julian calendar. It was a symbolic celebration of the king's coronation, for the gods to renew his lifeforce. To read a free short story the author created as a winter gift for her readers surrounding this time for Amenhotep III, visit her website and download "King's Jubilee."

- *Amun* can be spelled many ways—Amen, Amon, Amun—but it refers to the same god. Likewise, the *Aten* has also been spelled Aton, Atom, or Atun. The author chose consistent spellings for her series for pronunciation purposes.

- Ancient Egyptians did not use the words "death" or "died," but for ease of reading this series, the author used both in some instances. Rather, they would use alternative phrases to satiate the burden that the word "death" brought, such as "went to the fields of Re," "became an Osiris," and "journeyed to the west."

The author hopes you have enjoyed this story crafted from the little-known facts surrounding this period. She is hard at work writing. Find out what happens next with Ankhesenamun, Pawah, Ay, Horemheb, Mut, and the rise (or fall) of Egypt in the last book of the series, *Silence in the Stone!* Sign up at www.LostPharaohChronicles.com to receive the *Reader's Guide for Salvation in the Sun* or at www.laurenleemerewether.com to receive a free copy of her debut award-winning novel, *Blood of Toma*, and get alerts when new stories are on their way.

WHAT DID YOU THINK?
AN AUTHOR'S REQUEST

Did You Enjoy
Scarab in the Storm?

Thank you for reading the third book in **The Lost Pharaoh Chronicles**. I hope you enjoyed jumping into another culture and reading about the author's interpretation of the events that took place in the New Kingdom of Ancient Egypt.

If you enjoyed *Scarab in the Storm*, I would like to ask a big favor: Please share with your friends and family on social media sites like **Facebook** and leave a review on **Amazon** and on **Goodreads** if you have accounts there.

I am an independent author; as such, reviews and word of mouth are the best way readers like you can help books like *Scarab in the Storm* reach other readers.

Your feedback and support are of the utmost importance to me. If you want to reach out to me and give feedback on this book, share ideas to improve my future writings, get updates about future books, or just say howdy, please visit me on the web.

www.LaurenLeeMerewether.com
Or email me at
mail@LaurenLeeMerewether.com

Happy Reading!

Her future is pending.

The Mitanni Princess Tadukhipa weighs her options: happiness in exile and poverty, death in prison, or a luxurious life of loneliness. Cursed to love a servant and practice a servant's trade, Tadukhipa rebels against her father, the King, for a chance to change her destiny.

ACKNOWLEDGMENTS

First and foremost, I want to thank God for blessing me with the people who support me and the opportunities He gave me to do what I love: telling stories.

Many thanks to my dear husband, Mark, who supported my early mornings and late nights of writing this book.

Thank you to my parents, siblings, beta readers, and launch team members, without whom I would not have been able to make the story the best it could be and successfully get the story to market.

Thank you to Spencer Hamilton of Nerdy Wordsmith, who put this story through the refiner's fire, making this piece of historical fiction really shine.

Thank you to RE Vance, bestselling author of the GoneGod World series, who offered guidance in the series' framework and structure.

Thank you to the Self-Publishing School Fundamentals of Fiction course, which taught me invaluable lessons on the writing process and how to effectively self-publish, as well as gave me the encouragement and support I needed.

Finally, but certainly not least, thank you to my readers.

Without your support, I would not be able to write. I truly hope this story engages you, inspires you, and gives you a peek into the past. I've also created a Reader's Guide to help you delve into the history and into Book I a little bit more—just sign up at www.LostPharaohChronicles.com to receive it.

My hope is that when you finish reading this story, your love of history will have deepened a little more—and, of course, that you can't wait to find out what happens in the final book of the series!

ABOUT THE AUTHOR

Lauren Lee Merewether, a historical-fiction author, loves bringing the world stories forgotten by time, stories filled with characters who love and lose, fight wrong with right, and feel hope in times of despair.

A lover of ancient history where mysteries still abound, Lauren loves to dive into history and research overlooked, under-appreciated, and relatively unknown tidbits of the past and craft for her readers engaging stories.

During the day, Lauren studies the nuances of technology and audits at her job and cares for her family. She saves her nights and early mornings for writing stories.

Get her first novel, *Blood of Toma,* for **FREE**, say hello, and stay current with Lauren's latest releases at www.LaurenLeeMerewether.com.

facebook.com/llmbooks
twitter.com/llmbooks
instagram.com/llmbooks
bookbub.com/authors/lauren-lee-merewether
goodreads.com/laurenleemerewether
amazon.com/author/laurenleemerewether

ALSO BY LAUREN LEE MEREWETHER

Salvation in the Sun

(The Lost Pharaoh Chronicles, Book I)

This future she knows for certain—the great sun city will be her undoing.

Amidst a power struggle between Pharaoh and the priesthood of Amun, Queen Nefertiti helps the ill-prepared new Pharaoh, Amenhotep, enact his father's plan to regain power for the throne. But what seemed a difficult task only becomes more grueling when Amenhotep loses himself in his radical obsessions.

Standing alone to bear the burden of a failing country and stem the tide of a growing rebellion, Nefertiti must choose between her love for Pharaoh and her duty to Egypt in this dramatic retelling of a story forgotten by time.

Secrets in the Sand

(The Lost Pharaoh Chronicles, Book II)

1335 B.C. Egypt is failing. Allies are leaving. War is inevitable.

The power struggle for the throne should have ended long ago, yet it rages onward, shrouded in conspiracy and murder.

Pharaoh Akhenaten's plan to regain power from the priesthood of Amun is done, but his religious zeal has stripped the economy and the people's morale.

Whisperings of rebellion fill the streets as enemies close in on Egypt's borders, leaving Nefertiti to fend off political wolves as she attempts to stabilize the nation and keep her crown.

Silence in the Stone

(The Lost Pharaoh Chronicles, Book IV)

Reborn as Osiris, General Horemheb stakes his claim to the throne and takes his final revenge.

Receiving the crown with a Queen by his side, Pharaoh Horemheb knows all should be well in a flourishing and peaceful Egypt. *Yet* the position of Pharaoh is skirted and dishonored. The Amun priesthood suffers fear and restraint from the people who now know their past corruptions.

How will he do what needs to be done to reestablish the power of Pharaoh and keep authority over the priesthood? And how will he live with his overwhelming guilt and find love again?

Don't miss the Lost Pharaoh Chronicles Complement Collection.

Order now on Amazon or stay updated at www.laurenleemerewether.com

King's Daughter is the complement story to books two and three, *Secrets in the Sand and Scarab in the Storm*, and follows General Paaten and Nefe into the land of Canaan. To avoid spoilers, please read the prequels, ***The Mitanni Princess*** and ***Paaten's War***, first.

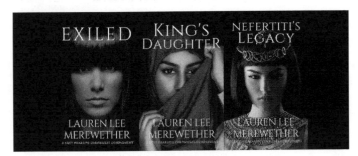

The Complement Collection

Don't miss the Lost Pharaoh Chronicles Prequel Collection.

Order now on Amazon or stay updated at www.laurenleemerewether.com

The Prequel Collection

The Mitanni Princess

(The Lost Pharaoh Chronicles Prequel Collection, A Free Novella)

Her future is pending.

The Mitanni Princess Tadukhipa weighs her options: happiness in exile and poverty, death in prison, or a luxurious life of loneliness. Cursed to love a servant and practice a servant's trade, Tadukhipa rebels against her father, the King, for a chance to change her destiny.

Grab your copy for free at www.laurenleemerewether.com.

The Mitanni Princess sits alongside four talented authors' stories in an anthology, *Daughters of the Past (available on Amazon)*.

If you have read both *The Mitanni Princess* and *Salvation in the Sun*, use the password: ATINUK!

This unlocks the secret bonus ending of *The Mitanni Princess* at www.laurenleemerewether.com.

King's Jubilee

(The Lost Pharaoh Chronicles Prequel Collection, A Free Short Story)

A secret. A brotherhood. A father's sin.

Crown Prince Thutmose's auspicious future keeps his chin high. Striving to be like his father, Pharaoh Amenhotep III, in every way . . . until his eyes open to one of his father's biggest failures.

What will Thutmose decide to do when he takes the crown one day?

Grab your copy for free at www.laurenleemerewether.com.

The King's Jubilee, a short story, also sits alongside sixteen other authors' stories in a young adult multi-genre anthology, *Winds of Winter*, available on Amazon.

The Valley Iris

(The Lost Pharaoh Chronicles Prequel Collection, Book I)

A forbidden love within a sacred village haunts her mind and troubles her future.

Even the vision granted to her from the goddess Hathor keeps Tey from the man she loves. Tey does not understand why her mother will not fight for her. She cannot see why his family does not accept her until it is too late.

Is Tey doomed to live a life with someone else or with no one at all? Can she pick herself up in the darkness of the starlit night and seek her own happiness?

Find out in this coming of age drama set in the New Kingdom of Egypt.

The Wife of Ay

(The Lost Pharaoh Chronicles Prequel Collection, Book II)

Temehu, the daughter of Nomarch Paser, is expected to live a certain life, marry at a certain age to a man of certain status, and have children.

But in her attempts to pursue what she wants for her life, she finds herself questioning the fate of her heart on the journey to the afterlife. Enduring the wrath of a new jealous step-mother and the nobility's harmful gossip and outcasting does not soothe her reservations either.

Is she reaping divine punishment for her deeds? Will she find peace for her eternal soul? Find out in this coming of age drama set in the New Kingdom of Egypt.

Paaten's War

(The Lost Pharaoh Chronicles Prequel Collection, Book III)

Injured in war. Captured by the enemy. Sold as a slave.

Despite his situation, Paaten believes his future is not in the enemy land of Hatti. As Paaten struggles to find his way back to his homeland of Egypt, he finds himself in an unforeseen battle waging the biggest war yet:

that of his heart . . .

Will Paaten's perceived enemy ensnare his love and loyalty or will he return to Egypt to fulfill his destiny and his oath to Pharaoh?

The Fifth Prophet

(The Lost Pharaoh Chronicles Prequel Collection, Book IV)

Power. Gold. Prestige. That is all he wants.

Young Pawah's life changes when he travels to Waset on his parent's hard earned savings to become a scribe at the temple of Amun. Facing discrimination in Waset for being the son of a farmer among the wealthy elite, Pawah discovers the ease with which he garners sympathy and subsequent pity gifts of gold with lies and deceit.

Growing into his own on the streets of Waset, how far will Pawah take his ever-expanding greed for gold and power that hides behind his charm and wit?

Dive into this coming-of-age thriller that chronicles the villain of *The Lost Pharaoh Chronicles*.

Egypt's Second Born

(The Lost Pharaoh Chronicles Prequel Collection, Book V)

Bullied by his brother and disregarded by his father, young prince Amenhotep seeks to belong. . . in some way. . . to some one.

Not expected to live as a babe, Amenhotep beats the odds only to find a life always in his brother's shadow and cast out from his father's glory. Turning to his mother proves a challenge and the noble girls seem to laugh save one, Kasmut.

Does Amenhotep succumb to the shadows of his father's great palace or does he rise above the ridicule to forge his own path?

Find out in this heartwarming tale of two royal brothers and their journey to love one another despite past wrongs and shortcomings.

Blood of Toma

Running from death seemed unnatural to the High Priestess Tomantzin, but run she does.

She escapes to the jungle after witnessing her father's murder amidst a power struggle within the Mexica Empire and fears for her life. Instead of finding refuge in the jaguar's land, she falls into the hands of glimmering gods in search for glory and gold. With her nation on the brink of civil war and its pending capture by these gods who call themselves Conquistadors, a bloody war is inevitable.

Tomantzin must choose to avenge her father, save her people, or run away with the man she is forbidden to love.

Lauren's debut work of historical fiction, *Blood of Toma,* won a Montaigne Medal nomination and a finalist award for the Next Generation Indie Book Awards in Historical Fiction and Readers' Favorite Award in Young Adult-Thriller.

Get this ebook for free at www.laurenleemerewether.com.

Made in the USA
Las Vegas, NV
13 April 2021

21309826R00231